Evald Flisar

TEA WITH THE QUEEN

Translated from the Slovene by
David Limon

Texture Press
Norman, Oklahoma
2015

EVALD FLISAR (1945, Slovenia). Novelist, playwright, essayist, editor, globe-trotter (travelled in more than 90 countries), underground train driver in Sydney, editor of (among other publications) an encyclopaedia of science and invention in London, author of short stories and radio plays for the BBC, president of the Slovene Writers' Association (1995 – 2002), since 1998 editor of the oldest Slovenian literary journal Sodobnost (Contemporary Review). Author of 12 novels (eight of them short-listed for *Kresnik*, the Slovenian "Booker"), two collections of short stories, three travelogues, two books for children, and fifteen stage plays (seven nominated for Best Play of the Year Award, three times won the award). Winner of the Prešeren Foundation Prize, the highest state award for prose and drama, and the prestigious Župančič Award for lifetime achievement. Various works translated into 34 languages, among them Bengali, Malay, Nepalese, Indonesian, Turkish, Greek, Japanese, Chinese, Arabic, Czech, Albanian, Lithuanian, Icelandic, Romanian, Amharic, Russian, English, German, Italian, Spanish. His stage plays are regularly performed all over the world, most recently in Austria, Egypt, India, Indonesia, Japan, Taiwan, Serbia, Bosnia, Bulgaria and Belarus. Attended more than 50 literary readings and festivals on all continents. Lived abroad for 20 years (three years in Australia, 17 years in London). Since 1990, resident in Ljubljana, Slovenia. His novel *On the Gold Coast* (published in English by Sampark, Kolkata, India) has just been nominated for the most prestigious European literary prize, the Dublin IMPAC International Literary Award. His other works published by Texture Press are *Tales of Wandering*, *My Father's Dreams*, *If I Only Had Time, Collected Plays, Vol. 1* and *Collected Plays, Vol. 2*.

*t*P
Texture Press

Evald Flisar

TEA WITH THE QUEEN

Translated from the Slovene by
David Limon

Texture Press
Norman, Oklahoma
2015

Originally published in Slovenia (European Union) as *Čaj s kraljico* (Ljubljana: Mladinska knjiga, 2004). Shortlisted for Kresnik, the Best Novel of the Year Award.

Published in the United States by
Texture Press, 1108 Westbrooke Terrace, Norman, OK 73072.

Editor
Susan Smith Nash, PhD

Sub-editor
Arlene Ang

Cover design by
Arlene Ang

Published with the financial assistance of Trubar Foundation, Ljubljana, Slovenia.

ISBN 978-0692356838 (Texture Press)

Rights are available from the European Literary Agency,
sandra@europeanliteraryagency.co.uk, or from sodobnost@guest.arnes.si.

Printed in the United States of America.

Texture Press
Norman, OK 73072
USA
texturepress@beyondutopia.com

PART ONE

1.

That year spring came early and, weary of delivering April down-pours, it turned to summer in the early days of May, with a bright sun in Europe's blue sky, with a warm wind that ruffled the brown curls of the French students on the Channel ferry heading for the white cliffs of the English coast *(There'll be bluebirds over the white cliffs of Dover!)*. I felt a little lonely on the crowded deck, where even the reserved English ladies on their way back from a pensioners' trip to Paris had come to enjoy the pale caresses of the sun. Well, perhaps not lonely – perhaps feeling that I had been inserted into a world where I did not yet belong, but as stubborn as the screeching flock of seagulls that accompanied us to the middle of the Channel and restless, excited at the thought of the adventure that I had embarked upon as (young men are allowed their dreams) the first foreigner since William the Conqueror to come to England with the intention of subjugating it.

It seemed that everything and everybody was in a hurry: the spring turning into summer; the wind blowing across the deck and through the ruffled hair towards the Continent, all the way to where I had left behind a bitter mess of failed plans (failed because they were too modest to mobilise the energy I felt inside me); the puffing steamship dashing across the dark green water; the French students in mini-skirts going to attend an English course in London to return as soon as possible – English spoken – to the streets of Paris or the sunflower fields of Provence; the group of German boys with rucksacks who would love to chat up some of these girls (but *no, merci* – and I liked that, since I felt, I don't know why, that they belonged to me, that soon everything would belong to me, everything); and the middle-class English trippers loaded down with French cheese and wine and cheap souvenirs, hurrying home to display their booty to their neighbours.

And I? Oh, nothing special: I was in a hurry to achieve riches and fame.

"Ladies and gentlemen, it gives me great pleasure to present Sir William Vaupotitch, the great British painter born in Slovenia, whose latest exhibition has just opened at the Tate Gallery." Yes! Yet another William to take his place in the wax museum!

Perhaps the feeling of accelerating time was triggered by impatience; perhaps time, which is relative, submits itself to the needs of the one in a hurry to achieve his goals – just as a black hole bends space and draws into itself all the mass, light and energy of the surrounding stars. But at the thought of the hidden traps lying in wait for me on the path to victory, the anxiety that was imperceptibly building inside me broke through the walls of my heart and entered my lungs, leaving me suddenly short of breath. I leaned over the rail and opened my mouth wide to catch as much of the wind as possible, but almost at the same time the ferry shuddered, as if a sea monster had blundered into it; I saw my fingers go white with the effort of holding on.

It was no monster, but rather the powerful Channel current that we had entered after sailing parallel to the French coast for some time; we were now heading directly for Dover, across the surging waves assailing the ship unevenly from all sides. My anxiety increased and I started to feel sick; when I once more gulped at the air, my gorge rose and brought up the half-digested sandwich that I had wolfed down before embarking. The friendly wind spat it back in my face, down my neck, across my shoulder and over my shirt – the ironed, light blue shirt, carefully chosen to make a good impression on the Dover immigration officers!

Behind me someone shouted, someone moved aside noisily, someone said *merde*. It was no use pretending that William the Conqueror II had not made a fool of himself, even disgraced himself (heroes do not throw up at the first swell of a restless sea), nor that the disgrace could be concealed, since I knew that I would have to turn around. But not immediately. With a nonchalant gesture, as if I merely wished to wipe my nose, I took out my handkerchief and carefully cleaned my face and my shirt. In fact, I did not actually clean my shirt but rather rubbed my vomit into the pattern, which was reminiscent of one of Cezanne's less successful early attempts.

That at least, I thought: always the painter! Every gesture, however stupid, an artistic one; every stain a work of art, from the spilled soup to the muddy trail on the carpet; it never happened that my smear was less beautiful than what I had messed up through my clumsiness.

Never, until that moment. For when I finally turned round there stood before me such a stunning young creature that my heart missed a beat. A vision. She was long-legged and slender, dressed in tight jeans and a white blouse beneath which the shape of her breasts suggested that no one had yet painted a bosom more beautiful, with the soft face of a not-so-innocent angel, a mixture of pickpocket on the prowl and a young lady who was quite capable of spending more than an hour in front of the mirror, black hair dancing in the wind, and fierce blue eyes that, half in anger and half in amazement, were staring at me as if expecting an answer to an unasked question: Why did you do that? On the more prominent parts of her blouse (carefully chosen to make a good impression on the immigration officers in Dover?) I noticed viscous traces of my stomach contents – remnants of cheese, ham and tomato – and in between drops of digestive juices, scattered in no discernible order to create an artistic pattern (but the vomit had been scattered by the wind, not I, and the wind is not an artist!).

Overcome with guilt I said sorry, reached out and with my dirty handkerchief tried to rub the stains from her blouse. It all happened so quickly that I did not really think what I was doing: I wanted to help. But to her, I was just some idiot who had first thrown up on her and was now trying to manhandle her breasts!

I even succeeded in this momentarily, but then her right hand took flight, as if one of the seagulls had swooped between us, and for a brief moment – all too brief – with a stinging slap made contact with

11

my cheek. It hurt – not her hand, which I would happily have kept against my skin, but the laughter that rippled round the deck. Only then did I notice that we had an audience. Some metal steps led to the viewing point on the bow of the ship and there, where she had evidently followed me, along with a few other passengers, we stood like actors on a stage, in a drama for two, drowning in a sea of curious eyes that were avidly and, it seemed to me, maliciously awaiting the outcome of our confrontation.

With the sense of vision that only painters possess, I judged that we were standing like silhouettes in front of the golden orb of the sinking sun, figures of hope on the way to imagining our future: to some, a couple who had just quarrelled; to others, strangers for whom a gust of wind had determined a common fate.

But my brush was too quick: in the eye of the observers I had painted my youthful desire for a starring role in my own life; what they actually saw remained a secret to me – in all likelihood (oh, how banal), a bevomited girl who in a flash of anger had slapped a bearded young man. She, too, showed no sign of wishing to fly with me into the dramatic world of imagination (how cold and solid the ground is – even if it is the swaying deck of a ship). When she realised that we were the centre of attention she looked flustered and rushed back down the steps onto the crowded deck, to become lost in the hustle bustle; she did not want to stand out.

No! I called after her silently, stay! Let us go hand-in-hand in the search for happiness, I like Parsifal looking for the Holy Grail, you as my Blanche Fleur; let us disembark as allies on Dover beach, *where ignorant armies clash by night;* pose for me, only me, and you will be famous until mankind grows weary of art. I shall portray you as a seductress, a mother, a little girl, a spoiled miss, Florence Night-ingale, a princess, Mother Theresa, Lady Macbeth, Antigone; I shall show you hunched over in grief, staring into the depths of depression, laughing with delight; your features, your soul will absorb all the archetypes and cover the walls of the National Gallery!

She was gone, lost in the safe shelter of the faces sinking back into indifference. Together we were interesting, the outlines of a story that could outgrow the moment, but without her beside me I was merely one of them, and the army of dreams that sailed with me and had touched them for a moment had, like the wind, become invisible. As had William the Conqueror II, who after a brief pause pushed his way along the rail towards the centre of the ship without anyone granting him more than a cursory glance; a clown for five seconds and then oblivion.

2.

In the men's toilets on the lower deck I first rinsed my dirty hand-kerchief. Then I tried to wash the stain from my shirt so as not to arouse additional mistrust on the part of the immigration officers (I had heard enough stories of unfortunates who had been sent back to the Continent on the next ferry). But more than the shirt, my interest was attracted by the face in the mirror, which for the first time in my life seemed unknown to me.

It had already happened before, when after a night on the tiles I had seen a monster in the mirror, although it still reminded me of myself; I had experienced a sense of deformation, a Picassoesque shifting of lines, but never a sense of alienation. This time, it seemed that the reflected person was not a part of my history; that he had nothing in common with me apart from the cowed look that we directed at each other: as if the mirror were ordinary glass and that on the other side I was looking at a stranger. Of course, he had a brownish beard similar to mine and long chestnut hair with a parting, and a light blue shirt which he was trying to clean with a wet handkerchief, but his features belonged to a man who was less reconcilable than I, less torn between irrepressible hope and a premonition of defeat, less willing to retreat from misplaced gestures. Quite the opposite: in his eyes there was a flicker of wounded vindictiveness, of hope replaced by stubbornness; any kind of retreat – honourable or dishonourable – would be met with fierce defiance.

Had my soul, upon its first collision with the unknown, split in two, created a double who would know how to overcome the faint-heart within me and force him through various trials with threats and violence? Which of us had more in common with William the Conqueror? The feeling took root inside me that there were suddenly two of us: Willy I and Willy II, to a certain extent allies, but in many ways the master and the servant who fears the master and yet relies on him. Was this the start of the schizophrenia that had been forecast three years earlier by my unrequited love, a student of psychology? At that time, it had seemed that she was merely looking for an excuse for withdrawal and that she could have found a better one. Her assertion that she feared a long-term relationship because I was fragile, as if woven by a spider from the dreams of thousands of children, struck me as insulting; her prediction that I would fall apart upon my first encounter with reality did not convince me. But was she perhaps right?

Whatever, upon returning to the windy deck Willy I and Willy II once more became a single person and my fears subsided; the external reality was kinder than the reality within, the wind had noticeably cooled, darkness was rapidly falling, above the English coast hung the long shadow of the clouds that had covered the setting sun and promised rain; in the port, lights were shining and we were approaching our goal, some passengers were already bustling with their luggage towards the staircase marked Exit, others were pushing their way into the duty-free shop for some last minute purchases. And my worries about my dirty shirt were unnecessary, since the cool of the evening permitted, even dictated, that we put on our cardigans, pullovers and jackets, which I quickly did, as I had my pullover to hand, having stuffed it into my shoulder bag on the train. Once more I was *presentable* (one of the first English words I had committed to memory) and I was also relieved to think that the same probably applied to the sick-stained beauty; all in all it had been nothing, a choppy sea, someone had thrown up, but not only one person, others too, as the sour smell of vomit was blowing from all sides; much ado about nothing.

I fought my way through the crush to the luggage racks to get my two suitcases, but searched in vain among the mountains of luggage that the other passengers (most of them had boarded the ferry *after* the impatient Willy) had piled up there; at the thought that my cases had disappeared I once more felt sick. It was good that I had completely emptied my stomach on deck, otherwise I would have once again thrown up over the white blouse of the dark-haired goddess who had (but where had she materialised from?) suddenly appeared next to me. Although Willy I felt a strong urge to run, he had nowhere to withdraw to, the crowd was too dense. The next moment Sandrina (why did I decide in a flash that she must be called Sandrina?) extended her arm and pointed into the depths of the heap of luggage.

"My bag," she said, with a soft but deep, almost masculine voice, "get me my bag." This was an order rather than a request, a penalty for the ruined blouse and at the same time, if the assignment was successfully accomplished, a peace offering, which opened for Willy further opportunities: friendship, alliance, love (oh, love!), but above all the end of loneliness on the shores of the unconquered land.

Which painter would know how to paint Willy during his fierce assault on the heap of luggage, which at first swayed and then collapsed beneath his determined claws? Suitcases, bags, parcels, packages flew in all directions, while it was not even clear to Willy what he was hunting for; only when the demolition job was complete and some of the other passengers were already grumbling did it strike him that he had entered battle for the goodwill of the alluring Sandrina in too random a fashion.

He turned and saw that the young lady was pointing towards a scruffy rucksack on the middle shelf. Impossible! The most beautiful of all beauties travelling to England with a shabby rucksack from the top of which protruded the handle of an umbrella? Well, her shoes weren't all that smart either: moccasins of some sort with the stitches coming loose. And her socks? One blue and one green! Where are you from, I wanted to ask when I handed her the rucksack, for it seemed that she was much poorer than me and in need of protection. At the last moment I thought better of it; the question would seem impolite and arrogant. Evidently she had been affected enough by the way I had looked at her rucksack, for with a contemptuous gesture

16

she swung it on her shoulder and started to push her way towards the exit without a word of thanks.

She suddenly turned, took two steps back and stopped in front of me. Another slap? I braced myself, almost offering my cheek. But no: her blue eyes softened, her lips formed into a smile, she reached out her hand and gently ran her fingers down my bearded cheek. And she winked, in the way that people wink when they discover that they have a secret in common that they do not want to share with anyone else. In that moment I could have ensured, with a suitable gesture or word, that we got to know each other and left the ferry together, and then the train to London and a shared future; but my plans were ruined by Willy II, who decided that it was necessary to balance obligingness with self-confidence. "I'm a very talented painter," he said, "you could pose for me."

She laughed as if I had told her the oldest joke since Cain killed Abel, and shook her hair as if embarrassed by my boldness; the next moment I also became embarrassed, since three passengers who were close by were looking at each other and smirking. I didn't move when she quickly, as if keen to be rid of me, started pushing towards the exit again; soon, I could see only her head among the multitude.

I eventually discovered my cases on the shelves at the other side of the ship. They were large, new, leather – the very opposite of the battered rucksack with which the beautiful-eyed Sandrina dared to travel. I thought that with her worn-out shoes and shabby luggage she would attract attention wherever she went, particularly upon entering Britain, which could be fatal for her. But after a few minutes my advantage did not seem so self-evident, for when the ferry arrived and we started to swarm up the stairs I was surrounded by a forest of rucksacks and I seemed to be the only one wearing brand new shiny shoes with gold buckles. And my trousers were the only ones that were so well ironed that the crease could be used to slice salami. Actually, in the midst of the crowd dressed in comfortable casual clothes, I looked as if I was on my way to a state banquet.

If anything did attract attention it was my suitcases, more suited for travelling in a Rolls Royce than on a grubby train and vomit-stained ferry. I had been convinced that upon entering Britain I had to be as smart as possible, but evidently I had gone too far and turned myself into a fop who stuck out like a sore thumb. In fact, I stood out so much that I could be spotted from a distance, which was far from what I had wanted to achieve. After all, this was the days of the hippies – no one went around like a mannequin that had escaped from a clothes shop patronised by bank employees, stealing two fancy suitcases on the way. The feeling that I did not belong in the world that I was entering then took on a new, even more painful dimension. What had the lovely Sandrina thought of me? A country bumpkin who had squeezed into his Sunday best to hide his sense of inferiority?

3.

While the motley crew from the ferry swept through passport control as if carried by the wind, I got stuck. The spotty light-haired officer, not much older than me, looked with surprise at my shoes, my trousers, my cases, then once again flicked through my Yugoslav passport and pursed his lips as if about to say: something isn't right here. Then he gestured for me to sit on the bench opposite.

"Wait over there," he said somewhat impatiently when I did not move.

Willy I was overcome with despair and almost staggered over to the bench, while Willy II was not there to lose his temper and raise his head in defiance. The blond officer smelt my fear and his suspicions only deepened; he left his counter and took my passport to consult with his supervisor, who sat behind a glass screen in a spacious office. They spoke, the supervisor leafed through my passport and then turned towards me; he gave some kind of instruction and the young officer nodded. Through the door at the back yet another officer appeared, an enormous man with cheeks like a St. Bernard, and the two of them came towards me.

But they did not stop, they went past as if they had forgotten about me, even though the first one still had my passport in his hand. I turned round and saw that some other poor unwanted souls were sitting there: a dark-eyed Arabic-looking boy; a young couple in winter coats who evidently had not realised that in Britain spring had already begun; a freckled red-headed young man, nervously chain-smoking; an older, bald man with a pot belly who was trying to calm himself by constantly shaking his left leg; and – my Sandrina! My feeling of loneliness evaporated; we were together again in misfortune, connected once more by the thread of fate.

I discreetly raised my hand and waved in greeting, but she did not respond. Perhaps she had not seen me waving, perhaps she did not want to show that we knew each other; she was waiting to see what the officers would do.

They went past her and stopped in front of the red-headed man, they said something and he stubbed out his cigarette, got up and followed them to the glass-walled office; as they went past me I could hear him grumbling and complaining.

"I knew you'd pick on me, I'm American and a writer to boot. Some years ago you maltreated Jack Kerouac here and because of that he fell ill and died, and before him Henry Miller. I really don't know why you have to be the most fucked-up country in Europe. I'm not surprised that my great-grandfather fled across the ocean, but a good job he did, otherwise I'd be one of you..." His voice faded and disappeared behind the glass, where they put him on a chair and started to question him.

The blond guy and the St. Bernard returned for a new victim. Since they headed straight for me I was convinced I was next, but they went past and got stuck into Sandrina. They asked some questions, she gave some answers, and then she picked up her rucksack and headed for the office. I hoped she would at least look at me, but no, she passed me as if we had never met – women are so cruel; and this was not the first time that Willy had found himself in the cold blast of their self-absorbedness. He knew how to portray all the nuances of their incomprehensibility, but he had never really understood what he was depicting, and although their stubborn mystery filled him with an insatiable desire to uncover and portray the depths of the female soul, he had often wished (and this was one of these moments!) that women would help him with this: to pull back at least one of the veils, to become somewhat less of an object of fear, of longing and hope, and somewhat more of a friend, a confidant, a comforter. But not so

20

much that they became maternal, since then for Willy (and his brush) they would lose their allure. Some other time, whispered Willy II, you can delve into the mysteries of the female soul some other time, now you need to stay alert.

But the moment stretched into a timelessness where events lost their beginning and end and order, and it seemed that everything was happening in parallel; I began to paint, not for real but in spirit, on the large canvas that has been stretched within me since the age of four, when the world first revealed itself as a teeming mass of lines and shades of colour; and the images became ever darker, Rembrandt-like, with the turbid glow of the harbour lights lurking behind us like the eyes of the guardians of a blessed child, restless in the wind that had changed direction and was now blowing from the sea, which was barely visible in the cloudy dusk of the May evening, gusting across the paved area in front of the brightly illuminated immigration office, overturning rubbish bins and rolling scrunched-up paper, empty cigarette packets and ice-cream cones, first in one direction, then the other – a suspicious, uncertain wind that was feeling its way around as if trying to sneak past the passport control officers, while every so often, to confuse us, spitting towards us a cold spurt of rain, which was falling outside with ever more determination and drumming on the metal roof above our heads in a rapid, breathless rhythm, arousing a sense of permanent dampness, stuffiness, perhaps rottenness in the country at the top of the high cliffs.

Meanwhile those waiting for entry – excluding me – were led into the office, seated on a chair beneath the glaring neon light and had to defend themselves before Her Majesty's exalted officials in the hunched posture of people who feel guilty and are prepared to do anything to have their sin, whatever it is, forgiven – except for the long-haired American, who was still tossing his red mane and waving his hands in protest. Then one of the Arab boys suddenly got up and dashed across the paved area beneath the roof into the rainy night; but he did not get very far since two of the officers were in hot pursuit, a uniformed bobby also appeared from somewhere, and the three of them threw themselves at him, knocking him to the ground like a sack of potatoes; they dragged him into the darkness round the

21

corner, laughing as they did so, while his fellow traveller in the office unsuccessfully tried to act as if this had nothing to do with him.

And so one by one they disappeared, heads bowed, slightly humiliated, teeth clenched, showing no anger, but glad that they could hurry to the platform where the next train was already standing. All except Sandrina, who was being dealt with by a strict, bespectacled woman that was asking her questions and carefully noting down her replies.

When I had already decided that they had forgotten about me, the St. Bernard came through the door and indicated that I should come to the office. I grabbed my bag and put it over my shoulder, picked up my cases, which now seemed heavier than anything I had ever carried, and like a broken-down beast of burden staggered towards the neon light, where I collapsed, slightly out of breath, on the chair in front of the blond guy and a tall, thin man wearing glasses, who had not been there before; it seemed that he had come from one of the back rooms just because of me, for there was no doubt that Willy represented the greatest problem.

I turned towards Sandrina in the hope that she would grant me at least a fleeting glance and a miracle happened: when she saw that we were the only two remaining, in spite of looking pale and exhausted, she gave me an encouraging smile. The interrogators noticed and looked at each other. The thin man with the glasses wanted to know if we were travelling together.

No, replied Willy II who, emboldened by her smile, determinedly went into battle with the defenders of the United Kingdom, we saw each other on the ferry, that's all.

The blond guy, who was leafing through my passport for what must be the twentieth time, wanted to know what I was planning to do in Britain. Now I was so much Willy II that my fear had subsided; what is more, I was floating on a cloud of rapture, convinced that I was invincible. Calmly and confidently, although in English so broken that it sounded as if I had turned over the luggage of all the ship's passengers to find it, I explained to them that I intended to do nothing other than what I had done so far and that was to paint, for I was an artist, something like their Turner, Constable, Francis Bacon and others; there was no need to worry about me stealing someone's job, I would earn my keep by selling my paintings.

The thin bespectacled one immediately took the wind out of my sails: "Painting is work, selling them is business, you need a licence for both. Do you have one?"

Willy II admitted that he did not, since he was convinced that he did not need one; painting was not work but art and the only licence for that came from God. It immediately became clear that his choice of words was not the best. The thin man turned to the blond one and asked: "Do you have it written down anywhere, John, that God has granted this boy right of entry to Britain?"

John shook his head and once more looked through the passport. "I can't see any entry visa signed by St. Peter."

Oh, but Willy II could not be defeated without once more opening his mouth: you did not let God in, in the sixteenth century you burned at the stake the German priests who had smuggled into the country the forbidden English translation of the Bible.

"Are we really without mercy, John?" the thin one winked at the other, who gave a sinister smile. "And what are you smuggling?" they both glanced at my cases.

In a flash, the cases revealed their secrets and in front of the hawk eyes of his inquisitors Willy laid on the desk three thick rolls of graphics, water colours and oil paintings. He carefully revealed to their astonished eyes sketches of faces, animals and Karst villages, the bold (too bold?) lines of female nudes and oil paintings that were like sudden explosions of colour, which attracted from other parts of the office and even back rooms at least ten immigration and customs officers. As they thronged the desk and began to look with wonder, but with ever greater suspicion, at Willy's best works they were joined by the strict woman who had been questioning Sandrina.

"Uh," she said, "I bet that lot's worth a bob or two."

Glowing with pride Willy noticed that the exceptional attention being paid to himself and his pictures had also made an impression on the lovely Sandrina; it was clear she would like to join the circle of admirers and she half rose but with one look her tormentor fixed her to her chair.

"The only problem," she said, "is that I've seen some of these pictures before. This one, for instance, these sunflowers. And this girl with golden hair rising from the water."

I'm glad, Willy praised her; the sunflowers were painted by van Gogh and the girl by Botticelli, her name is Venus.

"How did these paintings come into your possession?" spat the blond guy, as if catching the greatest art thief who had ever tried to smuggle his valuable loot through customs in Dover – and a dozen pairs of eyes latched onto me as if they could not believe my audacity.

Foolish Willy made another mistake – he burst out laughing. I got these paintings, he said, by painting them. The Venus in a few hours. Regrettably, gentlemen, these are not originals, which you might have believed for a moment, but copies, for the majority of people do not have millions to buy their favourite paintings, they almost always find a convincing approximation for a hundred pounds or so.

"If these are not your paintings," observed the thin bespectacled man, "then you are a forger, not an artist."

The ground shifted beneath Willy's feet; this was not going in the right direction.

I am an artist, he insisted, the majority of these paintings are mine. But for now I am relatively unknown and I do copies because I have to live off something. Copies are not forgeries as long as you sell them as copies; they would become forgeries only if I claimed they were originals, which I don't want to do and so I'm not breaking any laws.

But the group of gathered experts did not want to believe me: an animated discussion ensued, some saying that all the pictures were stolen and that I probably did not even know how to draw a daisy, that I was a smuggler who should be arrested forthwith; the others grinned at this and observed like connoisseurs that among the copies of well-known works there were some of my own pictures, although at first sight it was impossible to judge which; it was even possible, claimed a third group, that the supposed copies among my supposed works (or perhaps they really were mine) were in reality stolen originals that I was attempting in that way to smuggle into Britain. In any case, it was necessary to confiscate the pictures and leave it up to the judgement of the experts.

No, shouted poor Willy, you can't confiscate them, they're mine!

Look, I said and rummaged through my case. In a flash I had in my hands a sheet of paper and a piece of charcoal. One, two, three and the gathered officials were staring at the stunningly accurate sketch of their faces; I even managed to capture the shades of arrogance, amazement and contentious omniscience. Look, I said, and took out another sheet. One, two, three, and the stunned group had in front of it a sketch of the beautiful Sandrina, who was sitting not far away in exactly the same posture as in the picture, with her right leg stretched out and her left bent under the chair, leaning on the table with her chin supported by her left hand, with a strand of hair falling across her right eye.

The girl who would rather be elsewhere, I wrote on the sketch.

"The boy is not without talent," acknowledged the St. Bernard. Under the weight of evidence the others agreed with him, with the exception of the strict woman, who went back to Sandrina, saying over her shoulder: "I'd still like to hold on to the pictures and him until this is cleared up."

There is nothing to clear up, cried Willy I silently in his wounded soul. It is as clear as running water: I am an artist and no one on this Earth has the right to my work, apart from those who buy it or those I give it to!

Willy II began feverishly to roll up the pictures and put them back in the case, as if he was in a terrible hurry, but the thin one with glasses, evidently the one in charge, scratched behind his ear and said: "I'm sorry, but we'll have to hold onto the pictures. They'll be returned to you when it is proven that they are not stolen and that you are not breaking any rules by importing them; that's what we need to clarify."

Check now, said Willy II, I can't do anything without the paintings. For you that is confiscation, for me it is theft. I've got to live off something.

"If you've no means of support," said the Big Boss, "then we cannot permit you to enter, you will be put on the next ferry back."

The blond Hitler Youth zealously placed Willy's pictures in a plastic basket he pulled from beneath the counter; when he was about to add the drawing he had just done Willy grabbed his hand and said: Who did I steal that from?

The thin one with glasses indicated that he should put the others away, but leave those two; he pushed them across the counter towards me as if he was doing me a favour.

For the others I need a list and written confirmation that they have been confiscated and the reason, added Willy II, letting them know that he was not a complete pushover.

"Make a list," the Big Boss ordered the Hitler Youth.

The inquisitive ones had already drifted back to their places, only the St. Bernard was left at the counter. "I repeat once more," said the thin one with glasses, "if you have no means of support then we cannot consider letting you into the country."

Willy II slapped his canvas shoulder bag onto the counter, un-zipped it and pulled out a swollen wallet; he pushed it towards his tormentor, saying: Count it and you'll see that I have two-and-a-half million Italian lira. And before you ask me which bank I robbed, I assure you – so that you don't even consider taking my money, too, for clearly there is a great risk of being robbed as soon as you set foot on Britain's shores – that this is money *legally* earned by *legally* selling my pictures.

The Big Boss was visibly startled, whether because of Willy's cheek or the breathtaking sum that he did not know (unschooled in Italian hyperinflation) how to convert into eight hundred pounds, a modest amount and yet enough for a year in London. He suddenly became very polite, almost human; perhaps he was thinking of his salary and reflecting that being in charge of the immigration office in Dover was not such a gift from God as he had always imagined. At the same time he was looking for a new way to relegate me to the second division.

"It's not clear to me," he said, "what you want to do in Britain, when you are clearly already more than successful in your home country."

There was an embarrassed pause, since there were many possible answers to that question and each of them could make the situation worse. To explain that London was a somewhat larger arena than I had been so far accustomed to and an almost unavoidable stop on the road to the kind of success that every painter wishes for would mean that I was trying to form a trusting relationship with someone who had just seized what in London would enable me to enter the artistic world; not only would it not convince him, but I would feel that I was cooperating with his aim of humiliating me.

"Until I know what the purpose of your visit is, the rules demand that I do not permit you to enter," he said.

Oh, how he was enjoying himself! And poor Willy, how he hung his head. He felt his world beginning to crumble. Back on the ferry, back across the sea, back home, the end of his dreams. "If you at least had an invitation from someone who knows you and is willing to act as a guarantor," continued the official, unprepared for what was about to blow up in his face.

Someone who knows me? exclaimed Willy. Why didn't you say so? I'm going to visit a friend in Cornwall, I'm going to stay on her parents' farm for two weeks. My word of honour, I said, her name is Julia Denton-Barker.

The double-barrelled name sounded kind of aristocratic; I saw how he considered the possibility that some influential type would lodge a complaint if he sent me back across the Channel without a good reason. "Have you got an invitation?" he muttered.

I told him that I didn't have an invitation as such, I only had some of her letters from which it was more than evident that I was welcome there. The bastard wanted to see them straight away. And then they read them – him, the St. Bernard and the Hitler Youth, who had re-turned with a list of the confiscated pictures; they smirked and passed the letters around, winking, for in the chubby Julia's letters there were things that would have made her parents blush. They did this for quite some time in silence, while I sat there looking at Sandrina, who the strict woman was still tormenting with brusque questions (what was so suspicious about Sandrina that the woman had to write down all her answers?). She did not give her a moment to turn and look at me, barking questions at her as if cursing her and my Sandrina was looking ever more dispirited, ever more humiliated, less and less like the girl on the ferry, and I began to feel such indignation that I would have happily smashed everything, the whole office, the skulls of these brazen, conceited people who had to detain us while all the others would now be in London. And as in my thoughts I was destroying everything around me, cutting off heads and lifting Sandrina onto a white horse, I heard the question: "Are you going to marry this girl?" to which I replied reflexively: But I hardly know her.

"Judging by these letters you know each other pretty well," said the Big Boss, slipping the letter from the plump Cornwall girl back in its envelope. "If you are intending to marry, you should have arranged that through our embassy; you can't come in as a tourist if your real intention is to settle here permanently."

At that moment Willy II had had enough of these SS officers and I was all ready to jump up and start cursing them left, right and centre, when Sandrina got up, swung her rucksack on her shoulder, gratefully took the passport which the strict woman had stamped and headed past me for the exit.

I stood up so that she should not get away and looked for the words to detain her, but none came to me; and then I saw the drawing.

The girl who would rather be elsewhere, I said, holding the sketch out to her.

She was startled when she recognised herself, for Willy I is a master at capturing people in their most characteristic pose. "Oh," she breathed, "for me?"

Absolutely, I said, just let me sign it. I took the drawing from her hand and in the bottom right corner I scribbled *Piccadilly Circus, tomorrow at 11.00 a.m.*

She was confused; it seemed to me that she wanted to say no, but then she merely smiled enigmatically, said thank you and, drawing in hand, made her way towards the platform where the train was waiting. I watched the gentle, balletic sway of her hips until she disappeared behind a broad pillar; then the official voice of the thin man with glasses brought me back to reality.

"Do you have the phone number of the Denton-Barker family?"

No, I replied, they live on a farm, they don't have a phone.

"An English family without a phone is a rare thing," he said didactically about the unsurpassable standard of the country into which I, a peasant from the poor end of Europe, was trying to enter, one way or

28

another. "Bring the directory," he ordered the St. Bernard, while the Hitler Youth pushed in front of me a list of the confiscated pictures and instructed me to sign it. I absently scribbled my name, without really knowing what I was signing; I was much more interested what was going to happen to me, for I heard the whistle of the locomotive and then the noise of the train wheels on the tracks: the train was leaving and taking Sandrina to London – would I ever see her again?

It was still raining, but the wind had dropped and the brightly lit ferry had left the harbour and was heading for the French or Belgian shore. "The last ferry tonight," said the Hitler Youth, as if he wished to remind me that I was, although about as welcome as a plague-bearing rat, stuck on British soil.

"And the last train to London," said the Big Boss, looking at me as if he wanted to say: Now we're alone, now we can smash you against the concrete floor undisturbed. Meanwhile the St. Bernard had already dialled a number and tried to make contact with the Denton-Barkers (the shame of it, thought Willy, what on earth will they think, what will they say?)

"No answer," said the St. Bernard, hanging up. I was relieved, but on the other hand I wanted to shout: you have the letters, you have read them from beginning to end, is it still not clear to you that I am very welcome in her majesty's United Kingdom, how impatiently I am awaited by one of her subjects?

It then struck me that this might actually harm me, that they would not be indifferent, these frustrated individuals whose only real orgasms came from intimidating innocent foreigners, to the fact that I had deflowered one of their English roses (which Willy had in fact done, no offence intended), the kind that would not even condescend to insult them, let alone grant them a smile or offer the hope that they might on this side of eternity sit down with her for a coffee.

"What are we going to do, John?" asked the St. Bernard, turning to his boss, who was already sunk into some other paperwork unconnected with me.

"If you ask me, we've already done more than enough," muttered the blond guy, as if suddenly regretting all the trials they had subjected me to, even though he had played the largest part.

I know how it is, Willy II comforted himself: secretaries, bank clerks, pizza delivery men, hairdressers pose no threat to the former colonial superpower, a problem arises only when a genius knocks on the door – then gates are bolted shut, gun barrels appear through loopholes, boiling pitch is poured from battlements.

Don't be so conceited, Willy I reproached him; if you were more modest we'd be on the train to London now; it was *you* that fucked things up, *you* with your arrogance and posturing!

Before the dialogue between the two Willys could flare up the Big Boss tore himself away from his paperwork (it seemed that he was working on some daily record of passengers that was the bane of his life), reached out his hand and impatiently waggled his fingers; when the St. Bernard handed him my passport he went through it as slowly and carefully as if he was hoping to find on the empty pages an answer to all those questions that the hours of interrogation had left open. But the answer to the main question (how, without endangering his safety, job and mental health, could he cast me into the sea and watch with enjoyment how the *bloody foreigner* slowly drowned) stubbornly evaded him. Finally, he gave a nervous glance at his watch, once more flicked through the passport, opened it at an empty page and reached for the stamp. The sound was heard of an official seal of approval and then he wrote something important on the stamped page, scribbled his signature with a practised gesture, closed the passport and pushed it across the counter towards me.

"Thirty days," he said. "For an extension turn to the Home Office."

With that the matter was ended. But not for me.

"And my paintings?" said Willy II curtly, before Willy I had a chance to open his mouth.

"Your pictures are in safe keeping," said the Big Boss. "If we ascertain that there is no problem with them, then you will get them back. When that will happen I cannot say. Now, if you will allow me, I have other matters to attend to."

The blond guy, who had ended his shift and was in a hurry to get home offered to drive Willy, who had missed the last train, to Canterbury, from where he could catch another train to London Victoria;

that was his only chance of avoiding a long cold night on a wooden bench in the port. Thank you, said Willy I humbly, thank you very, very much.

And kiss my arse, added Willy II in a malicious whisper.

4.

On the train rushing towards London with comfortable, swaying speed, his mood improved considerably, perhaps because the few passengers in the carriage gave an impression of civilised politeness: lost in their newspapers, or their thoughts, or the night that was flashing past the window studded with lights, they showed no interest in Willy, who took the opportunity, after his battles with dragons, to relax a bit, with childish gratitude.

But the moment of relaxation expanded his inner space and both Willys now had an arena large enough to attack each other. Willy II suddenly slapped Willy I's head, claiming that his cowardly tactfulness was the reason for everything that had gone wrong, from the confiscated paintings to the merely one-month visa, to Sandrina, who had vanished for ever, while he could easily have asked for her name, citizenship, age and other details, and above all her contact address and perhaps even telephone number in England.

And what good would that do? responded Willy I. We cannot take possession of everyone and everything that crosses our path; we are artists, not collectors of experiences, people and opportunities. And she is sure to come to Piccadilly Circus tomorrow, even if only out of curiosity. You can jump on her there as soon as you set eyes on her and dig your fangs into her neck, you bloodsucker! And before we forget, remember that there is another lady awaiting us in Cornwall and that we should be feeling grateful to her that we are even on this

32

train, since without her letters, her invitation, we'd now be painting a five-pointed star on a fine arts building somewhere behind the Iron Curtain. Without hope and without an open door into the big wide world.

Willy II immediately revolted against what he heard. Fuck off, you blatherer, he said to poor Willy I, who liked neither vulgarity nor teenage angst, and shrank before such coarseness like a mushroom in hot butter. No doors simply open, you need to smash a door down if you want to enter the spaces that belong to you, and you create opportunity the way the two of us paint – with imagination, it's true, but at the same time audaciously, one, two, three, left and right, using the brush like a sword; what do a few bodies mean to a king on the way to a well-earned kingdom? Do you think that William the Conqueror gained the English throne by asking for it? She will not come to Piccadilly Circus, we have lost her for ever, we shall only be able to paint her from memory, let alone ever make love to her. The fat girl from Cornwall should be glad that we even bother with her; have you ever touched anything more like dough, half-cooked? Okay, good-looking I admit, but as lukewarm as rotting autumn leaves; what kind of women do they have here in England? From now on shall we have dealings only with foreigners? Although I suppose there is no lack of them in London: black girls from Nigeria, brown girls from Brazil, Chinese girls from Malaysia, Indian girls from Kerala – do you realise what is waiting for us? We shall paint only nudes. But you would rather hold these girls by the hand, chew over sentimental insipidity, talk of marriage and eternal faithfulness, sigh like a castrated Romeo, wouldn't you? You're going to be a great problem; more than an artist, you are someone who would like to create the impression that he is good and honest (even if you're not, it's the impression that counts), but that kind of person is a burden that an artist has to drag with him like the debts of three generations of predecessors. This can't go on. At some point we must settle this once and for all, and may the best man win.

Willy I could hardly breathe beneath the avalanche of threats and insults from his double (and, he had finally realised, his competitor!). He wondered whether it was even worth arguing with someone who attacked him in this way, without any sense of fair play, since reason never triumphs when confronted directly by irrationality – it has to lie low and wait for the moment when irrationality encounters its nemesis and burns out, only then can it crawl out of its den and begin to salvage what can be saved.

But there were still some moves available to him in this duel, which was travelling with me and within me towards London. The first was to remain stubbornly polite, knowing all too well that every bit of aggression that collides with the flexible wall of reconciliation sinks into the softness, is sucked in but then reflected back, confused and weakened. The other was strategic delay in the form of vague promises.

That's all true, he said meekly, so that Willy II did not sense the manipulation, but if we look on the bright side, you must admit that things are a lot better than they might be: our money was not confiscated, sooner or later we shall get the paintings back, we shall extend the month into a year and then five, and then we shall be famous and become knights of the British Empire and everyone will have to call us Sir William. If Sandrina, who probably is not Sandrina, but Melina Mercuriopulos or Claudia Cardinalis or Eva Horty or Melek Teglemeth, does not come to Piccadilly Circus tomorrow, we shall undoubtedly come across her some time later, for destiny never makes mistakes, it always knows what we need. And if we don't come across her, it's not the end of the world, there's still a possibility that we may be captivated by some other princess, since London, I agree with you, must be swarming with them. Plump Julia is a nice girl who really should not be put on a pedestal (not least because she herself has no such ambitions), but she can prove useful until she realises that she is wasting her time with us.

At the word useful Willy I was overcome with shame, whereas Willy II grabbed at it as a sign that perhaps Willy I was not his fanatical opponent, but an ally whom he wanted to deceive into thinking that he was more saint than sinner. This comforted and silenced him; he turned his attention to planning detailed viewings of the London galleries. Willy I happily joined him and the split within the fluctuating adventurer was healed. Willy I had won (again, and again in his

34

cunning fashion!), the door to the future was welcomingly open, there was no need to force it, everything was possible; the train was nearing London, hope and anxiety were in just the right balance to create a pleasant sense of excitement.

And who could remain unruffled beneath the arches of the famous Victoria Station, among the hustle and bustle of a colourful mass of people, such as Willy might only have dreamed about: tousled long-haired students, smart businessmen, confused tourists, shoppers laden down with bags, foreigners with every possible shade of skin and dressed in a range of outfits that not even the carnival parade in Willy's home village could match – it was breathtaking and all this just before midnight, when the normal world was asleep!

I was sucked in by the seething mass of untamed life, it embraced and hugged me like a generous uncle: you'll be alright here, I could almost hear the words being said, here life begins for real. Intoxicated by the turbulent colours and lines that almost swept me away, I had no idea which way to turn; it was clear to me only that I needed to spend the night somewhere.

My attention was drawn by a cluster of flashing neon signs: *Information, Hotel, Bed-and-Breakfast, Rent-a-Car, Sightseeing, Money Change*; there, I said to myself. I loaded myself up with my luggage (the suitcases were without wheels, the shoulder bag was slipping off my shoulder) and staggered along the platform to the arched concourse and through to the small counter on which a bored, yawning employee was leaning on his elbows.

Considering the splendour of the flashing signs I had expected about ten staff, very busy, and rows of waiting people, but the fatigued bald guy was apparently responsible for everything and in spite of that still had the time to be solving a crossword puzzle. With barely concealed astonishment he regarded the bearded and long-haired young man dressed in his Sunday best making his way towards him loaded down like a professional porter.

And thus upon his very arrival Willy discovered one of the secrets of the wide world in which he planned to reach for the stars: anything being offered, however modest, should shine with the greatest possible brightness, as if a space ship had just landed. In a way, this

35

bloatedness of what was on offer and suggestive teasing of expectations filled him with great hope; he thought that this was a game he
could master better than all the others and that the secret of success
was perhaps not only a question of quality, but also, if not primarily,
the manner of presentation.

"Good evening, Sir," said the bald man behind the counter with a
benign smile that was not terribly sincere but was at least obliging
and without the unyielding arrogance of the immigration officers.
Moreover, it was the first time that anyone had addressed Willy as Sir,
and that someone old enough to be his father; he was quite stunned
to learn that even a twenty-three year old had to be addressed with
the height of courtesy. What a country! Would he ever understand it?

But the learning process had begun and because he had, in spite of
his inner confusion, a good nose for hidden motives, the thought immediately occurred to him that the respectful addressing of potential
customers was part of the same game to which the neon signs above
him so eminently contributed. The customer is king!

"How may I help you?" continued the man behind the counter,
trying with a smile to encourage the awkward new arrival, who in
the face of such obligingness was beginning to show a slight degree
of mistrust. "A car, currency exchange, accommodation?"

A hotel, breathed Willy, a hotel for one night. Somewhere near,
since I'm travelling on to Cornwall tomorrow.

The gentleman, for that is what he undoubtedly was, since he wore
a tie, although knotted hastily with no feeling for symmetry, ran his
eyes appraisingly over Willy's suit, was slightly taken aback when
he noticed the gold-plated buckles on his shoes; then he assessed the
value and potential contents of the two leather suitcases that were unusual, Willy had noticed, even among the mass of luggage at Victoria
Station, and on the basis of these external indicators (very similar to
the flashing neon signs!) he tried to judge what could be extracted
from this inexperienced young man who had evidently arrived from
a planet at least a thousand light years away from the Earth.

"Yes, I do have something available, although it's not cheap, but
if it's just for one night it shouldn't be a problem," he decided on
Willy's behalf. He dialled the number, spoke quietly with someone

at the other end, put down the phone, folded his arms and said: "Ten minutes. Someone's coming for you."

Well, thought Willy, I won't need to pay for a taxi. But then it struck him that the man had not mentioned the price and he had not asked.

How much ...? he began, but the man, who was expecting the question, waved his hand. "Reasonable, very reasonable. We could look for something cheaper in North London, on the outskirts."

No, no, Willy shook his head. After the events in Dover harbour he could not face another insult. But he became quite bitter thinking about how much thinner his wad of Italian lire would be after this first night. He suddenly thought that the man might know what time the trains to Cornwall were and he did, giving him the details of the first departure at seven in the morning, the second at quarter past eleven and the third at two p.m. He told him he could buy the ticket straight away, or the next day before his departure, although there might be a queue.

Okay, I'll get it now, decided Willy, but just at that moment a short, middle-aged man (he might not have been much more than thirty, but to Willy everyone older than himself was middle-aged) approached and asked the man behind the counter something. He pointed towards Willy, whom the new arrival took in from head to toe at one glance. Then he turned to Willy's distinguished suitcases, picked up one of them, tested its weight, looked at Willy and said: "Shall we go?"

Willy joined him with the other case and together they walked through the arched exit to the car park in front of the station, where people were waiting in line for a taxi.

"First time in London?" asked the man, who had smooth black hair and a slightly swarthy, Sicilian complexion. When Willy nodded, he added: "Then you're going to see some very interesting things."

5.

The first interesting thing that Willy saw was the car in which the man loaded his luggage: it seemed unusually large, shiny, slightly old-fashioned, like a London black cab but more elegant, the black leather sighing softly when he sank into the seat. The man was not all that short, but he could barely see over the top of the steering wheel; his soft, almost feminine hands, adorned with a wealth of rings, did not look strong enough to steer such a car. In spite of that, it glided along the road without any problems, smoothly, as if guided by an invisible power, while the driver's face glowed with satisfaction.

"Have you ever ridden in such a car?" he asked. Willy shook his head. "And do you know what it is?" No, Willy acknowledged, he had no idea.

"Rolls Royce," said the driver, as if informing him that he had won first prize in the lottery. He turned and looked at him: "Surprised?"

Surprised? At first Willy could not open his mouth. Because he did not want to give the impression that he came from some village in the back of beyond and because he felt that the driver was taking too much delight in the shock on his face, he merely shrugged and said that he had not expected on his arrival in London to be met at the station by a Rolls Royce.

And that was the truth. But there were some unpleasant questions connected with this situation: who was this man, whose was the car, to what kind of hotel was he being driven for heaven's sake? Would the room cost him half the savings on which he had planned to live for a year? How the hell had he managed, after all that had already happened, to get himself into yet another such mess?

Suddenly, he felt like a complete idiot. He was just about to say that he was feeling sick and that he wanted to get out when the man behind the wheel read his thoughts and said: "Don't worry, the room with breakfast is only eight pounds. A small hotel, very basic. I'm the owner, there was no one else around to send for you, so I came myself."

Very nice of you, said Willy with relief, suddenly aware that he was being driven through the streets of London in the kind of car that the Queen rode in and when they stopped at some traffic lights the slightly tipsy young people who crossed the road shouted in admiration and peered through the windscreen, trying to guess which famous or rich person they might be lucky enough to see; a pretty girl in a mini-skirt winked and waved at Willy.

The luxurious car glided onwards and suddenly on the right there appeared the outlines of a magnificent building that Willy had already seen on countless postcards and photographs: "The Houses of Parliament," came the proud voice of the friendly driver, who was already behaving as if the whole of London were his and he was offering it to the young foreigner simply in order to bring a smile to his frightened, doubtful face. In taking ownership of such grandeur he was getting most enjoyment himself.

Your hotel is not very near the station, said Willy anxiously.

"We're not going towards the hotel," said the driver, "we're going in a totally different direction."

A totally different direction?! There ran through poor Willy's head at least ten different scenarios from murder mysteries that he had read when he was younger. He sat numbly on the leather seat.

So where are we going? he asked, barely audibly.

The obliging chauffeur was silent for a moment, frightening him even more, and then with his soft hand he patted his knee. "Since it's your first time here I decided to show you London," he said with a smile that suggested: you weren't expecting that, were you? "Now we are driving down Whitehall, on the left is Downing Street, where the Prime Minister lives, in front of us on that tall column is the statue of Admiral Nelson, which is shat upon every day by thousands of pigeons, and now we are coming to Trafalgar Square."

The dimensions of the square and the surrounding buildings filled Willy with deep admiration. Everything was illuminated, he saw the gigantic statues of lions that guarded the pools and fountains, and in spite of the late hour there were people everywhere – the middle of the night was the middle of life – while beside him sat a friend who was acting like his uncle.

He suddenly felt oddly intoxicated, everything spun around him as if he was on the leather seat of a slow roundabout: lights, buildings, immense statues, pillars, portals; the orange lights of pubs with people standing on the pavement outside, glass in hand; the rows of shops, their well-stocked displays full of light; the red double-deckers edging their way through the dense traffic one after another, the black taxis rushing in every direction and expensive sports cars in which long-haired hotshots drove long-haired blondes. All this will be mine, Willy boldly thought, it all belongs to me now although no-one knows it – I'm not even fully aware of it myself – but all that is now on offer to me here will one day, very soon, be within reach and I will be able to choose, accept, reject. This Rolls Royce could already be mine and this friendly chap my chauffeur, and I could be driving home from the opening of my exhibition to my villa in the most exclusive part of London.

He was so lost in his daydreams that he almost failed to catch what the driver (whom he had already in his mind christened Horatio, after Nelson) said next.

"And here is the National Gallery," said his benefactor, pointing somewhere to his left. Where? Willy turned and twisted his neck painfully so as not to miss the celebrated building: he caught only a glimpse of a steep staircase and the pillared entrance before the Rolls Royce turned to the right.

I'll be back, I shall return, this will be my second home, he said.

"Are you interested in art?" asked his friendly driver.

I'm a painter, said Willy in a tone of voice that implied: a Rolls Royce is nice, but what is it in comparison to the fact that I am a painter!

"I didn't know," said the driver in surprise and it seemed to Willy that his numerous rings first glittered and then darkened from shame. "Where are you from, then?"

From Slovenia, said Willy quietly. And then, with slight reluctance: from Yugoslavia. And he wished that the seat would swallow him up, for he would much rather be from France, Russia, Germany, Italy, even Austria. But he was not and he would make himself ridiculous by lying, since he knew that later in the hotel he would have to show his passport.

"I'm not English, either," said the driver without embarrassment. "I'm Polish, or rather a Polish Jew. There are quite a lot of us in London. In fact, it's quite hard to find an Englishman in London; it seems that there is gathered here the strangest assortment of people from every corner of the world. You're welcome, I'm sure you'll make a go of it here."

Oh, replied Willy, as if trying to rid himself of a burden, I'll paint, that's what I was born to do and there's nothing else that I'm good at. His friendly companion was listening in an amicable way and Willy wanted to make him happy (so that he did not think he was showing London to just anyone) with the image of a painter that would compel the man, the next day, to confide to a friend: you'll never guess who I was driving around yesterday. The words gushed out of him, particularly because now he was no longer afraid that the man would mock his English, since as a Pole his English could be nowhere near perfect.

And so there poured from Willy a bizarre assortment of biographical details.

My best known paintings, he said, are *Young Virgin Auto-Sodomised by the Horns of her Own Chastity*, *St. George Overpowering a Cello* and *Leda Atomica*. But they were all confiscated by the idiotic customs officers in Dover because they thought I was smuggling stolen great masters. I'm afraid I'll never see them again. My friends think I'm crazy because on the one hand I'm exceedingly timid, but on the other so demanding towards myself and others that it's often difficult to be in my company. And all this is because of the indescribable sin committed by my parents when they named me after

41

William the Conqueror, thus condemning me at birth to dream about the white cliffs of England and of the kingdom of art that I would establish on the island of Great Britain.

"And here," said the friendly driver, as if he was not even listening, "is Piccadilly Circus, with the famous statue of Eros, below which lovers from all over the world gather. Here on St. Valentine's Day John Lennon and Yoko Ono kissed in front of a crowd of people!"

Oh, recalled Willy, for me it is more important that tomorrow at eleven I shall meet here with my dear Helena Devulina Diakanova, Gala for short, although I prefer to call her Sandrina. In reality she is the daughter of a Moscow writer and the wife of the French poet Paul Eluard, but I mean more to her than anything in the world. When we met she said: My dear, we shall never ever part. I like painting nudes and she is my favourite model. But as I said: everything stayed behind in Dover. I don't know how some petty officials in a country that prides itself on its democratic credentials can steal the fruits of somebody's labour.

"Don't worry," said his new friend, "I'll get your pictures back, all of them. In return you can paint my portrait."

With pleasure, agreed Willy, it won't be difficult because you have very prominent, unusual features – even Holbein would be pleased with you.

The Rolls Royce glided comfortably along the wide tree-lined avenue towards an unlit building, which as it drew nearer grew ever larger and finally revealed itself to Willy as yet another one that he had seen on thousands of photographs. That's Buckingham Palace, he said.

"Excellent," said the driver, "unfortunately the Queen is currently not in residence, otherwise there would be a flag flying on the roof. She's probably in Windsor or one of her other castles – even she doesn't know how many she has."

They went round the palace, turning into a deserted street that led back towards Parliament. "In a few years when you're really successful, she will invite you to tea," said the driver."

If she wants, said Willy with a shrug, as if not particularly interested.

"I'm serious," said the Pole. "Every year the Queen organises a tea party to which she invites immigrants who have succeeded in Britain.

Many wait to be invited, but few are. Some wait their whole lives and then die; some get invited when they're only forty."

I don't really care, said Willy, I'm only twenty-three.

"Today," said the man, "but not tomorrow, tomorrow you'll be older. And then more, every day; time won't stop just because you're in London and your personal driver is driving you round in a Roller."

I don't want time to stop, said Willy, I just want my wishes to be fulfilled.

"And what do you want?"

Everything that a guy of my age wants, replied Willy, success, riches, fame.

"What about love?" asked the Pole with a glance.

Not too much, replied Willy. You find love incidentally, so it's not important. Although, he said, remembering Sandrina, there is also love that is not of the everyday kind but unique, misunderstood. But such love comes to few and among the few, one artist in a hundred thousand, so there's no point thinking about the unattainable and stealing time from what is.

"Success, riches and fame," repeated the driver, as if savouring his favourite Polish sausage. "Then you should be interested in tea with the Queen. That is the only proof that you have really made it – all the rest is nothing."

Oh, said Willy, a little agitated, I don't mean success that easily can be measured, nor riches that can be expressed in terms of share prices, nor fame of the kind where hordes of teenagers would chase me down the street. I'm talking about success in the sense that I could go to sleep each night in the knowledge that I had created works of art such that I daren't even dream about. Of the riches that the world would see in my paintings. About fame limited to the concealed admiration of other painters. All the rest is nothing, all the rest is just smoke.

Both Willys knew that this was Willy I speaking, while Willy II agreed more with the Polish driver's definition and was already secretly dreaming how in a chauffeur-driven Rolls Royce he was on his way to have tea with the Queen. And what about you, Willy turned to the driver, have you been invited?

"Me?" laughed the driver without sarcasm. "I'm no-one."

6.

Willy thought about precisely this when the car stopped in front of a two-storey terrace building with a broken neon hotel sign on which only the letters *o, e, l* were visible. What was the name of this *.o.el*? asked Willy, who could not hide his disappointment, nor his confusion about the disharmony between the car and the building.

"The hotel with no name," replied the Pole, suddenly a lot less friendly than he had been, as if he too was disappointed at the modest appearance of his property. But he immediately recovered with the statement that he had four hotels. "This is the cheapest. They said at the station that you didn't have much money."

But I do have some paintings that the customs officers did not discover, he boasted, although the next moment he regretted his candour. For when, with the other man's help, he had carted his luggage into the small hotel lobby where there was also a bar, he saw a group of men with furrowed faces such as he had before seen only in films about London's criminal networks. He had managed to land directly in a nest of burglars, robbers, prison escapees and drug dealers, who would not only steal the paintings from his case, but would probably cut his throat! And they were all staring at him ill-temperedly, like a pack of wolves at a lamb that has wandered into their midst.

"Is that the new guest?" asked a fat, bald guy whose hairy hands were resting on the bar. "A real gentleman," he said, looking Willy over from head to toe. "Gentlemen normally stay in better hotels."

44

"He's not a gentleman, but an artist," said the Pole, who was already behind the bar pouring himself a whisky. "His name is Salvador Dali. A little earlier he was telling me the titles of his best paintings." He raised his glass towards Willy and said "Cheers!"

Poor Willy almost collapsed under the shock. The friendly driver, who perhaps was the owner of four hotels, including this den of thieves, *knew* that his bullshit about Gala and Dali pictures was nothing more than the pathetic self-praise of one too full of himself. He knew and had said nothing! What kind of impression had he made? In England people were evidently *interested* in art. If even the owner of a shabby hotel, regardless of the fact that he drove a Rolls Royce, knew Dali's work, then he needed to learn a lot about this world that operated under different rules, not march into it with assumptions that reality immediately squashed.

And not with footwear that attracted such attention; now the amazed thieves were staring at them. "Nice shoes," said one of them. "Someone who wears shoes like that can't be badly off," said another. "Better off than we are," said a third. Then, as if under orders, they turned back to their game of poker. Was it just Willy's impression, or had they exchanged meaningful looks?

"Would Mr. Dali like a drink?" the fat man at the bar turned to the Pole.

"I don't know, ask him," came the reply. "Actually, don't," he added immediately, "I'll give him something, you go up and see if the room is alright."

"Which room?" asked the fat man.

"You know which one," said the Pole with a wink – or did it only seem to Willy that he had winked?

"Ah, that one," said the fat man with a nod and with heavy steps he went up the narrow staircase.

Silence fell. The Pole was looking for something under the bar, while the mobsters – there were five of them, all with distorted Picassoesque jaws, eyes and noses – carried on playing poker. Willy was frantically wondering what the response would be if he grabbed his luggage and rushed out into the night.

But what then? Alone on an empty street in London? He numbly had to admit that he was the prisoner of these people until morning.

"Here," the Pole offered him a glass of whisky. "Let's drink to the start of a glittering artistic career." Did Willy really detect a hint of sarcasm in his tone? Actually, he said, putting the glass down, I should ring the family in Cornwall, so that they meet me at the station tomorrow.

"You're going to Cornwall?" asked the Pole with surprise and the five mobsters turned their heads.

Willy explained that the family had invited him to spend a few days with them. The father was the chief of police in Penzance, Mr. Denton-Barker, from an aristocratic background. He had called from the station, but then he hadn't known exactly when he'd be arriving; now he knew and he wanted to let them know as soon as possible.

"At this time," said the Pole, smoothing his greasy black hair, "such a respectable English family will be asleep. They won't be pleased if you wake them up. Call in the morning."

I promised I'd do it today, Willy insisted and one of the mobsters laughed: "It *is* morning, it's two o'clock."

"In any case," added the Pole, "there's no phone."

A London hotel without a phone? Will said nothing, but the Pole, reading the question on his face, quickly added: "Of course, we have a phone but it's not working." He spread his hands as if to say what can you do?

Then Willy was overcome by a sense of numb surrender to fate; his soul left his body and he began to watch proceedings as if in the stalls of a theatre, following a drama with an uncertain outcome; everything seemed to be happening in slow motion, the glass of whisky that the Pole was once again offering him was travelling towards him as if it would never reach his hand, while through Willy's head there flashed recollections of the day. He was not searching for lost time, but the wrong step that had led, through a chain of coincidences, into a crime story, instead of the warm embrace of the love story he had dreamed about, or the role of romantic hero that had sent him into the world to charm it, or even to lift a spell.

He cultivated the hope that he was misreading the signs, but that was looking ever less likely, especially when the fat man panted back down from the first floor and announced that he had broken the key to the room and could not find another.

"I'll stand in front of the door and guard it," said one of the poker players, "otherwise the poor boy won't get a wink of sleep." His colleagues supported him with an obliging laugh. But the laughter was too hollow to be genuine: they all knew, and Willy most of all, that this was a charade – the key had not broken, it had been hidden so that he could not lock his room door. As soon as he fell asleep, tired as he was, they would rob him.

Once it became clear to him what was being planned he was not in the least surprised when the Pole suggested he should show them the paintings that he had managed to conceal from the customs officers in Dover.

"Of course," said the fat bald one, who must weigh at least a hundred kilos, "let's see what kind of artist this Mr. Dali is."

They wanted to see what was worth stealing; besides his money, of course, and his shoes.

Obediently, like a condemned man before the executioner, Willy bent over, opened one of his cases, pulled out three canvases and unrolled them right there on the dirty carpet. The first was an original piece of work that he was delighted had not been confiscated: three dancing virgins in veils that were swirling around them, like the misty edge of a galaxy that is densest at the centre, in front of an orangey red cloud that could be a fire or a stellar explosion, entitled *Bad Luck Comes in Threes*. The second was a copy of Gauguin's *The Spirit of the Dead Watching,* which Willy had painted to satisfy his longing for exotic places; the third was Leonardo's *Mona Lisa,* the same size as the original, suitable for the living room of some social climber from the lower middle class.

"Well," said the fat bald man, "who'd have thought it? The lad's got talent." Then Willy heard the rasping voice of one of the mobsters; he looked up and saw the five representatives of the London criminal fraternity standing round; some ash fell from the cigar of the one standing closest to him and Willy felt it burning inside his shirt collar. It was him who spoke: "Not only talent, but a need for love that he can't satisfy. He paints only broads!"

One of the others added: "For some it's not enough to touch women, they have to have a picture to look at all the time. Where's the boy from? In London it's easier to buy a porn mag."

The owner of the hotel, who had a third glass of whisky in his hand, now joined in. "Idiot," he rebuked the one who had just spoken. "If that dark-haired one with the enigmatic smile was an original we could get for it more than for the Duke of Westminster's share of Mayfair, no problem." The others looked stunned and exchanged glances, while the fat bald one said: "At the very least."

"I'm so unhappy," said the Pole, sipping his whisky, "to be surrounded by people who have never heard of the Mona Lisa. What have I done to deserve such a fate?"

The others muttered and shifted their angular shoulders, and then one of the bright sparks mumbled: "But if we could convince someone that this Money Leasing *is* the original then we'd be laughing, wouldn't we?" At these words they all turned to the Pole: only one person's opinion was relevant when it came to such matters.

And the Pole without hesitation responded: "Before you could convince someone of that he would have to receive a blow from the fist of some big idiot so that he became an even bigger idiot than the one who had hit him!"

"So," continued the proposer of the idea," we can give it a try, we're not short of fists."

"Oh my God," sighed the Pole "don't listen to them lad, they're not as stupid as they look, but rather a hundred times more. The Gauguin is a really good copy, better than the Mona Lisa. But the other one is yours, isn't it? That's the best. That's undoubtedly you. Does it have a price?"

No, Willy shook his head, that's a present for the girl I'm going to visit. And he was suddenly overcome by a tremendous weariness, not only physical, although he was on the edge of exhaustion, but psychological, since he felt that from the minute he had set foot on British soil he had been at every step the victim of manipulation, for which he could only guess at the motive, except in this instance, where it was crystal clear that the owner of the hotel was taking his side only to alleviate his suspicion and lull him into a false sense of security.

48

Willy lent forward, rested his folded arms on his other case and put his head on his arms as if on a chopping block: chop my head off, the movement said, but stop toying with me.

"The boy's tired" said the fat bald one.

"Of course," agreed the Pole, "he's had a long journey." Willy felt the man's hand on his shoulder, shaking him slightly. "Bedtime," he heard the voice, in which after all the cold irony there was once more some kindness. He almost felt grateful, although he knew it was not sincere.

He put the pictures back in his case, closed it and got to his feet. The whole time he was waiting for one of the thugs to hit him from behind, but they had already resumed their card game as if nothing of importance had happened. And perhaps nothing had, Willy thought, with his last ounce of hope; maybe they were just trying to be obliging.

But the very next moment his suspicions returned with redoubled strength. "Give me the list," said the Pole. "The list of pictures they seized in Dover. And you'll have to sign that you authorise me to act on your behalf if you want to get them back."

The list? said Willy in surprise. The list stayed in Dover.

"Did they sign it?" asked the Pole.

No, replied Willy, I had to sign it.

There was a short silence, during which the Pole cleared his throat. Then he said: "Did you hear that, boys? The lad signed for a list of pictures the customs seized from him. They didn't give him a receipt, but he gave them one!"

The mobsters laughed with one voice. "And I thought I needed a brain operation," one of them said through his laughter. To which another added: "Maybe the boy's already had one and that's his problem."

"Whatever," said the Pole. "Next time, be more cautious: not everyone in this country is honest and that also goes for state officials, sadly. In any case, write me an authorisation. I'll see what can be done."

And so poor Willy, now totally exhausted, at two-thirty in the morning, at the bar of a run-down hotel in God knows which part of

London, wrote down in error-ridden English, as the owner dictated, a declaration that he Vili Vaupotič, born on this date in this place, resident in this place, passport number this, authorises Mr. Richard Whitehouse, following the completion of the official procedure at the port of Dover, to collect the paintings confiscated by Her Majesty's customs officers, for they are the results of his own work and his inalienable property, regardless of the legal implications of their entry to the United Kingdom, in London on this date, signature.

Are you Richard Whitehouse? asked Willy, slightly surprised.

"My name is Palisander," said the Pole. "Richard Whitehouse is a friend of mine who has contacts where they are needed." To which one of the mobsters added: "And where he doesn't, he creates them." This was followed by the obligatory laughter.

"Get in touch in about a month," said the Pole, "then it'll be clear what the chances are." He turned to the fat bald one: "Take his luggage upstairs."

What about signing the register? asked Willy, but Mr. Palisander waved his hand: "It's not important, we'll sort it out."

Of course, if a guest registers then you have to explain where he has disappeared to, if he happens to disappear. This way you can claim that he was never there, which is certainly convenient if you have a plan to dispose of him!

This and similar thoughts were still running through Willy's head when he was installed in his room and he confirmed that the door could not be locked. The room was small, the bed wobbly, the mattress sunken, in places the wallpaper was parting company with the walls, the ceiling was stained with damp, the bathroom and toilet were at the end of the corridor, there was no sink in the room, no mirror, there was dust everywhere and the greasy curtains gave off a strange smell.

The only things that Willy was pleased to see were the cupboard, chest-of-drawers and table; with the last of his strength he moved them in front of the door, first of all blocking the door handle with the chest-of-drawers, then pushing the cupboard behind it and finally the table, at which he sat down on a tattered upholstered chair, resting his head on his arms. He knew that he would not be able to sleep

50

and should not. He got up and checked whether, in case of someone breaking into the room during the night, he could escape through the window. But the sash window had been so heavily covered with gloss paint that it was stuck to the frame and was impossible to open.

Thy will be done, said Willy, who suddenly remembered that he had been raised as a Catholic.

He opened the greasy curtains and looked out at the street through the dirty window panes. It was raining again and the endless row of identical buildings on the other side of the street, seen through the veil of water, looked only half real, like stage scenery. All the houses had dustbins next to the steps that led from the pavement to the front door. Below him, right in front of the hotel, stood the Rolls Royce. On the damp, deserted street it suddenly looked very small, just a parked car, one of many, nothing special. Willy felt overcome by something worse than tiredness: a deep, inconsolable sense of sadness.

Thy will be done, he said to himself. He sat at the table, intending to guard the door all night. Finally, he wrapped the belt of the shoulder bag in which he had his money around his head.

7.

I was awoken by the noise of someone trying to get into the room. The cupboard started to sway alarmingly and to push against the table on which I had been dozing. I heard raised voices, including that of a woman. It was very bright in the room, although not from the light that I had left switched on, but rather the daylight that was coming through the window behind me. I looked at my watch: ten-thirty! It seemed impossible to me that I could have slept leaning on the table for eight hours without once waking up and yet that was obviously what had happened, because the chamber maid was trying to get in, helped by the fat bald man.

"I've never seen anything like it since I've worked in this hotel," I heard him say. "It's bizarre." A guttural female voice added in a foreign accent: "If Mr. Palisander saw this what would he think?"

The next moment the door was wide enough open for her to stick her head inside: I saw that she was dark-skinned, a little older than me, with wiry hair and nervous eyes; she reminded me of one of Gauguin's Pacific Island beauties, with simple, clumsy, rounded, but nevertheless beautiful features and a strange innocence.

"Oh Jesus," she exclaimed when she saw me. I jumped up and tried to shove the pieces of furniture away from the door. Soon she was able to push her way into the room. "Why did you frighten us like that?" she said, wagging her finger at me. "We thought you were dead."

Oh, I thought, I can hardly believe that I am not!

"Breakfast is waiting for you downstairs," said her companion glumly and turned to go back downstairs. I don't have time for breakfast, I shouted after him, grabbed my bags and began to stagger down the stairs. I wanted to pay for the room and was already looking in my shoulder bag for my wallet. Then I would ask Mr. Palisander to drive me straight away to Piccadilly Circus.

The fat guy was standing behind the counter writing something on a piece of paper. I shuffled nervously from one foot to another, looking at my watch. "Eight pounds," he said finally, as if he had had great difficulty arriving at the figure, which had been completely clear from the beginning. I put the requested amount on the counter (for that price I might have found a table to lean on even at Victoria Station, I thought), then I impatiently looked around the empty space and asked: Where is Mr. Palisander?

I immediately realised that my domineering manner did not suit his temperament. He pulled a face, as if he had no intention of responding.

I'm in a hurry, I said, trying to soften my impatience somewhat and add a beseeching tone. It did not make any difference: when he spoke, he was puffed up with delight that he could disappoint me. "Mr. Palisander went on some errands," he sang, with a satisfied look.

How can I get to Piccadilly Circus in twenty minutes? I asked, as if really expecting an answer.

"Don't know," he shrugged. "However, I feel obliged to point out that Mr. Palisander is not a manservant charged with the transport of guests, but the owner of the hotel."

You can feel as obliged as you want, you moron, I thought and leaned on the counter in despair. Can you call me a taxi? I asked, deciding once more to raid my limited budget.

"Normally I could," he replied sweetly, "but I can't because the phone is still out of action."

And so it came about that poor Willy was forced to cart his luggage along the litter strewn pavement of the not very salubrious street of houses with peeling facades, to a junction with another street, along which taxis supposedly drove, past overflowing dustbins emitting the smell of rotting food. Hungry, unwashed and still half asleep, he stumbled across the uneven paving stones with grass growing between them, unpleasantly surprised at the down-at-heel appearance and unpleasant odours of the big city, feeling ever more out of breath, over-heated and perspiring from haste and effort, while he was getting increasingly wet because, in spite of the sunshine, a fine rain was pouring from the few clouds in the sky and it was being blown into his face by sharp gusts of wind, transforming his trousers into wet rags and his hair into lank strands.

Never in his life had Willy felt so disenchanted by his fate, which in its conspiracy against him had not overlooked the slightest detail and ensured that, when he arrived at the corner of the street, there was no taxi in sight, even though there were plenty of other vehicles roaring past, belching exhaust fumes, from lorries, buses and motorbikes to every other kind – even a horse and cart trotted by. But nowhere a vehicle that would take him to Eros, where Sandrina awaited him. And if he were to appear in front of her like a sheepdog that had been rolling in the mud, what would she say?

A taxi came along, but it was occupied, then another, also with passengers; it was raining ever harder and he was surrounded by rushing umbrellas, of which he had not even thought; he was prepared for almost any eventually, except for the fact that in England it was constantly raining. Then a taxi mysteriously appeared right in front of him; the driver looked at him until Willy shifted himself and crammed his luggage into the back, leaving barely enough room for himself, but the driver had already forced his way into the stream of traffic and was skilfully weaving his way towards the centre. Daytime London was bustling and honking and pulsing and teeming like an ant heap of unstoppable but strangely well-ordered energy, which in the middle of the night Willy had been unable to imagine; the city was literally roaring and the noise frightened the aspiring conqueror like charging cavalry with swords raised, yelling battle cries, fighting for their country.

He looked at his watch; ten past eleven – he was already late! How much longer? he asked the driver, who had to push back the small sliding glass partition in order to hear him.

54

"Hard to say," he shrugged, "what time's your appointment?"

Eleven, replied Willy gloomily, we're late.

"Eleven!" exclaimed the driver. "then you're going to be too early, it's only ten past ten." No, said Willy petulantly, it's ten past eleven.

"Maybe where you come from," said the driver somewhat haughtily, "but in England it's ten past ten. Look, on the right there is Big Ben, which is never wrong."

And then Willy remembered: when he arrived the previous evening, although he knew he was supposed to do it, he had forgotten to put his watch back! The sense of relief was indescribable: he could barely restrain himself from laughing out loud.

Then, with his elbows on his luggage, he perched on the steps below Eros, the traffic circling the fenced-off statue on Piccadilly Circus. He sat in the middle of a crowd of hippies and tourists from every corner of the world, each of them waiting for their own Sandrina, or perhaps they had come only to have their photographs taken in front of the statue, or perhaps just so that they could say they had been here, or for God knows what reason that Willy was not really interested in since all his attention was directed at when his One True Love would appear, walking gracefully towards him.

He already knew what he would say. "I've been waiting for this moment all my life." It was true that Willy II objected vigorously, saying none too politely that words like that are uttered on such occasions only by the heroes of cheap novels, which he had no intention of becoming, since this wasn't a time of romanticism, but only cynicism, opportunism and free love with no strings attached, but Willy I successfully defied him until the clock showed half-past eleven English time and it became obvious that the much-awaited one would not be making an appearance.

Even then, Willy I wanted to persist until midday, for she had perhaps got stuck in the traffic. The rain, which had stopped for a while, started again and the area in front of the statue began to empty. Willy, drenched to the bone, started to cough quietly. With a leaden weight on his heart he decided to look for a taxi to take him to the station.

And on the journey to Cornwall, as he stared through the window at the neat English countryside, at the fields bordered by fences and

55

hedges, at the houses, some with thatched roofs and tall chimneys, prettily clustered around a stone church, at the square, round, triangular or even figure-eight shaped copses, not an inch that had not been shaped by human hand, it seemed to him that in this land life was also carefully arranged; that everyone knew what they wanted; that everyone was where they wanted to be; that nobody lacked anything; that all the houses were fully built, mature, pleasantly aged, there were no building sites, no cranes, no yawning holes instead of windows; that here love was not longing, but rather a pleasant habit; that death held no fear because in a way it was already present in the fact that everything was already achieved, everything was optimal, everything was at rest even in movement, just as the landscape had already exhausted its depictive possibilities in the great canvases of Turner and Constable, who had, now one, now the other, like a warning and a revelation combined, configured in different shades of colour the passing meadows, fields, villages, clouds and the scarlet sun that here and there shone through the gaps between them.

"First time in England?" asked the brown-haired young woman who sat opposite with her silent husband and sleepy young son.

Willy was startled; for a moment he had forgotten that this was England; the image of England that he had brought with him still did not leave room for reality. Yes, he nodded eventually. I'm going to marry a girl who will be waiting for me at the station in Penzance. "Oh," said the woman, glancing at her husband, "how nice."

She would have continued the conversation but Willy gloomily pressed his face to the glass and concentrated on the scenery. Before the train departed he had spoken with the girl who was supposed to meet him at the station and her voice had oddly depressed him; it was friendly enough, but without warmth or enthusiasm, somehow empty and mechanical. And when at the end she had said how happy she was that they would see each other again after almost a year it sounded like one of those polite English phrases that were more a matter of manners than a way of communicating real feelings. He detected a hint of something more genuine in her voice only at the end when she said he was not to worry about her parents: her mother was very understanding and her father was so absorbed in himself and his work that he would not bat an eyelid even if a bomb exploded in his vicinity. What's more, her mother was a great watercolour enthusiast, so they could spend hours talking about art.

In spite of this, Willy was increasingly anxious about the meeting; not so much about the parents, but about her, since he did not know what she expected of him or what he could expect of her – what he actually wanted from her. It had never been as clear to him that he was not travelling towards Cornwall to deepen their relationship after a year of lukewarm correspondence, but rather to have somewhere to go, to get acclimatised, to weigh his options, to seek some advice about what to do – and then to London and action.

Julia Denton-Barker was just – and neither Willy suffered any illusions about this – a staging post on his journey. Willy I had a bit of a bad conscience about this, while Willy II knew that he was nothing more than a staging post on *her* journey: she was twenty years old and wanted some experience and fun, nothing serious. But what did she expect from him and what could he offer her now that he had been possessed by Sandrina? Would their friendship survive if he confided in her? Willy II thought it would and that if it did not, then so what – but at the end of the day, why even mention it? Willy I, however, thought that life was governed by an inexorable law of moral balance: the mistakes we make here and now we pay a price for elsewhere, while each small mistake, each compromise we make to ease our way forward sooner or later turns out to be an unconscious step towards perdition. And so to him absolute honesty, even if it brought short-term damage, seemed not only right, but also sensible.

We shall see, said Willy II, dismissing his scruples. We shall decide at a suitable moment.

Plump Julia, who was waiting at the station exit in a light spring coat, was somewhat different from how he remembered her, wider hips and heavier thighs, her feet turned inwards in shabby sandals, wearing a creased checked mini-skirt and strands of uncombed hair – a rather neglected country girl, decided Willy II. She welcomed him with a smile that required no explanation, it was warm and trusting, even timid, especially when, after a brief hesitation, she stepped up to him and gave him a hug, albeit a rather reserved one it seemed to him.

And then the usual avalanche of questions: how was the journey, how are you, are you very tired, for which Willy was grateful since he was able to respond in monosyllables, for his tongue felt curiously tied; and later, when they were sitting in her rattling Mini and driving along the narrow road through the hills, she did most of the talking, about the bad weather, although the sun had just come out, about college and taking a year off, and in passing she mentioned that she had been in Paris, where she "had got some additional experience of life".

This immediately caused some embarrassment to Willy; her immediate hint at sexual experience, the lack of which he had criticised her for when they first met, and the indubitable suggestion that he would be more satisfied with her this time, felt like such a burden to him, like an infringement of his rights, that he began to wonder if he wanted to continue with the relationship from which their friendship had grown. But from the way her eyes ran over his face to check his reaction, he felt that a lukewarm or even discouraging response would not suffice and so he gathered all his reserves of strength and lied as convincingly as he could: That's great! But he immediately felt that he had committed himself and so made an attempt to leave himself an exit strategy: And your parents?

"Oh," she said, "my parents are quite simple folk, but they are not old-fashioned."

And thus the beautiful-eyed Julia drove Willy in her Mini along the narrow road through the deserted pastures of the windy Cornwall hills like a trophy, a personal achievement, something to be proud of ("My friends would also like to meet you!") and satisfied that she would be able to show off a talented artist. What is more, she had also made plans for what the artist would be doing.

"You probably didn't notice that I've lost some weight. So you'll need less paint for your nudes!"

Willy ran his eyes over her ample body, squashed between the steering wheel and the seat. She did not seem the slightest bit thinner than she had been the previous summer, when after lengthy persuasion she had exposed herself to his brush behind some rocks in a small Adriatic cove.

58

Wonderful, he lied once more, with a sour smile that he hoped she did not notice. And what about the nude paintings, had she shown them to her parents?

She nodded. "To mother. Not my father. And of course my friends. Quite a few of my girlfriends are looking forward to posing for you!"

Oh, replied Willy, taken aback by such generosity.

"But I'll be there," she warned him with a smile, "to make sure that nothing untoward happens – one of them is very naughty!"

Willy was surprised how little the thought excited him, how little interest he felt in variations of relationships in a time of free love. He was taken, he was tied to a single vision: as soon as he thought about painting a nude then the image of Sandrina appeared in front of him and stubbornly persisted until he transferred his thoughts to the cows and sheep grazing on the melancholy hillsides.

So few trees, he thought. Hardly any. Had anyone succeeded in painting the low hills of Cornwall without sinking into depression and killing himself?

I'm really curious how your parents will receive the painting that I…

Oh no! Willy interrupted himself. Oh my God! Stop! Stop the car!

When the frightened Julia stopped at the side of the road he leapt from the car and stood there in the gusting wind that was almost strong enough to knock him over, wringing his hands. He ran along the road and put his head in his hands, as if he had just lost his mind. He had suddenly remembered that he had hidden the three paintings that had not been confiscated in Dover under the bed in the London hotel room. And he had left them behind. Should he go back? Why hadn't he left them in the suitcase? Why, in this strange world, did he have to fear himself more than others?

"Is that all?" said Julia with surprise when he told her. "Don't worry, you'll paint some more."

8.

In spite of this the evening, when we finally came to the isolated farm in a hollow between the hills, turned into a painful drama of clarification, repentance and the planning of steps to ensure that everything that had been forgotten, seized or stolen would be restored to its rightful place.

Mr. and Mrs. Denton-Barker were obliging listeners and each of them in their own way expressed outrage at those points in Willy's story where it was called for. The blonde, rosy-cheeked mother did this very vociferously, while the pale and extremely thin father restricted himself to restrained nods and affirmations. Although he was striving not to show it, he evidently did not like the fact that his daughter had brought into his house a strange foreigner who, immediately upon his arrival, spasmodically looking for the right words in his more than modest vocabulary, accused his majesty's officials of the sin of confiscating his pictures without reason and without giving him a receipt, of reading his private correspondence which in a country where the rule of law applied could only be done by a court investigating a crime, while in passing stealing two bottles of plum brandy that he had brought for his hosts!

(This was of course untrue, but Willy had to think of something when he realised at the last moment that he had forgotten to bring these kind people a present; moreover, with this detail his portrait of the "Dover mafia" became much more realistic.)

Even more thrilling was the story of the door without a key, of the hotel that had been a London underworld den, and the reasons that the paintings he had brought for the Denton-Barkers had remained under the bed. To top it all, he had only been given a one month visa; he had barely arrived and he was already having to think about returning home.

Julia said nothing, she sat to one side as if unsure whether she was more embarrassed by the behaviour of the British officials or because of Willy, who had brought into her home so many scarcely believable problems (and whom, as she said later, she had described to her mother as a sensitive young man in complete control of himself and his surroundings).

"We'll deal with it all," said the mother. "We shall write a letter of complaint to the Home Office, demanding the return of the pictures and the bottles, and request an extension of the visa with a letter of guarantee. They should give you at least six months and then we shall see."

The father gave his wife a meaningful unhappy look and asked: "Are you sure we're doing the right thing?"

"I've never been more sure," she replied without hesitation. "And we can immediately call this hotel and ask them to look for the paintings under the bed."

But with regard to the name of the hotel, Willy could only cite *.o.el.* Hadn't he asked what the hotel was called? No, it never occurred to him that it might matter, nor on what road it was, let alone to ask for a receipt when he paid for the room. The only thing he could tell them was that the hotel was pretty run-down and that the owner had brought him there in a Rolls Royce.

At this, his hosts exchanged a significant glance. Willy recalled that the owner had been a Polish Jew by the name of Palisander, that he knew quite a lot about art and that he had offered to try and get the seized pictures back through his contacts in Dover.

The story was becoming ever less credible and Willy was sounding increasingly like someone who was thinking up excuses because he had come on a visit empty-handed. Even the mother suddenly sighed. But the next moment she collected herself and asked: "What did you say? Palisander?"

Mr. Denton-Barker was not slow to observe that that was not even a Polish name, let alone a Jewish one, and certainly not a Polish Jewish one, but his wife dismissed this with a wave of the hand: "The only thing that interests us is his telephone number."

Unfortunately, a call to directory enquiries by the obedient Julia revealed that there was no one of that name listed.

"Then I don't know what to do," said her mother, admitting defeat. The husband got up and went outside. He did not slam the door but Willy thought that he closed it a lot more decisively than Julia and her mother were used to. There was silence in the room which, if he had to paint it, Willy would have depicted as a black cloud.

"Anyway," the mother broke the awkward silence, "you must be hungry."

Oh, not really, lied Willy, I ate on the train, or rather before I got on (in reality, he had gulped down a stale sandwich), I'm more tired than anything.

"I can understand that," she said, getting up. "Bathroom and then bed, I think. Julia, would you give him a towel?"

With these words she left the living room and Willy felt, not for the first time that evening, that the second phase of his invasion of England had ended in the same shameful defeat as the first. Head down, he followed Julia upstairs, where she showed him the room opposite hers and then the bathroom at the end of the landing.

"Shall I help you with your luggage?" she asked. No, no, it's okay, replied Willy. As if expecting such a response she wished him good night in a colourless voice and disappeared into her room.

Willy entered his. He could not summon up enough courage to splash around in the bathroom, so he decided to go to bed. He knew that he had not made a good impression. Quite the opposite: his general awkwardness had managed to cast a shadow on Julia who, responsible for his presence in the house, probably felt embarrassed in front of her parents, and hence her coldness towards him.

But they were friends, he could trust her, describe his fears, ask for advice; she was sure to help him since she had seen how clumsily he was trying to cope with an environment to which he was not accustomed.

He went quietly onto the landing, listened at her door, knocked. Silence. He knocked once more. Silence. He turned the handle, gently pushed the door and saw her lying in bed, reading. Her lower half was under the covers and she was wearing a white sleeveless top that emphasised the generosity of her half-exposed bosom. Her dark eyes peered at him with a mixture of politeness, fear, disappointment, anger and even, he thought, hatred.

"What?" she said.

Poor Willy, he himself did not know why he knelt beside the bed – perhaps to get closer to her or to avoid giving her the feeling that he was threatening her or had any expectations? He humbled himself before her, both literally and metaphorically (what had happened to the young man that had a year before confidently taken her virginity?).

But she interpreted his move, intended to express subordination, as reaching for her as if he owned her, to touch her, try to kiss her. She recoiled, raised the book in front of her as if in defence and moved back against the wall.

"I think you should go to bed," she said. "Aren't you tired?"

Was it only Willy's impression, or were her eyes, in spite of her timidity, really emitting a silent request not to take her defensive movements too seriously, but in spite of them to reach out for her? He did not receive an answer. In fact, he wanted to avoid it, for in that moment he needed more than anything spiritual closeness, but after her attempt to protect herself physically he could not tell her that; he sensed that she may interpret this as rejection of the body she was perhaps offering, even though she wanted to give the impression that she was defending it; she was offering herself in this way because she did not want to risk rejection.

And because after all that had happened, her body no longer tempted him and the thought of restoring their physical intimacy filled him more with a sense of duty rather than pleasure, he got to his feet, saying: You're right. Good night.

He remembered that he had in his suitcase a book of poetry that Julia had lent him a year before which he had to return. *Selected Poems of Matthew Arnold*. He took it out and opened it.

Joy comes and goes, hope ebbs and flows / Like the wave; / Change doth unknit the tranquil strength of men / Love lends life a little grace, / A few sad smiles; and then / Both are laid in one cold place, / In the grave.

Willy was suddenly overcome by a great wave of sadness; the dams broke and tears flowed, dripping onto the book, and he could not stop them.

Men dig graves with bitter tears / For their dead hopes; and all, / Mazed with doubts and sick with fears, / Count the hours.

Now he was sobbing out loud and shaking.

These dreams of ours / False and hollow / Do we go hence and find they are not dead? ... Hopes born here, and born to end, / Shall we follow?

The title of the poem was *A Question.*

He put down the book and rushed over to the window; he opened it gasping, feeling that he was suffocating, as if he was lying beneath a heap of earth in a freshly dug grave; he leaned out and offered his face to the cold wind that in the dark evening was gusting across the dark, grassy slopes, swirling round corners and knocking against something metallic. One gust that caught his face felt like a slap from a strict teacher dissatisfied with his homework. The next gust burst into the room and fluttered the pages of the book that Willy had left open on the table; he felt that the wind was turning to another page.

Had the wind brought him an answer to his Question?

He closed the window and returned to the table. He read the first verse of the poem *Urania.*

She smiles and smiles, and will not sigh, / While we for hopeless passion die; / Yet she could love, those eyes declare, / Were but men nobler than they are.

His tears subsided, a sense of relief arose, a new hope and with it gratitude. Sandrina took on a new name: Urania.

Yet she could love, those eyes declare, / Were but men nobler than they are. With this thought Willy crawled under the covers and as he slowly drifted off to sleep he contemplated the image of his Urania, to impress her for ever on his memory. So that she would become his beacon, guiding him through storm and tempest – to harbour.

9.

The next morning the grassy slopes were bathed in sunlight, the wind had dropped and not far from the house grubby sheep were grazing. Calmly, unceasingly, unhurriedly, they dipped their heads to the ground and chewed placidly and lazily, without fear that this green plenty would ever end. Slowly, thought Willy, slowly move forward; everything you need is already there, just wait and grab it when it comes to you; don't snatch at what isn't there, don't count on what is around the corner.

In spite of this, even more so because of the leisurely pace of the country, he felt in a hurry and that his first step towards the bathroom was a step towards London, for he was now sure that there was nothing for him here on this isolated farm where his hosts, he felt, would be unable or unwilling to incorporate him into their everyday routine. He knew that he should not be offended by this, since he was too different and foreign – even more so than he was to himself.

All this returned some decisiveness to his movements: he quickly showered and washed his hair, took some casual trousers and a corduroy jacket from his case, put on some canvas shoes, and he suddenly looked fresh and ten years younger than the night before, a proper representative if his generation. So much so that Mr. and Mrs. Denton-Barker were visibly surprised when they entered the kitchen. The lady of the house said with approval: "Now that's more like an artist."

Julia was not at home, she had got up early and gone to St. Ives to do some errands; her mother made Willy some bacon and eggs, coffee, rolls with butter and marmalade – the first real English breakfast he had enjoyed. And Willy knew that this would be the first of many, since he had never tasted anything so good before.

Mr. Denton-Barker wandered around the house, disappeared outside, came in again, went out once more, while his wife kept Willy company at the table and told him of the plans they had made for him while he slept. He had to write a request to extend his visa and as soon as he got to London he should sign up at one of the English language schools so that he would have an official reason for wanting to stay in Britain; the request for the return of his paintings and bottles of plum brandy was already written; as far as the mysterious hotel was concerned, he'd best forget about it. He was welcome to stay with them until he found his feet, for he had clearly suffered a much greater cultural shock than most new arrivals from the Continent.

And then her manner underwent a change. Her round, rosy-cheeked face, with its unsteady thatched roof of untidy blonde hair, bobbed in front of Willy like a sunflower. She wanted to know whether he had ever heard of *Subud*. No, Willy admitted, he had never heard of it, whatever it was. (Actually, he thought, he had never heard of most of the things that go to make up the world.)

Mrs. Denton-Barker explained that *Subud* was an Indonesian spiritual movement started by Bapak Subuh, and brought to the West by J. J. Bennett (of whom Willy had definitely never heard). *Subud* was based on the conviction that man can get access to God's power, which can heal and cleanse him. At the same time, it was an association of like-minded people who, through the spiritual practice of *latihan,* unreservedly gave themselves up to inner cleansing. Feelings of bodily and spiritual stress were ameliorated and then disappeared, to be replaced by an inner harmony that heals and makes whole. This state of healing facilitated deep inner communication with oneself and life became a quiet prayer, depending on your ability to give yourself up to life's spiritual powers. With time, this led to regeneration of your whole being, to the healing of inner wounds, making possible deeper spiritual experiences and harmony with the eternal.

Subud was not a faith, but a spiritual practice that constantly allevi-
ated inner stress, so that one could more easily attain one's goals.

What about Julia? asked Willy.

"Oh, Julia is still young and doesn't even realise that there may be
anything wrong with her or with the world. *Subud* is for people who
have lived a bit and who are faced with important decisions."

I am also young, thought Willy, but I'm still aware that the world
isn't right for me and I'm not right for the world. And more than
anything, I'm faced with some important decisions. But that doesn't
mean that some weird esoteric technique of inner cleansing is going
to help me. What do you take me for, dear lady? I cleanse myself
through art; my sweeping brush or – if you prefer it – vacuum cleaner
is my painting brush, which mixes the filth within me with the filth
of the world, and transfers both of them to the canvas as the distilled
essence seen by only myself and God. Art is alchemy, the making of
gold from base metals; he who has received such a rare gift may not
squander it by cleansing the world, which he wants to depict and must
depict so that others can also see it, although few do, the majority see
only colours, lines, outlines.

This all flashed through Willy's mind as he was mopping up the
bacon grease from his plate with a piece of bread. Out loud he said:
I should go, I have a great deal of work ahead of me. I need to learn
twenty new English words every day. And I need to get back to
painting as soon as possible. Last night I dreamed my life would be a
short one. Every moment without a paint brush in my hand is another
reason I don't deserve a longer one.

These words reminded Mrs. Denton-Barker that she had intended
to show him her "modest artistic achievements". She invited him
into an extension at the back of the house that she referred to as
her studio. There Willy encountered a stack of amateur efforts that
stunned him with their simple, almost peasant naivety. Stone houses,
sheep, clouds, meadows, seaside villages, cliffs, turbulent seas, a
lighthouse – in endless variations of approximate verisimilitude (and
failing even in this); copies of the visible without feeling for depth,
perspective, proportion, let alone the other, less obvious things that
transform daubs into art.

But how to tell the friendly woman who had just made his breakfast and on whom he was dependent for so many other things? Never had Willy so strongly wished to be somewhere other than where he was at that moment – even in prison – anywhere where he did not have to face such a cruel dilemma.

"I'm prepared for the worst," said Mrs. Denton-Barker, as if reading his thoughts. And she smiled meekly, resigned to her fate, with a hint of bitterness.

Well, said Willy, trying to decide what approach to take. He realised that he could lie about many things, but not about what is or is not art; here there was no room for compromise, regardless of the consequences.

Actually, he said, adopting the tone of a teacher giving instructions to a talented but wayward pupil, watercolours are by definition suited to amateurs. How many watercolours do you find in famous galleries? As far as I know, none. And if there are one or two, are people standing in line to see them? In spite of that this is all very… well, competent enough to lead to something a bit deeper… with the right kind of help. To something less reproductive and more connected to an inner vision. There is only one world, but each of us carries it inside us in our own special way. The secret of art lies not in our own particular vision, but in the way we transfer that vision to paper or canvas, following the established rules, but at the same time, and I must emphasise this, ignoring these rules in our own way. In your watercolours – and I speak as a young man who has no real right to give advice to a woman many years my senior – I see far too much of what we all see and too little of what you see. I allow for the possibility that you do not see more than do all the rest. If that is the case, then your pictures aren't all that bad. But they are not – and I hope you don't take this personally – art.

Willy was amazed that with his lack of English vocabulary and in a less than perfect version of Her Majesty's language he was able to express something so complex and in a way that the lady understood.

That she had understood there could be no doubt, for her flushed cheeks had become unusually pale and then greenish, and then dark reddish, a bit like the bacon that Willy had eaten for breakfast, and finally the yellowish tinge of a patient with liver disease who has lost the ability to metabolise toxins.

"I have never tried to be an artist," she said with a voice that was not yet trembling, but was vibrating slightly. "I paint to express myself. Not to make an impression, or to become famous, or make money. At my age I know that art isn't everything. Although I admire it greatly, it seems to me that the majority of artists, as in most professions, are maliciously conspiring against the lay public, that poets, painters, writers, as well as doctors and lawyers, normally fob us off with words we don't understand. What is there to understand? You yourself do not know. You hide behind your codes, like a freemason. In reality, something else is much more important. Honesty. Paint as you see and feel is my motto. And not just mine; there are many of us for whom honesty is the highest value – especially in art. And one more thing: of your paintings I have seen only nudes that my daughter posed for and I must say that they seemed rather makeshift. Don't expect me to be able to justify this, I'm speaking about feeling."

Poor Willy had to bend under the force of the counter-attack. His words had evidently touched a wound that the woman did not want to heal; perhaps she found it inspiring, uplifting, to carry the burden of a misunderstood artist.

But Willy wanted to defend his principles to the bitter end. Feeling, he told her, is not a reliable way of evaluating art. Everyone has their own. If we give up on general criteria, then we end up with the statement that I may not know much about art but I know what I like. In art, honesty is an easy way out for amateurs. An artist can neither lie nor be honest and even if he could neither would be of much help to him. We can be either honest or dishonest in personal relations. In art things are simpler: some things are art, some are not.

"Well," she said, "while we are on the topic of relations between people, are you always honest?"

I sometimes manage to be, sometimes not, replied Willy; sometimes I try to be so, sometimes not; sometimes I am dishonest unintentionally, sometimes intentionally, but complete honesty is only for saints. I'm certainly not that, I'm just a young man who likes to paint.

"I wanted to know whether you were being honest about your feelings towards my daughter, Julia," she said.

I don't know, Willy acknowledged. I'll be honest with you and say that I don't know what my feelings towards her are. We haven't known each other long enough. But we'll know sooner or later – not just me, but both of us.

"I wouldn't want her to get hurt because of you," said the girl's mother.

After this there was a feeling of tension in the house that I knew would never go away; sometimes it was so thick that you could cut it with a knife. Julia's father had taken a dislike to me from the beginning, but he had been polite enough when he spoke to me; now he merely tolerated me. Whenever we found ourselves in a situation where it would be natural for us to speak, he suddenly remembered that he had forgotten something and disappeared. Julia's mother tried to conceal her hurt behind an exaggerated but insincere friendliness that embarrassed me, annoyed Julia and drove her husband into silent, scarlet-faced fury. Julia was trying to be friendly, considerate, encouraging, but even she was filled with a quiet resentment that she was trying to suppress, although not quite succeeding. I felt that they were displeased with me, that I had done something wrong, that I was not what they had expected and that all of them, including Julia, would be happiest if I simply left.

And I increasingly wanted to do so myself. But I couldn't just leave – I didn't know anyone, where could I go? I had no choice but to try to win back their trust. I decided there was only one way: to create a work of art before their eyes that would astonish them; then I would give it to them as payment for my board and lodging. Then I would go, with head held high. Anywhere.

And so next morning Willy appeared in the kitchen as a new man: no longer frowning and reserved, but friendly, talkative and cheerful, the image of a young man who knows what he wants. Although this was merely a pose that he adopted with what remained of his strength, it worked: Julia and her mother exchanged surprised looks, while Mr. Denton-Barker did not withdraw under the pretext that he had forgotten something, but rather he gawped at Willy as if totally bewildered by his sudden metamorphosis.

"What has got into you?" asked Mrs. Denton-Barker "Did you have a strange dream?"

No, replied Willy, I have *awoken* from that dream and now I feel that the nightmare is behind me and that before me is a new life. Basically, since my arrival I have been ill, a stranger to myself. The main reason is that I have not been painting. Whenever I don't paint I am separated from my very nature, behind a door, in a waiting room, and so I do and say things that… I'm sure there's no need for me to explain. I am ashamed, angry with myself, and if you are kind enough to give me another chance then I guarantee that the discomfort that my presence in your home has brought about will tomorrow be just a memory.

And Willy would have carried on in this style if he had not noticed that the pleasant surprise on their faces was starting to change into the kind of discomfort that he was promising to dispose of. Evidently they weren't used to such theatrical outbursts. He stopped talking at just the right moment and Mrs. Denton-Barker (in the grateful hope that that he had pulled apart her daubs due to a momentary loss of reason) decided to rescue the situation with a wide smile.

"Then you must immediately get down to work. If there's any-thing you need Julia will take you to a very good art supply shop in Penzance and I could lend you a brush or two, although of course, as you said, watercolours are not art."

Oh, said Willy, grasping the opportunity, what I said about your paintings was not a concrete opinion but rather some general philo-sophising that I sometimes find it hard to avoid. I've no shortage of brushes, but I need canvas and maybe some paints, and a wooden frame and maybe an easel, and some sketching paper.

"I'd be happy to lend you an easel," said Mrs. Denton-Barker, "and my husband will knock together a frame, just tell him how big it needs to be. Julia will take care of the rest."

Mr. Denton-Barker coughed as if to object to the task that had been assigned to him, but he said nothing and his wife clearly felt no need to take any real notice of his protest.

10.

And thus began Willy's creative period in Cornwall, that landscape of gently sloping pastures, isolated farms, stone houses, high cliffs and picturesque – too picturesque – seaside towns and villages that he did not like to paint because in the end, in spite of his best intentions, they always became kitsch (no different from the mass produced pictures for tourists that he saw in the shops of St. Just and St. Ives). He preferred flocks of sheep or scattered herds of cows, drawn in silhouette at the tops of slopes against a cloudy sky, lost in the dimensions of the landscape whose rolling emptiness evoked a barely discernible but constantly present sense of approaching catastrophe. The long vistas, fine rain and gusts of wind were the things that Willy sensed would linger longest in his memory when he left Cornwall; and the cold – the middle of May was like winter and even the sun seemed unable to warm the air.

The days took on an apparent routine, which Willy had missed and in this foreign world replaced a feeling of homeliness. After breakfast he sat in his room copying words from the English dictionary and repeating them, delving into the endless variants of their meaning, while in the afternoons Julia drove him round in the search for views and sights worth depicting. In the evenings they explained to her mother (her father stared stubbornly at the newspaper) where they had been, whom they had seen and what Willy had painted. Surprisingly, his English got worse, rather than becoming more fluent; the more words he memorised, the less capable he seemed of linking them together coherently. He became aware that in his own language he used words almost automatically, without much reflection on their meaning, while each new English word wormed its way not only into his brain but also into the depths of his soul, into the foundations of his experience – as if he had rediscovered and for the first time really felt the meaning of something that had previously been only vaguely known.

And so one morning he came across a word that seemed to click with him, as if something had fallen into place. *Desolation.* He looked up the word in the English-Slovene dictionary but found little satisfaction. The original suggested distress, dejection, restlessness, gloom, melancholy, misery, sadness, pain, abandonment. The adjectival form *desolate* was even closer to the core meaning: abandoned, bare, barren, bleak, derelict, dreary, empty, isolated, lonely, uninhabited, unfrequented, unoccupied, abandoned, destroyed, forsaken, vacant, disconsolate, downcast, forlorn, devastated, disheartened; for some words he could find no equivalent in Slovene and in English they packed a much more powerful emotional change.

Willy best felt the true meaning of the word through its antonyms: *desolate* – inhabited, populated, cheerful; *desolation* – joy. The meaning of the original Latin *desolare* also seemed significant to him: to deprive, forsake, abandon.

The word captivated him, its sound reached all the way to his stomach, he repeated its derivations to himself and out loud, relishing the feeling it conjured up within him. He suddenly doubted in the essence of his art.

I'm a pedlar of desolation, he joked one evening at dinner.

"Why all the doom and gloom?" asked Mrs. Denton-Barker. "You are young, you should be bursting with joy."

Why, replied Willy with all the quiet certainty of one who had finally returned home, why even try to be the opposite of what I am by nature? We live in a desolate world, and my work is a celebration of that.

With this realisation Willy felt relief, as if for the first time in his life he could clearly see his goal. *My work is a celebration of desolation.* He repeated it both in his thoughts and out loud at least ten times a day, and each time he felt a weight lifting from his chest.

When late one afternoon he and Julia visited Land's End and looked towards the Longships lighthouse on the granite rocks about a mile from the shore, Willy was gripped by curiosity as to how precisely the dramatic scene would remain in his memory if he closed his eyes.

He did so, but nothing remained in his memory – he saw only darkness. He tried once more to capture the sharp rocks, the foaming Atlantic waves breaking against them and the phallic lighthouse: he tried to depict every detail on his inner canvas.

Once more he closed his eyes and once more saw only darkness.

This had never happened to him before and he feared that he had gone internally blind. He had never painted by looking at something and then transferring what he observed to canvas; he always looked, impressed on his memory, turned his eyes away and painted what he saw within. Reality was filtered through a sieve of expressive intention.

He feared that he had lost this internal filter and that from now on he would be condemned to the mere copying of the visible. Then he became aware of the power of the wind gusting from the sea. He felt as if it was passing through him and sweeping away the clutter of memories, fears, reflexes, habits. That it was leaving behind it an empty space, a hollow in his heart and soul, and in this hollow the vision of the lighthouse on the rocks suddenly shone bright and clear, complete, with all the shades of light and dark, all the nuances of colour – a picture to which nothing needed to be added.

And thus Willy discovered something fundamental: that as a painter he was a medium for the flow of those aspects of reality that the majority of people because of all their inner clutter could not perceive, and that to achieve maximum flow he needed to expose himself to the wind to empty himself, to push all the rubbish aside, so as not to disturb the rays of the vision that travelled only in straight lines and could not go round obstacles.

I am not empty enough, he told Julia. I'm too stuffed.

"Really?" she said in a friendly voice, without understanding him.

But who would understand? He saw no need for anyone to understand why he painted in this way; in fact, the secret of his creative strategy must remain a secret. It was enough that he himself knew what he was painting. And he did know. Each painting or drawing that he completed or half completed was titled by one of the synonyms of the word *desolation*. The little girl on the promenade in St. Ives, her arms outstretched and her face distorted by crying, running after her parents while they walked on as if they had forgotten about her became *Devastated*. The old sailor in the seaside village of Mousehole, where in Elizabethan times two hundred Spaniards from four ships of the Spanish Armada had raped most of the women and razed whole settlements, hunched over in the evening twilight repairing the mast on one of the three fishing boats, became *Disconsolate*. Lanteglos-by-Fowey, a 14th century church on a hilltop beside a solitary farm became *Unfrequented*. Even the American tourist in front of the gallery displaying the work of local artists on the promenade in St. Ives became *Disheartened*.

Julia's father, with a beret on his head, climbing onto a tractor in front of one of the outhouses and looking back at three sheep on the slope above, who with raised heads were staring somewhere into the distance, became *Lonesome*. Julia's mother, sitting in an armchair, bending over the book on *Subud* in her lap, with a sunbeam on the page that she had just turned became *Companionless*. Julia, bending over in a wrinkled mini-skirt with her rear end looking wider than she would like, taking a basket of shopping from the car became *Cheerless*. The picture filled her with feelings that justified the title even more. She stared at it in shock. This was no longer a nude depicting the emphasised curve of her breasts, thighs and mount of Venus; this was no longer a sexy young woman, the painter's bow to female beauty; this was a young woman whose posture and untidiness already hinted at the loneliness of old age; this was something that pierced her to the heart.

"Is that how you see me?" she managed to say in a tone more of bewilderment than criticism. I replied that I saw the fate that awaited her.

My pictures made a much greater impression than I had expected – not only on her, but also on her parents. Perplexity, concealed admiration, disbelief, awe were all blended together in a strange mixture

75

of distance and a desire for my company. Confronted by art springing to life before their very eyes, complete but almost effortless (a brush stroke here, a brush stroke there), they were rendered speechless and it was clear that everything that had happened before had ceased to have any meaning. At times I even discerned a trace of guilt in their eyes because they had seen me as an odd young man rather than an artist.

"The paintings are unusual," said Mrs. Denton-Barker one morning at breakfast. "I'm sure you've got a great future ahead of you. But life is not as dismal as that, and if it is so, is it not the artist's duty to leave us at least a glimmer of hope?"

No, I replied, hope and similar narcotics for the second-rate is the business of priests, psychologists and primary school teachers. The artist's duty is to transmit what he sees.

"Perhaps you'd see something different if you spent more time with people your own age," she said, looking meaningfully at her daughter.

And so Julia was given the task of presenting me to her friends, of introducing me to the local scene, of trying to show to me that the spirit of the times was different from my dark vision. I objected in vain that I did not see anything gloomy in what I painted, only the absence of false comfort, the truth without illusions; all three of them were convinced that I needed to be put into circulation to get me to feel at home, to help me get to know people who could help me sell some of my work.

11.

And so Julia began driving me on visits to friends, acquaintances and relatives. We drank tea, played football with the children, talked about my plans, about my shoes that they all without exception admired, about the horrors of life behind the Iron Curtain and how brave I was to have fled from it.

I got tired of explaining every day that I had not done anything so dramatic, but that I had simply crossed the border with my passport; I soon found out that the English are almost incapable of accepting certain things that deviate slightly from their preconceptions. And so if they saw in me a romantic escapee from a prison where people were starved and tortured, who was I to disabuse them? It was not my job to defend the honour of my homeland or to rid ill-informed foreigners of their prejudices. And of course, all of them wanted to see my paintings, since Julia never missed an opportunity to praise them.

When she had run out of relatives and acquaintances she started to take me to parties where they all smoked a little hashish, listened to the Beatles and conformed to the slogan of the times: *turn on, tune in, drop out*. One of them explained to me that this involved taking a rebellious stance towards the capitalist ethos, but above all leaving behind the society of false people and values. In short, you had to become a member of the international hippy fraternity that rejected conformism and lived for the moment.

I was told I could either be *hip* or *square*, a rebel or a conformist, a free person or an arse-licking member of the class that had too much money and exercised too much control over too many things. The main thing was to live your own life, to live freely, since any day one of the lunatics in Washington or Moscow could press the button and incinerate the world's entire population. Why then worry about what tomorrow may bring, act as if we might ever answer for the consequences of our actions or plan things that would only bear fruit in the future?

Everything you needed was already here – music, drugs, sex, the wind in your hair – all you had to do was stretch out your hand for what you need to drop into it. And to achieve this you did not have to kill, like those who set the rules. The heroes of the day were Timothy Leary, Alan Ginsberg, William Borroughs, John Lennon, the Rolling Stones and the London model Twiggy, a slight, fragile looking girl who was supposed to represent a new image of female beauty.

The parties attracted not only locals, for a lot of people came to Cornwall on holiday; nor were they all students: the most obvious hippies included young doctors, teachers, social workers and bank employees, which was definitely (at least in my mind – I also re-alised I had my prejudices) not in harmony with the philosophy of non-conformism. Although they were each in their own way serving the society that they loved to criticise, they saw this as a sacrifice, an attempt to reform things from the inside.

After many such conversations it became clear that hippies were fonder of contradiction than logic, that they feared consistency, that their ideas were left to the inspiration of the moment and that more than anything it was important to share feelings. In order to do that (and this was emphasised many times) you needed to be in touch with yourself, know your own desires, fears, frustrations, anger. *Only connect.* Drugs were not just an outward sign of revolt against a repressive environment, but also a means that made it easier to find yourself (*Are you in touch with yourself, man? Because if you ain't, we got nothing to talk about.*). They were a short cut to an alternative state of consciousness, to hallucinatory trips into the unknown, to the ocean of feelings, to connection with being.

At these parties I learned a host of new words and got an insight into the way of thinking of the generation that I ought to trust since I belonged to it (*Don't trust anyone over thirty!*), but it soon became clear that there was no place for me among the hippies. Not only because I came from a different place and preferred Mozart to the Rolling Stones: in the society that they disliked I was still a foreigner, an outsider. But now I knew that I would remain a loner among the alternatives, the psychedelics, the mystics, the rockers, the flower power youth, where I might be expected to find meaning and my goals.

To the usual questions about what I did, I replied that I did something extremely useful. *I'm a pedlar of desolation. I object to objection, I rebel against rebellion.*

"It's important to belong," said Julia, when I shared my doubts. Belong to what? I replied heatedly. Belong to whom? If there is a God we should belong to him and in every way, regardless of what feeble excuses our infirm minds come up with. But if there is no God then the problem is much greater, since we can belong to anyone and anything, and each day someone or something different. If belonging is a matter of choice then I'd rather belong to myself, or rather to the one who I think I am in the given moment. Basically, I would like to belong to my fate, which might be in total opposition to the spirit of the times, if the spirit of the times is what your friends represent.

"They're not my friends," she objected heatedly. "Being human means communicating with others, including with those who are different, because your fate is not just yours but is connected with that of others. And how can you communicate with anyone else if you can never share feelings or experiences? Why do you so stubbornly and arrogantly shut yourself off?"

Her offended tone of voice gave me a bad feeling. We were driving home from a hippy party. While dancing, which more than anything else was the uncoordinated wriggling of hips and waving of arms, one of her acquaintances had approached me. For a while he asked polite questions about my painting and my favourite artists. Because my answers were clearly of no interest to him I quickly surmised that he had an ulterior motive. And finally it emerged.

"What's wrong with Julia?" he demanded, as if expecting reparation for some kind of damage. "Don't you like her?" And he looked at me as if he intended at any moment to box my ears.

I shrugged. Of course I do, I said.

"So why are you ignoring her?" he wanted to know. "Look at her, a beautiful young woman that helped you come to England and now because of you she is suffering. Not a queer, are you?"

I was about to say yes and ask him for his phone number, but just at that moment my eyes strayed across the room to where Julia was dancing with some friends; I saw that she was looking at us with curiosity and guessed that he had been prompted to ask me these questions. Communication between us, once so natural that I only had to wink if I wanted a moment of closeness, had fallen so low that we had to talk about it through a third person.

Of course, it was all my fault, although I was not clear how. But our relationship, whatever it was, Platonic love or friendly sex, was no longer the main thing in my life. I had lost the will, I had lost the desire, I had lost my nerve. If she made the first move I would perhaps respond, more out of gratitude than desire, but she was evidently waiting for me to take the first step – and not just one, but two or three – to compensate for all the days when I had done nothing.

If she had known that in the middle of the night in the neighbouring room, barely three yards from her bed, I was masturbating and thinking about her and the time we spent together at the seaside, but that I did not have the courage to cross the landing and knock on her door, then the whole thing would have seemed even more strange to her.

I wrote her a letter in my mind; that was all I was capable of.

("Please accept the pain that I do not want to cause you but which there is nothing I can do to prevent, since it is part of your fate and perhaps your growth. Just as I accept the seed of love between us that was unable to germinate because we transformed it into a topic of correspondence and thus sucked it dry. Of course, there is still sex, that doesn't have to involve feelings, especially now when in the name of free love even complete strangers couple. I could probably still manage that, but only if you carelessly offered yourself to me. On my own I don't have the strength to reach for you, perhaps because not long ago I swore fidelity to another and I feel, at least at this moment, that I must remain faithful to her even if I never see her again. Besides, my time with you and your family is running out and sooner or later, perhaps very soon, I will have to take my leave and push off for London. Why introduce complications into our relationship that at a distance would only get worse? You cannot link your future to mine. My future is so unclear that I have no idea who or what I shall find space for. So let us stay friendly acquaintances or polite, lukewarm friends without illusions – in a year or two we will congratulate ourselves for it.")

Of course, this letter was composed by Willy I.

In the meantime, Willy II sent him a letter of his own. "Listen, you idiot. Are you really such a fool or do you just act like this for your own amusement? What do you get out of always being different, nobler than the rest, obsessed with the *idea* of women, instead of touching the *real* woman at your side? Can't you see that she's asking for it? Maybe she will turn you down two or three times so as to regain at least a modicum of the pride that you are trampling on every day, but your duty is to persist until she gives in. That's all she expects from you. How do you plan to get by in this world? Has everything the hippies told you fallen on deaf ears?"

Although in a way Willy II was right, I searched in vain for the will power and the strength to touch the offended girl; and I almost offended Julia because I did not find enough courage to invite her to me through some gesture or word. At night, I thought I could hear crying in the next room; I got up with the intention of going to comfort her, knowing only too well where that might lead, but at the door I reconsidered and went back to bed; I realised that our relationship was sealed and the only sensible thing to do was to remain friendly towards her without any ambiguity that she might interpret as a hidden promise.

12.

And so a sense of discomfort returned to the house and once more our meals together were accompanied by constraint and taciturnity, while the admiration for my artistic work had noticeably waned. It finally evaporated after Julia and I had gone round five galleries in St. Ives, St. Just and Penzance. No one wanted to buy my pictures.

"Almost professional, but too dark," said the first. The second was more honest: "The pictures are good, but they evoke pain, almost fear, and people don't like that." The third shifted the pictures around and examined them closely from close up and from two yards away, each for at least five minutes, before he said anything. Then he spoke such nonsense that I felt quite heated and felt inclined to punch him in the face. Actually, he did not even want to look at me but directed all his words at Julia. As if she had brought a dog into the shop that had dragged its paw across some canvases and was now expecting a reward.

"It's clear that the young man is not from our part of the world," he said. "The pictures are too tense, they exude a strange political dissidence, they are far too strained, I doubt they would sell."

For God's sake, Willy II almost screamed, what are you talking about? It's true my paintings are not as relaxed as most as the amateur junk that you offer here to housewives and their escorts who want to come back from holiday with a cheap souvenir, but they are art. Have you heard of it?

"Let's go," said Julia, blushing with embarrassment as she dragged me towards the door. I could do nothing other than bark like an excited dog at the frozen seller of kitsch from the doorway. How dare you call this shop full of daubs a gallery? I yelled, saliva spraying from my mouth. You are a disgrace to art and to your nation!

Only after we had gone round the corner did my rage subside. Sorry, I said to Julia, I don't know what came over me.

"I can understand," she replied, taking the opportunity to cautiously bring us closer again; she gently squeezed my hand and I reciprocated. "It was terrible. But you mustn't give in to disappointment."

Anger is not disappointment, I said somewhat haughtily.

And added: I'm not disappointed that these fools don't like my pictures; I'm disappointed because in this country that I have so long admired there are so many fools.

"They're not fools," she said in their defence, "they're just dealers who sell a certain kind of product. These are tourist resorts. I'm sure that in London people will be fighting to get their hands on your paintings."

Although I wanted to maintain my faith in my future, at that moment I was incapable of believing in it. But the next gallery owner, near the quay in St. Ives, was friendlier. He liked the pictures, he nodded and for each of them he found a word of praise. "Dramatic, moving, challenging," he said, piling them up.

Because he had thick glasses perched on his perspiring nose I thought that perhaps he could not even see the canvases and that he was merely throwing out the odd cliché out of politeness. But no, he said he was really interested in the pictures and that he was honoured that we had brought them to him rather than someone else. Of course, he could not buy them outright, but he would gladly take them on commission of fifty per cent.

What does that mean? I asked Julia.

"That means that the pictures stay here and you get paid when any of them are sold. Then you split the money fifty-fifty with this gentleman."

Impossible, I said, I get only half? But I painted them!

"That's how it usually works," said the man, wiping his thick lenses with a black cloth. I saw that without them he was almost blind.

Okay, but not all of them, I said. I'll leave three and take the rest with me to London.

"All or nothing," said the man in a friendly but decisive voice.

I looked at Julia and she shrugged. "You decide. They're your paintings."

I began to think about how I would benefit if a small gallery (and it really was tiny) in a small town on the coast of Cornwall sold ten of my paintings. Not a lot: I would earn some money, but the pictures would disappear as if swallowed up. Nobody would 'discover' me here or introduce me to one of the influential art dealers – after all, that is the fate of most artists' work. I was very proud of some of them, but almost all I could paint again from scratch very easily.

Okay, I said, how quickly do you think the pictures will sell and at what price?

"It's hard to say," said the man, barely concealing his glee beneath a forced negativity. "Some hang around here for a year or two, others go very quickly. I would recommend ten pounds apiece."

I grabbed the paintings from the counter, stuck them under my arm and, head raised, stalked outside.

"What is it with you?" demanded Julia when she caught up with me.

Listen, I said: for that sort of money you sell sausages, umbrellas and bread rolls. I'm not a butcher, or an umbrella-maker or a baker, I'm a painter. The lowest price for one of my works is a thousand pounds and that's for the ones that are nothing special. The other, more valuable ones, I wouldn't let go of for less than five thousand.

"You're not living in the real world," she said, as I marched glumly towards the car. "Prices like that are for painters who have already made a name for themselves. No one knows who you are."

No problem, I replied, they soon will. I threw the pictures on the back seat, got into the car and slammed the door.

"We can try somewhere else," she said in a conciliatory way and drove me down some narrow streets in the old part of town. She stopped in front of a door saying The Little Gallery. I immediately thought that the owner was probably a hippy with unkempt hair and beard, and precisely such a person awaited us inside.

"Hi," he said, "I'm John."

I quickly ran my eyes over the pictures that were hanging on the walls or standing on the floor leaning against walls or furniture. I immediately saw that the young man (he looked my age) had more taste than all the other gallerists put together.

"What can I do for you?" he asked "Are you looking to buy?"

We're selling, I said. I lay my work in front of him and waited for his response.

"Oh," he expressed pleasant surprise even when looking at the first picture, a girl who has lost her shoe running after her parents. "Did you inherit these?"

"My friend painted them." Even Julia was becoming a little impatient now.

The hippy looked at me and gave a guilty smile. "I find that hard to believe. Nobody paints like that today. These pictures are from before the war."

Julia turned to me, saying: shall we go?

No, I said, first I'd like to show this guy something.

I took out a felt tip pen, grabbed the painting of the girl who had lost a shoe, turned it over and on the back sketched the gallerist using about twenty lines. I placed it in front of him. Now do you believe that I painted them?

"No," he replied, evidently dissatisfied with his portrait. "There are thousands of people who know how to do quick portraits. Go to Leicester Square in London and you'll find at least ten failed artists who try to make a living doing sketches of passers-by. On the basis of this portrait I would say you could become an average caricaturist. These pictures are not yours, I daren't put them on sale. Unless they are excellent copies and then even less, since I don't sell fakes."

The feeling of shame was even greater because Julia was with me. As we drove home I could barely stop from crying. "Come on, now," she tried to comfort me. "You can't expect everyone to like your work. Especially not here. Cornwall is the appendix of England. It's my home, but apart from picturesque seaside villages and weird people there is nothing here. Don't get me wrong, I haven't grown weary of your company and at the moment even my parents are in no hurry to see the back of you, but as you can see, there's nothing for you here. My friend's mother rents out rooms in Bedford Park, the nicest part of west London. She's very friendly, she likes to help, she knows a lot of people. Her youngest daughter goes out with the son of an eminent art critic. He could undoubtedly give you some good advice. In any case, I really should start studying if I'm going to pass my exam."

She glanced at me sideways to see what effect her words had had. I feel sick, I muttered, please stop the car.

I scrambled over the wooden fence at the side of the road and ran up the slope, towards the top, in the hope that there I would see a different, friendlier world. I heard Julia slam the car door and run after me. "Willy," she cried, "Willy, wait, what's the matter?"

My strength failed me before I got to the top, but not because I was unfit: I realised I was running towards nothing, aimlessly, and I felt drained of will power. I fell onto the grass and put my head in my hands. I sensed how, out of breath, she stretched out on the grass beside me.

"Willy," I felt her warm breath in my ear, "you're being very child-ish. I don't know what image you had of England, but if you want to succeed you'll have to be a lot stronger."

I stubbornly remained silent, head in hands. I wanted to sink into the earth, burying myself and my shame; but I also felt offended and I wanted to revolt and show them who they were dealing with. But who? I realised that I could not accuse anyone of anything, no one had done me any harm. Just as I couldn't demand of people that they like my eyes, I couldn't force them to like my pictures – some did, some didn't.

I felt her hand clumsily ruffling my hair: she wanted to stroke me, but she did not want to do that without a possibility of retreat. "It'll be okay," she whispered in a soft maternal voice for which at that moment I was endlessly grateful. "You'll win in the end. But it won't be as easy as you're used to. There are different rules here."

I don't know what came over me; perhaps I felt that my shame was so great that I had nothing left to lose; or that the fall from the ramparts on which I was so aggressively defending my dignity had rid me of all my fears and reservations. I suddenly threw myself on top of Julia and began kissing her.

"No," she finally managed to push me off with both hands, "what are you doing?"

I thought that this was one of those no's that mean yes, so I reached for her once more. This time her hand fluttered like a bird and I felt the sting of a slap that I think surprised her more than it did me.

"Sorry," she said, "but you can't simply climb on top of me as if you owned me."

I began to explain that I really didn't think of her like that, I simply hoped that we could carry on where we had left off a year ago.

"Now," she said in disbelief, "now you want to carry on, now when you're leaving! What was wrong with me until today?"

I don't know, I acknowledged. Something held me back, something kept me from you. Maybe it was the presence of your parents, staying in their house, and fear that you would reject me, and a hundred other things for which I can find no reason. But now I know that I would like to carry on where we left off. After all, on my arrival you indicated that you had acquired some new experience in Paris.

"Maybe I did," she said, sitting up and hugging her knees.

She stared at the slope opposite, her soft face showing traces of real sadness. "But you've no idea what women want. When we first met you knew how to court me, albeit in a rather arrogant, self-centred way, but it worked there, I said to myself this is how it is, this is how men here behave. Besides which, I was on holiday, a long way from home. Here I am surrounded by different expectations, different rules. Even so, at the beginning I hoped we would get over the awkwardness that had come over both of us. But you did nothing to make that happen. And so everything inside me froze. I'm afraid our moment has passed. I'm sorry if that hurts. I'm still your friend."

Thanks for that kind of friendship, I thought, but said nothing. If friendship means rubbing salt into fresh wounds, kicking a person when he is down, then it is obviously a new, hippyish kind of friendship that I have yet to master. But we all need to adapt, why shouldn't I?

We drove home in silence. Mrs. Denton-Barker immediately sensed that something had happened, but she didn't ask any questions, since she had some news that she thought was more important.

The Home Office had returned my passport with a three month residence permit. "That's certainly good news," she said. "Now for some not so good news."

She handed me a letter, also from the Home Office, which stated that the pictures confiscated by Dover customs officers had been collected under my authorisation by Mr. Richard Whitehouse and that I should therefore turn to him.

"I can't believe," she said, "that they would hand over the pictures to a stranger who has obviously forged the authorisation letter!"

No, I said, that was the name I wrote an authorisation for on the advice of Mr. Palisander. But that's not important, since we now know that that gentleman does not exist. If he's not in the phone book, then he's not real. And if by some miracle he's not a figment of my imagination, I'll give him my latest pictures as well, since there's no danger of him selling them, he'll just make a fool of himself carrying them around.

Mrs. Denton-Barker directed a questioning glance at her daughter, who shrugged and said: "Later, mum."

Willy locked himself in his room and succumbed to restrained sobbing. He knew that his hosts were talking about him downstairs, so each time his sobs grew too loud he stuck his head under the pillow. He also knew that admiration for his art was changing into contempt (the experts know what they are talking about, don't they; and what balm that was for the wounded pride of an amateur watercolourist!)

He also knew that they were wondering how to get rid of him as soon as possible. He decided to make things easy for them: the next morning he would take the train back to London, find a hotel room for a few days (after all, he had saved quite a bit of money here), look for a room with a studio and then... carry on painting?

He was almost surprised that his painful experiences had not broken his will. The more he suffered, the more determined he was to persist, to "show them", to break down their resistance. He was offended and that hurt, but at the same time he knew that this did not mean the end of his ambition, especially not his painting, since he felt that he would neither want nor know how to do anything else.

His sobs gradually subsided. He reached for Arnold's poems, opened the book at random and read: *Weary of myself, and sick of asking / What I am, and what I ought to be, / At this vessels's prow I stand, which bears me / Forwards, forwards, o'er the starlit sea.*

He looked at the title of the poem: *Self-Dependence.* He thought: ever since Julia left me this book when saying goodbye last year, Arnold's poetry is like my horoscope, the interpreter of my mental state, the corrector of my mistakes, a signpost telling me where to go – how unusual! And perhaps even my adviser, my guide on the path of destiny, my book of prophecies.

He turned some more pages and read: *I must not spring to grasp thy hand, / To woo thy smile, to seek thine eye: / But I may stand far off, and gaze, / And watch thee pass unconscious by, / And spell thy looks, and guess thy thoughts ... Ah, might I always rest unseen, So I might have thee always near!*

And the title: *Calais Sands.*

We boarded in Calais, Sandrina and I, and from there sailed together towards our respective fates; mine has gone somewhat sour – where has hers taken her? Has it raised her up, trampled on her? And if I saw her again (hope refuses to die), would I know how to remain invisible so that I could keep close to her?

I thought: how far from nobility I was today. How unworthy of my goddess. And I even intended to cheat on her! But you will, whispered the malign voice of Willy II. If not today, tomorrow, if not tomorrow, the day after, and it's right to do so, for this woman is a phantom and you can't cheat on a phantom, you are just cheating on yourself while you persist in following principles that even she would see as archaic. What do you want to be: a saint or an artist? Both, replied Willy I, I can be both. Okay, just you try, said Willy II scornfully, and then sell your metaphysical daubs to the angelic art collectors! And what are you even doing on this farm for a third week, you parasite? Don't you know how to look after yourself?

13.

I didn't go down to dinner. First Julia knocked on my door and then her mother. I didn't open it, but said that my stomach hurt, good night. The next morning at breakfast I indicated that I was leaving for London, would Julia drive me to the station in Penzance? They all looked at each other, Julia and her mother twice. I sensed that the previous evening I had been their main topic of conversation.

"Right now?" asked Mrs. Denton-Barker.

As soon as possible, I said, I would like to catch the first train

"What has upset you so much?" she continued, with a slightly sharper tone.

This surprised me. I thought they would breathe a deep sigh of relief, stick me in the car and take me by the shortest route to the station. *Bye-bye, Willy – forever, we hope!*

"You should stay till the end of the week," said Julia.

"A shame," added her father in the background, nervously rustling the morning paper.

"Things can't be so bad that you can't stay a few more days." Mrs. Denton-Barker's tone became even sharper. "Perhaps the food isn't good enough."

"Mother, please," Julia threw her an imploring glance. Then she looked at me. "Mrs. Hudson will have a free room from Sunday. You remember: my friend's mother. She knows a lot of people, I think it would be useful for you to stay with her."

"Certainly more than here," added Mrs. Denton-Barker, who had never been so caustic.

"Mother, please!" Another imploring look.

But the lady would not be put off. "The only problem is that Mrs. Hudson is very fond of young boys," she said. "Don't imagine that you'll be able to spend all your time painting."

"Oh, mother," said Julia in embarrassment and left the kitchen. Her husband folded the paper, threw it down and followed her. I remained alone with Julia's mother.

"Oh well, let's have breakfast," she said, suddenly more amicably. "Drink your coffee before it gets cold."

I obeyed without a word; I was totally confused.

"I'm not going to do anything horrible to you," she said with a smile, since she saw that I expected the worst. "I'd like to tell you a couple of things now that we're alone, that's all. Not that I want to hide anything from my husband or daughter, but my husband's level of mental development is about the same as his tractor's and Julia is involved with you in such a way that she wouldn't understand that her mother has a life that is not connected only with care for her family. That I am not only a mother, but a woman with dreams. Who had dreams. Which after twenty years on this farm have disappeared under a layer of cow, sheep, goose, chicken, pig and dog excrement. Perhaps you will say that everyone has their destiny and perhaps you would be right. But the fact is that I've never been satisfied with mine. Above all, I never knew how to refer to it. Now I know. *Desolation.* All the paintings you titled with variants of that word say something about me. All show aspects of a soul that has dried out in the Cornwall winds. All of them are chapters in the sad journey of a lively girl towards being a pedantic, melancholy middle-aged woman who until your arrival was not even aware that there existed a world outside this gloomy farm in this gloomy hollow. Your pictures showed me so unequivocally the colour of the despair in which I have persisted for so many years that I have approached the edge and something in me has moved. No more, I said to myself. No more will I allow others to trample all over me. I will do everything in my power to rescue the girl who drowned in this fat, clumsy woman and allow her some life."

91

She fell silent and looked at me, tears appearing in her eyes. "In short, after that long introduction, which was necessary otherwise you would not understand me, I can finally tell you what I want from you. Before you leave here for ever, I want you to teach me to paint."

I remained silent, sipping at the dregs in my coffee cup; I felt my hand trembling slightly. It was a long time since I had been the target of such an outpouring of emotion and none had affected me so much. A good minute passed before I dared say anything.

I don't feel good enough to be your teacher. Julia told you the reception that my paintings got – they seem worthless to all those who know anything about these things. And I don't even have anything to teach you, your pictures aren't bad, in fact they're very good, as the gallery owners would no doubt...

"Stop talking nonsense," she interrupted. "Cornwall gallery owners have about as much idea of art as pigs do of algebra. Surely you're not going to listen to fools. You should be concerned if they had received your pictures with enthusiasm. Both you and I know that they can change someone's life, like they have mine. Sooner or later someone in artistic circles in London will see that and they'll be all over you. And as far as my amateurism goes, we know what it is like. Be honest with me like you were when I showed you my paintings."

Oh my dear lady! I thought.

The sense of relief that flooded through me washed away the weight of all the fragments of concrete, all the decaying autumn leaves, my blood started to flow again, my heart to beat normally and to fill like a reservoir of strength and fresh hope. I could not find the words to express all that but the expression on my face was eloquent enough; she gave a soft, conspiratorial smile and reached across the table to give my hand a conspiratorial squeeze.

But I felt that I had to say something.

Mrs. Denton-Barker, I began but she immediately interrupted me. "Penny," she said. "Call me Penny. Short for Penelope."

This will be hard, I thought. If nothing else, I still saw her as an extension of Julia, more as a mother than a separate person. But as soon as I thought about calling her Penny, she became miraculously younger in my eyes. I dared not ask her directly how old she was, but I imagined something over forty. She did not seem as dumpy as she did when she was just a mother, when I had not looked at her properly; she was of course well-rounded, but no more than Julia, in a curvy, pleasant way. And her features were surprisingly beautiful, clear, modelled; her short light hair was no longer the crow's nest that I had retained in memory from when I first met her, but an untidy, youthful mop of hair that gave the impression of a rebellious gesture. In a flash "mum" fled from the drawer of fixed images into which I had closed her and in front of my eyes became "woman". It struck me for the first time how much what we see is dependent on what we want to see. Perhaps she was illuminated by a ray of my gratitude, but in the light of it she seemed more beautiful than her daughter, who at that moment came through the door, followed by her father.

"Right," said Mrs. Denton-Barker in a false official tone, beginning to clear the table. "We have a deal. We won't charge for board and lodging as we had intended, because the lad has no money. We have agreed that in return for our hospitality he gives me painting lessons; he agrees and I am happy that someone is going to teach me how to use oils. We shall start today, won't we Willy?" Her look told me that it would be wise not to object.

And so the following five days Willy and Penny (short for Penelope) devoted their time to art. The husband thought the whole thing was a waste of time, which he also said out loud, but only once, since his wife's reply ("Was breakfast to your satisfaction, was it as good as all the others over the last twenty years, or was lunch better?") left him no room for further objection.

At first Julia was delighted ("Super, mum, it'll be good for you, a wise decision."), then she began to wonder, then she became suspicious and eventually slyly cynical. Almost every day she came up with some errand that meant she could go out early and come home late in the evening. This suited her mother. She disposed of her husband by reflecting aloud each day at breakfast what needed doing in remote fields. Mr. Denton-Barker had no choice but to take her hints and so the budding artist and her mentor had time in abundance.

At first they felt slightly awkward, because they were not sure how best to make use of this time. But art soon revealed its power and sparked the imagination of both, although the pupil more than the teacher. It seemed right to Willy that she took the lead and he followed: after all, she was the initiator of the project and probably also knew what she wished to achieve. Blissfully grateful, he was bursting with a desire to considerately and patiently pass on the secrets that separate an artist from an amateur, while she was itching to learn in five days what he had spent four years learning at the academy.

They threw themselves into painting as if they had dived headfirst into a refreshing lake. They did not start with oils but with marker pens and drawing paper: they sketched sheep, cows, the house, slopes, toes, fingers, a spade, a rake, a pair of muddy boots – for, as Willy said, before we tackle painting it is necessary to master the secrets of perspective, depth, ratio, shading. Although he soon noticed that Penny was not so adept (her little finger was always stubbornly larger than the middle finger and the cows on the hillside were always the same size, regardless of their distance) he did not get angry. Nor did he say anything, for he knew it would not go down well: she was doing her best and to demand more would be an act of violence.

But he had to say something and since he knew that it did not really matter what he told her, he wanted to remain friendly. Not bad, he said. Much better than I expected. Of course, she did not believe him, for it could not be denied that her sketches were amateur squiggles. But because she could not speak about this, her disappointment with herself was transformed into exaggerated praise for what he produced. He remained tactful to the last and did not tell her that what she so admired was simple craft, exercises from the first year of the academy.

They found themselves in a quandary that miraculously (of itself?) triggered a redemptive process of distancing from the set targets, in both a thematic and geographical sense: each day it was less the case that he watched her work (and offered tactful advice), and each day he drew and painted more. She became increasingly his companion, admirer and assistant, who took care of the easel, canvas, palette, paints, brushes.

And each day they went further from the house: first to the top of the hill, then behind the hill, then to the next one. When the time for

94

oil paints arrived Penny, within the space of two hours, progressed from potential artist to artist's model, almost (it seemed to Willy) with a sigh of relief, as if this had all along been her real goal. And what a relief for Willy! He no longer had to stroke the fragile ego of the artist manqué; from now on he could stroke her image with a brush, without worrying about her expectations.

Her image, with only slightly exaggerated curves, turned his imagination to the great masters of the past: with no great effort he saw in her Rembrandt's *Bathsheba* or *Woman Bathing in a Stream,* Boucher's *L'Odalisque,* or Velazquez's *Rokeby Venus,* and finally Rubens's *Leda and the Swan.* It amused him to paint her in similar poses and to think that he was actually copying (from memory) these famous nudes. Each time, he changed the face so that the figure became Penny.

The lady herself was charmed; she spent long minutes staring wordlessly at her features in the embrace of art history, distant, honoured, but at the same time gripped by the unknown fear that her soul would separate from her and become part of eternity. Eventually she asked: "Why do you borrow the bodies of the models of other painters if you want to paint me? I'm not so shy that I wouldn't be willing to pose naked."

And she did. She unrobed for the first time on top of the hill behind the house, at precisely 2 p.m., two days before his departure (he looked at his watch since the scene so strangely captivated him). Like a sign of God's grace, the sun broke through the constantly cloudy, windy Cornwall sky just at the moment when she stretched out on the blanket that she had brought with her to put on the wet grass. She adopted the pose of the Rokeby Venus, admiring her own reflection in the mirror that Cupid had offered her, and how quickly Willy managed to sketch her outline (how ripe and alluring is the body of a middle-aged woman, he thought, excited by the discovery that life does not end at thirty). Meanwhile, these unusual goings on attracted the attention of a small flock of sheep and a sheepdog that gingerly came closer. Willy was not sure whether the sheep were following the dog or whether he had herded them there. They stood in a semi-circle (the dog slightly further forward, in the centre, with a lamb on either side and the sheep behind, an enormous ram with proud horns among them). They paid no attention to Willy and his magic brush, but stared devotedly and dully at their mistress, slightly confused, it seemed to Willy, as if thrown by her nakedness, for they had surely never before seen her like this, so glowing and rosy, lying on her side, resting on her elbow.

Willy did not know whether the composition had been gifted to him by God or whether it had never actually existed and it was the fruit of his imagination, but he did know that he was creating one of his best paintings. He worked quickly, but in spite of his haste there was nothing compulsive about his movements, which were relaxed and divinely simple, as if someone was dictating them. Since he felt that Cupid somehow did not belong among the farm animals he placed the mirror in the sharp, snarling teeth of the sheepdog. This, he thought, is art. Thank God, after this picture the deluge. *Venus with Dog and Lambs* he subtitled his victory, when he made the last brushstroke.

"But we must hide this picture," said Penny, more to herself than to Willy, when she knelt in front of it with the expression of a sinner, "we can't show it to anyone."

Perhaps not, thought Willy. Who would understand? Render unto Caesar the things that are Caesar's, unto God the things that are God's. "Oh, Willy," breathed the immortalised Cornwall housewife, "no one could deny that you are a genius."

Mrs. Denton-Barker hid the picture beneath her marriage bed, but the next day she wanted to pose again; she wanted to keep fornicating with the history of art; she had succumbed to an incomprehensible, almost wanton greed; she wanted to become every woman that had ever been depicted by a painter of genius. After breakfast she almost took the car by violence, saying that she and Willy simply had to paint some seaside villages as a souvenir (Willy was leaving in the morning!) and as she drove down the gravel driveway to the road Willy saw in the rear view mirror Julia and her father standing in the farm yard like frail, abandoned figures who cannot comprehend what has possessed there hitherto normal and caring adherent of *Subud*. In spite of his sense of triumph (Hey, I've hijacked wife and your mother!), Willy felt terribly sorry for them and their hunched posture shocked him. And in his imagination he sketched a new work in the *Desolation* cycle.

The previous night his voluptuous muse had leafed through the *History of Art* that she had borrowed from the local library and wanted to become Goya's *Naked Maja*, the Venus of various artists, but particularly Botticelli, as well as *Odalisque, Bathsheba* and *Leda*. Her pink cheeks were even rosier, she had become a young girl, a child; she was once again learning the alphabet of life. And when in a shady cove, surrounded by vertical rocks, she shed her clothes as if they were so much rubbish, Willy decided for Leda, when her lover Jupiter visits her in the guise of a swan. Without knowing why, Willy gave the swan his own face and he called the painting, which was actually a faithful copy of Rubens, *Self-Portrait with Leda*.

When Penny, the quintessence of all female models through the ages, crouched in front of the painting as if honouring the unattainable god of art and saw how the swan with Willy's face was lovingly and passionately burrowing between her legs, Willy knew that there was no going back and that it was his own fault, although he had merely opened the door to the storm that would in any case have torn it from its hinges.

"Is that us?" she whispered after what seemed like an eternity.

Yes, replied Willy, that is us and all the lovers in the world. Then on the sand, that was now in deep, late-afternoon shade, he experienced the released passion (and delights) of a mature woman who (like him) realised that life would never again be the same as it was before the (innocent?) desire to play undermined the dam that kept back the floodwaters. They knew that the lonely farm in the isolated valley in the extreme south-west of England had been visited by something superhuman, something that was not a sin, although others would not understand this.

Since they both realised that the touch of the gods may be only a temporary delusion, the following day they said their goodbyes formally, politely, almost coldly – so that the daughter and husband would suspect nothing.

"Thank you for the paintings," were the last words uttered by Leda, enriched by Jupiter's seed.

Thank you, for everything, came the polite reply from Willy, who was driven to Penzance station by Julia's uncle, who had happened to drop by (Julia making the excuse that she had an exam to revise for).

A painful, unforeseen, laughable farewell.

At the station the uncle took from his van a bundle of canvases tied up with string. "A present from Mr. Denton-Barker," he said, before driving off. The bundle contained all that Penny had wanted to hide and keep for the future. Willy pushed it under the train seat, together with the bundle from the *Desolation* cycle.

PART TWO

14.

My second arrival in London was different from the first, which the rainy night, mistrust and the trauma from my experiences in the port had painted with the blackness of uncertainty and fear. This time the sun was shining and the second half of May had already decorated the western suburbs through which the train passed on its way to Paddington with lush greenery and blossoms: wherever I looked the endless expanses of greyish roofs were interrupted by the bold colours of late spring. At moments, it seemed that London consisted only of parks, gardens and avenues of trees, while the rows of red brick or white houses among the greenery gave the impression of not belonging there – that in spite of their Georgian, Victorian and Edwardian past they were a late human interpolation, a persistent, aggressive, but unsuccessful encroachment into the primary environment.

Since I came from a part of Europe where grey concrete reigned and greenery was represented by dwarf pines and uncut grass, I found this English cohabitation between the natural world and architecture amazing. Certainly, some of the buildings, especially those along the railway line, were seriously neglected, damaged, covered in damp and sorely in need of a fresh coat of paint, but the patina of time was also harmoniously incorporated into the way of life. For the first time I was touched by the spirit of the past, which here (in contrast to back home, where history extended no further back than to the mythical World War 2) was present in innumerable layers and a hundred different ways – the whole of London was history. What a city! I thought. Millennia of history and not long ago the capital of a great empire, and now the city of my future!

Perhaps it was the lively colours that filled me with hope: in the middle of burgeoning gardens, beneath the May sunshine, in the gentle light without deep shadows it would be a sin to think that my wishes would not be fulfilled. All around me I smelled promise, opportunity, possibility. When I first started to think about, dream about London it was always foggy or gloomy and so my encounter with the colours of the city which only came to full expression in the late May sunshine evoked in me an indescribable rapture. Even the greyness was not uniformly grey, but had more than a dozen shades and there was not that much of it even in the central parts of the city, where the facades of venerable buildings offered almost the whole palette of colours: from snowy white to gentle orange to soft greenish to wild terracotta, and in between at least a hundred combinations that would be almost impossible to capture on canvas.

When I got into a taxi outside the station and asked the driver to take me to Chiswick I knew that in London, in addition to everything else, perhaps more than anything else, I would paint, perhaps obsessively, urban landscapes. In the bold but at the same time moderated, ordered colourfulness of the city I felt a primary challenge. Of course, it was not very sensible immediately upon my arrival (for the second time already) to indulge in the luxury of a taxi, but I had too much luggage to use buses or the Underground, and insufficient patience to look for the connections that would bring me to my goal: as soon as possible I wanted to set up a base from which I could wander round the city like a vagabond. Besides which Willy, who was still in love with his image, wanted to arrive like a gentleman; what would Mrs. Hudson say if he arrived at her door sweating and out of breath like a dockworker who has just finished a long shift?

No, a good first impression seemed too important to Willy to sacrifice it to the principle of frugality, especially when the taxi turned into Abinger Road and the driver mentioned that Bedford Park was one of the most select areas in West London. Here it would be a sin to walk, let alone to cart luggage along the pavement. No one had warned me that I would be staying at the end of the street of fine houses surrounded by large gardens.

"What, no tip?" exclaimed the taxi driver when I counted out the exact amount shown on the meter. Of course, in such surroundings a tip was self-evident: I reached into my pocket and added a pound so that he would not think he had driven a beggar. ("What are you doing?" suddenly blurted out Willy II, who had not made an appearance for quite some time. "You'd like to play the gentleman? Then tell the driver to carry the luggage to the door.") But Willy I was too enthusiastic about the house in front of him to want to play at anything: alone, he dragged his luggage piece by piece up the path to the front door.

His enthusiasm visibly waned when there appeared at the door the infamous Mrs. Hudson; he had imagined someone more beautiful or at least sexier than the black-haired woman who opened the door and (judging by her expression, quite disappointedly) ran her eyes over him. He was most bothered by the fact that the stocky 42 year-old widow with relatively short legs and lumpy thighs was wearing a mini-skirt; she would have looked better in jeans.

But Mrs. Hudson evidently wanted to retain a youthful appearance in spite of the lines that had already made their mark on her neck; she tried to compensate for her fading looks with youthful movements. With rapid short steps and exaggerated wriggling of her bottom she showed me the living room and dining room, the back garden, which had a small pond, and the first floor, where there were four bedrooms: one belonging to her twenty-year-old daughter Ana, the second to her teenage sons Gerry and Christopher, the third to a young lodger Harry, while the fourth, relatively spacious with a view of the back garden, awaited me.

"You can paint in the garden," she said, "it's impossible to get oils out of the carpets." She showed me the bathroom, which was not particularly luxurious and rather dirty. "There's only one bathroom for everyone, so please clean up after yourself, because I have enough work already cleaning up after others."

She evidently saw an unspoken question on my face, so she looked me straight in the eye and said: "If you're wondering where I sleep

I'm afraid I'll have to disappoint you. On a mattress in the dining room, which at night is separated from the living room by sliding doors. I can lock the door from the inside. So after eleven you are not allowed in the dining room. Unless I invite you."

There was nothing to indicate that an invitation would be forthcoming soon and as far as I was concerned she could wait indefinitely, regardless of the fact that, without friends or acquaintances in the big city, I felt an almost painful need for human closeness.

"I'm not going to call you Willy," she said, "because you are not funny enough for such a name. In any case, you probably know what *little willy* means in English."

I shook my head.

"You don't know?" she asked in amazement. "It's what you have in your trousers."

Oh, responded Willy II quickly, that should be *big willy*.

Willy I blushed in embarrassment, while Mrs. Hudson shook her head and said: "Englishmen are usually a bit more discreet when they boast. You've got a lot to learn."

That's why I'm here, said Willy I in conciliatory fashion, to learn as much as possible.

She once more weighed me up and decided: "I'll call you Zhivago. You remind me of the actor in the film." I found no reason to object: which young man would not be flattered if a middle-aged woman said he reminded her of a young Omar Sharif? In her friendliness I also saw the first outlines of a manoeuvre that would undoubtedly lead, sooner or later, to an invitation to the dining room after 11 p.m. and I was not too happy about that.

Perhaps I could have let myself be invited into the bedroom of the daughter, Ana, who I met a couple of hours later at dinner; but she was very reserved towards Zhivago and her mother never stopped emphasising that she had a serious boyfriend, a computer programmer and thus by definition intelligent, who was on top of that the spitting image of Paul McCartney.

Gerry and Christopher were alright – they wanted to know whether I was a famous painter (of course, I said) – whereas Harry, the other tenant, was not at all enthusiastic about my arrival, staring at his plate and every so often, half mournfully, half sullenly, mumbling a polite question ("How do you like London? So you're planning to become a painter? Is that well paid?") Although my kind of age, he was completely bald, with an oval, pallid face and the look of a stricken dog, drooping shoulders and awkward fat fingers with which he could not quite control his cutlery – he was twisting it around as if he had only just learned how to use a knife and fork. The scar on his left cheek reminded me of an old joke that Willy II repeated with alacrity: "Do you know why all the emergency wards in Irish hospitals are full on Mondays? Because at the weekends the Irish learn how to eat with cutlery."

Unhappy Harry became slightly less pale, which probably meant that he was blushing, and Mrs. Hudson immediately leapt to his defence.

"Harry has a problem with the joints in his fingers: Heberden arthrosis. It usually attacks the old, but he got it when he was young. He has to live with severe pain, so it seems that he is always in a bad mood, which isn't at all true, is it Harry?"

Harry said nothing, while Willy got the feeling that he was seen as a threat because Harry was an occasional, if not a permanent guest in the dining room after 11 p.m. and was afraid that he would now have to share that privilege with Zhivago.

Dear Harry, I thought, as far as I'm concerned that privilege can remain yours exclusively and indefinitely, or at least until I move somewhere else. When and where was not too clear, but sooner rather than later, not only because the food (meat pie & two veg with roast potatoes, and a glass of tap water) was decidedly below the level one might expect in such a classy neighbourhood and for thirty pounds a month, but mostly because of the disabling unease that I felt in the bosom of this family.

I got up relatively late; Ana was already at work, Harry too, the boys at school. Mrs. Hudson served me and then sat at the table watching me enjoy my breakfast. In a loose tracksuit she was strangely more attractive than in a mini-skirt and her pointed nose no longer bothered me so much.

"I thought you'd be more talkative," she said.

105

I replied that I *have* moments when it doesn't bother me to hear my own broken English and then I *am* talkative, but often I prefer to say nothing because I fear that I cannot take part in a conversation on an equal basis.

"Oh come on," she said, "you speak better English than many Englishmen. Certainly better than Harry, who has no education and is here only because he pays rent."

Like me, I replied.

"You are something special. You are an artist. You are in touch with eternity, while Harry sells vegetables in Covent Garden market. So don't crack jokes at his expense. He's already not too happy about you coming here. The poor lad has got it into his head that there could be something more between us than me cooking and washing for him. An absurd idea, but now he's convinced that he has a competitor." And she directed her greyish blue eyes directly at me.

Poor Willy found himself on the horns of a dilemma. She had set the trap for him so skilfully that he would be caught whatever he said. Willy II was all for telling her outright that Harry had nothing to fear, but Willy I held him back: it did not seem wise to insult the landlady. When you are in a strange city and friendless you should be friendly to everyone who crosses your path, and that includes making promises that you have no intention of keeping. That's not very nice, it's true, but as the English saying goes *beggars can't be choosers*. On the other hand, Willy I did not want to create the impression that he understood Mrs. Hudson's hints so well that sometime later he would not be able to call upon the fact that he had misunderstood her.

His solution was to ask what Dr. Zhivago would say in this case.

The lady immediately spotted his manoeuvre and was not at all pleased that the young arrival had not grasped her offer with both hands; irritated, she got up and began to clear the table. "And what now?" she asked from the kitchen. "Are you going to start painting straight away?"

No, replied Willy, sipping the last of his coffee, first I'm going to see London.

"At least show me a picture or two before you go," she said, "so I can see what they are like."

Okay, replied Willy. He got up and went towards the door to go up to his room. And then it hit him.

Oh no! he cried so loud that Mrs. Hudson rushed in fright from the kitchen. No, no, no! This is a nightmare! It can't be real!

I fell to my knees, put my face in my hands and started to groan. I felt rather than saw how she stood behind me with a tea towel in hand, helplessly wondering what on earth had happened. And suddenly all the brakes were released and it poured out of me – a long babbling narrative, a wave of garrulousness, in a tone that was at first one of self-accusation, then despair, then fear and finally a plea for help.

I had left the bundles of canvases and drawings that I had done in Cornwall on the train! I had been so captivated by how the May sunshine bathed London, I had been in such a hurry to travel its streets, that I hadn't once thought about my latest products that I placed beneath the seat before the train's departure so that they would not get damaged. And I had even told myself that I must not forget them!

Before leaving for Cornwall I had left another load of paintings in a hotel near Victoria and before that more than a dozen paintings, some of my best work, had been seized by the customs in Dover. As if someone had decided that nothing I painted should stay in my possession. What did this mean, what was happening? Had I subconsciously become a saboteur of my own goals? Was I afraid of the success that on the other hand I so strongly wished for? Was I trying to undermine or at least delay it until I was strong enough to live with it without the risk of destroying the only thing through which I could achieve it – my talent?

In the hush that followed my torrent of suppositions and questions, I could interpret her silence in only one way: she did not believe me. And why should she – I wouldn't believe myself if I hadn't known that I was speaking the truth. Suddenly I felt a light touch on my right shoulder.

"Poor Zhivago," she said. "You really are unlucky."

That was all that she said. Politely sympathetic, cold, false like only the English know how to be. Once again I felt a hand on my shoulder, which could not decide whether to squeeze or stroke me. Then its owner went over to the couch, sat down and transferred the tea towel from her right hand to her left. With her freed right hand she patted the seat beside her, as you would to call a cat or a dog.

"Come here," she said.

And Willy, the wet, beaten doggy Willy, shuffled on his knees towards her. He bent over and put his head in her lap, as if he could not go on without a friendly word from his mistress. And he started sobbing. Poor Willy, hungry for consolation, lost in a strange world, gave in to an unstoppable flood of tears, and just like the shipwrecked sailor lets the power of the tide carry him to the shore, knowing all too well that the shore is merely an illusion, he knew all too well that the hand that was now almost mechanically stroking his hair was not offering sincere comfort but was only using (abusing) this moment of weakness to prepare the ground for the final phase of the manoeuvre – an invitation to the dining room after 11 p.m.

Willy was most surprised to realise that it did not matter, and that false consolation works as well as that which comes from the heart. Even better, since false consolation means no obligations, makes no demands for repayment. Is that possible also in art? he wondered. That in certain situations the copy is more authentic than the original?

"Don't worry," said the owner of the slightly rough hand that was still smoothing his hair as if stroking a dog newly brought from a refuge. "We'll get your pictures back. We'll call the lost luggage office, we'll call that hotel, we'll call the customs in Dover; it'll all be alright."

No, thought Willy. No it won't.

15.

But I was still not without hope and my first trip to the city centre became a kind of detective story. I thought that the man with the tie in the information office who had (in the distant past) telephoned the Pole with the Rolls Royce *must* know who he had phoned: even if not friends they must have a business agreement – ten per cent for each client, for example.

However, at the information desk, instead of the man with the tie, sat a frowning middle-aged woman. What man with a tie? There was nobody like that working there. Impossible? Was I accusing her of lying? Was I saying her memory was bad? Was I perhaps saying that she did not know what was going on in the office where she had worked for twenty years?

Sorry, I said, I'm not accusing you of anything, I just wonder if there is a possibility that there works in this office, besides yourself, a middle-aged bald gentleman who has perhaps put on a tie at least once in his life, or perhaps someone who stood in for you when you were sick, since you can't be the only person who works here, considering that the office is open *round the clock*.

The woman bristled like a sensitive hedgehog poked with a stick. I'm never sick, she said, her voice almost breaking, and no one has ever stood in for me. There was a gentleman working here until recently, but he was dismissed and the reason is not something that concerns you, if you get my meaning.

Your meaning is very clear, I said. Now just tell me if on the list of hotels where you send clients there is one owned by a Mr. Palisander, who comes for guests in a Rolls Royce.

The woman sat bolt upright. That was confidential information that she didn't give out to just anyone. She looked over my shoulder and piped: "Next, please."

I turned round; behind me there was now a long queue of travellers hungry for information. But I was still at the front of the queue and Willy II had decided that Sherlock Holmes was not leaving the counter until he received a polite answer to a polite question.

Madam, I said, a month ago I was picked up from here by a Mr. Palisander, who was called by your former colleague. He took me to a hotel somewhere near the station and in the room of that hotel I forgot some things that are very important to me. Hotel addresses, as far as I know, are not confidential information. Please, could you take another look.

Hearing the word please she softened. She pulled out from beneath the counter a large hard-backed notebook and opened it. She ran her finger down a long list of addresses. Palisander, I repeated. She turned a page and then another until she came to the end of the list.

She closed the notebook and put it back under the counter. "That name is not on our list," she said. "Next," she repeated over my shoulder.

Madam, I responded quickly, perhaps Mr. Palisander is not listed under that name, but in one of the hotels on your list I left behind some very valuable, very personal things; at least give me the addresses of all the hotels near the station. "I'll tell you what I am going to do," she said, reaching for the phone, "I'm calling security to have you removed."

It struck me that one of the taxi drivers might know of the .o.el, since Mr. Palisander surely did not come personally for every guest. There was a long queue of taxis in front of the station, but the drivers were about as friendly as the woman at the information desk. "I need the name of the street," said almost every one of them, "there are about a hundred hotels in this part of town." When I mentioned the two missing letters they smiled; when I mentioned Mr. Palisander they shrugged indifferently.

I went to the nearest newsagent's and bought an *A to Z*. I drew a circle around Victoria Station and decided that I would check all the streets inside the circle until I found the rundown building where my paintings were probably still lying under the bed. But it soon became clear that the distances were much greater than the map book suggested and that the streets were so similar that I walked down some of them twice, perhaps even three times. Only then did it occur to me to mark each one I walked down on the map. I moved as if through a great labyrinth, up one street and down the next, left and then right, diagonally and then in a semi-circle, along wide, noisy roads busy with traffic and long apparently uninhabited streets with rows of empty, dilapidated houses – through a strange urban landscape, where ordered affluence often gave way around the very next corner to neglect and poverty, misery and splendour living cheek by jowl in deep-rooted interdependence.

Every so often I stopped and asked a passer-by, including two postmen, but no one had any idea about any *.o.el*. "In London hotels are always opening and closing," said one of the postmen, a garrulous Irishman with a red nose. "A week doesn't go by without one going bankrupt. As soon as letters go missing from the sign then bankruptcy is very near. Owners also go missing and with them many other things – profits, loans, alimony payments, young chamber maids. Some end up on the beach in Brazil, others open a new hotel at the other end of London under a different name. In this city anything is possible."

After four hours walking in the May sunshine and two short breaks – one for coffee and one for a sandwich – I was soaked with sweat and so tired that I could hardly lift my feet. When I finally ticked off the last street within the circle I literally collapsed, not only physically (on the steps of the house on the corner), but also deep inside, since I felt more than ever that I was not in control of things: that I did not even know how to take care of my paintings, which after all were the reason for me coming to this indifferent city, nor could I remember where I had been, where I had spent the night or who I had paid.

I closed my eyes and for some moments listened to the sounds of the urban landscape. Through the cacophony of ringing, rattling, crackling, creaking, horns blaring, brakes squeaking, engines roaring, and occasional thumps, bangs and crashes, there emerged, if I listened carefully, less aggressive sounds: birds chirruping, cooing, warbling; the rustling of the leaves on the trees that swayed in the wind between and above the buildings; the suppressed hum of thousands of conversations; the tramping, rushing and sliding of thousands of feet; the surge of the crowds heading in and from all directions, ceaselessly, without a moment's pause or silence.

Everything that according to the laws of nature should be moving but was not immediately became disturbing, suspicious – including the black guy that I suddenly noticed standing motionless on the corner, two yards from me. His skin was not completely black, but a reddish olive colour, with a high, sloping forehead and a gently curving mouth that could be a woman's, although it was evidently a man standing there: quite tall, thin, around thirty years old, staring mutely, not at the traffic on the road, but somewhere beyond it at the invisible centre of the sea of sound, the diminishing waves of which reached to the invisible end of the world. He was wearing a bluish-grey tunic that reached to his knees and shabby sandals.

He suddenly stirred and came up to me. "This city is too big," he said. "There's no centre anywhere. Wherever you go, you get the feeling that you should be somewhere else. There are ten million people here. Can you imagine? The same as in the whole of my country, Ethiopia. And the distances – they're lethal! I was sent here to study. How can I study if I get lost ten times a day? I've been here six months and I don't know anyone. So I speak to strangers who are more lost than I am. Are you an Englishman or a man?"

Neither one nor the other, I replied.

"What, then?" he asked with concern. "The devil?"

Not far off, I thought: driven by the devil, led by the devil, betrayed by the devil. I'm a painter, I said. A painter who has not got one painting to show.

"Then you are a success," he said, "if you sell everything straight away."

No, I said, they were all stolen, or lost, or forgotten; my fate is to paint and to remain without paintings.

112

"Oh shit, man," he said, sitting beside me. "And what do you intend to do?"

I'm not clever enough to know, I admitted.

"Oh shit, man," he repeated, almost with compassion, quite glad to have come across someone with worse problems than him.

"I don't like dispensing advice," he said, looking up, "but I'll tell you something. Get to know the city. Master it before you start work, otherwise it will constantly threaten you. I don't have time for that, but you do. Where's Camden Market? You don't know. Where's Crystal Palace? You've no idea. Neither have I. But that's no good. When my uncle stopped sending me money I wanted to become a taxi driver. Into a car and around. No chance, man. Did you know that to become a London taxi driver you have to pass an exam that they call *the knowledge* and that you've got to spend two years riding around the streets on a moped to remember which is where? I don't have that much time. Especially not now, when my uncle is again sending me money. Where are you from?"

I told him I was a Tatar from Nizhny Novgorod; I had neither the will nor the strength to deal with my origins, my past, my identity. Actually, I added when I saw that he was trying to believe me but finding it difficult, it's only my mother who was a Tartar, my father was a German prisoner-of-war.

"Oh shit," said the Ethiopian. If that's what he really was. If he had not, for reasons similar to mine, fabricated his origins just for me.

So how is Haile Selassie? I asked him. If his skin was not reddish brown I could have sworn that he blushed.

"No shit, man," he exclaimed. "You know my uncle?"

I emitted a short laugh that was eloquent enough on its own. If I had thought it worth saying anything I would not have said *no shit* but *bullshit.* However, I did not want to hurt his feelings, so I asked in a friendly, surprised voice: Haile Selassie is your uncle?

"Of course," he almost shouted. "Every month he sends me money for my studies. In my country anyone who gives you money is called an uncle. The money is called a scholarship. Haven't you got one?" No, I said, I've got some savings, but they're rapidly disappearing,

113

as fast as my paintings, but when my money runs out so will I and that will be my graduation. End of comedy.

"I'll tell you something." He laid his right hand on my knee then speedily withdrew it. "In my country it is usual when you come to a village to visit a relative or someone who is dear to you, such as the woman you are courting, to first call in on others. You sit here, sit there, chat as if you had all the time in the world, listen to people's problems, offer advice, eat something, drink something. Only in the evening, when you have met the whole village and you know all the paths, all the stories, do you knock on the door of the person that you really came to see. Now you are ready. Now you see that person for real. Not only through your eyes, but through the eyes of the people around him. Now you see him as he really is – objectively, they would say here. And then there is no risk of you being wrong about him or your feelings towards him. This doesn't only apply to people, but also to places. It was always my greatest wish to see the waxwork museum in London. Think about it: you can stand next to Napoleon, Churchill, Stalin, Marilyn Monroe. You can hold their hand – secretly of course. Now listen to this: I have been in London six months, but do you think I have been to see the museum? No, for now I just walk around the town, I listen, I talk, I ask questions, I found out how to get there, I'm in no hurry. When I finally do go to see it I won't be trembling with anticipation. I've got far enough to know that I won't stand next to Marilyn Monroe, that I won't be holding her hand, but some wax. A little longer and the waxworks will stop being anything special. That will be the right time for me to visit it. Or maybe I won't at all. And you? What do you most want to see in London?"

The National Gallery, I said. And the Tate. And the Hayward. And the British Museum.

"I advise you to save them until the end. Otherwise you'll be disappointed. Forget you are wearing a watch. It keeps driving you, but it's not your master, you are its master. In your shoes I would take it off and give it to the first beggar you meet. First spend two years going around London on a moped gathering *the knowledge*. Only then should you realise your greatest wish."

He reached into the breast pocket of his tunic and pulled out something small. "Give me your hand," he said, reaching for it.

I opened my hand and when he placed the small item in it I saw that it was a tiny wooden carving of a gazelle. "Do you know this animal?" he asked.

Of course, I said, who doesn't know a gazelle?

"Let it lead you," he said. "A gazelle runs swiftly, but only when it is being chased. When it is grazing it is relatively still. Follow its example."

He walked off with long strides, disappearing into the crowd.

Only a minute later I realised that my watch was missing. Surprisingly, I felt no anger: I thought that he had not stolen from me, but rather liberated me from my "master". And he had paid for it with the little gazelle. And with the wisdom that was just what I needed, for with the disappearance of the *.o.el* I had lost my last support and I really had no idea what to do next. The encounter with the Ethiopian, who had not told me his name and perhaps was not even Ethiopian, pointed me in a new direction and filled me with an almost unbelievable sense of relief. Even my physical tiredness diminished by a half.

"Did you have a good day?" asked Mrs. Hudson at dinner.

At first not so good, rather fruitless, but in the end good, I replied. Not only good, but excellent. Tomorrow I shall start to conquer London.

"That means you'll start painting. Good for you. London will leap to its feet and then fall to the ground."

No, I said, I shall only start to paint when London lies at my feet.

"Are you really a painter?" asked Ana, with a barely discernible grin. Her crooked, slightly mocking smile (the corners of her thin lips first rising and then falling) annoyed me. I pushed my plate away, unfolded the paper serviette, dipped my finger in the gravy boat (nice gravy, I said, very tasty) and with a few rapid but calm strokes sketched Ana's face. Altogether it took less than a minute, but the result (that Willy had never doubted) more than achieved the desired effect; when I picked up the sketch and showed it to her the mouths of all those present gaped in amazement.

So, I said, what shall we call this? *Ana in Gravy*? *Saucy Ana*?

"He really is an artist," gasped Mrs. Hudson. Her eyes moistened as if she heard above her the flutter of angels' wings and I could see how she had renewed her desire to invite me into the dining room after 11 p.m.

I reached across the table, pulled the serviette from beneath Harry's plate, dipped my finger in the gravy and one, two, three, sketched his sullen expression. I took Gerry's serviette and sketched on it both his and Christopher's face; they immediately tussled for the work of art and in doing so pulled it to shreds. "What about me?" asked Mrs. Hudson with an expectant look.

I said that, sadly, she had already screwed up her serviette and put it on her plate.

"I can bring another," she said, half-rising, but I insisted: serviettes are for wiping your fingers on – she had used hers, I mine.

"Don't worry," commented Ana, getting up. "You'll get a nude."

She left the table and went into the garden. Harry cleared his throat a couple of times and then went to his room. The boys followed him.

"Well?" Mrs. Hudson raised her bright eyes across the table. "Am I going to get a nude?"

First London, I said. Then for a long time nothing and only then, possibly, art.

16.

Even on the first day it became clear that I had perhaps bitten off more than I could chew. The size of the city filled me with respect, bordering on fear: the geographical scope of the built-up area exceeded anything I thought possible. First I wanted to master the celebrated Tube or Underground, whose spider-like limbs stretched across the suburbs although everywhere it was depicted in regular, different coloured lines. In the outer suburbs it ran above ground and then it was nice to observe the endless expanse of reddish brown and dark grey roofs. When the trains whizzed past each other they did so with a loud clap and a sudden change in air pressure that shook the carriages, but nearer the centre (although still far from it), where the lines disappeared underground, the noise of the wheels became darkly rumbling and at moments deafening; here, it often seemed that we were getting nowhere, that we were merely swaying on a large stationary fairground ride, for outside the windows was only darkness, while within they stubbornly displayed the clear, at moments unpleasantly distinct reflections of the passengers. It was painful to observe oneself, sitting between a large black guy and a slight lady with a plastic carrier bag in her lap, or between a young girl and her boyfriend, or a German tourist and a smart Indian gentleman wearing a tie on his way to work.

When, usually in the middle of the day, the trains were almost empty and in the reflection opposite I saw only myself, the feeling was no more pleasant, since this forced encounter with my own reflection triggered the uncertain question as to who was observing who, and above all the awful feeling that I was alone in the world, shut inside a swaying underground train, alone with myself, Willy I and Willy II. On some lines the distance between stations was greater and the duration of these encounters comparably longer; but on every line, sooner or later could be heard the squeal of brakes as the train slowed down, usually with a jerk that threw us forward and then back again, while to left and right flashed the lights of the station, the doors opened, some people got off, some got on, a moment of relief, new faces on the platform, a change of passengers. And then onwards.

At certain times, usually towards the evening when everyone was rushing home, the crowds on the platforms were like an impenetrable thicket shaken by the gusts of the underground wind; the most impatient pushed their way onto the train before others could get off and tempers frayed, insults were voiced, some were left disappointed on the platform, while those on the train were squashed together like sardines – men against women, men against men, young against old, white against black, beautiful against ugly, tall against short, fat against thin, rich against poor, clever against stupid – in a tense, erotic atmosphere that they all contrived to ignore, but which could not be overlooked, since it was so thick that you could have cut it with a knife. Of course, they all considerately turned their heads and looked into space, but the feeling of belonging to the same dream, of having the same needs regardless of age, education, appearance or social status was so strong as to border on conspiracy. The close physical proximity was all the more disturbing because the bodies were unknown to each other, because contact was coincidental and for each contact there was an alibi.

The tension persisted in another form on the escalators, especially at the deep central stations such as Piccadilly Circus, Leicester Square and Oxford Circus, where from the bottom you could hardly see the top and the moving stairs seemed to be travelling to the surface in stages from the centre of the Earth. Those descending towards the platforms came into view and into judgement like goods on a conveyor belt, an endless selection of features and figures and hairstyles and clothes and skin colours; and towards them, in a similar way, travelled those who were ascending from the underworld. Across the gap in the middle in any one day there were exchanged at least a million curious, evaluative, fleeting or less fleeting glances. In my case at least, the feeling was always the same and, although misleading, endlessly uplifting: an awareness of a limitless number of possibilities and opportunities.

Also above ground, on the streets, London was unable to forego a profound erotic pulse; wherever I went – past large shops in which girls were trying on skimpy tops and mini-skirts; through the streets of Soho, where ladies of the night stood on every corner; past shop windows boasting, in addition to pornographic magazines, dildos and vibrators and every other kind of gadget for improving your sex life; or past public toilets where young boys offered themselves to passing men; or through the park where young couples lay on the grass kissing – I was accompanied by the thought that this city contained enough of or perhaps too much of everything, and that at least some of it was for me (although in the midst of the mass of pretty girls the image of Sandrina again took on clear outlines and attached itself to the face of every passing woman).

Sometimes, when almost alone on the platform or in the midst of a crowd, waiting for a train and inhaling the deeply stuffy smell of the tunnel (through which the train always approached with a distant and then growing rumble, often accompanied by a powerful blast of air that it pushed before it, ruffling our hair like a sudden gust of wind), I saw her face everywhere: on the advertisements pasted to the walls, in the air before me, even on the rails below the platform. All the women waiting with me or who got off the arriving train with at least one detail, hairstyle, hair colour, way of walking, perhaps a hand gesture or a turn of the head reminded me of her, of the one *who could love... / Were but men nobler than they are.*

I kept seeing and at the same time kept looking for her on the London streets, on the squares and promenades, in the markets and bookshops, in the cafes and pubs, among the tourists in front of the famous buildings, in the cinema and theatre queues, on the red double-decker buses with which I criss-crossed the city, observing from the top deck the architecture and life on the pavements (in the hope that I would at any moment catch a glimpse of her), in the spacious parks that stunned me with their tidiness and majestic greenery, in the department stores of Harrods, Selfridges, Fortnum & Mason, Liberty's, where I walked through every floor in the hope of spotting her among the shoppers, in the museums where every unknown female visitor first looked like her from the back; even in the suburbs, where I was led by my desire to master London, in Southall to the west, peopled almost exclusively by Indians, or in East Ham to the east, where mine was the only white face, it did not seem impossible that she would suddenly appear in front of me, crossing the road, entering or leaving a shop, getting on a bus, sitting down beside me and saying: "I found you."

(Then the little devil Willy II sat on my shoulder and whispered in my ear: How can she love you when you are sentimental instead of noble? Above all you are stupid, as if you had stitched up that hole in the head you were born with yourself. You know all too well that you'll never find her in this swarming mass and if you did she wouldn't even remember you; in these weeks she's probably passed through about a hundred men's hands; who the hell do you think you are? Especially since you failed to remain faithful to her and never will, which is right. More than anything, you are a great bluffer and deceiving yourself: you're not looking for her, but using her to fuel your ridiculous exploration of London, which you would already have tired of, since it's clear that you can't stuff it in a box and then pull it out and wind it up like a toy whenever you feel the need to master something. There are things that cannot be mastered. And in any case, isn't it better to live in a city that constantly surrounds you and threatens you like an ungraspable mystery, full of opportunities and dangers?)

Although I felt that Willy II was right, I continued my hunt around London with undiminished energy. Each evening I returned home more tired and I sometimes even nodded off during dinner. I had already stopped responding to the usual questions (Where were you today? What did you see? What happened?), as well as to the question as to why I was avoiding galleries when "as a painter that's precisely where you should be going". Mrs. Hudson kept trying to convince me to open an account at her branch of Lloyds Bank (she would give me a letter of recommendation), to put my money in and start using cheques because it was safer. She said that she did not know where I was keeping my money since she didn't go poking around my room, but it was only a matter of time before the house was burgled. Then what would I do without any money? London is a fairy tale while you have money in your pockets, but when that is no longer the case it is the cruellest place in the world: no one cries if some foreigner is dying of hunger.

I replied that she was right, that using cheques was safer, but if she had no objections I would wait until I finally felt at home in the city, when London became "my town". She replied that that was how dogs tried to make a territory their own, by weeing on every corner, but that people already start to feel at home when they know the main Tube lines and bus routes. And the majority of people don't actually live in London, but in one small part of it where they have everything available, from shops to doctors to post offices to banks to restaurants to cinemas; they go to "London" only to work, to the theatre or to go shopping.

But I persisted, since there were so many things I had not yet seen. "If you can afford to be a permanent tourist, then so be it," said Mrs. Hudson, unconvinced. I allowed her to register me at the local library, realising that I should know at least a little about the things I was seeing. The books revealed to me that I knew nothing. Above all, I did not realise that I would best feel the pulse of the city if I put my finger on its main artery. I overlooked the Thames until I began to tire of the underground and the overground, and said to myself that this self-imposed examination should now end and that the grade would have to suffice for a student who had got the top grade in every subject except citizenship studies and maths.

In fact, I became aware of the Thames only in the late afternoon of my thirteenth day of exploration. So exhausted that I could barely lift my feet, I was returning from the South Bank across Westminster Bridge. Somewhere in the middle, feeling faint, I leaned against the railing and looked eastwards down the river. The sun was going down behind me and on the surface of the water I saw the shadow of the bridge and the tiny head of Vili Vaupotič. It struck me that it reminded me more of a speck of dust on the back of a mosquito rather than the demented conqueror of something as indeterminate as the "spirit of the city".

I am nothing, I thought. In this city I am less than a mouse dropping, whether I have mastered it or not. When in search of some kind of mental support I looked further down the river that lay before me gilded by the sun, the buildings on either side pushed their way into my field of vision, also bathed in sunlight, almost glowing, all the way to the dome of St. Paul's and beyond.

And just at that moment, as had become customary in my life, a stranger stopped beside me who I had slowly begun to suspect was my guardian angel, appearing (each time in a different guise) whenever I stood at a crossroads and did not know which road to take. This time, he had adopted the guise of a small bespectacled man with a battered briefcase under his arm. Evidently it contained something very important, since he kept nervously checking whether it was still there. During a period of five minutes he transferred it several times from one side to the other, as if unable to decide where it was safer.

"Have you worked out how many bridges London has?" he asked in a deep voice inconsistent with his slight frame; I thought that perhaps he sang bass at the London opera (possibly hidden behind the scenery while onstage, because of authenticity, a larger male figure mimed to his voice).

He saw me hesitating, so he answered the question himself. "Twenty-seven!" He announced this with pride, as if he had built at least three of them himself. "And this one, Westminster, was built in 1749, only the second on this spot. Can you imagine that the bridge the Normans built in the eleventh century sufficed for six-and-a-half centuries? But the others followed at ever shorter time intervals."

Interesting, I said.

"The purest symbol of progress is the building of bridges. Between river banks, between people, ideas, faiths. Between man and God. Between the sexes, between members of the same sex, between people and animals. To bridge is the most noble word in the dictionary.

122

To bridge a divide. The two of us are different, aren't we? But the river flowing beneath this bridge and beneath all the others brings us together. The river is the heart of this city. Engrave its image on your heart if you want to feel at home here."

He did not even look at me, but turned and walked on. It was as if he had carried out some daily ritual, for he seemed satisfied with himself, raising his head and starting to whistle. I followed him with my eyes until he was swallowed up by the crowd near Parliament. He had spoken with a foreign accent, but I had too little experience to judge where he was from. Judging by his appearance, he could probably come from any European country, East or West, North or South. But that did not interest me too much – more important were his words, which sounded like advice to the lost. I decided that I would *engrave its image on my heart* in a similar way to how I had tried (unsuccessfully) to internalise the city on its banks.

I began the very next day. Although the Nile and the Amazon are twenty times as long, although the Danube flows through six countries, although the Mississippi carries considerably more water, in many English eyes the Thames is the "greatest river in the world". This is in spite of the fact that it is only two hundred and fifteen miles long, that its flow is less than 2400 cubic feet of water per second, and that it contains no impressive waterfalls, dangerous rapids or pools. To the English it seems great because it is theirs. One Roger de Coverley, who among other things said that one Englishman is worth three Frenchmen, described it as the "noblest" river in Europe. There is barely a poet or writer who has not honoured it with some admiring epithet. It winds like a silver stream, it has silver feet, it is the mother of all rivers, the wind longs for it, for its love, it is deep yet clear, gentle yet not boring, powerful yet never angry.

Perhaps the poets sensed its geographical and historical significance. For without the Thames there would be no London. Without the Thames there would be no port, which for centuries was the trading centre of a global empire. Once the water was clear and teeming with fish, especially salmon. In the seventeenth century even kings and queens drank its waters, while the Portuguese transported it to Lisbon in giant barrels. Then Antwerp declined as the financial centre of the old world and ever more international trade routes diverted to London. Soon the volume of traffic on the water became untenable. In a port intended for 545 ships, more than 1700 were anchored. At times the river was so crowded that ships were unable to reach the port or to leave it. The general chaos was made worse by the hundreds of smaller boats transporting cargo from the anchored boats to the shore and back. It could take weeks for a ship to unload. And the whole time thieves were on the prowl: the organised gangs who became known as "night relievers", "light cavalry", "heavy cavalry" and so on struck fear into the heart of every captain waiting to unload.

The Elizabethans, who generated their wealth through trade, respected the Thames, almost revered it; they saw it not only as the main artery, but also as an adornment of the capital. The Victorians were interested only in profit, so they turned their back on it and along its banks, instead of palaces and fine townhouses, built warehouses and factories. In the former marshes and fields of East London, across distances of more than six miles, there grew up in half a century black, smoky masses of industrial complexes and impoverished workers quarters that early socialists described as "the shame of the civilised world".

In the early nineteenth century a London fisherman caught the last salmon. The water became so polluted that anyone falling into it would die from poisoning before they drowned. But with the decline of empire, cleaner water began to return to the Thames. At the time of my arrival it was more brown than black, nor was there any longer thick fog – there had not been for quite some years – and it was said that even fish were beginning to return. Each year the water was a little clearer, each year it contained a little more oxygen, each year the fish were able to venture a little further. The port complexes were avoiding the city and moving towards the mouth of the river; Londoners were returning to the "silver-haired Thames"; abandoned warehouses and factories were being demolished and in their place were appearing housing complexes with gardens on the river bank and flowers on the balconies.

The river, which I had noticed upon my arrival but not felt, began to obsess me. Not only because it flowed in two directions: towards the sea and then, with the tide, back upstream; and not only because of its imposing bridges, although I could not get over the imagination shown by their builders. Even the magnificent views of the city available from the water were not the main reason for the excitement that gripped me like a mysterious ailment. No, I was captivated by the spirit of the river: a combination of its tangible presence and its past, which I learned about from books, but it breathed within me as if the centuries past were still alive and connected to the present like a double photographic exposure.

That which I perceived through my senses was of course more intense and thus became disturbing, while at the same time I was aware of an increasing desire, almost a sense of duty, to somehow reinforce this conditionally contemporaneous past, to "tie" it to the present so that it would be there all the time and not only in occasional flashes.

I knew I had to paint it.

17.

When I told Mrs. Hudson that I needed a boat I could use whenever I wanted, at any time of day, whatever the weather, to travel up and down the Thames from one side of London to the other, she felt my forehead with her hand. "You've no temperature, yet you're talking as if you were ill."

Yes, I admitted, I was ill, increasingly so each day, but this was not a new illness, it had attacked me many times before and each time I could only get over it by succumbing to it. This illness, to use a stale word, was inspiration. I wanted to paint all twenty-seven London bridges. (I dared not tell her that I wanted to paint the past; at that moment even to me that seemed like a premonition of madness, although I knew that this need, which had become the driving force of my life, could not be denied.)

"Do you know how far it is from one end of town to the other? More than forty miles! And who would buy pictures of London bridges? You can get them for a few pence on postcards."

I replied that I didn't care whether anyone bought them or not; it might happen that I would not even want to sell them. I wanted to paint them because I had no choice; that is what I had been commanded to do.

"You're an odd lot, you artists," she said, yet without a hint of criticism – almost, it seemed to me, proud that she had one of these rare creatures under her roof.

And it is true that in his impatience Willy, characteristically, completely neglected the practical aspects of the planned river trip. For instance, you cannot hire a boat as easily as you can a car. And no one is allowed on the Thames without a licence. In any case, you need a boatman if you want to paint on a boat; without a firm hand on the tiller, the current will in minutes carry you away or send you crashing into a bridge pillar or into another boat. And at the end of the day, bridges can be painted from the riverbank, so why do you need a boat?

No, Willy stuck to his guns; anyone can paint bridges from the riverbank, he wanted to paint them from the water, from below, while in motion.

"I can of course ask," she replied, "I'm a member of Chiswick Rowing Club." And her eyes flashed darkly, as if to say: you see what an ally you have in me. In her look Willy once more recognised the hint that any possible help or service rendered would need to be paid for in some way – that was the way of the world, there is no free lunch in a free-market society.

With surprise, he realised that in spite of all his reservations he would be prepared to do that: my kingdom for a boat. But Mrs. Hudson, in addition to any possible reward for herself, had in mind financial payment. "It will be hard to get anything for less than twenty pounds a day."

Willy was taken aback, but he immediately did some calculations in his head: he would need at least two weeks, fourteen times twenty, maybe an extra day, three hundred pounds, a half of what he had left. Although he knew what that would mean (if in a few months he did not sell any pictures, he would have to starve or admit defeat and return home), he said without hesitation: okay, can I get a boat for tomorrow?

Mrs. Hudson could not help but be amazed at his zealousness. In her eyes he sensed a shadow of fear, mixed with respect, for in her ritually empty suburban life she had never encountered someone who so clearly felt the strength of divine inspiration.

"Right," she breathed, like a sentimental young girl. "I'll see what I can do."

127

That same evening she invited me to the rowing club on the banks of the Thames in Chiswick. She asked me to dress nicely and to wear my shoes with gold buckles, although I had long ago discovered that I looked ridiculous in them. But I realised within five minutes of my arrival that the rowing club was a meeting place mainly of snobs. The women spoke in a metallic, elevated tone, which to my ears at least sounded as if they were impersonating and mocking someone ("Oh, really?", "Oh no!", "Great!", "Charming!", "Oh, I can't be bothered!", "Singularly uninteresting!", etc.), while the men grumbled and mumbled, and in general acted as if they were the women's paid servants, although from the snippets of conversation I overheard it was clear that they were the ones who earned the money and decided about most things.

"This is Zhivago," Mrs. Hudson introduced me, proud of the tenant who immediately drew friendly glances from the women present, while in the eyes of their husbands I noticed a mistrustful evaluation taking place as to whether this long-haired boy could be a threat of any kind. Willy suppressed his desire to throw his chest out and win some compliments from the ladies; instead, he kept a low profile, as it was more than clear to him that it was the men who decided what happened to the boats.

The whole evening, Mrs. Hudson spoke only of me and in doing so offered many half-truths and lies in the desire to transform me into a romantic hero (although I did not know whether it was to get a boat or to raise her club status, as it quickly became clear to me that most of the ladies present and also quite a few of the men thought that the interesting lodger was actually her lover). Thus I had not only *fled* across the border under the cover of darkness, but on the way I had *strangled* two border guards, not out of a desire for freedom and a better life, but out of fear of a *life sentence* in a harsh communist prison, since out of honour, as dictated by my environment, I had killed the soldier that had raped my young wife who was three months pregnant with my child and who then, out of shame, *killed herself.*

"Oh no," exclaimed the ladies. "Amazing!", "Well done!", "How brutal!", "Poor boy!", "What a story!" And one of the men added: "Good chap!" The myth that in less than half an hour Mrs. Hudson wove around me had obviously gone so beyond the bounds of the absurd that there was certainly no one in the club who really believed it, but at the same time no one was able or allowed to show it, as a certain amount of exaggeration was a generally accepted ingredient of club life. Although I myself was also prone to exaggeration whenever I wove a story designed to improve my image, the unreal description, almost a caricature of my past, shamed and ridiculed me; I really felt like punching the stupid woman on the jaw and marching out of the club in as dignified a fashion as possible.

But the need for a boat was so acute that I quietly accepted my loss of dignity in an environment that I knew I would never visit again. In fact the whole thing, the club and the people in it and their conversation, was so like a nightmare that not a trace of embarrassment managed to worm its way inside me, but remained as a sort of unpleasant smelling sticky substance on the surface of my skin. The only real thing was the boat, but that was becoming increasingly unreal the more Mrs. Hudson explained why I actually needed it. If the club members were prepared to believe, with a large pinch of salt, the story about my breaking through the Iron Curtain, my idea of painting bridges from a rocking boat on the Thames seemed so "impractical", "excessive", "extravagant" and even "loony" that in the end there was no one who would be prepared to put themselves forward as a patron of art, even for twenty pounds a day.

At least, not among the grown-ups. Luckily, the seventeen-year-old son of a Chiswick bank manager was there, a timid lad with protruding ears by the name of Jimmy who was, as befitted a seventeen-year-old in such company, extremely taciturn and who, whenever he had anything to say, acted like he was competing in a hundred metres sprint over hurdles of words that due to his stutter he knocked over, stepped on and piled up so badly that almost no one could understand what he was trying to say. Of course, the unwritten rules of the club membership would not allow anyone to talk about this as it would involve admitting that the boy had a speech defect and this would, I learned later, border on "bad taste", which the middle class, emulating the habits of the upper class, could not afford. So they all pretended to understand what poor Jimmy was trying to say, nodding amiably in agreement, although no one gave a specific response to his words, with the exception of his father, who at least half understood his son's stuttering.

As I had the feeling that only Jimmy believed all the details of my flight, it did not surprise me that he offered to take me along the river on his father's boat. Of course, I could not follow his tumbling words, but got the gist of his offer from his father's objections.

"A nice gesture, Jimmy, but you can forget it straight away. First, you don't have a licence yet; second, you have to help your mother; third, it's not without its dangers; and fourth, the whole thing's ridiculous, no one in their right mind would plan such a thing. In any case, everything the young man wants to paint has already been painted and reproduced a million times."

He pointed to *The Thames Boating Calendar* on the wall, which really was made up of paintings of boats by English masters which also featured bridges.

"Don't you agree, Maria, that it's all a bit of a joke?" he said turning to Mrs. Hudson.

The poor thing wilted under his withering gaze and obediently nodded. I did not hold that against her, as she had done everything within her power to get me a boat and had probably lost face simply by bringing me to the club in the first place. But Jimmy, God bless him, was not convinced by her humble retreat (perhaps it reminded him too much of moments at home when his mother had to give way under the weight of his father's "arguments"), so he sulkily, almost in tears, turned to me for confirmation.

I felt as if the eyes of everyone at the club were upon me. What would Willy do? Would he show that, in spite of his background, he qualified as a potential member of an English rowing club or, as seemed to be expected, would he embarrass both his landlady and the father of the unhappy boy? I could feel them all holding their breath. Equally strongly I felt how Jimmy wanted someone (at least me, if no one else dared) to challenge his father's objections, which he was so unhappy about.

I went over the calendar and unceremoniously tore off the page for May. I did not even look at the reproduction. It's the thirty-first,

130

I said, tomorrow is the first of June, you won't be needing this anymore. They were all so astonished that no one said a word, except for an elderly lady who could be heard to mutter somewhere in the background "What a cheek!" Some of the others were charmed by my audacity, including Jimmy, who sensed that it was largely for his benefit.

I sat back down at the table, placed the page from the calendar on it blank side up, pulled a marker pen from my pocket and began to sketch with rapid, practised strokes. In a flash, most of those present congregated behind me, including Jimmy who was literally breathing down my neck. I saw Mrs. Hudson light a cigarette in a satisfied manner and wink at me: she knew what I was doing, she knew what the response would be, she knew I was also doing this for her, and she was both grateful and proud of me – we were allies.

In less than five minutes, before the eyes of the amazed observers, there appeared a drawing of a boat on the Thames with London's famous Tower Bridge in the background and in the boat two figures – a bearded young man standing at a painter's easel and a seventeen-year-old boy sitting at the rear of the boat holding the tiller. The boy looked so much like Jimmy that a gasp of amazed approval arose from those gathered behind me. I wrote *Jimmy, the painter's boatman* on the drawing and handed it to the boy.

"D-d-d-addy," he stammered, rushing over to his father, who had stubbornly turned his back, "d-d-daddy, look!" But daddy did not want to share his son's enthusiasm: in fact, he did not even want to look at the drawing, throwing a cursory glance at it and turning away. "Jimmy, I've said what I have to say and that's the end of the matter."

Head bowed, the boy brought the drawing back and laid it on the table in front of me.

It's yours, I said to him. I wanted to tell you how honoured I would be if you were to be my boatman and how sad I am that you are not to be.

He sniffed and with tears in his eyes withdrew from the empty table to the most distant corner of the room. He leant over the drawing, sobbing.

131

"So, that's that then," exclaimed one of the gin-and-tonic ladies, while the boy's father turned to Mrs. Hudson and voiced his displeasure: "Maria, I'm sorry but this simply isn't *fair*. Every member may bring a guest, but this time you were insufficiently choosy. Nothing personal."

"Look here, Malcolm," said Mrs. Hudson picking up her handbag, "you may rebuke your bank employees, but not me, as I've been a member of this club longer than you have. You know as much about art as next door's parrot, and even less about the wishes and needs of your son. Shall we be off, Zhivago?"

And so, as the evening's undoubted victors, we went down the stairs, knowing all too well that they would not quickly forget us.

Thank you I said, squeezing her hand.

"Any time," she replied. "I really don't know why I bother with that bunch of snobs. Most probably because I am lonely and don't know anyone else."

We were already in the car park when Jimmy came panting up to us. He was nervously waving his hands around as if he wished to touch me, but at the vital moment lacked the courage.

"Calm down, Jimmy," I said, giving his elbow a friendly squeeze.

"T-t-tomorrow aftern-n-noon," he managed to stutter. "Here, at t-t-two. I'll g-g-get the b-b-boat. I'll get the boat." Amazed that he had been able to say this without stuttering, he repeated: "I'll get the boat. Tomorrow at two." His face broke into a satisfied grin, he straightened up and was suddenly several inches taller.

"Jimmy," said Mrs. Hudson, "you'll get into trouble."

"From mummy," he shot back. "M-m-mummy has a b-b-boat. Tomorrow at two. Here." He turned and ran back to the club. En route he executed several little jumps, like a frolicking young buck.

"It's too risky," warned Mrs. Hudson, after we had got in the car and driven off. "The boy is not yet of age and in this country people who wish to make mischief can accuse you of many things. Besides which, he has twice tried to commit suicide."

But what can they accuse me of, I thought; that I brought some pleasure into the life of a boy who probably stammers because he is completely under his tyrannical father's thumb? Well let them, I'll tell them what I think of them.

I did not say this out loud, but only: Thank you from the bottom of my heart, Mrs. Hudson.

"Please don't keep calling me Mrs. Hudson," she insisted, "it's Maria; we are much less formal in England than on the Continent."

Maybe not, I acknowledged, but you are much more screwed up, as I found out today.

"We really are different," she acknowledged. "But you don't know us well enough to start criticising everything. One day soon I will explain to you the importance of the social classes in England and the differences among them, and even if you reject that, as I'm sure you will, it will at least be clear to you where you are and what awaits you. At the moment it is not. So you are making terrible, terrible mistakes. And suddenly I am doing the same, just because I want to help you. I don't know if I'll be able to show my face in that club again. And what do I get out of it all? Nothing."

No reproaches, please, I muttered. I'm the sort of person who needs time. First I have to establish myself, to feel at least partly in control; and only then can I deal with everything else.

"And I, of course, come last," she observed sharply.

No woman comes last in my life, said Willy, elegantly trying to save the situation; with each one it is as if she is the first.

"Well, then it's worth waiting," she said, looking at me.

I dared not tell her that it almost certainly was not.

18.

The next day at 2 p.m. with my easel over my shoulder, a roll of canvas under my arm and my palette, brushes, paints and dirty overall in a holdall, I was waiting for Jimmy in front of the rowing club. I had arrived too early, so I was carefully examining the large boats chained to the wooden docks, and the many small ones that lay on the mud, waiting for the tide, speculating as to which was to be part of the painting project of the century (and thus already written into history). When Jimmy had still not shown up at a quarter past, my enthusiasm began to wane and I thought that the boy had no intention of keeping his word; perhaps I had represented only a convenient means of defying his father.

I had already written him off and turned to leave when he came rushing along the paved riverside path towards me. "S-s-sorry, s-s-sorry," the words tumbled from his lips; his face was hideously contorted out of fear that he had disappointed me.

"The main thing is, you're here now," I said. He was trembling with relief and I knew I had a friend for life. "Th-th-there," he pointed, pulling me along. Two hundred yards down the river at the foot of some steps that led down to the water was a boat that was so small that I was almost overcome with laughter; Jimmy, I wanted to say, what did you think you were transporting, a Chihuahua?

Fortunately, it looked small only from a distance; when we came closer I realised it had everything a boat needed: two seats, two oars

134

and a small outboard motor, as well as enough room for the two of us and everything I had brought with me, including my easel. The only thing now missing was a wooden frame to fasten the canvas to, which I had completely forgotten, but without hesitation Jimmy said: "I kn-n-now where."

He untied the boat, pushed off with an oar, started the motor and we were soon chugging upriver to the west. A riverside carpenter in Brentford quickly knocked me up a solid frame and nailed the first canvas to it, while for the others he gave me a bag of nails and a hammer, all for free ("M-m-mummy's c-c-cousin," explained Jimmy, as we carried the frame to the boat.) The weather was ideal for painting: soft light, scattered heavy clouds that floated across the city in a leisurely fashion, hiding and uncovering the sun in a dramatic sequence of darkness and light, a freshness of water and air that gave a sharp edge to reality, not a breath of wind, a calm surface, barely discernible rocking; bliss.

Jimmy, I said, as we are in Brentford we'll start here, because it was here that in 54 BC Julius Caesar and his legions forded the Thames. And in a flash, the rapidly applied layers of paint on the canvas began to depict something that Jimmy observed with increasing wonder: ranks of Roman soldiers with plumed helmets wading across the Thames, some with water up to their necks, others to their mouths, with their spears and swords and shields held high above their heads, and a little below them the cavalry swimming to the north bank on horseback; on the first horse, sitting tall in the saddle, resting on the stirrups, young Julius, his head thrown haughtily back in a half commanding, half cajoling posture, with his sword in his left hand aggressively pointing towards the bank, from where the tattered rabble of British defenders had already begun to withdraw and flee. And all illuminated by the sharp rays of light breaking through the clouds: a composition of flashing helmets and shields, as well as a golden glint in the point of Caesar's sword.

"Oooh," breathed Jimmy, "ooh."

I should have warned him not to use up all his admiration on my first attempt; he should save some at least for what was to come. But I was too absorbed in my vision to be able to speak. So Jimmy, when

135

his wonderment should have reached its peak (when behind the Romans crossing the river there appeared the outline of Tower Bridge, built more than fifteen centuries later, and in front of it to the left the dome of St Paul's), he was completely exhausted from admiration and could react only with barely audible whistling, imbecilic open mouth and vacuous stare.

This picture we shall entitle *Simultaneity*. In fact *Simultaneity I* because there will be more. With some brush strokes, Jimmy, we have changed two thousand years of history into a single moment! *A wanderer is man from his birth. / He was born in a ship / On the breast of the river of Time; / Brimming with wonder and joy / He spreads out his arms to the light, / Rivets his gaze on the banks of the stream.*

"M-M-Matthew Arn-n-nold," said Jimmy, "we have him in sch-chool."

How nice, I thought, that as well as art we are brought together by the poetry of an old-fashioned poet.

Over the following days we criss-crossed the Thames in our boat, looking for images for the *Simultaneity* sequence, stopping whenever our hungry eyes spotted a view worthy of depiction, most often before, beneath or behind a bridge, and I painted as if condemned to death and only brush strokes were keeping me alive – exhausted, hungry, dehydrated. Meanwhile Jimmy, instead of growing weary, became as obsessed as I, trying to stop the boat from rocking as I painted, or the current from carrying us off, or the boat running aground at low tide or turning in a circle or running into another, and making sure that he did not catch my legs with the oar when he had to row.

A great lad!

The canvases that each day, as the sun began to set, we carefully carried from the boat and locked in the unused store room of the rowing club to dry soon become a public secret. Some club members wanted to see them but we turned down every request, saying that they would be exhibited when the series was finished and the canvases dry. I would not even comply with Mrs. Hudson's request for a quick look. So as not to offend her, I told her that I was superstitious:

if someone saw the paintings before I had exhausted my current vision the magic would disappear in a flash. "Artists," she said with exasperation and gave up.

Jimmy used the same excuse to keep his mother at bay, a melancholy but extremely attractive woman with smooth hair, who came one evening to see what was happening. It was actually thanks to her that I had a boat and she was also the one who had given Jimmy the (only) key to the store room, so I was prepared to meet her request that she be allowed to see the pictures; but Jimmy (using my excuse) insisted that she could not and because I did not want to create the impression that he was not an equal partner I backed him up. This pleased her even more than being allowed to take a look. She invited us for a drink in the nearest pub; we did not want to go to the club.

"Jimmy is completely transformed," she said. Her eyes were on me the whole time: they travelled over my features, observing me with warmth and indulgence, but at the same time shrewdly and with curiosity, in the fear that she would come across the shadow of something false, calculating. "He's never been so enthusiastic about anything before. He's never been so good tempered. He keeps reciting a Matthew Arnold poem; he never liked him before. And each day there are more words he can say without difficulty. As if something has opened for him, something new. As if he has started to believe in himself, and it's thanks to you."

Ah, I waved my hand and winked at Jimmy, why shouldn't he, there's nothing wrong with him; I'm the one who should be grateful, to him and to you, for without the boat and Jimmy I would never have had the opportunity to paint the bridges between the past and the present. What Jimmy and I are engaged in is actually a philosophical exploit: we are showing time to be false, mocking transience and celebrating God's omnipresence.

"Are you religious?" asked the beautiful melancholy lady, who I felt an increasing desire to paint (perhaps as the Virgin Mary, with Jimmy as Jesus in her lap). I replied that I believed in innocence and the purity of natural beauty and in the ecstasy of the soul and in the gentle harmony of the spirit, all of them undoubted attributes of God; whenever I painted my hand held a brush and God held my hand.

"And who holds God's hand?" she said with a warm smile.

My vision, I said, returning her smile.

We both knew that we must see each other again, that Jimmy was our child, that he was safe with me as with her, and that I, although only six years older, was his surrogate father.

"My husband moves in the world of money," she explained. "To Jimmy and I less tangible things are more important. So your arrival brings joy to my heart. I don't know how to thank you."

There's no need for thanks, I said, it is enough that you look into my soul and see it as it really is. If you really want to do me a favour, once this phase is over you can pose for a portrait.

"Oh," she was confused and blushed slightly, "I'm afraid that... But no... I don't know why I should be afraid... Perhaps I shall."

At this point Jimmy came out with an avalanche of stammering worse than ever before, perhaps because he was in too much of a hurry; all that I could make out from the unstoppable flow of fractured words was the urgency with which he wanted to convince his mother of something.

"Jimmy," she tried to calm him with her hand, "you know it's no good. Your father wouldn't allow it. And Willy is staying at Mrs. Hudson's, we can't steal him."

Excuse me, I said, I'm the one to decide when and under what conditions I'm going to be stolen – if at all. Can you tell me what you're planning to do with me without my knowing?

Once more the lady blushed charmingly (oh, how quickly Willy was falling in love with her, how much he would like, right there in front of Jimmy, to stroke her cheek and smooth her hair and say to her: Let's kill the bank manager!). "Jimmy thinks you should move in with us, into our guest room. I gave him at least two reasons why that is not possible; you give him another one."

I replied that I would only cite one of hers and that was the first, which was more than enough to stop us contemplating this tempting offer.

"I must go," she said, getting up. "You, too, Jimmy, so that you'll be rested tomorrow."

138

And it really was increasing tiredness that threatened the successful completion of our project; tiredness from stress rather than effort; from the stress of wondering what we would carry to the store room at the end of the day. We were very satisfied with some pictures, in some cases so enthusiastic that we danced right there in the boat, almost tipping it over. Jimmy had got used to dedicating lines of Matthew Arnold to each completed painting, usually reciting them in ceremonious fashion before we removed the canvas from the frame to take it to safety; he had such a knack for choosing appropriate lines that I could hardly believe it and when he was reciting he did not stutter at all, but pronounced the words clearly and with deep feeling.

The weather remained friendly, only once did rain fall from a black cloud and ruin a half-finished picture; but we both saw this as a sign of God's benevolence, as he seemed to be saying: you realise that I could send such a downpour five times a day? But soon from inland a breeze began to blow, which the next day became a wind, until the river became so choppy that the boat was constantly swaying. It was hard to keep a steady hand and my brush often strayed a fraction of an inch from the spot on the canvas where it was supposed to slide. At first this disturbed me terribly, but I soon realised that a new style was being born before my eyes, a kind of jagged, trembling representation that most reminded me of the Expressionism of Oskar Kokoschka, of his impetuous, spontaneous and apparently coincidental but controlled brushstrokes, although my style was still somehow original: people and buildings and trees and water and boats somehow tattered, torn at the edges, at the same time in duplicate, even in triplicate, full of a mysterious energy that jumped right out of the canvas.

Jimmy, I said, do you know how Impressionism was born? Monet got cataracts and suddenly everything he saw was blue. And what he saw he painted. At the same time, he was convinced that he was painting what others also saw. But others saw in his paintings something new, a new style and he became famous. After an operation, when the sight in one of his eyes returned to normal he was horrified at the paintings and wanted to destroy them. Something similar is happening to us, Jimmy. My inspiration charmed God into sending a westerly wind in order to rock the boat so as to knock my brush and before our very eyes a new era in the visual arts is born. Shall we carry on painting in this jagged style or shall we wait for the wind to die down and the river to settle?

"C-c-carry on," said Jimmy without hesitation.

Okay, I said. We shall risk the worst that can happen to an artist: that he becomes immortal because of capricious weather.

"N-n-no," he violently shook his head. "*As is the world on the banks, / So is the mind of the man.*"

Jimmy, I said, are you at all aware what wisdom you have spoken through the words of a poet from the past? You and I are of the same ilk, we are both at odds with the time in which we live –we live in all times and are synchronous. We should be listening to the Beatles, going to parties, smoking dope, putting our hands up girls' very short skirts, criticising the boring bourgeois society, living from one day to the next, rebels without a cause. But we go our own way. If we had the same mother she would be very proud of her two sons.

"M-m-my m-m-mother could be your m-m-mother," he struggled to say, the nicest offer I had ever had. Of course, I did not tell him that his mother could be many other things besides my mother, so I said nothing, but quickly, almost embarrassed, smoothed his ruffled hair, the generous boy. Thanks, Jimmy, I said, we'll ask her what she thinks of the idea, but while this sweet wind is blowing we must make use of every second to produce the works of art that will wake the world from its slumbers and confront it with the truth about itself.

And we continued: Jimmy steering the rocking boat up and down the river, sometimes with the tide flowing from the sea to the interior, sometimes with the current flowing towards the sea, the rocking taking the brush pretty much where it wanted to go, but always recognisably within the boundaries of my intentions. From day to day, the number of paintings in the *Simultaneity* sequence multiplied; from day to day, I increasingly mastered my "trembling" style; and ever nearer came the moment when we could (both gratefully and inconsolably) acknowledge that we had finished.

In every painting, in various guises, a bridge spanned the river (not every bridge, but the most interesting of the twenty-seven); in all of them there was the panoramic presence of modern London buildings,

140

while the historical moment was different in each and in each the combination of imagined and observed told a different story.

Against a backdrop of Kingston-upon-Thames, now one of the most comfortable nests of the middle classes, I painted the stone throne on which were crowned the Saxon kings of England: between 900 and 979 Edward I, Athelstan, Edmund the Magnificent, Edred, Edwig All-Fair, Edward the Martyr and Ethelred II. From the rapidity with which seven kings occupied the throne in 79 years I judged that life in those times (especially the life of kings) was nasty, brutish and short and, judging from the roughness of the throne, very uncomfortable, so I painted two stone thrones and duplicated the kings: on the first throne they were crowned, on the second beheaded, one after the other. The icing on the cake was Henry the Eighth who, in the background, in the infamous Tower, himself beheaded his wives. This was *Simultaneity VI,* subtitled *Origins of English civilisation.*

In Teddington, to where the tide reaches (Tide-end-town), the flora and fauna change; swans and ducks give way to seagulls. From there to Hammersmith along the left bank of the river there were, in the seventeenth century, ranks of plantations and vegetable gardens through which ran the road to Hampton, covered in ankle-deep mud even though the king travelled along it several times a week. In the bushes beside the road lurked highwaymen, ready to rob carriages and pedestrians. Now two main arterial routes cut through these suburbs: the Great West Road, built in 1925, and the first British motorway the M4. The painting *Simultaneity VIII*, subtitled *The more things change, the more they stay the same,* showed a half-muddy half-tarred road; on it, in the foreground, masked highwaymen were robbing a carriage in which sat terrified medieval nobles, while in the background traffic police were breathalysing the driver of a Jaguar.

To Jimmy, this picture seemed the best, but to my eyes it was almost a caricature, skilfully executed but poor in terms of content. I was much more proud of *Simultaneity IV, VII, IX, X* and *XIII*, which showed the "wedding of the centuries": 18th century river pirates with daggers in their teeth climbing the cruiser Belfast (preserved from World War II, moored in the Thames as a floating museum), while on the Tower in the background fluttered a flag bearing a swastika;

141

the unloading of exotic goods from a mass of mid-19th century ships with the skyscrapers of the Square Mile in the background; William the Conqueror, riding up the Thames in a motorboat, staring up in wonder at Waterloo Bridge, while his soldiers rode behind him on the backs of giant salmon (Jimmy, God bless his soul, could not get over how much William looked like him); and the beautiful Hammersmith Bridge, across which drove twenty completely full red London buses, while from the bridge were hanging a number of figures, including the Beatles and, with a guitar around her neck, Queen Elizabeth I, in whose right hand dangled a half-size Shakespeare. (I called that picture *We all live in a yellow submarine*, which Jimmy thought was terribly funny.) And so on and so on: after two weeks twenty-three canvases were drying in the rowing club store room in Chiswick. Some were already dry enough to be stacked, the others I spread out wherever I could.

19.

I had three unpainted canvases left. Only after the events which followed did I remember how important it is to quit at the right moment and how different my life would have been if I had not tried to add to the *Simultaneity* cycle. As long as I felt that something was driving me, pursuing me, and that I was painting because I had no choice, God was with me and every brushstroke was imbued with his breath. When I began to think that at the end I should paint something else for Jimmy, for his mother and for myself, I subordinated the artist to the dealer in emotions and created the conditions for irremediable errors.

I wanted to paint him as a Welsh prince on a white horse who has waded to the centre of the river and with his sword beheaded twenty river pirates; his mother as a mermaid gazing wonderingly at the Houses of Parliament, to where the tide has brought her; myself as Odysseus who has sailed his boat through the fog on the Thames and is staring in astonishment at the crowds of people thronging both banks of the river holding up placards with the slogan "London is Ithaca". None of these ideas seemed anything special in themselves – until I had the idea of showing them all on the same canvas!

Jimmy, I cried, I have an idea thanks to which the three hundred greatest painters of all time will be turning in their graves with envy! "H-h-hooray!" he responded excitedly and asked for details.

No, I said, this will be a present for you and your mother, so let it remain a secret and then the surprise will be that much greater. But

I had overlooked the fact that after one encounter I did not recall his mother's features clearly enough; before starting work I would need to meet her at least once more.

Jimmy, I said, I need your help.

The very next morning I was invited to tea. Mrs. Hudson, reticent and slightly ill-humoured, drove me to the door of the distinguished house next to Ravenscourt Park. The lush greenery that embraced the dark brown brick walls, the fragrance of the roses beside the entrance and the spacious park that seemed to have no end overshadowed even the fine house in which I was staying, and Mrs. Hudson knew this so she slammed the door of her dilapidated car, threw a "Thank you for the ride" through the window and drove off.

I understood her distress; I was going for tea with a woman who was more beautiful, somewhat younger, richer and better educated than her; I had bathed, washed and carefully combed my hair, put on a clean shirt, dabbed a few drops of her perfume in my beard; what was she to think? Besides which, I had shrouded myself in a mysteriousness which was only likely to increase her suspicion that I was getting into something that I was denying her.

This was of course far from the truth. I could have fallen in love with the gentle consideration and melancholy amiability of Jimmy's mother, but not even in my wildest dreams did I dare to hope that this would have touched her, as she more than likely made a similar impression on every man that had the opportunity of chatting with her. Besides which, she was the mother of my only real friend in London; this friendship was sacred, I would not want to jeopardise it for anything.

Henderson, was written beneath the doorbell.

Jimmy, I asked, what is your mum's name?

"Stella," he replied without effort and then, as if this was not enough, tried to repeat the name, with considerably less success: "St-t-tella H-h-hender-s-s-son." To my ears (and sense of rhythm, which I was not short of) the name sounded like an erotic dance, like a quick, harmonious tango on the polished deck of a ship: Stella – Willy – Willy – Stella.

144

We found her in the back garden, sitting at a wooden table beneath a tree, somehow fragile, brittle, almost girl-like in comparison with the woman I recalled from our first meeting, perhaps because she was wearing a short black skirt that made her almost snow white legs seem highly vulnerable and a light blue, carelessly buttoned blouse which offered glimpses of the roundness of her mature breasts, which barely imperceptibly sagged, but which, because of the history of breast-feeding and sex that they testified to, were much more attractive than the untouched breasts of a young girl.

"Willy," she greeted me, putting down the book she was reading. I caught a glimpse of the title: *Therapy for Speech Defects*.

When she got up I was surprised how much smaller she was than I had imagined: obviously at our first encounter she had worn very high-heels, which I had not even noticed; now she was wearing sandals.

"Tea?" she smiled. I said I would rather have coffee, if it was not too much bother; where I come from we do not drink tea with milk.

"Sugar?" she asked.

Two, please, I said; I already knew the ritual.

"Jimmy, will you ask Conchita to bring it?"

Jimmy obediently went, while the fragile Stella invited me to sit. She ran her eyes over me two or three times. "You're very well turned out today," she said approvingly.

We painters are strange ones, I replied: when we paint we sweat, when we are seeking for inspiration we smell sweetly.

"You do smell nice," she smiled slightly at the women's perfume that had evidently wafted her way. "Is that why you came? Because you are seeking inspiration?"

As well as undoubted opportunities, the question offered too many pitfalls for a quick reply, so I decided to wait until a less risky moment. I became engrossed in the beauty of the garden, in the blossoming exuberance that contrasted so sharply with the fragile, breakable, already slightly faded beauty of Jimmy's mother, and in this contrast, that underlined the melancholy of her blue-grey eyes and the gentle resignation of her broad mouth, with its down-turned corners, I felt (perhaps under the influence of the sonorous sounds of Barber's *Adagio* emerging from the open French doors to the living

145

room) something familiar, something that I had obsessively painted in Cornwall. *Desolation.*

When I have finished on the river I shall start to paint English gardens, I said. Although they are so beautiful that it is painful, it seems to me that this is because in their natural, untidy luxuriance they absorb the sadness and traumas of the people who live among them. In the midst of this luxuriance, which seems overdone, I sense so much pain, so many muffled cries of resistance, so many suppressed wrongs, so many faded hopes, so many shattered dreams.

I looked at her and saw her flinch, but she clearly did not want to take the bait, it was either too early or too un-English to reveal to someone she was meeting for only the second time her inner desolation, although I felt that the idea excited her, perhaps filled her with hope that a moment may come when such an obstacle was no longer in place. But she had to say something, and because she could not say what she wanted to say, a sense of awkwardness began to arise between us.

Fortunately it was interrupted by Jimmy and Conchita (the spotty Spanish au pair), who brought a tray of coffee and tea. Then Jimmy joined us and we chatted about neutral things, although it was so only on the surface: when she talked about what she liked to read, what music she liked to listen to, how seven years earlier she had left a well-paid job in advertising to retrain as a teacher in a school for children with speech defects (that Jimmy had just completed), and about her husband, who had at first opposed the idea, although he had accepted it in the end and now ensured the family's material comfort, she increasingly approached the line beyond which her words would become a confession and a cry for help.

She knew what was happening; she knew that I also knew what was happening; we also knew that Jimmy, who blindly trusted both of us, did not know; and suddenly we were drawn together by this secret which, alongside striving to protect Jimmy from it, became a stronger and more dangerous connection than could be established through thousands of words. Our awareness of this sudden closeness was like a spark ignited within both of us at once; with fleeting glances we told each other everything.

146

Once more she began to talk about Jimmy: how he had never had a real friend; how he spoke about me the whole time, although he kept stubbornly quiet about what we were painting; and how we artists had the power to come into people's lives and completely change them, even if we did not want to do this and even if the people concerned resisted the changes. Perhaps because we see further and feel more than most people allow themselves to see or feel.

"Mummy," said Jimmy, "stop talking like that, you'll embarrass him."

We both burst out laughing. "You see," she said, "seven years of private school did less then you have achieved in ten days. I'm quite afraid of what will happen when you stop painting and don't need the boat anymore."

Obviously Jimmy was even more worried, since he glanced anxiously at me two or three times to gauge my reaction.

But I'll need Jimmy, I said, I'll be painting other things; I won't be able to carry an easel, frame, canvas, paints, brushes and everything else on my own; if he has the time his help will be very welcome. And from every picture I sell he will get twenty per cent.

Jimmy emitted a strange sound – half cry, half muffled gasp – and in his embarrassment jumped up and ran to the far end of the garden, where he busied himself with the flowers of the wisteria, nervously rearranging them, although they were already hanging as they were meant to and nothing he did would make them hang any differently.

"He feels awkward," said Stella in explanation, "but from happiness. He often cannot control his emotions. I get the impression that he feels everything – pleasure, sadness, whatever – twice as strongly as normal people."

She fell silent and looked at me. "Are we normal?"

Upon reflection I said: if normality means suppressing what we feel inside and distorting the dreams from which we draw energy into messy compromises that are acceptable to others then we should be less normal. Regrettably that is often impossible. But there are moments when we can afford such luxury without a feeling of guilt.

"But is it possible to live without a feeling of guilt?" she asked. "If you have a son like Jimmy?"

147

It's not your fault that he stammers, I said.

"It's my fault that out of a need for security and comfort I stayed with his father, who was never able to accept him and whose rejection only made his problem worse. You are the first to show him a way out: you have shown him that he doesn't have to stammer. When he is convinced enough of this, he will stop. I'm not exaggerating when I say that I shall be eternally grateful to you."

I'm not a healer, I said; I am simply what I am; every moment I am myself, although these selves differ from each other; I get the feeling that there are too many of them, although two prevail and the rest are perhaps only their incarnation.

"I too," she looked at me brightly, "I too have more than one self, and I have no idea which one is now telling you this. I only know that they are all equally grateful."

Her emphasis on gratitude began to fill me with the thought that she would probably not be able to say no if I took her at her word and demanded a reward. Perhaps by harping on about this she was only trying to give me the courage to make the demand without fear of being rejected. Fortunately, at this moment Jimmy returned. He had recovered from his overdose of delight. He sat down and looked at me.

"T-t-tell mummy why you came," he said. Stella looked at me: was there anything behind my visit other than courtesy?

"T-t-tell her," Jimmy insisted, beginning to fidget restlessly; once again he was gripped by impatience, once again he was in too much of a hurry for his words to jump the hurdle without tripping.

I confessed that for the last picture in the *Simultaneity* cycle Jimmy and I were planning a painting in which his mother was the central figure. As I could not remember her features sufficiently clearly after our first meeting I wanted to meet her once more before starting to paint and commit to memory every detail of her face, down to the very smallest. I was not completely sure, but she seemed to blush slightly. That I was not mistaken was confirmed the next moment when her blush became obvious.

"My face is nothing special," she said.

On the contrary, I said, the first time I saw it your face reminded me of one of the faces from the history of art, a portrait by one of the

148

immortal painters – perhaps not a whole portrait, but only a feature of one of the female figures that appeared so frequently in the old masters. I'm really annoyed that my memory, which is normally so reliable, has let me down. If I had to hand an illustrated history of art I would find the face of which you remind me in less than five minutes.

"We have one," she said, "upstairs in the library. Shall we go and have a look?"

I jumped up before I had time to think that my haste may create the wrong impression. But she had risen equally quickly, and judging by her expression with the same thought. "I'd like some more tea and you probably more coffee; Jimmy, will you see to it?"

Jimmy nodded and went towards the kitchen, while we went through the living room to the stairs and up to the first floor. She went first; the stairs were steep and near the top she made a long enough step and opened her legs enough for me to catch a glimpse beneath her black skirt of white silk panties. Although I was very young I was still experienced enough to know why at that moment my head began to spin: not because of the speed of our ascent, not because of a change in blood pressure. I began to feel the blows everywhere: in my stomach, in my veins, in my head, in my trembling hands, in my knees which felt weak.

"Are you alright?" she asked, turning to face me at the top of the stairs; I still don't know whether she lengthened that last step to show me how young she still was, or deliberately to expose herself to the young man walking behind her. "Come on," she reached out her hand and pulled me up as if I was a winded old man, "what's wrong with you?"

The coffee, I said, if I have too much caffeine I sometimes get quite dizzy, maybe there's something wrong with my heart.

"Ah," she replied, going into the library. Still somewhat confused I followed her, but as soon as I entered the library my confusion was replaced by amazement. The room had large windows looking onto the garden and measured at least five yards by four; three of the walls were covered to the ceiling with wooden shelves full of books, which were so exquisitely arranged that it seemed someone had ordered them not alphabetically or in terms of content, but rather for maximum decorative effect.

Wow, I said. I could see she was both proud and satisfied.

"One of my little vices," she acknowledged. "Books that I collect because they are beautiful. I haven't read them all and probably never shall, but it's nice to know that they are here and that any moment I can choose a new one. Having the possibility means more to me than making use of it, do you know what I mean?"

In the middle of the room there stood a glass-topped table, similarly full of carefully placed books, beside it a comfortable couch and two armchairs – a paradise for an addicted reader. In the right-hand corner opposite the door the shelves passed over a semi-circular writing table on which stood a large oval mirror that reflected the library as a continuation of the space or as a new, identical space with the same layout of shelves and furniture. Above the mirror the shelves came together again, forming the same semi-circle as the table below them.

"Jimmy also likes to explore this treasure house," she said. "My husband never. He has only been in here about twice. He is happy enough with the Financial Times in front of the television in the lounge. Ah, that's what we are looking for."

With rapid steps she approached the corner table and reached for a large book that protruded a fraction of an inch from the first neat straight row on the first semi-circular shelf. As it was too high, she placed her left hand on the table for support and leaned forward, but she could still not reach. I rushed to help her; standing right behind her and with my left hand on the table I stretched for the book, which I reached easily, but before I took it from the shelf I felt how I was leaning on Stella from behind, that I was actually leaning against the curve of her behind.

The next moment my hand, instead of removing from the shelf *The Illustrated History of Art,* grasped hers, which was still stretched out, and pulled it down to the table; now we were both leaning on the table with both hands and in a position that had nothing to do with books, although we had found ourselves thus by chance and without the slightest thought about what we now needed to decide.

150

Our eyes met in the mirror. No, hers warned silently; alright, mine agreed. But we were in deep shock; neither of us could make the movement that would separate us. By then, being pressed against her behind had had its effect and she also must have felt my sudden tumescence; now the question in our eyes was repeated; her answer was still no, mine still alright. But we had both absorbed a strange sense of alarm, almost a feeling of panic that we would not be able to resist the temptation into which we were sliding. Each of us waited for the other to withdraw, and each of us feared this.

Probably I would have taken a step back if two things had not happened. First the sun, which was approaching noon, came so far that its first beam shone through the window, and that ray of sunlight fell straight on Stella's face in the mirror; it was so sudden, so sharp, that she shuddered and blinked. And almost at the same time I thought I remembered who that illuminated face reminded me of: not of some famous portrait to be found in *The Illustrated History of Art,* but of the girl on the ship, *the girl who would rather be elsewhere,* and who was now elsewhere, God knows where. It was this girl (my Muse, to whom I had pledged my everlasting fidelity) who had in some incomprehensible way become embodied in the woman whom I was now, from behind, swollen as never before, pressing against the table.

I do not know to what extent, during the last look we had exchanged in the mirror, she had realised that my attention was no longer only on her, but also on some other, lost although eternally present woman – the only one, and the real one that I had not wanted to let go of, but had wanted to make her mine forever. All this happened so fast and without any awkwardness, as if we had been rehearsing precisely this event. But I was granted only one deep, smooth, tight thrust, for as soon as the head of my penis hit the neck of her womb and I pulled back for another thrust we saw in the mirror, where our misted eyes met once more, something move, and realised that Jimmy had appeared in the doorway.

He froze, just as we did.

A rescue mission followed, which could not have been better organised if we had planned it. A few hand movements did it all: placing my penis back in my trousers, zip up, panties up, skirt down, hands – hers and mine – almost simultaneously reaching for the shelf. "I'll do it" (Willy), "I'm not tall enough" (Stella), and then, when the book was in my hand, "Thank you. I don't know how it found its way up there".

"Okay, let's see," she said, reaching for the book, "who I remind you of."

The next moment she started as if she had only just seen her son. "Oh, Jimmy," she said with as normal a voice as possible, although I could tell how upset she was. "Are the tea and coffee ready?"

Jimmy nodded and withdrew; it was completely impossible to judge what he had seen and what he was thinking.

When we returned to the garden he was not there; on the table sat a tray with tea and coffee.

"Conchita," called Stella, "where's Jimmy?"

For quite some time there was no reply and then from inside a hoarse voice coloured by a strong accent said: "I think he's in the toilet."

We sat and pretended that everything was normal; we knew that we would need to play the game to the end, without confusion, with no let up, with no uncertainty. When Jimmy returned to the table he appeared completely normal. It was hard to say who was more relieved, his mother or I.

"D-d-did you find anything?" he asked.

"Nothing for now," his mother replied, "what have you got there?" And she pointed to Jimmy's t-shirt, which was full of greenish stains that had not been there before.

"N-n-nothing," he said, "I was s-s-sick."

"You were sick," she almost shouted, "why?"

Jimmy shrugged and looked at the ground. "I d-d-don't feel well."

"Then go and lie down," she almost shouted once more; when she heard herself she moderated her voice and wearily, almost on the verge of tears said: "Go on, Jimmy. Go and lie down, until it passes."

Jimmy got up and went off, head down. "Oh God," she sighed.

He did not necessarily see anything, I tried to comfort her; maybe he really is feeling sick.

"He's never sick!" She was almost hysterical.

152

Then she gathered herself, leapt to her feet and said: "You'll have to go. I'm sorry, but really, this moment. I don't know what will happen now but you cannot stay. Collect the paintings from the store room, return the key to the club, I'm sorry, I hope you understand. I'll let you know what is happening."

She accompanied me to the door and almost pushed me over the threshold. "God," she said with tears in her eyes, "what have I done?"

And she closed the door without even looking at me; for her I was already someone from the past, an intrusion about which she needed to forget.

20.

For two hours I wandered around Ravenscourt Park, sitting on benches, lying on the grass, shocked at the thought that in less than ten minutes my life had been turned upside down. It had an air of unreality, the images mingled inside me like a scene from a bad film. I looked towards the house, waiting for Jimmy to come running out the door and for us to take to the Thames. The more I thought about who was to blame, the clearer it became that no one was: what had to happen happened and at the most an unfortunate set of circumstances could be held responsible. Although I helped create the pictures in which my life (and Stella's and Jimmy's) changed, the main brush strokes came from a more elevated artist. And again, more than ever before, I was seized by the desire to uncover, get to know, define this artist who so arbitrarily painted and repainted human destiny; I felt that recently he was all too often meddling in my affairs, almost making a fool of me.

(Oh come on, said Willy II, not that religious impulse again – deal with it some other time, this is really not the right moment. Look at the sun in the sky and what it is shining on: you'll see that your life is no more than a speck of dust. You're no one, Willy, no one and nothing. But at the same time you are more than all the rest: you are a painter, and when you become a painter you forego the right to sentimentality. The great painter in the sky is your competitor: show him that you're better than him, that he can't get to you, that you can correct all the daubs he puts on canvas and cover them with *your* strokes. Don't fool yourself into thinking that God is with you when you paint: he may be there, but only to hinder you, since he cannot bear it if one of his little men improves upon his vision. Suppress those idiotic feelings, take a step back while you can, otherwise you will fall into a mire of moralising from which you will never be able to extract yourself. Remember what the Buddha said about the meaning of life. Carry on.)

I had never felt any particular wish to follow Willy II's advice, but this time I found in it great consolation. The only consolation. I squinted into the noon sun and thought that it was shining equally unconcernedly into the library where Jimmy lost a friend and his faith in his mother; on the people around me emerging from offices to munch their lunchtime sandwich on the sunny lawns or in the shade of a tree; on the children who, under the watchful eyes of concerned mothers, were screaming in the nearby sandpit; on the geese and ducks criss-crossing the pond; on the crowds of people in the streets of London; on Julia and her mother in Cornwall; on Mrs. Hudson, who was probably sitting on one of her wickerwork chairs in the garden, biting her nails as she wondered what I was up to; even on my mother and father, who were perhaps sitting on the balcony of a small block of flats in a small town in Slovenia; on the friends and acquaintances who were already fading in my memory; and on the thousands of towns and villages, and the millions of people, each with their own story, wrapped up in themselves as if there were no other stories, as if there was only one centre of the world – wherever "I" am – and all the rest is just a space given to me so that I can see myself reflected in it and confirm my own existence.

The renewed awareness that I was only one of many brought me no comfort; within me there remained a painful void that I would have preferred to fill with lines from Arnold, but because I did not have his book to hand, the words of another Matthew came to mind: *Ye are the salt of the earth. But if the salt hath last its savour, wherewith shall it be salted?*

Maria Hudson was surprised that Jimmy and I had finished so suddenly, since I had been saying all along that we still had quite a bit of work in front of us, but although she probably guessed that something had happened, she did not probe at all and was visibly pleased when I said that Jimmy and I would not be seeing each other again, because he had other things to do. In as much as she saw Jimmy's mother as a potential competitor for my affections, she was now relieved. She was happy to help me collect my canvases from the store room. There were so many of them that we needed two trips and she offered to return the key herself to the caretaker of the rowing club (evidently she wanted to make sure that that part of my life was really over).

The canvases were too big to keep in my room, so I left them in the dining room; the last ones that were not completely dry I carefully leaned against the wall. "Unusual", was Maria Hudson's only comment, "very, very unusual. Is that all you painted in two weeks?"

(Is that all?! Twenty-four large oil paintings?!)

I have to rest, I said; my head hurts, maybe from the sun. And I went to my room, locked the door, slumped onto the bed, pulled the cover over my head and fell into a tortuous state where I wanted to sleep but was unable to do so. Finally, it must have happened.

I was awoken by voices coming from the living room; Harry and Ana were evidently back from work, Gerry and Christopher from their wanderings. But they were louder than usual, making a real noise, talking, swearing, exclaiming, enthusing. I heard certain words and phrases: "amazing", "look at that", "it's history in the making", "what precision", "unforgettable", "it's like a dream".

Evidently they had discovered my paintings and from their reactions I could only conclude that they were enchanted, astonished, charmed. Of course, I had not expected a less than enraptured reception, but it still did me good to hear that even the restrained Ana was not sparing with her superlatives ("I can't believe it,", "it's such a shock", "you must really have to be someone special to do something like that").

Oh, Jimmy, I thought, how I wish that you were present to hear how the world lies at our feet.

Gripped by the sudden fear that one of the pictures would get damaged, I got up and rushed downstairs. In the living room I witnessed a scene that at first my eyes refused to believe. The pictures were

156

where I had put them and the family were sitting together watching the television.

"Come, Zhivago," said Mrs. Hudson, beckoning me, "you shouldn't miss this for the world". In spite of the fact that my legs almost refused to obey me, I managed to take three steps into the room.

"The Americans have landed on the Moon," explained Christopher. On the screen a buffoon in a bulky space outfit hopped around. In the background stood a strange space vessel and beside it another buffoon was making awkward movements.

"Just think," exclaimed Gerry, "on the Moon an elephant would weigh less than a mouse on the Earth."

"Oh no it wouldn't," was Harry's sagacious contribution.

"Come and sit down," said Mrs. Hudson, moving over to make room for me on the couch.

I saw the paintings, neglected behind their backs (like so much old junk gathered there ready to be thrown away). The Americans had landed on the Moon. Then I must have seen them, since I landed there before them! Or rather not, since I had landed on the dark side. Or they had landed on a different moon. Whatever, art remained on Earth, literally on the ground, and one of the still wet paintings that I had leaned against the wall had fallen over and was probably already making a mess of the carpet without anyone noticing.

I don't feel well, I said, I'm going back to my room.

"Dinner will be later than usual," called Maria Hudson, when I was already at the top of the stairs.

I surreptitiously left the house and went to Ravenscourt Park, which was almost empty in the evening and I saw only joggers and dog walkers. Hidden behind the bushes, I crept towards Jimmy's house on the northern edge of the park. The bank manager was evidently already at home, since a silver Jaguar stood on the driveway. The house was in darkness, whereas in most of the others the lights were already on. I would have given my right arm to know what was happening inside at that moment. Every few minutes an Underground train rumbled across the viaduct that divided the park into two unequal parts, stopping at the platform high above me and disgorging passengers returning from work, before rattling onwards.

In the clear but darkening sky I could already see the pale image of a waxing moon. It did not seem possible that people were walking on it. It seemed equally impossible that this did not excite me, as if it was connected with another world. The Americans had landed on the Moon, but life on Earth followed its usual course, as if infinitesimal feelings and small personal goals were more important than the history now being made. Not only art, but suffering had remained down below.

I walked down to the Thames and wandered along it to Hammersmith Bridge and then back to the rowing club in Chiswick. I sat for half an hour with a beer on the pub terrace where only a week before I had sat with Jimmy and his mother. That felt like God-knows-when, in the distant past. Imperceptibly, simultaneity had become the pain of loss. I went on, once more walking from the bridge to the rowing club. I felt like a criminal returning to the scene of the crime, hopelessly looking for a way to turn the clock back, at least to the point where a different decision could have been taken and been followed by a different life. More than ever before, I felt how fateful moments in life can be.

I returned home through the narrow streets, avoiding dinner, and closed myself in my room. And I tried, while the others were in the living room watching the Americans on the Moon, to find some consolation in Matthew Arnold: *And the calm moonlight seems to say: / Hast thou then still the old unquiet breast, / Which neither deadens into rest, / Nor ever feels the fiery glow / That whirls the spirit from itself away, / But fluctuates to and fro, / Never by passion quite posses'd / And never quite benumb'd by the world's sway? - / And I, I know not if to pray / Still to be what I am, or yield and be / Like all the other men I see.*

Half an hour later Mrs. Hudson knocked on the door. "Zhivago," she called, "time for dinner."

I did not reply, I held my breath, I was too weak to return from timelessness to a time that I had not chosen, that belonged to the lunar Americans.

"You really are a strange young man," she murmured and went downstairs.

I felt as if I had moved away from a world that I no longer knew nor dared to touch into a protective circle of silence, beyond which the commotion outside lost its edge. I became deaf. Deaf to the world and the cries echoing within me.

The next day I slept until eleven, missing breakfast, and I would have missed lunch too if Maria Hudson had not persisted in rattling the door handle and knocking on the door. "Zhivago, come down, there's a big surprise waiting for you."

Numb at the thought that it was connected with Jimmy or his mother, I went down to the dining room, only to encounter a smiling middle-aged man with thinning, slicked down hair, dressed in trousers too narrow for his age and his physique, which boasted a well-rounded stomach, and with a yellow cravat tied around his neck and tucked into the neck of his blue shirt.

"Mr. Alan McClelland," Mrs. Hudson introduced him with pride, "art critic and seeker of fresh talent for eminent collectors and leading London galleries."

I am not sure whether the man, on catching sight of me, really winced or whether it merely seemed like that since all his movements and gestures were rather exaggerated, but he became at once extremely friendly as if trying to create the impression that he was more refined than he actually was; in doing so, he only succeeded in making me wonder whether he could be trusted. My first response would be no.

This feeling was strengthened when he offered me a soft, almost feminine hand and held mine somewhat longer than was necessary for a mere handshake. When he spoke his voice seemed false, as if he was trying to caricature himself; and this fed my doubts even more. Another Palisander, I thought.

"Maria has told me everything," he said. "I won't call you Zhivago, let that remain her dream, to me you shall be Willy."

"And that is your dream," murmured Maria Hudson, in spite of herself. The man threw a reproachful glance her way, which he tried to hide from me, but I could not help but notice that there was a certain tension between them.

159

"Whatever," he said, turning to me, "I'm Alan. Your paintings are inspired. And please don't think that I'm trying to be friendly – far from it. Even yesterday I sensed that today would be a special day, but when Maria called me and described your work I never imagined that I would see something so original. These pictures will trigger a real earthquake on the London art scene, you mark my words."

Take them, I said carelessly, I was thinking of destroying them anyway.

"Zhivago!" Mrs. Hudson rebuked me.

"No, no," said Alan, springing to my defence, "I know of no painter who at some point does not want to destroy one of his paintings. And quite a few of them have done so. Your pictures are a real statement, almost a confession, undoubtedly connected with deep personal wounds. You do of course have the right to destroy them, they're yours. But I would recommend something better than that. I know at least three gallerists who would be happy to sell them on commission, frame them at their own expense and give you an advance payment of at least a hundred pounds."

"Well?" Maria Hudson gave me a triumphant look.

Okay, I said, turning to leave.

"Don't be like that," she said, pulling me back by my shirt sleeve. "Alan is trying to ease your path into a world that is closed to most young people, however talented they may be. And for foreigners especially it is hermetically sealed."

"Regardless of the fact," added Alan, "that art speaks all languages. Sadly, even art cannot get by without money, so it is important who presents you, to whom and with what. In this instance one could not hope for a better combination."

I didn't know what to say. I felt that I should be happy, but looking at the *Simultaneity* cycle, into which Jimmy and I had invested so much faith and enthusiasm, so much pure and at the same time conspiratorial energy, brought on a deep, dull pain somewhere in my bowels that subsided as soon as I looked away. The pictures did not belong to me, they had become alien, unpleasant, dirty. Just take them, I said and returned to my room.

21.

I stopped washing and combing my hair; I stopped leaving my room and asked Mrs. Hudson to put sandwiches in front of my door if she could be bothered – if not, no problem. I made no effort to establish how much my behaviour was hurting her or how much of a nuisance I was being, but every time she left a sandwich and a glass of juice in front of my door she tried to persuade me to come down.

"Why are you punishing yourself?" she asked "Why not tell me what's tormenting you? You'll feel better for it."

Maybe I don't want to feel better, I shouted. Maybe I don't want any more contact with people.

"You need help," she persisted. "Depression is a serious illness."

I'm not ill, I shouted back. Don't worry about the rent, I'll pay it.

"There's no need," she said. "I got a hundred pounds advance from Alan for the pictures. I can give you the money or keep it for future rent."

I don't care, I said, you keep it. It's far too much for those pictures, anyway.

"I didn't give him all of them," she said. "I kept one. I had it framed and it's hanging on the wall in the dining room."

Which? I asked.

Come and look.

No, I replied.

"Aren't you interested which is my favourite?"

No, I yelled, I'm not interested, those paintings are not mine.

She kept trying to lure me out of my den. She even threatened a couple of times to have Harry break the door down with an axe and drag me out. But nothing worked; the pain of the wounds that I wanted to heal before venturing out once more into the world was too sweet not to prolong it; I was discovering unexpected new shades of suffering – as if uncovering new colours that I could use to cover the old, tired picture inside me with a fresh new, albeit grotesque image.

Through the window I saw a blossoming, fragrant summer; from neighbouring gardens came the sounds of children shouting, dogs barking and playful adult voices. But although close, this was also beyond reach, as if happening on a film screen. I felt that a sense of reality would not return (if it ever did) gradually, but with a sudden jerk and this is what happened when Maria Hudson knocked on the door and said she would be out for a while because she was going to a funeral.

"You could go as well," she said. "Jimmy was your friend."

No, I screamed, leaping up. No, no, no, I repeated when I opened the door. No, I groaned, when I saw that she was standing at the top of the stairs in a black dress. I fell to the floor and put my arms round her knees. Please, no, I repeated, on the verge of tears, although I knew that this was what I had been waiting for, what I had had a foreboding of.

"Look at you," she said. "You can't go to the cemetery like that, it would be an insult to the family. And I can't wait for you as I'm late already."

Where, I shouted after her, where, where?

She did not reply, since she did not want me turning up rumpled and unshaven at the funeral, where I would disgrace myself in front of the members of the rowing club and Jimmy's family.

I dashed back into my room, threw on the first clean clothes I found, rushed out of the house without locking the door, ran with long, gazelle-like strides to the main road, hailed the first passing taxi and, panting, told the driver to take me to the cemetery in Chiswick.

"Which one?" he asked. "There are several."

One at a time, I said, but quickly.

162

The first was deserted. At the second there was a funeral taking place at the chapel of rest near the entrance. But there were so many mourners that I thought: this can't be the right place, Jimmy can't have had so many friends. Then I saw behind the coffin, which had just been brought outside, the black clad figure of Stella Henderson. Her face was covered by a veil, she was bent over and leaning on her husband's arm. Around her I saw sombre faces, most of which I remembered from the rowing club, including Maria Hudson's; but more numerous were the boys and girls who had evidently been Jimmy's schoolmates. The vicar was saying something, quoting from the Bible, for dust you are and to dust you will return and similar nonsense, but I was not listening: all my attention was focused on my partner in crime.

When she raised her head and looked in front of her I got the feeling that she saw me, although I was crouching behind a cypress near the entrance. But no, she was staring into space, through the arched entrance gate towards the road, devoid of expression, giving no indication that she was feeling anything. At that moment her face did not remind me of anyone, certainly not of Sandrina. One of Jimmy's classmates stepped forward and announced that on behalf of the class she would recite a verse of a poem by Matthew Arnold, who was Jimmy's favourite poet. The verse had been chosen by Jimmy's mother.

This is the curse of life! that not / A nobler, calmer train / Of wiser thoughts and feelings blot / Our passions from our brain; / But each day brings its petty dust / Our soon-choked souls to fill, / And we forget because we must / And not because we will.

This time Mrs. Henderson did not succeed in maintaining her composure: her knees gave way and if her husband had not caught hold of her she would have crumpled to the ground. She let out a short breathless cry, very similar to the sound emitted by an animal whose throat has just been gripped by a lion's jaws. Was I the only one who heard it? The mourners gave no indication that the sound had affected them and the next moment Stella Henderson was once again calm and collected, as if her thoughts were elsewhere and she was only attending the funeral out of a sense of duty.

163

I slunk back to the road and got into the taxi that was waiting in front of the entrance to take me home. I dragged myself to my room and crawled under the cover. I cried convulsively, then got up and started to pack.

When I had put almost everything into my bags I remembered how Maria Hudson said that she had kept one of the *Simultaniety* cycle and hung it in the dining room. I went to check; I was determined to cut it from its frame and carry it off, for after all it was mine. She had not been lying: on the wall hung Julius Caesar with Tower Bridge in the background, *Simultaneity 1*.

Why did she choose this one in particular? It was not bad, but the others were much better. I stood in front of it and looked at the details that I had managed to paint in the grip of my vision: Caesar's foot in a sandal, bent in the middle so as not to slip from the stirrup; a tendon in the neck of a turned head; the teeth of the whinnying horse whose head Caesar, rising from the saddle, was pulling back with the reins; a flash of sunlight on the point of a sword that had struck armour and bounced off it like a secondary, weaker flash; the splashing of water beneath hooves.

I stood there wondering how I had managed to capture so many details I had not even been aware of as I made my quick brushstrokes. I went into the kitchen to look for a sharp knife. But when I returned to the dining room I felt that the one standing in front of the painting was not the artist who had created it, but rather a thief who wished to steal it – another person, unknown to the artist.

I fell to my knees before the painting as if paying homage to a holy image. Matthew Arnold's words began to reverberate in my head: *This, or some tyrannous single thought, some fit / Of passion, which subdues our souls to it, / Till for its sake alone we live and move - / Call it ambition, or remorse, or love - / This too can change us wholly, and make seem / All which we did before, shadow and dream.*

I took the knife back to the kitchen and then returned to my room. I opened my suitcases and travel bag and put my belongings back where they had been. As I did so, I straightened things as if to emphasise that I was not going anywhere. I put the money back beneath the mattress. I took a frame and fastened one of the remaining canvases to it, then put it on the easel so that I could look past it at my reflection in the mirror on the chest-of-drawers. Then I began to paint my portrait.

Before I made the first mark I already knew what the picture would be called. I wrote on the bottom edge: *Who am I?* I had not yet used painting for self-enquiry, but I felt that this was a way that I might arrive at some answers, especially if I allowed my subconscious to paint instead of me. And so I moved the brush mechanically, without reflection, without any effort to fill the movements with vitality; I just painted and did not even give the paints too much attention.

Although at some level of awareness I knew what was being created, the painting did not interest me until right at the end; only when I had filled the canvas did I dare to look at it. The portrait was recognisably mine, but my face was made up of badly glued together pieces of a broken plate, perhaps two plates, so that the left eye was lower than the right, the forehead drooping, the nose lopsided, the mouth broken in the middle, the beard unconnected with the moustache, and the left ear growing straight out of the cheek. What is more, on three of the larger fragments that made up the mosaic there was the same face, reduced, but repeated down to the last detail.

I sat on the edge of the bed and stared at the image in front of me. More than the picture itself I was interested in the story the picture told; a story of broken pieces that had failed to come together again as a whole. The door opened and in came Mrs. Hudson, dressed in black, funereal. I remembered that I had last seen her at the cemetery.

What had I been doing there? And what had she been doing, who was she mourning?

Silently, she came closer and sat on the edge of the bed beside me. First she removed from my hand the brush, from which yellowish paint was slowly dripping onto the carpet and wrapped it in a paper tissue she took from her handbag. Then she took another tissue, bent over and tried to clean the paint stain from the carpet. She soon realised that she was actually rubbing it in, and so she stopped and threw the crumpled up tissue onto the window sill.

Only then did she look at the painting.

"Is that you?" she asked.

I shrugged, remained silent for a while and then said: no, that isn't me, that is me, that isn't me, is it me?

"I've stopped hoping that I will ever understand you," she said in a quiet voice, without reproach. "But there's no need for us to understand everything and everyone in this world, is there? Today, at Jimmy's funeral, I realised that I no longer understood myself. That I never had, however firmly I had believed the contrary. A broken plate? Well, a badly glued together one is sitting beside you, one that has not only been broken once but a number of times. Do not think that your pain, your confusion is anything exceptional. It's true that you are an artist and that you know how to express it, and thus perhaps push it away, to paint it out of you, and then perhaps you feel easier and can pick yourself up again. I don't have those capabilities and no one beside me to confess to, I have to pretend the whole time that there is nothing wrong with me. Imagine the effort involved in that. And the price I pay. When I finally lost hope that the future may hold some sort of love for me, even fleeting and unimportant, everything started to get on my nerves. Even things that I once liked. Birdsong in the garden, the footsteps of a stranger on the street at night, Mozart. Believe it or not, I really enjoyed listening to Mozart. Now I hate every kind of music, any kind of noise, magazine ads, the smiling faces of people in shops; I even hate my daughter's boyfriend because he looks too much like Paul McCartney; I even hate – but this is just between the two of us – my own daughter for boasting about this. As if it was thanks to him or her, their achievement, that he looks like Paul McCartney. I have a stupid daughter, I am surrounded by idiotic people, I try to ensure that no one notices how much I am suffering, so that they don't feel my intolerance but rather my love, which does not really exist. Wherever I go, whoever I talk to, I am only doing what is dictated by my memory of the time when I knew why I was doing what I was doing. I am ashamed to say it, but I act like a perfect member of the Chiswick rowing club. Form, dear Willy, form is the essence of Englishness. I don't know why you had to come here, why you didn't go to Paris like most painters, but I feel obliged to offer you a piece of advice: do everything in your power not to become English. There would be no benefit in it, only great harm. I discovered that today at Jimmy's funeral. Poor Jimmy, who perhaps had only two friends in his life – you and his mother – made of his death the most un-English ritual it is possible to imagine. In spite of the almost cheap comicality it was tragic, grand, majestic. After your visit – and perhaps you will confide in me sometime what happened – he first attacked his mother with a kitchen knife and would have killed her if the Spanish au pair had not grabbed him by the hair and pulled him back. Then he turned and stabbed her, not to death, but a deep wound to the left thigh – she is now in hospital. His father, who had rushed back from work, wanted to call the police, but Jimmy's mother begged him on her knees not to. If he had not listened to her then Jimmy might still be alive. She also realises that. Then he ran down to the river, jumped in his mother's boat, aimed it at one of the pillars of Hammersmith Bridge and crashed into it with such force that the boat was reduced to matchwood. I dare not even think in what state they found Jimmy. I warned you, but you would not listen. But okay, you are not involved, nor can I be accused of anything. But it is amazing how quickly these things spread around London when a respectable English family is involved. That is how the Irish and Italians are supposed to behave, not the English."

She fell silent, looking sideways at my expressionless face.

Then she raised her hand and briefly stroked my hair. "You are dangerous, did you know that? You release the floodgates within people, you release the held-back feelings that the English are not allowed to show. You infect them, so that they start to dream how things could be different, more alive, warmer, more real, bloodier. Some will be grateful to you, but most will hate you for it. But they will all be afraid of you, even the ones who are grateful. I know that from myself. I won't tell you how much you stirred me up, how grateful I am that you awoke the corpse that lay unburied within me. And how much I am afraid, because I don't know what awaits me."

She got up and once more looked at the picture of the shattered plate. "You captured me very well," she said. Then she left, quietly closing the door behind her.

I dashed to the bathroom and returned with some nail scissors. I took the canvas and began to cut out the fragments of plate along the edges where it could be seen they were stuck together. I laid each piece on the bed. Piece by piece, I removed the parts of my face – the nose, forehead, mouth, ears, and above all the eyes, to which I had paid most attention; I removed them with a kind of stubborn contrariness, as if I wished to blind myself, to see no more, to paint the world black, to disappear, to be scattered in the dark.

When I was completely torn to pieces, I scattered the fragments of myself on the bed and lay down on them, closed my eyes and wandered through the gloomy world of my memories, sorting them, stringing them together into images that might mean something, might tell me something, for more than ever before I felt that I needed an Answer. While doing this I drifted off and sank into an unpleasant swamp of sleep. I was awoken by a clap of thunder and through the window I saw that a summer storm was sailing across the western suburbs of London: fat drops were hitting the window pane, the wind was shaking the trees, the lightning flashed now to the left, now to the right.

Someone knocked on the door. I knew it was Maria Hudson and since I didn't have the strength for another confrontation I turned on my left side and pretended to sleep. I heard her open the door, gasp and say "Oh my God!"

This was followed by the carefully cultivated voice of Alan Mc-Clelland, who with false astonishment asked: "What happened?"

"He destroyed the painting," said Maria Hudson and then she began roughly shaking me by the shoulder. "Zhivago, wake up, what have you done? Do you realise that Alan came here to buy the picture?"

No, I didn't, I said sitting up and then squatting on the bed like an enraged dog. Why would he want to buy something that he hadn't seen? How does he know that I painted something? Who informs him of my every movement? And what gives the person who is keeping him informed the right to do so? May *I* and *I* alone decide *what* I paint, *what* I do with the paintings, *who* I give them to and *when*?

"Well, that's nice," said Maria Hudson, starting to cry. "I pave the way for you into the world of art because I think that's what you came for and that is the thanks I get! That's the last thing I ever do for you!" She turned and stormed down the stairs.

Alan remained. With his ever insipid smile he approached the bed. I knew that he would sit on it before I felt it give beneath his weight.

"Women are so emotional," he said. "And always when it suits them. We men know how to be more understanding, regardless of what storm is raging inside us."

Really, I said colourlessly, merely to have something to say. I felt that he was trying to get me on his side, to lure me into some kind of conspiracy against Maria Hudson, offering me an alliance, two against one. Why?

"You're making progress," he said. "The last time I was here you were only threatening to destroy your work, now you have carried out the threat." He picked up a piece of canvas and examined it. "A wild, inward looking eye," he said. "Very much yours, the eye of an enraged Tartar. Do you feel better now?"

Absolutely, I snapped, like a dog defending its territory. I feel on top of the world.

"That isn't the best thing to feel," he said. "A fall from the top of the world lasts infinitely longer than from an ordinary chair, and before you hit the ground you have a great deal of time to reflect on how much wiser it would have been to stay on the ground in the first place."

Fuck off with these contrived phrases of yours, I thought. Where do you take them from – fresh out of your arse? Out loud I merely said: Really?

"Why do you assume that people are against you before you have a chance to find out whether they are potential friends? Basically, you are short-changing yourself."

And why shouldn't I? I asked defiantly. After all, I know myself better than anyone, what I deserve and what I don't.

"You know yourself a lot worse than you dare to admit," he said. "I can tell you what you deserve. I can show you if you come with me."

169

I can't go anywhere, I answered reflexively – and almost at the same time felt that I was rejecting something that could represent an escape route from the vicious circle I was in, so I added: At least not as I am. I haven't washed for ages.

"Then do so," he said, getting up from the edge of the bed. "I'll wait for you."

22.

When his steps faded at the bottom of the stairs I rushed to the bath-room, showered and washed my hair, showered once more with cold water to rouse myself, put on a clean shirt, summer trousers, sandals, combed my long wet hair and realised I looked like Jesus caught in a storm, put on my sunglasses even though it was still cloudy outside, but I hoped that I would at least then be able to look people in the eye without having to immediately avert my gaze, and then with head raised, like some poser, I went downstairs. I had no idea from where I took the energy that had shortly before been conspicuous by its absence; suddenly, I felt that I was taking a first step towards something new, unknown, far from the environment in which, like a nervous echo, I still felt numb.

"Look at him," exclaimed Alan admiringly, measuring me from head to toe with his gaze, "what a beautiful young man!" Evidently he was trying his hardest to put me in a good mood, although his comment seemed a bit over the top, since I had never heard a man say something like that about another man; Maria Hudson also pulled a wry face.

"Right, you two go and do what you have to do," she said, disap-pearing into the kitchen.

"Take care of yourself," she whispered as she went past. And then more loudly from the kitchen: "I assume you won't be dining at home this evening."

"I'll take him to an Indian restaurant," replied Alan on my behalf, as if I was an object the ownership of which had just quietly changed hands.

First, he drove me to Chelsea in his rickety old Jaguar, an artists' quarter, he emphasised, one of those that I had neglected when conquering London, perhaps because it had no Underground station. When we got to Kings Road, "the centre of new fashion and art," the streets seemed oddly empty and abandoned, and I was not at all enthused.

"Wait a little," said my guide, who was dressed somewhat invasively, like a dandy, in a white jacket and green shirt, and of course with a carefully tied cravat, with his thin, almost distastefully thin legs in dark grey jeans, in which his manhood was particularly noticeable because he had stuffed a crumpled paper tissue in his pocket which at a fleeting glance gave the impression that he was better endowed than he actually was (my God, I thought, what kind of people are these art critics?).

"Look," he said when he had parked at the kerbside. He gestured towards a broad window in which there hung some framed pictures. House of Art, it said above in large letters. "Don't you see?" he asked, amazed.

Only when we got out of the car and went closer did I notice that among the pictures were two of the *Simultaneity* series: Elizabeth I with a guitar around her neck and Shakespeare in her hand *(We all live in a yellow submarine)* and Henry VIII, chopping off his wives' heads *(Origins of English civilisation)*.

"Well?" Alan took me by the elbow, which I hurriedly withdrew. "How can you be so cold? You're worse than the English. Your paintings are hanging in one of the most eminent sales galleries in London and your response is zero?"

More out of politeness than enthusiasm I shrugged and said: Thank you. Where are the others?

"Those are inside, in the store room. He can't have only yours in the window. But if you look closely, you'll see that he has two of yours, but only one each of the others."

172

He invited me inside to introduce me to the owner, but he was not there: behind the counter stood a strict-looking young woman with a large nose and flat chest, who said that Mr. Hamilton had just popped out and would be back in about an hour.

As we walked to the Indian restaurant I felt the urge to write Alan a letter in my head. There were things I needed to make clear to him.

("Dear Mr. Alan McClelland, who is trying to give the impression that he would like to be my friend. Forget it. I had a friend and I drove him to his death, and with him were buried all my hopes. And as Matthew Arnold said: *which leaves the fierce necessity to feel, but takes away the power ... by drying up our joy in everything, to make our former pleasures all seem stale.* If my paintings had been hanging in a gallery *before* that event, you would now be walking along the street with a different Willy, the former one, who always avoided compromise or any unfairness that would benefit him. But the Willy who created *Simultaneity,* about whom I have no opinion – absolutely none at all because he has nothing to do with the Willy now walking beside you – that Willy is no more. Together with his friend, he smashed into Hammersmith Bridge and only splinters of him remain. To be honest with you, I have no wish for that Willy ever to return, even if it means that I will no longer be an artist. The Willy who is walking beside you and who won't let himself be sucked off by you – please get this into your head – must only begin to learn to paint. And if he does not succeed he won't be disappointed, he will simply do something else in life. The awareness that he *doesn't have to be* a painter is currently the only thing giving him a sense of freedom, so please don't try to trap me in your web by promising to help me get access to galleries, organise independent exhibitions, write flattering reviews, find rich buyers for my work, enthrone me as a new star; at the moment, none of that moves me in the slightest – just so that you know. But I won't say no to dinner – I've never tried Indian food.")

In my head I sealed the letter and posted it. The telepathic post worked quite quickly, for during a tasty meal of different spicy dishes that pleasantly burned my mouth and throat, Alan did not utter a single contentious word or drop a single hint of a sexual nature. In fact, as he uninhibitedly chatted about this and that I recognised that he was actually an extremely intelligent, perceptive, likable interlocutor. He told me that in addition to the son who was going out with Ana Hudson, he had a younger one who had run away from home and refused to have any contact with him, as well as a thirteen year-old daughter, Marisa, who lived with him; that he and his wife, who had a drink problem, had split up ten years ago; that he knew many people, but few to whom he would confide his innermost thoughts; that he was fifty-three years old and not as fit as he would like to be; that he saw himself as a tolerant person, but that certain things and people he simply disliked, even hated, including politicians, actors, Protestants, feminists, prostitutes, the English (with some exceptions, he himself was from Belfast), the Welsh (without exception), foreigners (with some exceptions), Americans (with some exceptions), fox-hunters (without exception), Blacks, Indians, Pakistanis, the Chinese, Spaniards, singers of popular music, the Beatles and all those who listened to them, BBC employees, tax inspectors (without exception) and painters (with some exceptions).

And why don't you like painters? I asked.

"Because they are capable, in a single day, of unwittingly causing more problems than those who devote their lives to problem-causing manage to achieve in a whole year. Because they are dirty, argumentative, drunken, self-centred and have an opinion about everything that they are unwilling to discuss, however infantile it is. Because each and every one of them is convinced that he is at least Leonardo, whereas among them there are more amateurs than in any other profession. Because they spit on every eulogy that you publish about their work, saying that it is insufficiently sincere and for every sincere critique they want to crucify you. Because they read nothing, because the world does not interest them, because they never tell you anything worth knowing."

He looked at me as if expecting my agreement, even approval, and as if I was not a painter myself, or that I fell into some other, special category.

When he observed my doubt he added: "I said that I don't like painters, with some exceptions. The exceptions are few, but you are among them. Your art contains something that I miss in the others.

174

And I don't mean your technical skills, which for a young man of your age are amazing. I mean the courage, that you are probably not even aware of, with which you freely combine established styles into a kind of collage that works like a new, original style, although not to the experts. But sooner or later, of this I have no doubt, this combination will give birth to something that is really, uniquely yours. And then your name will become known, overnight. I will make sure of that. Although there will be no shortage of opportunists who will claim to be the first to have discovered you."

With bowed head, I ate the rest of my curry and tried not to show how extremely upset I was by his implication that my pictures were primarily the result of skilful imitation; I did not believe this, since at home I had heard completely the opposite view from people whose opinions I valued, but it hurt nevertheless, particularly because he threw out the idea as if it was self-evident, unimportant, before passing on to another topic. I was not listening to him then, the pain went too deep, along with the hot curry that was eating away at my insides.

Actually, I interrupted him in contrary fashion, painting is over for me. Next week I'm going home and I'm going to get a job as an art teacher in a primary school. A smart person knows when to stop.

"Your reaction is completely understandable," he said. "I know about Jimmy, about your relationship – Maria told me everything. But that in itself is proof of the deep humanity that pervades your work. Perhaps you don't know it, but your paintings are moving. Perhaps not in the same way that we are moved by the perfection of the great masters, but more profoundly, as a direct communication from one person to another. The message of your paintings is: suffering is not an individual thing, suffering is our common destiny. You must never forget that, although it is only the first, perhaps small step towards immortality. Don't be impatient, take your time, wander round the city, chase girls, or boys if you prefer them, visit the galleries and learn from others. In that way you will more quickly extract yourself from the mourning that is filling your head with silly ideas."

I don't need consoling, I said, and Maria has no right to go spreading stories about me and Jimmy, since she knows nothing about it and every word she utters is a stain on a friendship that was ours and *only* ours. More than anything, it is an insult to Jimmy. In fact, it is also an insult that galleries are selling pictures that rightly belong to him, are in memory of him.

"But you know Maria: an unhappy widow who finds solace for her loneliness with young boys, doing both herself and them a lot of harm in the process. If you feel that living in her house is hindering your creativity, then you are welcome to stay with me; Marisa will be delighted, Myles will shortly be moving to his own place; the house is big enough, you can set yourself up a studio. It will be easier for me to monitor your work and to more effectively play the role of agent, which I would love to be, if you agree."

I replied that I was not some sickly boy who needed protecting from an unhappy widow. As for moving, I could not afford anything better than what I had now, regardless of the advance he had so generously paid.

"My dear Willy, we are not understanding each other," he said. "I'm inviting you as a guest, as a friend – I don't rent out rooms, I don't need a lodger. I'm not rich enough to be your patron in the medieval sense of the word, but I can help in a small way and your presence would also encourage me to work."

He surely saw, master of manipulation that he was, how his offer was invading me through every pore, spreading through my body like snake venom that has hit just the right spot and how it would finally reach my brain and perform its duty; at that moment I felt that I should resist with all my might, reject him even with a certain measure of insolence. But somehow I did not succeed: I merely said that I would think about it, although I was in no hurry to go anywhere. With this, he obviously smelt victory; he showed this with an indulgent smile of the type that was far too often on his face. I have never met anyone who smiled as much as he did and without any real reason – as if he was afflicted by some strange nervous disease which produced a false glow and shining eyes. In the darkened restaurant it seemed that his face was pulsing like a firefly.

I wouldn't like to feel under any kind of obligation to anyone, I added; neither a borrower nor a lender be, is my motto.

"You know all too well that with Maria there will be a price to pay. Although you are paying her rent she will soon demand the extra payment and when you reject her you will see what Shakespeare had in mind when he wrote *hell knows no fury like a woman scorned*. In my opinion it's better to avoid the problem by beating her to it and leaving *before* she has you in check. If it's not too late already, of course."

I deliberately left him in doubt; I felt he was interfering too much in my life; I had already half decided not to move to his place. In spite of that, or precisely because of it, I did not object when he proposed a small detour on the way back, stopping off at his house, saying hello to Marisa, a glass of whisky, so that I would have at least an idea of what I would be missing if I did not manage to escape from the clutches of the unhappy widow.

I don't know why I thought that Alan's house would be as distinguished as that of Jimmy's parents; it just seemed to me that someone who was an influential art critic, who dressed like a dandy and drove around town in a Jaguar could not live in a terrace house with crumbling plaster on a bare street near Paddington Station, where the metal dustbins smelled of rotting food and every thirty seconds a train thundered past the back, causing the window panes to rattle in their decaying frames.

The basement room, in which Marisa, a slight girl with a timid look who was squatting in the midst of the disorder with a book in her hand and who barely acknowledged my presence, emitted an odour of damp and decay; the ground floor kitchen was strewn with unwashed dishes among which Alan searched in vain for a clean glass for the proposed whisky (which he eventually realised he was out of); the first floor room where I would work and have my studio was no bigger than the room at Maria Hudson's, with the only difference being that here, instead of looking out on the garden, I would have a fine view of the railway lines.

I was surprised to see that there were no interesting pictures on the wall. As if reading my mind he said that there were about five break-ins per day in this area and that all his pictures – and there were quite a few – were locked in a special room in the basement. Regrettably

177

the light bulb had gone a couple of days ago and he hadn't got round to changing it; he'd show me on my next visit.

I said that I was very tired and would like to go home. Without objection, friendly as always, he drove me back to Chiswick. During the drive I decided that there would not be another visit.

23.

The next morning something shifted inside me. I felt a clear end to the sense of being suspended in the air and knew that my life would start moving again, without getting bogged down in details – more rapidly, as if depicted with large smooth brushstrokes, *free from the sick fatigue, the languid doubt ... from fluctuating wildly without term or scope*. I decided to forget about London, fame and riches, and return home. Perhaps this was mainly because of a visit I made to the cemetery, where Jimmy's gravestone, on the fresh grave, bore the line from Arnold: *Thou has not lived, why should'st thou perish, so?* In the warm glow of atonement I felt that I must tidy up after myself, settle my debts, recompense all those who deserved it, not only because of my promises, but because of their wishes and expectations.

I waited for Maria to drive to the shop and then I carefully took apart the frame in which there hung on the dining room wall the picture of Caesar in the middle of the Thames and laid the canvas on the table. I brought my brush and paints, and in less than half an hour I had changed Caesar's features into Jimmy's. I could not help gazing at him: a muscular, broad-shouldered general on a white stallion, a man of aristocratic posture in the moment when he rises in the saddle in order to turn to the legionnaires behind him; I felt that I had connected Jimmy with his dreams. I painted over *Simultaneity* and titled the picture *Eternal Life, Amen.*

179

I waited for the fresh paint to dry sufficiently and then I rolled it up so that it was not folded where the face was. I hurried with it to the end of the street, ran down Bath Road to the entrance to Ravenscourt Park, past the pond with the ducks, swans and geese, past the exposed bodies soaking up the sun, along the embankment of the Underground line, through the gate in the green fence, along the narrow street on the left side of the park, until I got to the bell beneath which it said Henderson. Afraid that at any moment it would open and Stella would emerge, I leaned the rolled canvas against the stone doorway and then returned home by the same route.

There I found Maria Hudson staring at the empty frame. "Don't I deserve a single painting?" she said with an accusing look.

I had to take it to the gallery, I lied, they wanted the set. You will get something better. A nude. We can start right away.

"Not now, for heaven's sake," she said in an annoyed voice, to conceal her astonishment and elation. "Ana and Harry will be back at any moment. Not to mention my sons. After eleven, when the dining room becomes a bedroom."

Yes, that's what I was thinking, I said.

She looked me straight in the eye for some time. I could not swear to it, but I think she was blushing slightly. "What has happened to you?" she asked.

A lot of bad things and a lot of good, I replied. Perhaps more bad and that's what I'd like to redress.

"Look at the time," she suddenly said. "I've got to cook dinner for six people. Then I have to bath and wash my hair. Are you serious or joking?"

The time for joking in my life is past, I replied. Now I have to go into town again for canvas and the paints I need.

"Buy enough brown," she said. "I want to look tanned. As if I'd just come back from Majorca. I don't want you painting me as white as I am."

I'll paint you so that you will be able to sit in front of the picture for the rest of your life, admiring your own beauty. "Go," she said, picking up her shopping bag.

And that's what I did. I took a taxi to Chelsea, got out at the House of Art and told the taxi driver to wait. I went inside and asked the strict-looking, flat-chested assistant to call Mr. Hamilton. She said that Mr. Hamilton had just popped out and would be back in about an hour. He seems to do a lot of popping, I replied.

"I don't understand," she said. "Weren't you here yesterday with Mr. McClelland?"

Exactly, I said. Do you have a pen and a sheet of paper?

"You'll find the stationer's at the other side of the street," she said. "We sell paintings."

I know you do, I said, including more than twenty of mine, which I don't want you to continue selling. I want you to withdraw them from sale, because I have given them to a person who deserves them more than any of your customers, regardless of taste or the size of their wallet. Am I making myself clear or do we need an interpreter?

"I can't decide about something like that," she said, offended, "it's up to Mr. Hamilton. Come back tomorrow morning."

Tomorrow morning, I told her, I will be on the way back to Slovenia, if you happen to know where that is and if you don't I can tell you it's a kind of dead end, an extension of the Kamchatka peninsula, which I'm sure you've heard of.

"As a matter of fact," she said, her head slightly raised, "I'm not much interested in foreign countries, I don't see why I should be."

You're right, I said, abroad is just a hoax, a strange miasma, an illusion of sorts, I've also noticed that, so let's stay here, where thanks to the basic principles of democracy things are equally simple for all, including for the poor in spirit or, to put it more simply, the retarded. In other words, I need a sheet of paper and a pen!

"Across the road," she pointed and then turned her back on me.

And so Willy – the old Willy, who had filled the decision to say goodbye to all that with the much-missed *esprit* for which he was well known on the dead end of the Kamchatka peninsula – had no choice but to expose himself to ridicule and meaningful glances in the stationer's across the road when buying a ballpoint pen and a single sheet of paper. But this no longer bothered him. Since he realised what he actually wanted, it was almost as if he was floating on air.

181

Okay, he said, when he returned to the gallery, now I will borrow your counter, if I may, so that I can write a statement.

He bent over the sheet of paper and wrote: "Dear Mr. Hamilton, Mr. McClelland, who is presenting himself as my representative without my authorisation, offered you more than twenty oil paintings by the painter Vili Vaupotič. Sorry about the name. I would like to inform you that those paintings are my work and that they are not for sale. Their presence in your gallery is a kind of theft and they belong, according to my express wish, to Mrs. Stella Henderson of Chiswick (please check the address in the telephone directory or call her husband, who is a bank manager – no, forget that, don't call him! – deliver the pictures to Stella Henderson in person!). Thank you, Mr. Hamilton. I know you are an art lover and understand that in this world everything, contrary to how it looks, is not for sale. I enclose one hundred pounds, which you kindly paid as an advance. If the money came from Mr. McClelland, then please return it to him. Thank you and goodbye."

Right, I said, pushing the folded paper towards the flat-chested individual of increasingly indeterminate gender. If Mr. Hamilton does not receive this the moment he walks through the door, you will regret it for the rest of your life. And I smiled. Job done. Have a nice day.

And then the nude. So as not to clatter around the house at night with an easel, frame, brushes and other equipment, I heeded the advice of the excited model and carried them all into the dining room before the evening meal, under the pretence that I wanted to paint the family eating. Then I would come up with some excuse – such as that I had forgotten to get one of the basic colours – so that I could eat with them and by the next day they would already have forgotten my promise.

But an opportunity to paint the *Last Supper* seemed too good not to take advantage of, so I painted with my right hand and every few minutes I took a piece of beef from my plate with my left hand and chewed it while painting, giving me an excuse to ignore the stupid comments and even more stupid questions that flew from the table.

The members of the family posed so wholeheartedly that they almost forgot to eat. Not one of them guessed that this really was our last supper together. The whole time they maintained a stiff, absurdly noble posture, as if I was photographing rather than painting them. Since I wanted the painting to be my going-away present, I succumbed to the pressures of benevolent imagination: I depicted Harry as an upright, distinguished naval officer in an Austro-Hungarian uniform; Christopher and Gerry as long-haired rock musicians, one of them beating wildly on a drum, the other thrashing a guitar; I transformed Maria into the light-haired Julie Christie as Lara in the film *Doctor Zhivago*, leaning her head on the shoulder of a young Omar Sharif (who had my face); and Ana I painted (perhaps with a hint of malice, because she never liked me) as the serving maid of this noble family, standing by the table with a platter of food.

They all wanted to see the result immediately, but I rejected their pleas with the explanation that I needed to make some corrections and I never showed a work until it was really finished. Maria began to clear the table a lot earlier than usual, saying that she had a headache and that she wanted an early night, so why didn't we all go to our rooms, including me; I could leave the painting on the easel and finish it in the morning.

An hour later I tapped on the sliding door that separated the dining room from the living room. She opened it just enough for me to slip through. "What took you so long?" she whispered.

There's no hurry, I said, the night is long.

"Too short for me, who has been waiting for this from the day you arrived."

She was wearing a silk robe beneath which she was evidently already naked and ready to pose; she had placed a freshly cut rose in her freshly washed and brushed black hair; she had made up her face and although she had over-done it a bit, this did not really matter anymore – I was paying off my debts and had foregone the right to be critical.

I removed the *Last Supper* and stretched a new canvas on the frame.

"Thank you for Zhivago and Lara," she said. "I'm glad that you married us on canvas, although I would have been more suited, as you well know, to the role of serving maid."

How do you want me to paint you? I asked when I'd finished setting things up. In the style of a famous nude such as Naked Maja, Leda, the Odalisque, Venus?

"Paint me as you see me," she said, "I want to see myself through the eyes of an artist."

I replied that we artists do not always see what is in front of us or what the majority of other people see, but much more often a projection of our suppressed desires, dreams, atonement, generosity, even self-punishment. Painting is a kind of dialogue that can be many things – loving, offended, argumentative, seductive.

"Let it be loving," she said, "let it be seductive – don't you think that I deserve it at least a little?"

Why? I wondered. Because for two months you have been cooking meals for me that are more fit for pigswill and you charge me twice as much as you do Harry? But no, I didn't say this out loud, although Willy II hinted that I should say goodbye in precisely this fashion.

We rarely get what we deserve, I said, trying to sound wise, but tonight you will get everything.

"I'm feeling so nervous," she said. "Can I smoke? When I'm posing, of course."

Better pose while smoking, I tried to amuse her with a variant of the old joke, but the poor woman was trembling so much that the cigarette fell from her fingers onto the carpet. What was she afraid of, what has she hiding beneath the silk robe?

When she finally removed her robe and lay on the sofa, put her right hand behind her head and with her left hand, in which she held a cigarette, partially covered her breast, I did not see anything unusual: an average female body, neither too old nor too young for her age, slightly too wide for its length, with large already sagging breasts, with hips that could not deny that they had been forced apart by three new lives, the thighs big and lumpy, the slightly rounded stomach emphasised by fat and folds, and toes that crossed each other rather than pointing straight; the latter seemed the most original part of her.

"Disappointed?" she looked at me like an animal awaiting slaughter.

Not at all, I said, a painter is enthused by everything he sees and disappointed only by his own work.

184

"I meant as a man," she added, with a hint of impatience.

Oh, I said, whenever the painter is at work the man is safely locked away in a steel-lined cell; however much of a fuss he kicks up, he won't be let out until the painter decides that he can't cause any more disruption to the task in hand.

"How long will it take?" she asked, blowing smoke at the ceiling.

I don't know, I said. Which do you prefer: immortality or five minutes of puffing and panting, and an average orgasm?

"I don't know," she replied, noticeably surprised at herself. "Perhaps we could change the running order?"

We already have, I said. Although we have not acknowledged this explicitly, we both know that men are ten a penny, whereas a true artist is born once every hundred years. Believe me, in comparison with a gifted brush, *every* penis is a poor little pimple.

"So begin," she said, stubbing out her cigarette and putting her left hand behind her head as well.

This movement suddenly made clear what she had the whole time been quietly reminding me of: Paul Delvaux's *Sleeping Venus*. For the composition to be more accurate I asked her to let her left leg hang slightly over the edge of the sofa. She did as I asked.

"But don't make the whole thing too obscene," she said, closing her eyes. She evidently knew that the movement of her leg had revealed her pubic mound, which was almost hairless and which aroused me about as much as seeing a five-day-old bread roll on the table. This was of course no longer Delvaux; it was more reminiscent of a magazine cover in a Soho shop window. I didn't mean quite like that, I said; let just the lower part of the leg hang over, but keep your knees together.

She tried to do as I asked, she readjusted her pose, but it still was not right; eventually I realised that the whole angle was wrong and that I should move the easel. Now it's okay, I said. Now we can begin.

"Can I close my eyes?" she asked.

It really doesn't matter, I replied. You can fall asleep if you wish. As long as you don't move.

I used chalk to create the basic outline of the body, mixed some paints and began. Although I was working quickly I knew it would take quite some time, perhaps all night; there was plenty of opportunity for her to fall asleep in the meantime. She kept opening her eyes and asking how I was doing and whether I was close to finishing; each time I answered that posing, too, is an art of a kind and that those who radiate resigned patience usually appear more beautiful in the painting.

"I'm so tired," she said, "devoid of energy."

The more I painted, the more there grew within me a sense of fellow-suffering. The naked woman stretched out before me represented all women at a specific point on their journey through a life of wasted and trampled dreams to bitter persistence in feeling responsible for what life had brought: a child, survival, reputation and surviving hopes, right up until wrinkled old age, illness and the end, the coming of death, which Delvaux depicted as a skeleton in front of the sofa. I thought of sparing Maria Hudson the skeleton, but decided that without it the picture would be incomplete – for dust you are and to dust you will return, youth is but a shadow flitting past.

In consolation, instead of the bitter face of a disappointed housewife who has to make a living by renting out rooms, I painted an image of eternal youth, the strikingly beautiful harmonious features of my unforgotten Urania. I titled the picture *The Body Dies, Beauty Remains*. When I finished at around three in the morning the tired lady was asleep – in that state more frail, more human than at any time since I had come into her home. I quietly opened the sliding door, then closed it behind me, went to my room and locked the door. I began to pack. In two hours everything was ready. I lay on the bed in my clothes and fell asleep.

At eight o'clock Maria was rapping on my door. "Zhivago, come out. I want to know who you painted!"

You, Maria, I sleepily replied.

"That's not me. Don't make fun of me. And what's that skeleton doing there?

That is the question, I silently quoted Hamlet, but out loud I said: I'm tired, I have to sleep, I'll see you at lunch.

"Well, that's nice," she sighed and went downstairs.

I knew that after breakfast every morning she went shopping, and before that she took Christopher and Gerry to music school, where

186

one was learning piano, the other guitar. I listened until I heard the key turning in the door. Then the slamming of car doors, the sound of the engine retreating into the distance and the house was mine. In fact, I needed only enough time to call a taxi, carry my luggage down, lock the door, drop the key through the letter box and drive off.

24.

Just over two hours later I was already in Dover harbour, dragging my cases and travel bag (exactly the same luggage with which I had arrived, containing nothing that I had not brought to England) towards the queues for passport control. Behind one of them I saw the blond haired guy who (when? it seemed like years ago) had driven me after hours of interrogation to Canterbury to catch the London train, and suddenly like an electric spark came a moment of *simultaneity*: I was overcome by the feeling that I was *again* and *still* waiting to come into England, that London was in the future or that there was waiting for me a different, more friendly city. I was overwhelmed by the mixture of feelings that had accompanied my first arrival here. As if everything that had happened was the result of hallucinating while I waited to enter.

Perhaps the stuffy air in the building was to blame, but my head began to spin and I started to feel nauseous; I left the queue and found just enough strength to drag my luggage to the nearest bench. I collapsed onto it and everything swam before my eyes. For the first time I was truly aware that nothing had come of my time in London, it was all wasted; that somewhere along the line, God knows where, I had made a catastrophic mistake, spent my time on everything other than what I should be doing; that I had (because I was afraid of being alone?) become strangely diluted, I had let others sidetrack me. I had been insufficiently determined, insufficiently dogged, too soft; I had soaked up the environment, rather than permeating it with willpower and energy. It seemed almost impossible that I was leaving without a single painting, without at least one as a souvenir, as evidence that I had even been in London.

I became aware that someone was sitting beside me on the bench, unpleasantly close, hip to hip and shoulder to shoulder; there was actually not much room because I had my travel bag beside me. Towards me there floated a discrete, expensive male perfume. Whoever it was seemed very intrusive – he could easily have sat on another, empty bench – but I didn't even look at him; I was staring straight ahead, towards the large clock on the wall, that was flowing and dissolving and then coming together again, as if I had something wrong with my eyes. I felt them filling with tears and then the drops running down my cheeks, but I made no sound, as if I was not crying, as if water was simply overflowing.

I reached into my left trouser pocket where I normally kept a handkerchief, but there was nothing there; I checked the other pocket but it was also empty. Evidently in my rush to leave I had simply thrown all my things into the suitcase. I sensed a movement to my left, a hand brushed my elbow, retreated, reached for something. The next moment I saw before me an open hand on which lay a scented, pinkish, carefully ironed handkerchief, folded hexagonally as if taken from a breast pocket.

"I'm glad to be in the right place at the right time," said the man, who was no other than (as I had somehow sensed, although it seemed impossible) Alan McClelland. I accepted the handkerchief and wiped my tears, but then started crying for real, shuddering, sobbing, sniffling and with a muffled wailing more suited to an offended schoolgirl than a bearded young man.

"There's no reason to feel ashamed," Alan consoled me on the drive back to London. "Women burst into tears over every trivial matter; with men, crying means that a great shift has taken place, that the landscape has changed. You'll see, everything will be different now. At some point he who is called to do great things always resists that call, although not for long. Usually there is some older, more experienced person on hand to ease the young hero's way forward."

I must paint, I said. That's the only thing I must do – paint, paint, without rest, night and day.

"Your words are music to my ears," he said. "In between, two or three hours sleep, some pleasant moments in the company of friends, visiting exhibitions, conversation with spirits, conversation with souls, these things are also helpful."

We agreed that there would be little point in my returning to Maria Hudson's, although it was she who informed him that I had gone. She was terribly offended that I had fled, although she admitted that I had left no debts behind.

I did not run away, I said, I left after she fell asleep while I was painting her portrait; that is an insult to a painter.

"Yes, she said that she wanted to talk to you about that portrait. She actually called it a nude, but if she did fall asleep in the middle of it, it must be a portrait or she's not the same Maria that I know. I don't want to poke my nose into your relationship with her, but once or twice she even hinted at the possibility of marriage, saying that you'd proposed to her so that you could move to England permanently."

I don't ever want to see her, I said, I don't like women who lie so shamelessly!

He promised that he would not tell her the truth; he would say that because of an accident on the road he had got to Dover too late and that I was already on my way home.

There's another problem, I reminded him.

"That has also been dealt with," he said with a smile. "Hamilton called me yesterday evening and informed me of your demands. Early this morning I took the pictures personally to Stella Henderson. She was not at home and I handed them over to the maid without any lengthy explanation – that seemed the best thing to do. And thanks for the hundred pounds. I would still like you even if you hadn't returned it. Since you have, you are forever engraved on my heart. I don't know of anyone who in such circumstances, determined to leave, would think of something like that."

Life in the house beside the railway line began encouragingly and my traumas were swallowed up by mass of hazy memories; the only thing that occasionally struck me like a shockwave of fear was the thought that I could have left and spent the rest of my life cursing myself. For this reason, the gratitude I felt towards Alan was perhaps a bit over the top. And because he did not take advantage of this, my sense of gratitude increased daily until it got to the point where I was convinced that I owed him for nothing less than a new beginning, a rebirth, a new Willy. When I mentioned this he was almost moved; he softened and stroked my hair like a father would a son. "I'll never forget those words."

I recoiled violently at his touch, letting him know that I felt threatened. At the same time, I mentioned as if in passing that I could not work if I did not have a feeling of security. He took this warning – which was perhaps somewhat churlish – to heart and never bothered me again. Since he kept insisting that I was a guest in his house and that I did not have to contribute anything, even for food, I could afford to spend slightly more on painting materials. He also helped me with this, taking me to shops where he knew people and where I was often able to get a discount. Soon I was stocked as never before and needed only something to compel me to start painting again.

This is where I got stuck. Nothing special came to mind; the will to paint was general rather than specific. It had never happened to me before that I felt a kind of emptiness inside, almost hollowness, and what seemed like fear of the paint brush.

"Don't worry," Alan consoled me, "it happens to everyone. The calm before the storm of great creativity. It will come. In the meantime, you can keep your hand in with copying. Hamilton is not short of customers willing to pay for copies of well-known works. Not everyone can afford an original."

I can't do that, I said, it's humiliating.

"Oh," he said in annoyance, "are you so rich that you can forego a guaranteed source of income? And a lot of painters through imaginative copying have come up with new originals. Joan Miro, for example, copying a picture by Hendrick Sorgh. You did it with one of your *Simultaneities,* which in terms of style and colour is very reminiscent of Andre Derain's *Pool of London.* Another *Simultaneity* recalls Atkinson Grimshaw's *Night on the Thames.* "

I replied that I did not know these paintings, but he immediately came back with: "You don't need to know them. *Simultaneity* means more than what you wanted to express. It means also the simultaneity of different artists' visions, the affinity of viewpoints that can connect the centuries."

Okay, I said, I will paint copies of the great masters, why not? After all, at one time I did do that, quite successfully. But I will only paint them to order and none for less than a hundred pounds.

This seemed to him excessive, almost conceited. "If they are good, then Hamilton may be able to manage twenty for the large canvases and fifteen for the smaller ones – you'll never get more than that."

Twenty-five for the big ones and twenty for the smaller was my final offer.

"I'll see what he says," he conceded.

Two hours later he came back very pleased with himself and with a large painting in an awkward antique frame. It showed a dark English landscape in the style of the young Turner. "Hamilton wants a trial picture, to see what you are capable of. He has a commission for Gustave Caillebott's *Young Man at His Window.* He has sent this old canvas that is almost the same size and from the same era – late nineteenth century."

But I'll destroy the painting, I protested.

"Thank God for that. Hamilton gets these pictures from people who are clearing out their attics."

It wouldn't feel right, I replied.

"It is nice that you are so sensitive, but that's just superstition. Look."

And he laid in front of me a large fat volume entitled *The Art Book,* which included five hundred reproductions of the most famous paintings of all time, including some that I had not seen before. When I saw *Young Man at His Window* it at first seemed impossible that someone would want to have a copy of precisely this painting on their wall, considering that they could have ordered anything. It seemed to me a too dark, too gloomy portrait of loneliness. A young man in a dark jacket stands at an open window with his back towards us, his hands in his trouser pockets, staring at a Paris boulevard. The stone balustrade in front of him separates the dark interior from the pale sunlit world of the almost empty street, on which we can see only two carriages and the outline of a lady in a long skirt crossing the road. In the glass of the open, right-hand side window we see a reflection of the man which works as an added presence, almost his alter ego, a visible shadow of his loneliness.

"Will it be difficult?" asked Alan.

I don't think so, I replied. I think it will be one of the easiest.

25.

Once I began, I soon forgot that I was covering over the work of an anonymous nineteenth century painter; the method of applying paint on rough, already dried oils was different from painting on fresh canvas and called for different, more cautious strokes. I told myself that I was not destroying the painting, merely covering it with a new one, beneath which it would remain unchanged albeit unseen. Alan suggested that I paint in the living room because there was more space there, but I wanted to be alone. In my room, between the bed and the window, there was just enough space for the easel.

Of course, I did not remain alone for long because Alan kept coming to check on my progress, each time staying for half an hour, sometimes even an hour before he remembered that he had errands to run or his own work to do. In between he chatted without pause about nothing in particular, nervously smoking and dropping ash on the floor, which I did not like, but I did not feel able to say simply leave me in peace. His speech was fortunately so monotone that I soon only half heard him, like a radio somewhere in the background. In any case, every few minutes a train rumbled past the window, drowning out his words, which as the train retreated into the distance returned in successive waves, until I could hear them clearly again; but fortunately, each time they then merged into the background once more.

"I know that you're not even listening to me," he reproached me a number of times, "but I can't help myself; some things within me can only be sorted out if I say them and hear them."

Okay, I said, sorry, but this requires concentration, I work better in total silence. "Then it's better that I leave you in peace." And he went, but never for long.

When he was not there Marisa would come, timidly at first, asking whether I needed anything, coffee, tea, juice, an apple; then she became more confident and entered the room, stood behind me and watched me work in silence; then she returned with a book and asked if she could sit behind me on the bed and read, which would certainly not disturb me since she would be as quiet as a mouse, but it would mean a lot to her. She had never watched a painter at work; the odd amateur, perhaps, but never a *real* painter, she emphasised, as if to find favour with me.

Okay, Marisa, I said. You be here and read.

Of course, she remained quiet only for a while and then started asking questions, at first warily, fearing that I would drive her away, but when she realised that her fragile presence had a strange calming effect on me the questions multiplied until she became almost as garrulous as Alan. But her words were at least genuine and full of grace, so I even answered her while painting; as a matter of fact, through our conversation, which happened almost in parallel, a fresh, innocent energy flowed into me, for which I was grateful to her.

"Have you done a lot of paintings?" was one of her questions.

Far too few, Marisa, far too few; too few of the right kind and too many of the wrong, and this one won't be the right kind either.

"How do you know that a painting is right?"

Feeling, Marisa, that's all you can rely on in life. That applies to everything, not just painting.

"Then is it right if my feeling tells me that daddy is a lot happier since you've been staying with us?"

That I don't know, I said, since I didn't know him before; I can't imagine that he was ever *un*happy; and I've no idea what I might have contributed to him not being.

"Daddy was very unhappy," she said. "Mummy drank a lot and left him, then he began to drink, and since he did he has succeeded at almost nothing he has attempted."

I haven't noticed him drinking a lot, I said.

195

"Not now," she said. "He gives a great deal of importance to what you think of him. So I hope you'll stay. At least until I grow up."

I can't promise that, I said, you're barely thirteen.

"Now that Myles has moved out you could be my older brother," she said.

Difficult, Marisa, difficult, I said. Not long ago I took on a similar role and it didn't end well, so don't tempt fate. But I can be your friend.

"A real friend?" she asked.

To the best of my ability, I replied. Don't you have many friends?

"I've got some at school. But it's summer now and I'm at home most of the time, looking after daddy. And reading. I read a lot. What about you?"

Not really, I replied, I somehow don't find the time; whenever I reach for a book my hand somehow finds a brush. The only thing I read is the poems of Matthew Arnold, which I know almost by heart.

"I don't like him," she said. "they force him down our throats at school. I prefer novels. I'm just reading *Wuthering Heights*. It's great, have you read it?"

No, Marisa, we can talk about art, which I know a little about, but literature has somehow passed me by, though I must admit I've never tried very hard.

"Daddy reads a lot and knows a lot. He would be the best father in the world if he didn't have an inner demon. Do you know what a demon is?"

Roughly, I said. Perhaps we all have one – to a different extent.

"No," she said, "you don't, I can feel that. I don't either. But daddy has, a terrible one. Whenever it wakes up I want to die; then I don't even recognise him."

What does he do? I asked.

"He yells at me, breaks things, swears, brings home strange people and the house is full of drunks. Usually he has no money then because he's wasted it all on drink and his horrible friends. Until now Myles, who has a good job, has always helped, but now that he's no longer around I don't know what will become of us when daddy goes crazy again. Do you promise you won't leave when it happens?"

It's hard to say, Marisa, I said. It's hard to say what will be tomorrow, let alone next week; at the moment I'm also a little lost.

"If you promise, I'll be your friend forever," she said and I felt her gentle touch on my elbow.

Okay, then I promise. I don't have many friends, either. But I find it hard to believe that he is ever short of money – after all, he is a well-known art critic.

"Oh," she said, "no one takes him seriously. They used to, but not anymore – now some people even laugh at him and that hurts so much. Don't tell anyone I said this. What's this picture called?" she asked, directing her attention at the canvas in front of me.

Young Man at His Window, I said.

"That's you," she said.

No, I replied, it's the younger brother of the French painter Gustav Caillebott.

"No, look. There's a window in front of you, you are standing at the window with your back to me, like the man in the picture. You are the young man at the window."

With the difference that outside there is no Parisian street but a tangle of railway lines, along which the next train will rumble at any minute, I said.

"It's not a street in Paris, but it could be. If I close my eyes I can see it."

I can't close my eyes, Marisa, your daddy's friend wants an exact copy.

"But I like to close my eyes and pretend how things would be if they were not how they are. Now I'll go, I'm disturbing you too much."

And she slipped from the room as soundlessly as she had entered it.

But her words stayed with me, sank within me, attached themselves to my nerve endings, breathed with me. I thought: "imagine how things would be if they were not how they are", is that not the most beautiful definition of art that I've ever heard, regardless of the fact that it came from the lips of a thirteen-year-old girl? Or perhaps because of that?

197

Suddenly my faithfulness to Caillebott vanished, the brush went its own way (just like that, for fun, I thought, to see what happens; if I'm already painting over one picture I can later paint over whatever appears). The painting became increasingly similar to the scene that Marisa had observed from the bed behind me: a young man standing in front of a canvas on an easel, painting what he sees before him – a canvas on an easel, a window behind it, outside the window railway tracks, beyond them a greyish brown wall, above it the flat roof of the industrial building on the other side and the first carriage of a train just entering the picture. I painted not only the canvas but also the painter before it, transferring the whole image of my painting onto the painting in the picture. Instead of the stone balustrade a dusty wooden window sill, instead of the Paris street a tangle of rails, instead of elegant buildings the shabby façade of the modern industrial age. No reflection in the glass; its role was taken by the repetition of the big painting within the frame of the smaller one in the painting. All that remained of Caillebott was the sharp separation between the gloomy interior and the pale, sunlit exterior, although I added to the latter only one ray of sunshine, reflecting off the roof of a carriage.

"What in God's name have you painted?" asked Alan upon his return.

Young Man by a Window, I replied. A kind of self-portrait.

He stared at the picture in astonishment and I got the impression he was blushing slightly. "That's… it's… I don't know what to say. Hamilton will have a stroke, but it seems to me that… that you have created a work of art. Are you aware of that?"

For now, no, I acknowledged. I got carried away, I followed an instinct, I couldn't help myself. I can still scrape it all off and paint a copy of Caillebott.

"God forbid," he said. "First I have to show it to Hamilton."

It turned out that Mr. Hamilton did not have a customer for the Caillebott, he had chosen it on a whim to see how good I was at copying. He said that the "copy" was completely worthless, while the picture itself first confused him, then annoyed him, then excited him and ultimately charmed him (at least, that's what Alan said). In fact, it not only charmed him, but convinced him to buy it on the spot for two hundred pounds! Alan counted out the money in five pound notes onto the table.

A hundred for you, I pushed half back across the table. I wanted to add, my contribution for board and lodging, but I caught Marisa's eye in time and said instead: after all, you are my agent, you deserve your commission.

"No agent gets fifty per cent," he objected, pushing fifty pounds back across the table. "And I now have two new copies for you, this time for real: Gian Lorenza Bernini's *Ecstasy of Saint Teresa* and Marc Chagall's *Above the Town*. Hamilton will send you two canvases by forgotten amateurs of the right size. Will you begin straight away or do we have time to celebrate?"

I shrugged and Marisa exclaimed: "Celebration!"

Alan imagined that we would go across the road to the Irish pub, The Great Western, but Marisa (God bless her) had in mind something much more celebratory: a meal in a restaurant of the kind that would not let us in if we were not dressed appropriately; a visit to the zoo, especially the aquarium; a drive round the city, for there were surely many interesting things that I hadn't yet seen; and lastly ice cream in the company of the hippies in Trafalgar Square, where we could watch the world go by until midnight.

"Marisa," Alan pointed out, "Willy doesn't have that much time. In any case, the point is not to spoil you but to celebrate Willy's success. Why don't you ask him what he wants?"

Exactly what Marisa mentioned, I said.

"Hooray!" she shouted and started getting dressed.

Sadly, it all ended with compromises that made her in particular miserable: in Trafalgar Square, instead of the hippies there was a crowd carrying banners, preparing to protest against the Vietnam War; because of this some of the streets in the centre were closed and we could not get to the restaurant that Alan said was the most exclusive in London; the ice cream that we bought from a vendor at Hyde Park Corner was obviously off since we all started getting stomach cramps in the middle of our meal at a Chinese restaurant in Bayswater, where Marisa left all the food on her plate; we ended the evening in the pub across the road, where Alan debated in a loud

voice with his compatriots the situation in Northern Ireland, while
Marisa and I sat in the corner, drinking our beer and juice and playing
a strange game with our fingers that she had made up.

At one point she leaned towards me and whispered: "If daddy
drinks more than three whiskies I seriously recommend that you lock
your door tonight and pretend to be asleep if you hear him knocking."

Why, I wanted to know, but she shrugged significantly and said:
"You'll see."

Since Alan did not stop at three whiskies but got as far as seven,
it seemed sensible to take her warning seriously, so before going to
bed I bolted the door. Then I waited to see what would happen. Since
nothing did, after an hour my anxiety faded and I fell asleep.

But not for long: first of all I was woken by a couple of trains
that, in spite of the late hour, rumbled past the window one after the
other in opposite directions; and then, before I managed to get back
to sleep, I heard strange noises outside my door. It sounded like a
muffled conversation, a man and a woman, then the rattling of keys
and then knocking.

"Willy," I heard Alan's voice, "what's this, locking yourself in your
room?"

His words were noticeably softened and lengthened; it was obvious
that, after we came back from the pub and Marisa and I had gone to
bed, he had consumed a few more whiskies. "I've got a friend here,
Bee Duffel, who would like to meet you. She came especially to
shake your hand. I told her that you had made a big impression on
all my friends in the art world with your insight into human beings
and their problems. She really needs some advice."

I stubbornly pretended to be asleep. This was becoming increasingly difficult because Alan had raised his voice and was almost
shouting. "How dare you? This is *my* house, that is *my* room, you are
my guest – what gives you the right to lock the door in my face."

Suddenly, he attacked the door with his hands and feet: blows and
kicks rained down on the decaying wood and it seemed that at any
moment it would come off its hinges. The woman tried to calm him
down: "Stop it, Alan, let him sleep, it's one-thirty in the morning."
But he didn't give up and was now banging on the door with a heavy

object. "Oh, the ingratitude! I'll die of misery. I always make the same mistake."

The blows ceased and I heard sobbing. And a woman's voice trying to comfort him. "Come on, you're not a child. You just drank too much. Are you in love with this boy?"

"I'd like to make this boy," came his distorted voice, "into a painter, but he rejects me, ignores me. I won't tolerate it. Tomorrow I'll throw him out of the house and he'll see how nice it is to live in London without friends."

"I'm sure you won't do that," said the woman. "Go to bed. When you wake up it will all seem different."

There was a short silence and then I heard footsteps going down the stairs. "Careful, or you'll fall," said the woman, "lean on me." And his voice, increasingly hard to make out: "I worship him. And I'm afraid of him: I'm afraid of his talent, which is unbelievable, although he is eaten by uncertainty. He is split as if with an axe and he heals that split through painting, although he is not aware of that. Do you know that he painted all twenty-seven bridges on the Thames? Don't tell me I'm wrong, I know my Jung…"

26.

The next morning I stayed in bed until ten. The house was unusually quiet. Even though I was terribly thirsty I dared not go downstairs; I opened *The Art Book*, found Bernini's *Ecstasy of Saint Teresa* and began painting. At the same time I began thinking where I could move to as soon as possible. I painted until I heard a gentle knock and Marisa's mild voice quietly saying: "Willy, can you come down?" And then after a long pause: "Please. You said you were my friend."

When I came downstairs I found them at the dining table. They were sitting at opposite ends, gloomily staring into space. Alan looked totally spiritually flattened. When I sat down Marisa glanced at me and said: "Daddy has something to say to you." She looked down the table at her father and prompted him: "Daddy?"

Alan was quiet for a good five minutes. He compulsively squeezed his hands together on the table top, he bit his lip and, as far as I could tell, his tongue as well, all the while striving to avoid my eyes. The colour of his face ranged from scarlet to deadly pale.

Marisa waited patiently, as did I. Eventually she got up and went over to the suitcase standing in the middle of the room that I had not noticed before.

"Marisa," said Alan quietly, "please."

Marisa obediently returned to her seat and once again began staring towards her father.

"You say it," he asked her. "I am too ashamed."

Marisa turned to me; I had never seen such a grown-up, mature, resigned, martyred, but also calm and controlled face on a thirteen-year-old girl. "Daddy would like to apologise to you," she said. "When he drinks, he becomes a monster. He deeply regrets what happened last night and begs you not to leave us because of it."

And that suitcase, what's it doing there?

"My things are in it," she said. "I wanted to leave. Daddy begged me on his knees to stay. I said yes, on condition that he apologised to you. And promised that what happened last night is never repeated. If it does, I'm leaving for good and daddy will never see me again."

It was nothing really, I said. Some noise outside my door that I didn't even hear properly, since trains were going past the whole time. I just remember someone shouting something. I thought I was dreaming. I don't see why your father should apologise to me. What happened, did he fall downstairs?

Marisa maintained eye contact with me for some time. We both realised that I was sacrificing myself: for her and for her father. We both knew that we had finally become brother and sister.

"Okay, then I'll get breakfast ready," she said, getting up. "Daddy will pop to the shop on the corner for milk, won't you daddy?"

I'll go and have a shower, I said and hurried up to my room.

Life ran on, as if the early morning incident had been only a short-lived nightmare. Alan, a hostage to his daughter's threat that she would leave if he said one wrong word, was considerate and polite as never before; I, a prisoner of my promise not to leave them, continued to maintain the pretence that I did not know what had happened; Marisa, our young overseer, once again became an obliging and friendly girl who knew almost nothing about the problems of the world, let alone one who could control the relationship between two grown men. But that is precisely what she did; the wary looks with which she accompanied the goings on in the house escaped neither me nor Alan, and although we did our best to hide it, the knowledge that we had a supervisor somehow brought us closer again. And made us feel more relaxed. Especially Alan, who spent hours and hours in my room (as if he had nothing better to do, which he probably did not), nervously smoking and babbling in his unstoppable Irish manner, as if his life depended on it.

"When I see you with a brush in your hand," he prattled, "it always reminds me of a friend in Dublin, James Joyce's cousin, or at least that's what he claims, although I've never checked, who isn't actually an artist but a house painter and the occasional author of unpublishable verses. Of course, for house painting you have to use a much bigger brush, but your way of moving the brush around, how you both apply paint with particular caution but at the same time certainty, like a priest laying the host on the tongues of the faithful during holy communion – in that you're incredibly similar. One more proof that we are all in some mysterious way connected. When I watch you, I can't get over the gift with which God has blessed you. First you will be celebrated in Britain, then America. It will all happen when you are ready; if I may quote Hamlet: readiness is all. I have met a great many artists and I think I know how they progressed as people and as artists, and how important their private life was to this progress. I see how important were the hours in their life when they looked back and regretted past mistakes, and how this hindered their progress. All the attempts to restore messed-up relationships, to start anew, all that attachment to people, property, rights – all that is negative, there's no doubt about it. I don't know anyone who has not longed for the certainty of true love, but I do know a lot of people whose lives have fallen apart because they kept the wrong company. I know that you are capable of great love and you have already shown great understanding and perhaps that scares you because you are so young, perhaps sometimes you doubt – I hope I'm not mistaken. An artist must perceive things quickly and equally quickly put them in the right drawer if he wants to avoid wasting time. I, of course, am unable to do that since I'm a slow learner, so I have to come to terms with the fact that over the past ten years my career has not developed in the way I might have hoped. I spent too much time looking back, picking over old wounds, feeling sorry for myself because I had to raise three children on my own, in return for which one of them doesn't even want to know me. But Marisa, who esteems you more than anyone she has ever met, our dear Marisa outweighs all the bad things that have happened to me. We cannot disappoint her. I've done that more than once, but for you it is not too late to become a steady light in her life. And I promise that I will dispose of at least two of my burdens: the pain of the past and sentimentality. I know what I want and every day I pray that my wish be granted at least to some extent – I'm not greedy, a minute's happiness a day is enough for me. And for you, too, as you doubtless know. Nobody will ever understand your profound sadness like I do; and I am perhaps the only one who sees in you a hidden comic, satirist, clown. That will also come to the forefront in your work; when the copying is over your personal vision will once more reappear, we shall be stunned by the optimism that shines from your paintings… there's someone at the door, I've got to go, I think it's Louis MacNeice's cousin asking for a cigarette and a free lunch. I'll go and drive him away and say: *fuck off, there are two artists in the house who need peace and quiet and want to be protected from all the fucking bores…*"

The rare moments when he wasn't there were, as before, exploited by Marisa, who was content to sit quietly on the bed behind me, reading a book. In between, she sometimes sidled over to the easel to see how the painting was progressing. I found that her silence bothered me, so I soon began to initiate conversation myself.

Do you like the smell of oil paints? I wondered.

"Not too much," she said.

Does it bother you? I asked.

"If it doesn't bother you, who sleep in the room, why would it bother me, who comes here just to visit? You could of course sleep somewhere else, like in Myles's room, which is empty and which daddy wants to rent out. And it's on the other side, so you wouldn't hear the trains."

Let him rent it out, I said, this is quite enough for me and the trains don't bother me anymore, which means that I would even get used to Hell eventually and that's a great consolation to me as that is where I'll probably end up.

"How do you know? To end up in Hell you have to have committed a mortal sin, but you don't have that on your conscience. Or do you?"

205

For now, no, I said, but I don't know how things will be tomorrow or in twenty years.

"Aren't the opportunities for mortal sin fewer the longer you live and the more you learn?"

Not necessarily, I said, we learn bad things just as fast as good ones – even faster.

"I often wonder where I'll be in ten years' time. When I'm the same age you are now. You probably think of yourself as still young, but to me twenty-three seems very grown-up, very responsible. Not to mention daddy, who as a fossil from the age of the dinosaurs should have a great sense of responsibility, but actually has none at all."

You father is fifty-three, I said, a youngster compared to my grand-dad, who is ninety-three. A sense of responsibility has nothing to do with age: in this house the most responsible one is you.

"Maybe I am," she said. "But you're not, because I can see your painting is again changing into something else, even though you promised to do a copy."

I can't help it, I replied, it seems as if my hand is following its own ideas.

"Wait a minute," she suddenly slid off the bed and came closer, "that woman looks just like me!"

That's not a woman, Marisa, that's an angel, I said. It's true she has your features. Don't ask me why, I wouldn't be able to tell you. And that isn't even a painting, but a photograph of a marble statue in the church of Santa Maria della Vittoria in Rome. I don't know who would want to have a painting of a statue hanging on the wall, but it is true that as an image it is very strong, powerful. Saint Teresa looking in ecstasy at an angel who is piercing her heart with a golden spear. Rapt in physical and spiritual devotion to God, she sees the angel as God's herald and in the spear that will wound her as a symbol of God's love.

"And why does Saint Teresa have my daddy's features?" she wanted to know.

Oh, I said in surprise, I didn't even realise. But now that you mention it, you're right. You are the angel thrusting the point of the golden spear into your father's heart, preventing him from committing a mortal sin. You know what, we'll call the painting *Daughter Saves Father with Love.*

"Hamilton will smash it over daddy's head," she said.

Nothing like that happened; once again Hamilton was enthused by what I had produced and although he did not buy it he agreed to sell it at the relatively low price of three hundred pounds, minus thirty per cent commission. For the Chagall he said he wanted a copy, just a copy and nothing but a copy; if he did not get one he would be forced to conclude that I was incapable of copying, which would have negative consequences for both of us, so he was giving me a last chance.

"I'm not saying anything," said Alan. "I'll just say what anyone who is not indifferent to you and your future would say: be yourself. People are always wanting something from us so that we become what we are not and I gave in to a large extent, perhaps because God blessed me with three children who I have to get educated and employed. You can resist, so why not do so? I'll back you up."

Right, I said, I'll do a Chagall and if this time higher powers intervene I will stop.

I began immediately, even though Marisa said I should go out a bit, around the streets or maybe to Hyde Park to get some fresh air, of which there was very little in the house. Besides which, she would like to show me the statue of Peter Pan in the park, her favourite character who reminded her a little of me.

First I must finish the Chagall, I said, then perhaps Hyde Park. Where does your father publish his reviews? I asked. I haven't seen any of them yet.

"Nor will you," she said, "he hasn't published one for more than a year. And he hardly ever goes to exhibitions because he has offended just about everyone and is banned from quite a few galleries. When he writes about less well-known painters he can be really rotten; one of them once attacked him on the street and knocked out three of his teeth."

What about the paintings he has locked in the cellar, why does he never show them?

"Because they're not worth anything," she said. "He's always bringing something home and stuffing it into that room which is

207

already overflowing – one picture at a time, like a rag-and-bone man. Perhaps he thinks he'll be able to sell one of them if he really runs out of money."

Have you ever seen them?

"No, because he keeps it locked. I know where he keeps the key, but I wouldn't want to do anything behind his back. What is that you're painting?"

I told her it was *Above the Town*, one of Marc Chagall's best known paintings, which makes use of images from Russian Jewish folklore, although he spent most of his life in Paris and the USA. Above a town of simple houses, painted with child-like naivety, fly two fairy tale figures, a man and a woman. Since his left hand is on her right breast, they are probably lovers fleeing from a world that wants to come between them.

"Why would they want to come between them?"

Perhaps they went against the customs of the place where they live; perhaps she's married to someone else, or he has a family that he is fleeing from – there could be dozens of reasons. Looking at her rounded stomach, the woman might be pregnant. Perhaps they are fleeing their destiny. But they are definitely fleeing, since the man is looking back to check how close their pursuers are.

"Have you ever been in love?" she asked.

Oh, I said, I don't know how to answer that.

"Don't be coy," she said, "I'm old enough not to be embarrassed, I already have my periods, I know that babies are not brought by the stork."

It's not that, I said. Until not long ago I would have said without hesitation that I had been in love many times, maybe too many times. But on the ferry from France to Dover something happened; I got to know – actually, not got to know, but had a fleeting encounter with – the girl of my dreams, my muse. Sooner or later every artist meets a woman who begins to embody all that is beautiful and good in this world, all that is elevated, worth striving for, sacrificing for.

"And can you decide which woman will do that?" she asked with more insight than I had expected.

No, you can't, that's the problem. No, it's not really a problem, it's the only way it can be: you are destined to have a particular muse, otherwise she has no power. There is only one muse that is only yours and irreplaceable.

"And," she asked after a short pause, during which I got the impression that something in my words was bothering her, "did you sleep with her?"

Only in dreams, I said. In my dreams. And perhaps we never shall in reality, because since that encounter I haven't seen her. And I probably never will, although I'm still not completely without hope. She vanished into the London crowds.

"But if you did meet again you would sleep together, wouldn't you?" she wanted to know.

I don't know, Marisa. On the one hand I want to, on the other I don't. A muse is most powerful from a distance. When she is once beneath you, sweating and crying out, she becomes too earthly to be a source of inspiration.

"Poor Willy," she said, "are you suffering terribly?"

Only when I betray her in one way or another. And even then, not as much as artists used to suffer in more romantic times.

"Have you been unfaithful to her?"

In my mind and my heart, never, I said, while for every other sin she is indirectly to blame, for the sin is intended for her, a kind of worship.

"You men always know how to arrange things so that they are to your advantage," she said. I was startled. "I've noticed that with daddy. He always does the worst with the best of intentions."

You're unusually grown-up for your years, I said. Do you know that?

"Someone's got to be," she said, with a hint of bitterness, "so that the world can move forward."

She came closer and looked at the picture "That woman is nothing like the one in the reproduction. And the man looks very like you. And the city below them is London. You've broken your promise again."

It's true, I acknowledged. It looks as if my career of a forger is just about over.

"Is that her?" she asked, turning to me.

I nodded. But I don't do it deliberately. There are moments when every woman becomes her, takes on her features.

"Funny," she said, put her head down and left the room.

Marisa, I whispered rather than called after her, I love you, too.

I titled the picture *Fleeing One's Own Fate* and Alan took it to Hamilton. To begin with he evidently got worked up, saying that his gallery was not a dumping ground for adolescent wit, but eventually he agreed to sell this new Vaupotič on commission.

"I think you're on the right path," said Alan. "Although it's true that old Hamilton has had enough and when he says that he'll give you one more, really one last chance, he's not joking."

He gave me a list of seven paintings that he wanted copying for "reliable regular customers". This time he did not bring any old canvases, because Hamilton said he didn't have any and that I should use whatever I could get my hands on, if nothing else sacking, since copies are not worth anything better.

And so over the following days I painted faithful copies of Egon Schiele's *Sitting Woman with Legs Drawn Up,* Walter Sickert's *Ennui*, Frans Snyders' *Still Life with Dead Game*, William Turner's *Snowstorm*, Vermeer's *Lady Seated at a Spinet*, Anders Zorn's *Dagmar* and *Virgin and Child* by Dieric Bouts. Finally, Marisa found in the book a self-portrait by Marie-Louise-Elisabeth Vigée-Lebrun and said: "And now one for me."

Looking at this picture I experienced a real shock: from the image of the artist with a brush in her hand Marisa stared out at me, similar in almost every feature to the popular eighteenth century portraitist – the same gentle smile and open look in her green-grey eyes. "Do you believe in reincarnation?" she asked.

Of the soul, not the body, I replied. Maybe the soul. Have you shown this to daddy?

"It was him who showed me it in the first place," she admitted. "He told me to ask you to paint a copy. He daren't ask himself."

Why not, for heaven's sake? I asked.

210

"He's afraid of you," she said quietly. "You mean too much to him and he wouldn't want to lose you. Me neither."

But for you I won't do a copy of a portrait of some other woman, I said, for you I will do a real portrait. You can pose for me.

"Will you really?" she said, giving a little jump for joy. "But not here, I can't relax in this house, somewhere outside, somewhere in Hyde Park."

Okay, I said, we can begin tomorrow morning.

"In front of the statue of Peter Pan," she said. "You can call it *Marisa and Friend.*"

27.

At dinner, for which Marisa had made spaghetti bolognese that Alan
praised as the best ever, she burbled on about how tomorrow would
bring a new phase in my development as a painter. In a few minutes
she had come up with a whole narrative: how I would be painting her
portrait and how the passers-by would be so taken with it that they
would ask me to paint them too, also with Peter Pan. And although
Peter Pan belonged to her and only her she would be glad, for the
sake of me and my future, to lend him to others and thus I would soon
become celebrated as the "portrait painter of Hyde Park", a London
tourist attraction, people from all over the world would come to me
wanting to be portrayed in front of the statue of Peter Pan, there
would be a waiting list months long, like in London hospitals for
operations, the price of a portrait would rise in line with demand and
part of the money would be channelled into a fund for the building
of a Peter Pan Gallery beside the Serpentine in Hyde Park, where
all my paintings would be exhibited and where she would work as a
curator. "And you," she said to Alan, "will renew all your contacts
and promote the gallery. Can you think of a finer future?"

I realised that Alan, although he listened to all this with a fatherly
smile, was not particularly enthusiastic about her raptures. As if her
escape from the bitter melancholy that had been her basic tone filled
him with concern and even fear that something was happening over
which he had no control. Evidently, for the first time since I had

moved in, he was aware that his daughter had overtaken him in the struggle for my inclinations. He suddenly felt redundant and in the plan that Marisa had unveiled, which was really an expression of adolescent fantasy, he discerned a silent conspiracy.

In order to correct this impression I said that it would probably start and end with one portrait that would hang on the wall in Marisa's room, unless Hamilton managed to sell it for ten thousand.

"Never," exclaimed Marisa, "my portrait with Peter Pan will never be for sale, not even for a million. If you don't mean to paint it for me and only for me, then I'd rather not pose."

Of course I'll paint it for you, I said, and hand it over to you alone – with a signed statement if you want.

"I don't want a signed statement," she said, "I just want your word. If that's not enough then I was wrong about you, in which case my portrait would not really mean anything."

Marisa, I said, stop arguing.

"You carry on," said Alan getting up noisily from the table, "a quarrel between lovers is a good thing – it usually clears the air and creates the conditions for even more intense love. I'm meeting an old friend from Belfast, I'll be home late. Good night."

And with a strangely red face he left.

"What's up with him?" asked Marisa, as if she no longer under-stood her father. I shrugged – Alan's reaction seemed stupid and terribly unfair. "I didn't know we were lovers," she said. "I thought we were friends."

And so we are, I said. What's wrong with him, he knows you are only thirteen years old.

"That doesn't matter," she said. "Girls can fall in love a lot earlier than that. What does matter is whether you're in love with me."

No, Marisa, I said, I'm not. If I was, we couldn't be friends, which is a lot more precious. And I told you I had my muse, who I may not, must not be unfaithful to. Why are we even talking about it? Let's stop.

"A bit late, don't you think? Now that daddy has stupidly planted the idea in our heads, we'll be thinking only of that."

I won't, I said, getting up. Nor will you, if you want to have a portrait with Peter Pan. I'm going to clean my brushes and then have an early night.

"You know what," she yelled after me, "you're blackmailing me."

No, Marisa, I shouted back, quite the opposite: you're blackmailing me. And friends don't do that!

I went to my room and lay on the bed. It was quite some time since I had felt so confused, so close to despair, which was reaching out its long limbs towards me from the dark corners of the room like a poisonous spider. Never in my life had I thought of the possibility of being in love with a thirteen-year-old, except perhaps when I was that kind of age myself. But at that time they were the fantasies of a growing boy, whereas now I was looking at a real situation. Unless I had got it all wrong. But no, her hints were all too clear and Alan's reaction was even less ambiguous: evidently it did not seem impossible to him that something like that would happen, evidently he knew his daughter better than I did. And perhaps something similar had happened before. Perhaps Marisa had fallen in love with one of his "friends" in order to spite him, or perhaps she had lured someone away in order to protect him from an entanglement that would bring him only pain.

On the one hand, I felt that I had to avoid the danger at any cost; on the other, I felt increasingly inclined to go along with things and to flee only when there was no other choice. Willy I wanted to be honest, Willy II wanted to live, to appropriate the world, to experience adventure and as far as suffering went, let each one take care of themselves.

Suddenly I heard knocking and Marisa's voice.

"I won't come into the room, I'll tell you from here. Can you hear me, are you asleep?"

No, I replied, I'm awake.

"Then remember this. I don't need your permission to be in love with you. That's entirely my affair. For the time being I can reassure you that I am not, but I can't promise you that things will stay like that. If you don't understand that, then you don't even know what love is and then you're not much of a painter either – then even your best paintings are merely fakes."

Okay, Marisa, okay, I said. Anything else?

"I know that you don't care too much about my feelings; I know that you don't take me seriously; I know that you think only of yourself. But don't imagine that you can just withdraw or run away. Daddy and I won't let you. Ever. If there's no other way, we shall share you. And don't think that it would be the first time."

Don't talk nonsense, I said. Imagination is a fine thing, but it is starting to lead you into wickedness, far from Peter Pan. Stop going on about it, otherwise I really will start thinking about leaving. I like it here, I like you, but now things are getting a bit complicated.

"In short, you don't like me," she said after a while. "Perhaps I'll manage to come to terms with that by the morning. But know this: you give yourself too much freedom. You only take, you give nothing. You even deprive me of my right to have my own feelings."

I heard her going down the stairs.

It all wearied me so much that I slipped into a strange half-sleep in which a raging torrent of disjointed images from the past flowed through my head and I tried to put them in some kind of order, as if I was going to stick them in an album; while doing so, I must have fallen asleep since the images faded and melted into the darkness, but then they returned, equally disjointed although from among the swirling mass the image of Sandrina gradually became sharper, walking towards me through a tall meadow full of flowers, with rolling but coordinated steps, with an enigmatic smile on her lips, provocative but at the same time embarrassed.

She came to me and we found ourselves in a tight embrace, I felt the pressure of her breasts on my chest, our tongues gripped each other like leeches trying to suck blood; the next minute we were lying in the scented grass, I on my back with a strong, almost painful erection, she with her lips covering the head of my penis, which she suddenly began to suck and lick. The sensation was indescribable as I thrust my hips towards her to push my penis further into her mouth; but not wanting to rush, she gripped it with the long fingers of her left hand and restrained it, so that her mouth could work on it in a

215

rhythm of her choosing, alternately gentle and forceful, relaxed and tense, stroking and almost painful.

I heard a loud noise that was soon repeated and I realised that a couple of trains had rumbled past, and the rattle of wheels was now receding into the distance. Suddenly, I was awake, but the head of my swollen penis was still gripped by firm lips, I could still feel the skilful movements of a caressing tongue – as if I was not quite awake, as if I wanted to drag the most seductive part of my dream into wakefulness and fix it there for all time. Then another train went past and I realised with a shock that I was not dreaming; that someone really was caressing me and I felt two elbows resting on the mattress on either side of me.

Marisa! I thought. Along with the sense of horror, I felt a desire to succumb to the strange experience, which was more beautiful than I had ever dared imagine. I felt myself close to orgasm, I started to moan slightly and then I came, spurting into the unusually greedy mouth all that had built up inside me since my arrival in London, all the tortuous moods that had had no opportunity to disappear, all the suppressed desires, all the concealed resentments, all the unfulfilled hopes, all the weight of the past, and I felt that I was cleansing myself, that I was being flooded with relief and a sense of freshness, while the mouth sucked, kissed, drew it all in, swallowed, oh Marisa, I sighed, Marisa, Marisa, I love you!

I reached out my hand to grab hold of her hair – her thick, curly brown hair – to draw her gentle, innocent little face to mine and to smell the scent of my semen in her mouth, to suck it into me and thus to seal the love between us that we had not been able to avoid.

But my hand felt a bald head and protruding ears. No, I thought, this is still a dream, a very vivid dream that is turning into a nightmare – it was not her that came to me, it did not really happen!

Then I clearly heard Alan's voice: "Do you see now that it makes no difference whose mouth it is, whose vagina, whose arsehole? You have proven to yourself that only the feeling matters. You still don't want to admit that all men are queer?"

I leaped up and started to beat him wildly about the head. Damn you, I yelled, damn you! Then I felt that I was beating the edge of the bed and I heard the key turn in the lock, and the following words came from the other side of a locked door.

"You are damned, since you will never again emerge from that room. Only love will save you. Not for Marisa, but for me. For me, is that clear?!" And then silence.

I started to sob desperately in the darkness. The sobbing changed into crying reminiscent of the howling of a beaten animal. It was drowned out by a train rumbling past. Desecrated at last, I thought. Finally punished for my self-obsession. For the pride of an artist who is convinced that he can play with love as with a drop of paint at the end of his brush.

Never again.

The door was indeed locked; Alan was determined to make me a prisoner. He held all the cards: he could accuse me of trying to seduce his thirteen-year-old daughter, even of trying to rape her. I had no doubts about how far he would be willing to go if I did not submit to his demands. The irrationality of his obsession shocked me; if I had not experienced it first hand, I wouldn't have thought it possible.

But there was no time for brooding, I quickly put on a shirt and trousers and then I began – cautiously, so as not to make any noise – to put into one of my suitcases the most necessary things: some clothes, some brushes, some paints, three pairs of shoes. I realised that I would have to leave most of my stuff behind.

I looked at the clock: it was two-thirty in the morning, a time when the railway lines beneath my window were almost completely quiet. I carefully pushed up the lower part of the sash window and leaned out. In the dim light of the stars and the lamp on the viaduct on the other side, I judged that it was about twelve feet down to the ground; if I climbed out and hung from the window sill I would reduce that to about six.

First I dropped my suitcase down, then my travel bag and then my shoulder bag with my money and documents; finally, I climbed out myself, said goodbye with a look to the room and slipped into the depths beneath me. I landed on the suitcase, almost smashing it with my foot; in doing so, I twisted my ankle, which started to hurt so much that I could hardly walk. I knew that I was risking my life, since at any moment a train could come rushing along the tracks, while in the tunnel in front of me there was not enough room at the side to press against the wall. But I also knew that Paddington Station was only a few hundred yards away and if a train (assuming that they were even running at this time) should through happy coincidence avoid the track I was walking along towards the tunnel then I would have a good chance of staying alive.

There was no other way, I could not go back, and so carrying my luggage I marched along the outer track on the right-hand side towards the tunnel. Almost at the same time I heard the rumble of an approaching train; I froze and frantically tried to work out which track it was on. The next moment I saw rapidly approaching lights that almost blinded me; it was too late to get out of the way. So that's it, I thought, completely calmly, as if something was taking place that I could not influence. Then the lights were in front of me, above me, then darkness and a noise disappearing into the tunnel, and then the lights at the rear of the train, rapidly retreating. I'm still alive, I thought with relief, but also with a hint of regret, as if the darkness that had yawned at me from the depths of the tunnel had offered the best solution to my problems.

Almost as soon as I entered the darkness of the tunnel I saw the light of the platform at the other end; the station was even closer than I realised and in less than ten minutes I was safe, while in another ten minutes I was already in the main station concourse. I looked for the left luggage office, handed over my suitcase and travel bag, returned to the concourse, lay down on one of the empty benches, put my shoulder bag under my head and fell asleep. But before I did I thought: so now I'm a vagrant, a sexually abused vagrant.

I slept longer than I had intended, evidently I had been terribly tired. I managed to sleep through the morning rush hour and the noise of the mass of people hurrying to work. When I opened my eyes, the first thing I saw was a large station clock showing ten to ten. After a quick breakfast in the buffet I took the Tube to Sloane Square and walked from there to the House of Art gallery. Instead of the flat-chested young woman, behind the counter stood an elegant

218

middle-aged man who slightly disdainfully examined me from head to toe as soon as I came through the door.

"What can I do for you?" he asked.

Very little, I'm afraid: the artist responsible for some of the pictures you have on sale has just walked into your gallery. I'm a painter, Mr. Hamilton. I assume you are Mr. Hamilton?

"Definitely," he replied, without altering his supercilious tone, "And you are?"

Vili Vaupotič, I said.

He frowned and shrugged. "If that somewhat odd sound that I just heard is your name, I must say that it is completely unknown to me, so I think our business is finished for today, don't you?"

No, I said, our business is not finished, it hasn't even started. I want you to return the paintings that Alan McClelland brought; I have a feeling that they're not safe here.

"Oh," he said, "those paintings. I'm afraid you're too late, Alan took them away a half hour ago."

Where to? I shouted, They're not his!

"I know nothing about that," said Mr. Hamilton, wiping his glasses with a small cloth he took from a drawer and symbolically washing his hands of the matter. "He brought them, he took them away; if he stole the paintings from you then I suggest you call the police – that's the only advice I can offer you."

No one can do what they like with my paintings, I objected, although it was becoming increasingly clear that I was attacking the wrong man.

"Perhaps not," he said, "although that is a matter of agreement between the two of you of which I know nothing. Why don't you speak to him, would you like his address?"

No, I said after a long pause, my head down. What do you think he has done with them?

"Perhaps he has given them to someone else to sell, perhaps he has found a buyer, perhaps he has taken them home; as far as I know, he likes to collect paintings – for a rainy day, as he says."

Mr. Hamilton, I said after brief reflection. You ordered from me at least ten copies of great masters. I'm ready to supply you at the rate of two a week.

"Supply them to someone else," he said. "Your work did not convince me. I took the paintings as a favour to Alan. Now, if you don't mind, I have other matters to attend to." And he turned his back on me.

I wandered out of the gallery, walked to the corner and leaned on the wall. On the other side of the street my eye was caught by a sign saying: Accommodation Agency – Rooms to Let.

Right, I said. Let's go for it. Let's start again.

PART THREE

28.

In spite of the mass of visitors in London, there was never a shortage of rooms to rent. It seemed that half the population was making a living from renting out rooms to the other half (and to a certain extent this was true). Unfortunately, this did not mean that you could just make a phone call or knock on a door and you would have a roof over your head, since the offers in the windows of newsagents or agencies involved very selective criteria. Some did not like men with long hair, some smokers, others Blacks or Indians, or foreigners in general ("English only"), some disliked men, some women, and so on. If you took into account all the exclusions, then every seeker of accommodation would sooner or later come across a "sorry, room taken" sign: not only those with the wrong appearance or skin colour, but even the English – "Sorry, no English" I saw in two ads (perhaps the rooms were being let by someone Irish, Black or Indian who wanted to give the English a taste of their own medicine).

With greyish blue eyes and light brown hair, I had just the right qualifications for most racist landlords, but I did have a recognisably foreign accent, which in many cases immediately led to a colder tone on the phone, and long uncombed hair plus a goatee beard, which deterred many on the threshold. But the most negative responses were no doubt due to my response to the question "And what do you do, Willy?" There seemed to be little point pretending to be a bank clerk, a programmer or a physical education teacher, since it would sooner or later become apparent that I was a painter, so I always admitted it at the start.

"What kind of painter? A house painter?" No, I at first objected with indignation, but then ever more contritely and eventually with a feeling of guilt, a real painter, an artist. Ooh… and great surprise. "That probably means a lot of mess with paint, doesn't it?"

I always put old newspapers on the floor was my standard reply, but evidently it was insufficiently convincing, for after an embarrassed pause there always followed an implausible response: from the fact that the room had been taken half an hour earlier, to the more understandable claim they were *actually* looking for someone with a regular job who would not be around during the day, to the barely credible assertion that paints are inflammable and that their presence in the house would pose a fire risk.

Quite a number of potential landlords I excluded myself, because I didn't want to live with a family again and face the burden of unclear relationships, expectations and abuses of one kind or another; after my last experience I wanted to be left in peace and to live alone. After two days of exhausting telephoning and looking at rooms all over London, I got the feeling that, in spite of the apparent limitless offers, I would never find anything suitable, for each time either I didn't suit the room or the room didn't suit me.

"So tell them you're a house painter," said Willy II. I decided not to do that: the difficulties that would follow were too obvious and the lie would only bring a few days grace.

But sleeping on a wooden bench at Paddington Station could not go on for ever, while my ever more crumpled and unwashed appearance was not bringing me any extra points, so it became clear that I would, at least temporarily, have to seek a compromise. I decided to sacrifice that which I needed most – space; at that moment privacy seemed more important. I ended up in a long, narrow room on the fourth floor of a red brick terrace house between Earls Court Tube station and the Exhibition Centre. Nevern Square. I thought: if I take away an n I get Never Square and, considering the circumstances in which I found myself, this coincidence seemed to me a natural part of Fate's message that I would never, ever achieve the goals that had brought me to London (although I had clung to them with increasing stubbornness as my grip slipped).

Almost every other building was a hotel, but ours (very impressive on the outside, anything but on the inside) was a boarding-house: a labyrinth of rooms in a basement, a raised ground floor and four other floors, which the owner had multiplied by dividing the existing rooms into two or three using thin hardboard walls. Some were larger ("double rooms"), but most, including mine, were twelve feet long and six across: enough for a narrow bed, a small table and chair, a cupboard and a kind of shelf on which stood an electric plate for heating water.

Ideal for a painter who likes big canvases!

But I was at the top of the house and my window offered a wonderful view across the rooftops to the north; I had already painted the view in my mind and had begun to quite like the room. Moreover, I had already worked out that I could place a large canvas on the bed, leaning against the wall, and paint sitting on the wobbly chair: romantic. And I soon discovered a particularity that finally made me fall in love with the place: I could climb through the window onto a stone ledge and from there onto the flat roof of the building – in fact, the whole row of buildings. From there I had a marvellous view all around and felt like the master of all I surveyed: the whole of London was mine.

In spite of all its shortcomings, the room was well worth the five pounds per week just for this access to the roof. But at the beginning it was the shortcomings that occupied me most. It did not bother me too much that there was a shared bathroom (one for the five rooms on the same floor), which was filthy (the layer of dirt in the bathtub had been years in the making), and that through the dividing walls you could hear everything your neighbours were doing – from coughing, farting, taking deep breaths, muttering and rustling the newspaper, to more delicate sounds such as gasping before and shouting during orgasm, to perhaps even the agony of dying, for one day a corpse in a body bag was carried down the stairs. What bothered me more was the caretaker, a desiccated old Irish woman, always the worse for drink, with an enormous bunch of keys on a steel ring, who at all hours of the day and night tramped up and down the stairs, knocking on doors, asking or demanding something, arguing with or generally upsetting the occupants, without it ever being clear to me exactly what she wanted (she never knocked on my door, although I suspected that she came into the room and went through my things when I wasn't there).

One aspect of the privacy that I enjoyed after a long absence was the silence, or at least relative silence, and so the racket caused by the drunken caretaker brought me real pain, but I could never summon up enough courage to go out onto the staircase and rebuke her: "Mrs. O'Riley, allow us to live here in peace and quiet!" As if sensing my ill-temper and determined to provoke me even more, she started using a small transistor radio that every other day, when she cleaned the staircase, she put in the pocket of her overall, from where, step by step and floor to floor, it shrieked out the news, pop music, dog-racing commentaries and every other form of sound torture. If the sun was shining I took the opportunity to retreat to the roof, where it was more pleasant to listen to the roar of the London traffic, while if it was raining, which it sometimes did five days in a row, I stuffed my ears with cotton wool, which I bought at the corner shop precisely for this purpose.

There were about thirty rooms in the building – too many for the tenants to greet each other. The most you could hope for was to say "hi" in the hallway, where we met while searching through the chaotic post, half hoping that there would be no reply, because a reply, or even just a hint of one, would mean an obligation, a first step towards making contact, which we were all – or at least that's how it seemed – terribly afraid of; it was as if we were all inclined towards solitude, if not even misanthropic; as if each of us had brought with him (and was determined to do whatever it took to keep to himself) a great secret, great sorrow or an unpleasant disease.

I thought that perhaps we had been pushed into this extreme form of self-containment by the slightly morbid, creepy atmosphere in the house. But whatever the reason and in spite of our chance encounters on the stairs, there was less human contact among us than would have arisen if we had all sheltered under the same awning for five minutes during a downpour. Perhaps we were unconsciously conforming to the instruction in faded letters that someone had taped to the wall of the hallway: "Mind your own business." It was never clear to me who had thought it necessary (or morally instructive) to display this notice; certainly it was not the caretaker, who was the only one to brazenly ignore it.

It was also possible to rent a room for a short period, with a minimum of three nights, so the faces on the stairs were always changing, which was an additional reason for us to avoid each other; as a matter of fact, it was like living in a cheap hotel. Nevertheless, the atmosphere was unusual, oppressive and almost always disturbing, simply because we were all young, single people living under the same roof.

In this situation the rooftop, which was exclusively mine, was a blessed retreat – and even more refreshing since, in spite of the privacy it offered, it was completely open. I realised that I no longer felt the urge to go into town: it was enough to see it spread out beneath me like a sea of colours stretching on all sides to the horizon – so big that the visible part represented at most only a quarter of it. I spent hours and hours on my "roof of the world", in the sunshine, on cloudy days, even in the rain and often at night when the lights swarmed like millions of fireflies. Among the moments of rapture there were moments of dejection that were particularly painful when I thought that in this endless sea of humanity I knew only three people: Alan, Marisa and Mrs. Hudson. After three months I was completely on my own in London, unknown and uncared for. This affected me much more than the thought that I would probably never again see the paintings that Alan had locked in the cellar (or all the others that I had lost or forgotten). As several times before, I was faced with the decision whether or not to start afresh.

I felt a strong urge to visit the parts of the city that I had abandoned, to prove to myself that I already had a past in London, a history, and that I was in spite of everything a part of it, at home in it. I walked along the street parallel to Abinger Road and, hidden behind some shrubs so that no one could see me, I peered from around the corner at Mrs. Hudson's house. I saw Harry, gloomily sunk in his own unimportance, returning from work, clumsily opening the gate, equally clumsily trying to extract the key from his pocket and then struggling with the lock for at least five minutes before, with rounded shoulders and bent like an old man, he stepped inside. Of course, he could have rung the bell, but he was trying to be a "gentleman" and not disturb anyone, let alone admit that there was anything wrong with his hands. An icily cold feeling shot through me that we had much in common: I too had recently only "tried to be" a painter; I too refused to admit that there was anything wrong with my hands, or rather what my hands produced. Now that we were no longer supposed competitors and fellow sufferers under the same roof, I felt sorry for him. Poor Harry, I said. Poor Willy. Poor Mrs. Hudson.

I saw her emerging from the house in her mini-skirt and white cardigan, looking through her handbag with a solemn face until she found her car key, getting behind the wheel of her ancient Rover and driving off to God-knows-where – perhaps to the shop to buy something for dinner, perhaps to a restaurant, but not the rowing club, since it was too early. She filled me with a troubling sense of compassion; now that I was no longer dependent on her goodwill and her designs, her life, in spite of the nice house, seemed modest, empty, swathed in illusions of lost youth and a lifestyle that alone, as a mere housewife, she could not afford. If I was suffering, how much must she be! Distance had given me the capacity to sense people's inner colours much more than when I lived in close proximity to them. This sense of compassion, which was a new feeling for me, contained a hint of nostalgia, as if part of me still wanted to be back there, from where I had fled, as if I did not want to leave the fragments of my life to the past.

The same feelings came over me in Paddington, when from inside the Great Western pub I stared at the façade of Alan's house across the street, agitated by the thought that at any moment he or one of his friends might come in (it was almost as if I wanted it). The whole episode appeared to me like a painting and if some elements had been different I might still be there, close to the channels leading to the galleries and the art establishment; and still close to Marisa, who had offered me innocent joy and could really have been my younger sister if things had not turned out the way they had.

I did not know who to blame most: Alan, who forced upon me something I could not accept, or myself for not wanting to accept something which I might (at least temporarily, through gritted teeth) have been able to. For some time I toyed with the thought of waiting until I was sure that Alan was not at home and then ringing the bell and asking Marisa to open the cellar in which her father had locked my paintings. But then it seemed like too great a risk. No, that part of my life was irrevocably behind me. I slunk off to the Underground and returned to Earls Court, to the house full of strangers and loners, my new home.

29.

The next day I popped to the Art Shop on Kensington High Street and bought some canvases, drawing paper, chalk, brushes and oil paints in small glass jars. I realised that nostalgia would not get me far and that I needed to start again as soon as possible – the only other alternative was slow decay. When I emerged from the Underground onto the street I saw that there was a thunderstorm: fat raindrops were bouncing off the pavement, there was rumbling overhead and I thought that at any moment hailstones would be pounding on the roofs of the cars.

But the downpour diminished and the city unwound like a snake and slithered onwards. I ran round the corner and across a small park towards home. From a distance, I could see a young woman sitting on the steps. When I reached her I saw that she was soaking wet: her long black hair hung in bedraggled strands on her shoulders, her white shirt was stuck to her skin and her light blue jeans were dark with moisture. The drops of water even seemed to be running down her cheeks, until she raised her deep dark eyes towards me and I saw that she was crying.

"Have you got a key?" she asked, her tone almost suggesting that she really wanted to say "What took you so long?" I could not tell from her accent where she was from, but her smooth olive skin and well-rounded figure suggested the Mediterranean, perhaps Greece or Sicily.

Why didn't you ring the bell? I asked. Mrs. O'Riley would have let you in.

"No, because she's just gone off somewhere. She's never there when you need her. And of course today would be the day I lose my key."

But someone would have let you in, I persisted.

"Are you stupid, or what?" she said. "It's all men here, what if I got someone who just wanted to get me into their room?"

Aren't I a man? I asked. Or can you tell from just looking at me that I pose no threat?

"You?" she said, evaluating me. "You don't look at all dangerous."

Well thanks, I replied. If I wanted to return the insult, I'd say you weren't the kind of girl to make me dangerous.

"Yes, go on and insult me," she said. "The whole world insults me, why should you be left out?"

I unlocked the door and stood aside to let her into the dark hallway. She was so wet that water was dripping off her. And what now? I asked. You probably lost your room key as well, didn't you?

"Yes, it was on the same key ring. I don't know what I'll do now. Do you have any suggestions?"

I wanted to say: you'll catch cold, you need to get out of your wet clothes and dry yourself with a towel, but she probably would have got the wrong message, so I simply shrugged.

"Just what I expected," she said. "I guess I'll just have to wait here until Mrs. O'Riley comes back."

That could be a long time, I said, you'll catch cold.

"And why do you care?" she said reproachfully. "It wouldn't matter to you if I caught pneumonia and died. In any case, that would probably be the best solution for me."

Oh dear, I sighed to myself, then said out loud: I don't have much time. If you want, you can dry off and get changed in my room; you can put on the coat I wear for painting. If not, the only other option is to wait here. Unless you want me to break down your door. Where's your room?

"There," she pointed down the narrow corridor. "Past the stairs. What about you?"

231

Right at the top, I said. I can get through my window onto the roof. There's a wonderful view.

"Especially now, when it's raining."

It's stopped, I replied.

She considered for a moment and then she said: "If you swear that you don't see me as the type of woman that you will jump on as soon as I step through the door, but only a fellow human being in distress who needs your help, then… maybe."

From where do you get the idea that I see you as a woman? I asked. Don't be silly. In fact, your figure is more of a man's. No offence, but I just want to show that you're safe with me.

"I'm not offended," she said. "No. As a matter of fact, I am."

Her hand suddenly flew through the air and landed on my cheek. I turned and went up the stairs. I reflected that in my life so far I had received only three slaps across the face: the first from my father when I was young and rolled a barrel of wine into the cess pit, the second from Sandrina on the Channel ferry and the third one now. Did they have anything in common, could any pattern be discerned? I could not see one: from three slaps it is hard to draw a map of one's destiny. But I got a brilliant idea for a painting entitled *Three Slaps*.

As I reached the last flight of stairs I saw that the soaking wet Mediterranean girl was following me; perhaps she had decided that one blow was not enough. I speeded up to reach my room as quickly as possible, but before I managed to find my key she had caught up with me and was standing right behind me.

What? I said, instinctively shielding my face with my elbow.

"You said I could dry off in your room."

I unlocked the door and invited her in.

"Oh," she said in surprise, "I didn't think that any room could be smaller than mine."

Big dreams are at home in small rooms, I said just to pass the time, but she liked the statement so much that she cried out: "You should write that down, so you don't forget it. Are you a poet?"

I'm a painter, I said. If you like, I can paint you changing your clothes.

"Just you try it!" she replied. "A pity you're not a poet, you could have recited one of your poems while I got changed. I like poetry."

I can recite some lines of Matthew Arnold, I said. Do you know him?

"No," she said, "I only know Hafiz and Omar Khayam. What have you got that I can put on?"

Just this, I said, offering my stained painter's coat.

"Oh my God," she said in disgust, "everything of yours is so dirty. And that thing is too small for me anyway."

No it's not, I insisted.

"Of course it is, you're smaller than me."

I'm not smaller than you.

"Look, I'm half a head taller. How tall are you?"

Five foot eleven, I stubbornly persisted.

"Let's say you are," she conceded. "I'm five foot ten, which means you're bigger than me, even though you only come up to my eyes. Evidently where you come from they have different tape measures."

You're too tall, I said, too tall for a woman.

"For a woman, perhaps, but not for a queen."

Oh, I didn't know you were a queen, my apologies. What is your name, your majesty?

"Cleopatra," she replied, rising to her full height. "Queen of Egypt, so you know who you're dealing with. But you can call me Cleo."

Very kind of you, I said. Not long ago I painted one of your lovers, Julius Caesar. I didn't know then that we would meet.

"I don't know what you're on about," she said "and I'm starting to get cold, so give me a towel, a clean one, and turn your back."

I didn't have a clean towel, but one of the two I owned was slightly less dirty and it was in my suitcase, so my assurance that it was clean did not sound like a lie.

"I hope that I won't catch anything," she said, shifting the towel from one hand to another as if unable to decide. "You men suffer from all sorts of horrible things."

Including rude women, I replied, a little angrily, what have you got against men?

"Nothing that any other woman wouldn't have against them," she said. "Now turn round and look out the window until I tell you that it's okay."

Okay, I said, in the mean time I'll read to you from Matthew Arnold so that you don't get bored. And I reached for the book.

"Read whatever you want," she said, "but if you take even a peek at me out of the corner of your eye, you will feel the wrath of an Egyptian Fury."

Are you really from Egypt? I asked. An Arab? A Muslim?

"What's so strange about that?" she asked in surprise. "Are you racist or religiously intolerant, or both?"

Neither, I said, I think it's great that you are a Muslim and an Arab and an Egyptian; I've never met one before.

"There are plenty of us," she sighed. "Well over fifty million."

But not like you, I said. I'm sure you're something special.

"I think so, too. Thank you for noticing. But don't think that gives you any special rights. Now please turn your back and read me those poems."

I did as she said. She did not know that in the mirror on the shelf in the corner I could see almost everything that was happening in the room behind me and that I was able to watch her undressing, drying herself with the towel and then putting on my painter's coat. I pretended that my eyes were on the text, but in fact I knew the poem by heart.

I must not say that she was true, / Yet let me say that she was fair; / And they, that lovely face who view, / They should not ask if truth be there.

"Go on," she said, "It sounds nice."

I had never liked voluptuous, well-rounded women, I had always been attracted by light, slender gazelles such as Sandrina, but what I saw in the mirror did not disappoint me; she really did look like a queen and her breasts looked as if they could nourish twenty hungry babies; her hips looked strong enough to fell a tree.

"Why aren't you reading?" she asked.

I turned some pages, pretending to be looking for some suitable lines and then, my eyes still on the mirror, I continued. *Truth – what is truth? Two bleeding hearts/Wounded by men, by fortune tried/ Outwearied with their lonely parts/Vow to beat henceforth side by side.*

"I can't believe it," she said. "A strange boy is reading love poems to me and I'm undressing. But you can turn round now."

In my painter's coat, which she tightened round the waist, she looked even more seductive than when she was naked. When she raised her arms and started to dry her wet hair, the lower edge of the coat lifted just enough above her knee that the lower part of her thigh was visible and, as often before, I reflected that, rather than nakedness, it was this kind of revealing that was erotic – teasing the imagination, which is happiest when it can fill in the missing parts of the whole.

You know what, Cleo, I said, if you really are Cleo, you should pose for me some time for a picture of Cleopatra, the real one, who you could well be very similar to. I'll paint you with a crown on your head.

"You can forget that," she said. "In Islam portraying the human figure is forbidden. Why don't you make me some tea and tell me about yourself?"

30.

And so in the house of lonely people I no longer felt so alone; Cleo became my friend. "Just don't touch me," she warned at the beginning, "and everything will be alright. And don't talk too much, I don't like men who want me to be their mother, I prefer those who listen."

In spite of that, in the first few days I told her all about my life, my childhood, the anguish of my first love, my goals, Sandrina, and everything that had happened to me in England – about Jimmy, even about the incident which led me to jump down onto the railway lines and the strange set of circumstances that meant I was unable to show a single one of my paintings.

"You really are a fool," she said, "someone should look after you."

She told me a lot less about herself and what she did tell me I was not sure whether I should believe. Her parents wanted to force her into marriage with one of her distant cousins, but she had resisted because "he stank of garlic and was as hairy as an ape". Her father, quite a sophisticated dealer in precious stones, did not want to punish her by banishing her from the family; instead of that, he had given her enough money for four months in London on condition that she look for a respectable and wealthy husband.

And she was looking, "if possible, for an aristocrat, or at least someone upper class". She was placing ads in different magazines and meeting up with the men who wrote to her, but they were "all the same, they only wanted one thing," they did not want to accept that a Muslim girl must enter marriage as a virgin, otherwise she would be rejected by her husband. Men were a strange bunch – even those who gave the initial impression that they were different turned out to be regular bastards. She was feeling ever more inclined to stop placing ads, since it seemed she was unlikely to find the right one that way – if such a person even existed.

On the other hand, she was not sure what to do, for without a bridegroom who would meet her father's high standards she could not think about returning to Alexandria. At the same time, he had to satisfy her criteria: at the very least, he had to be gentle, friendly, clever, educated, handsome, funny, generous, innocent, sincere, faithful – in short, the type of man for which most women would circumnavigate the globe on their knees.

He must also be a good lover, I said, but how will you know, if he isn't allowed to touch you before the wedding?

"Don't provoke me, or I'll give you a slap" she said. "I'll know how to tell, we women are not stupid."

And how rich does he have to be to make it onto the shortlist? I asked

"Are you thinking of yourself?" she laughed. "If you came for me in a Rolls Royce, gave me a diamond ring worth a hundred thousand pounds, took me to a house with at least twenty rooms and as many servants, gave me a horse that was a regular winner at Royal Ascot, then maybe I might be willing to check out the other qualities that I mentioned. Until, of course, I came up against the first real flaw, which would happen with you on the first day. And then any amount of riches would not help you."

Don't I remind you of your fellow countryman Omar Sharif?

"You?" she burst out laughing. "Yeah, you could be twins."

Don't you have the feeling you are expecting too much, I asked, considering what you have to offer in return?

"What more could anyone ask for?" she said in an offended tone. "Whoever gets my love will have everything. I'm a queen, would that not be enough for you?"

You know what, Cleo, I said, you are like a modern female Don Quixote, you've read too many women's novels, you mistake fantasy for reality and now you've prepared the ground for a great disappoint-ment. And you're going about the whole thing in the wrong way: for-get about ads, go out among people, to parties, to exhibitions, horse races, to the theatre, where you might meet at least the shadow of the man you're looking for. And unmarried? And willing to become a Muslim? My God, doesn't your project seem even more unrealistic than my desire to become a world famous painter in less than a year?

"You just have to believe and it will all come true," she chided me. "Your problem is that you don't believe in yourself. That's why you keep running away. Destiny has already plotted your road to success, but you are avoiding it, you want to outsmart it. And me. And if you're so clever, help me, take me out, to exhibitions, parties; introduce me to men that you think might like to marry me."

Okay, I said. But not in that baggy shirt and jeans – you're not looking for a hippy. Dress so that they are struck dumb when they see you.

"I will," she said with an impatient wave of the hand. "You sort yourself out if you want to accompany me. Look how you're dressed: I can't believe how neglected you are."

I am an artist, I said. I'm not looking for a husband who earns as much as the Duke of Westminster. I'm past the phase of paying much attention to what I wear. Now I wear jeans, a creased shirt and scuffed shoes, which is more suitable for what I want to be.

"Okay," she said. "Then tell me what to wear."

In her room, where she invited me only five days after our first meeting, she had nothing that would attract the attention of the afflu-ent, except for a tight white t-shirt and black mini-skirt. "That's the last thing I'd dare to put on," she said, "my father would kill me and Allah punish me."

So why do you buy such things, I asked. "How stupid you are for an artist. Do you never dream? Maybe one day I'll be brave enough, or someone will persuade me that it is not a sin to dress like that. Wouldn't it be terrible if at that moment I didn't have those things to put on? It's good to be ready for anything."

Part of this preparedness was obviously also the ten pairs of shoes beneath the bed, from leather moccasins to sandals to stilettos.

Listen, Cleo, don't you think you could do with more shoes?

"Ten pairs is the most that a prudent woman can afford," she explained, as if she had not discerned the irony in my voice. "It's enough for now and when I find a husband he will decide how many pairs of shoes a day he wants to give me."

We soon established that she had nothing suitable in her modest wardrobe, so I suggested that we go into town and buy her something. *I* shall buy you a dress, I said. Not long ago I earned a little with my painting. My treat.

"Oh," she said, brightening, "maybe you're not as useless as I thought. But don't think that you'll get anything in return," she warned me. "In any case, you're not interested in me: there's only one woman for you, the one from the ferry, whatever her name is, although you'll probably never see her again."

You're not jealous, are you Cleo? I teased.

"Me? Who of?"

We visited all the expensive shops in London – Harrods, Selfridges, Fortnum & Mason, Harvey Nichols – as well as more than twenty exclusive boutiques where the prices really shocked me. But there was no risk of me going bankrupt because the Queen of Egypt could not make up her mind, everything was either too tight or too loose, too short or too long, or the wrong colour – everything was made for "skinny dwarves" and even XL was too small for her.

You're not a normal woman, I said, you're a giant. Accept that you are not built for ladies wear. There must be a shop for big women, Mrs. Big, like Mr. Big for men; that's probably the only place you'll find something suitable.

"If we weren't standing in the middle of Oxford Street," she said, "I'd punch you on the nose. You keep insulting me. I am what I am, should I have myself reduced or what? There's nothing wrong with me, most men are too small and those that aren't are either ugly or stupid or poor or coarse or weird or obsessive or sometimes all those at once. Don't worry, I'll find the right one."

You will, Cleo, you will, I said, but I can't devote as much time to this project as you because I have my own and I must start painting.

"Go on, then," she said with a pout. "There's no need for you to waste your time with a stupid Arab woman. You just go, I mean what are friends for – to leave each other alone, aren't they?"

Oh, Cleo, I said, you are one of the most difficult women I've ever met.

"I know," she murmured. "I'm surprised you haven't shaken me off. Why haven't you?"

Because, I said, you know how to make a man feel so guilty that he'll do almost anything for you.

"I don't want just anything," she began to cry in the middle of the street. "I just want you to help me find a husband."

Of course, it didn't work out, this search for a handsome millionaire with a longing for a female Arab weight lifter; wherever these rare creatures where, when we looked for them they were conspicuous by their absence. They did not go to the cinema, or the theatre, or to obscure little exhibitions, or classical concerts, or the zoo, or for walks in the park. And if we happened to spot someone that might fit the bill, we never found a way to approach him in a non-intrusive manner, as such types always seemed to be in a hurry.

You know, Cleo, I said, they all think that I'm your boyfriend, so it's better that you go around on your own; I wouldn't approach a woman who had a dangerous-looking bodyguard with her.

"You?" she laughed. "You wouldn't even frighten a cat."

In any case I have to start painting, I added. I'm a painter, as you probably noticed.

"No, I haven't," she said, "although it's true that you're always going on about it. Your painting has something in common with the man I'm looking for."

The following few days, perhaps the whole week or even more, we did not see as much of each other. I finally started to daub a bit and she returned to grading the replies she got to her ads and to meeting with the men who got most points and seemed the most interesting (and safest) at least for a coffee or (occasionally) dinner.

Whenever anything interesting happened she came and told me about it. Usually this was late evening and we went on the roof, lay on a large blanket that I had spread out on the tiles and, watching the stars and the twinkling London lights, talked long into the night, sometimes even to dawn. Occasionally she appeared in the afternoon with a small plastic bag of dates that she kept chewing on ("I need something sweet in my mouth in this bitter world.") as she stared at my paintings, small canvases that were drying wherever I could find space for them, shaking her head and tut-tutting.

"You really are a Silly Billy, why are you painting London roofs, isn't it enough that you can see them through the window? And they're all twisted and your houses look as if they're about to collapse at any moment. Why didn't you go to some kind of art school before you started painting?"

Thanks, Cleo. Why don't you want to pose for me, I wouldn't paint you twisted, I'd paint you knobbly and rounded.

"Pose yourself, you poser, and stop insulting me because I'm deaf to your comments," she said, sticking out her tongue.

We often also climbed on the roof during the day to enjoy the view while she told me about various Johns and Marks and Trevors that she had met, the stupid things they had said, and increasingly often we recited together Matthew Arnold's poetry, which fascinated her more and more, especially the love poems, and she learned quite a few of them by heart. And it wasn't long before she added Arnold to the exam that her suitors had to pass; to each of them she recited some lines and if they guessed who it was they got three points.

Cleo, I said, you clearly enjoy this game. In reality, you're not looking for a husband, but you like toying with men, leading them on, while you have a good time, for they certainly take you to some fancy restaurants and bring you expensive presents...

"Really?" she interrupted me. "Have you seen anything in my room that looks like an expensive present?"

Maybe you've got another rented room somewhere, I said, where you stick all your trophies. Maybe you're just waiting until there's enough and then you'll open a gift shop.

"You're an idiot," she said bad-temperedly, but the next minute she smiled: "Now and then you do surprise me with a good idea, although I'm not thinking of becoming a shopkeeper. I'll keep waiting for my prince, he's sure to come eventually. Maybe I should post more ads."

241

Or relax the criteria, I suggested.

"Why would I do that?" she asked. "Why do *you* keep dreaming of the ideal woman, who you met only once and then so fleetingly that you don't really know her, and remain faithful to her, although you know all too well that you'll never meet her again? And if you do and it turns out that she is stupid, boring, wicked, selfish, what then?"

That can't happen, I said. You don't understand: I'm looking for something that I already know, that I experienced; you're looking for a combination of your projections. I'm looking for something that exists, here, in this city; you're looking for something that you won't find anywhere on Earth. If you really wanted to find a husband you would have done so long ago, and even probably one that satisfied your choosy father's criteria. But no, you don't want to. You enjoy acting as bait, and when you flee you enjoy them chasing you and making fools of themselves. Your father should put you across his knee and spank you."

"You try it, if you dare," she said. "If not, there's something you can tell me. What does *fellatio* mean?"

Hang on, I said in surprise; why are you teasing me?

"I'd like to know," she said stubbornly. "Okay, I'll ask someone else."

Not a good idea, I said. Why don't you look in a dictionary?

"Because I don't have one," she said. "Why would I bring an English dictionary to London? I speak English, I went to the best private school in Alexandria, and that isn't even an English word."

Why do you want to know what it means?

"Because quite a few men I've met up with have mentioned it and I didn't want to give the impression that I wasn't a sophisticated modern woman. I had to pretend I knew what it meant."

My God, how did it come about that they were even using that word?

"Almost half of them sooner or later get round to trying to persuade me to do the bad things that men do with women. I of course tell them that it's out of the question – because of my religion and my culture I have to be a virgin when I marry. And then they say: what about

242

fellatio, that won't affect your virginity, isn't that a possibility, it's no big deal. And I say: no, it's not such a big deal, maybe. Or something like that. And then they say: right, my place or yours – you know, like in that film we saw. And I say: my place is very small. And they say: and mine is very big, but don't be afraid. And so on. It's very embarrassing because I don't know what we're talking about."

So how do you manage to get out of it, I asked, because you obviously haven't done it with any of them otherwise you'd know what it means.

"I say I'm suddenly not feeling well, let's wait until next time. I always leave with a guilty feeling that I'm not generous enough to these gentlemen when some of them are very generous to me. And although I really must keep my virginity for the right one, perhaps a bit of fellatio, if it's not such a big deal, would be worth considering. Last time, for instance, I met this Lord – a bit old, but so refined and polite and elegant that I was really unhappy that I couldn't oblige him. He said: a slow, gentle bit of fellatio would please me immensely. And I, like a fool, could only say: no problem, but not today, because it's my birthday and that's the only day of the year when fellatio is out of the question."

I couldn't help laughing out loud and I'm sure the whole of London could have heard me.

"What?" she asked innocently. "Did I say something funny?"

No, Cleo, actually something sad; now it's clear to me what kind of men you are meeting. Public school, military service, horses, country house, stiff upper lip, the most notorious kind of English gentlemen, wankers, all of them, into rubber and other kinky stuff, but they use fancy foreign words instead of simple Anglo-Saxon ones. Cleo, you need protecting.

"Exactly," she said, "that's why I need to know what the word means. Otherwise I'll lose all credibility. Already some of them refuse to believe that I'm from a wealthy Egyptian family. It would be nice if you taught me this fellatio, so that I wouldn't keep making a fool of myself."

Wait a second, I said and crawled to my room for the Chambers Dictionary. When I got back, I opened it at the relevant page and put

243

in in her lap. First read that and then tell me if you want me to teach you.

"*Fellatio*," she read out loud. "*A sexual activity in which the penis is stimulated by the partner's mouth. To perform fellatio on somebody.*" She closed the heavy dictionary and put it down.

Well, I asked. Does it still seem like no big deal?

"It isn't," she said coolly, "because my virginity would stay completely intact. But I don't know if you're the right person to teach me."

Of course I'm not, I said. We've had too many nice times together to spoil our friendship with something like that.

"Are you saying that fellatio isn't nice, that it's unpleasant?"

Oh, Cleo, I sighed, I didn't say that. I'm talking about my specific experience – I told you what happened to me. Come on, let's forget about it, you can't be serious, you're surely not going to go around sucking the cocks of depraved rich guys!

"On the other hand, it's probably safer if a friend teaches you. At least he wouldn't be exploiting you for his own pleasure."

No, he would suffer, I said. He'd suffer because fellatio is just foreplay that inevitably leads to copulation, if you know what that means, and of that you would happily deprive him.

"If he was a real friend, he'd understand and it wouldn't bother him," she replied, as if talking to herself.

Oh, Cleo, please, go away, I said. Go and read your suitors' letters and the next time one of them mentions fellatio, give him a good kick in the shins beneath the table.

"I know what the problem is," she said. "You don't want to betray your muse. She means more to you than I do. I'll find someone else to teach me." She rolled onto her knees and started to crawl backwards towards the ledge below the roof. "There's this American guy on the second floor who'll be interested."

Cleo, I called. She slipped down off the ledge, crawled through the window, unlocked the door and left. I hurried after her but at the door I stopped. No, I said to myself, I must paint! I must paint!

I locked the door and grabbed a brush.

But the very next moment I put it down again and rushed downstairs. I knocked on her door. Cleo, I called quietly, so as not to disturb the other occupants, let me in, there's something I want to tell you. For a long time there was no reply and I thought that perhaps she wasn't even in the room – maybe she'd gone into town. Then I heard her voice.

"You're an idiot, Silly Billy," she said. "You simply don't understand women. Go and paint roofs, they are less complicated."

Cleo, I said, open the door.

"Go away," she said in a weary voice, "our song has been sung."

Cleo, I persisted, don't talk nonsense, you know we've gone through too much to end things just like that.

"Ah, harsh flatterer!" she shouted, *"let alone my beauty! I, like thee, have left my youth afar. Take my hand, and touch these wasted fingers – See my cheek and lips, how white they are!"*

31.

The next morning I knocked on her door again, but there was no answer. Until midday, I sat on the stairs, wandered up and down the pavement in front of the house, or waited in the hallway so as not to miss her if she came out of her room or returned from where she had gone. In between, every now and then, I knocked on her door. Cleo, I shouted, let me explain, you misunderstood me. Several times one of the other doors opened and hostile eyes glared at me: "Cut it out," came the warning, before the door slammed and the key turned in the lock.

Towards evening, Mrs. O'Riley knocked on my door for the first time. "Listen, sonny," she said, blowing cigarette smoke into my room. "I'm getting complaints that you're harassing one of the residents on the ground floor. I don't know where you're from and I don't really care, but in this country that is a criminal offence. You stop it, or I'll be forced to call the police." She exhaled once more, straight in my face and parted with a toothless smile that said: Got you, didn't I?!

I could not summon the strength to carry on painting, so I climbed onto the roof and spent some time staring over the edge at the pavement down below in the hope that sooner or later I would see Cleo returning from town. But there was no sign of her. It was as if she had vanished from the face of the Earth.

What are you playing at? piped up Willy II, who I hadn't heard from for a long time. Every day you have less money, every day you're further from your goal, every day you care less about the future, and now you'll waste time on a silly Arab girl who has no idea what she wants and who would consume you like a praying mantis if you let yourself get close enough. She's unhappy, objected Willy I feebly, unhappy precisely because she doesn't know what she wants, because she's caught between two cultures. Someone has to steer her in the right direction, help her differentiate between what's real and what isn't. And how to give blow jobs, sniggered Willy II, as if she didn't know how to do that already – can you really not see how cunning she is? And as for differentiating between what's real and what isn't, you're the ideal teacher – talk about the blind leading the blind!

Shut up, replied Willy I. There are things that you know nothing about, matters of the heart and human needs, which can't always be directed like traffic. But you don't direct anything, said Willy II excitedly. You'll end up in jail or on the street or back home with no future, and all because of your uncontrolled sentimentality. Look at your "studio": what a joke, no room to swing a cat, with a few paintings that you couldn't even sell at the Sunday amateur art market on Bayswater Road. Meanwhile, your real pictures are being sold by others.

I can't help it if people take advantage of me, said Willy I, that's just my fate, so I don't want anyone taking advantage of Cleo on account of her naivety; she's got no idea of the risks she is running. Oh, laughed Willy II, I'm sure she can look after herself. And you are left feeling responsible for a fantasist who doesn't even want to open the door to you because she has realised what a waste of space you are. What is it with you? Go into town and look at the galleries, be among people who can help you, make some contacts, sort yourself out – that's your duty, not helping women who are quite capable of looking after themselves.

But I like her, said Willy I. She's good fun and, in spite of her arrogance, pretty helpless. And deep in her heart she's so pure.

And what about Sandrina? said Willy II. Is it the end of ideal love? That's something else, replied Willy I. Sandrina is like the sky above me, she is always there; Cleo is like a change of seasons, like

247

the spring that arrives and makes everything warmer and fresher, including the sky. Wonderful metaphor, sneered Willy II. Now that you can no longer paint maybe you could become a poet. Go to hell, responded Willy I.

We're both heading there, said Willy II and fell silent.

I spent the next few days lying idly on the roof. Whenever it got too hot I clambered back into the room. I stared at my latest painterly products, wondering why I seemed to have got stuck, looking for ways out of my fix, making plans and immediately rejecting them, pacing to and fro like an animal in a cage, waiting, as so often in my life, for something to happen, anything that would shatter this feeling of being trapped and push me forward.

The neighbouring room, which had hitherto been occupied by two quiet, considerate and almost invisible shaven-headed men, obviously gay, received a new occupant. He was much noisier, forever clattering about the room, banging into furniture, throwing things on the floor, arguing with someone – probably himself – sometimes crying or howling like a wolf, speaking in two different voices as if learning by heart a play for two actors, then there was nothing for quite some time except the sound of a typewriter, then wild cries, among which I could make out "Fuck!", "Shit!", "Merde!" and similar expressions of dissatisfaction with the world and himself.

I often also heard a woman's voice, usually late afternoon or at night; not always the same one, although they all shared a kind of respectful caution, as if they knew they were visiting someone who could at any moment do something unpredictable. And he usually did speak to them in a kind of domineering, explanatory tone, while he was the only one who said much – the women hardly got a word in edgeways. Once there was a woman there who spent the whole time laughing stupidly and another time one who cried non-stop. Although I put my ear to the wall I was never able to discern enough individual words to be able to work out what they were talking about. Just once, when one of the visitors was leaving, did I hear what she said, but that was after she had closed the door behind her and was making for the stairs. "I'm not coming to this filthy hole again," she called through the door, "if you want to see me, you'll have to come to my place."

248

I didn't know why these women were coming to him, since I only heard the muffled sounds of love-making a couple of times, and perhaps both times with the same woman. I was really interested what my new neighbour looked like; I had already been at his door once to ask him if I could borrow some sugar, but at the last moment I thought better of it. The next morning I ran into him in the bathroom, which he hadn't locked; he was squatting in the dirty bath, spraying water on his head with the shower attachment and half murmuring, half singing a Russian folk song. Actually, I saw only his hunched skinny body, his bearded and long-haired head, half turned to the wall, and a large hand with bony fingers, a real paw, waving the shower fitting around; the next moment I closed the door and withdrew.

I waited until I heard him emerge from the bathroom and return to his room. But no sooner had I entered the bathroom and bolted the door, than I heard him rattling the handle and shouting: "Hang on a second, I forgot something, open the damned door, what kind of house is this where a man can't even shower in peace?"

His thick accent was distinctly Russian and when I opened the door and saw him I got quite a fright: my first thought was that Rasputin was standing in front of me. He was well over six foot tall, his long black hair hung in wet strands on his shoulders, his face was almost completely concealed by his beard, which was chestnut brown, his piercing eyes were dark and he had a large wart on his nose which only increased the distinctiveness of his appearance. He was also built in a strange way: his left shoulder seemed to stick up and his right shoulder to lean downwards, his left arm was longer than his right and his legs were noticeably twisted outwards at the knee.

"What are you looking at?" he asked. "Never seen a man before?"

Then he suddenly offered his hand: "Aleksej Ivanovič Solouhin. My English friends call me Dostoyevsky."

Why, I asked, as my hand disappeared into his bear-like paw.

"Because it's easier to pronounce and because I'm a writer."

Interesting, I said, I'm a painter.

"A painter from where?" he demanded.

Slovenia, I said, convinced he wouldn't have the slightest idea where that was. "Slavic brother," he muttered. "That's all I need.

But you Slovenes are something special; as far as I know you are the only European nation that never had its own nobility. That's evident from you – a complete lack of manners, you still haven't told me your name."

Vili Vaupotič, I said.

"Poor you," he laughed. "What problems you must have in this country where they can't even pronounce Maskva – they all keep saying Moscow. What do they call you? Willy? Wow Potty! You won't get far with a name like that. In fact, I see you haven't, otherwise you wouldn't be living in this luxurious residence."

The same goes for you, I said.

His eyes darkened, he reached over my shoulder and took the towel he had forgotten from the hook in the wall. "We'll talk about that some other time," he said and with long swaying strides headed back towards the open door of his room, which he slammed behind him.

I kind of hoped that I would never see him again, but as soon as I had showered and returned to my room, he knocked on my door, opened it and came in.

"Willy Wow Potty," he said in surprise, "your studio is not as big as I expected. Are those your paintings?" he gazed sceptically at the canvases that were leaning everywhere where there was something to lean against.

No, they're not, I said quickly, starting to turn them towards the wall, those are old cheap canvases that I got almost for free in a junk shop – didn't you know it's best to paint on top of existing paintings by amateurs?

"There are many things I don't know," he said, "including why these paintings are so similar to the panorama of London I can see through the window. Do you think that by some strange coincidence the unknown amateur painted precisely in this room?"

The panorama of London is pretty much the same everywhere, I said, trying not to blush.

"Where is one of yours?" he asked, looking about the room.

I currently don't have any, because I sell them as I go along, I said, but I've been having a creative crisis for some time now.

"You too?" he was almost pleased. "Two artists in crisis, and neighbours; a significant coincidence, don't you think? Why are you in crisis?"

It's a long story, I said.

"Tell me, I like stories."

Some other time, I said, trying to get rid of him.

"I've got a proposition for you," he said. "You're obviously suffering here. You can't work. You must move in with me. My room is more than twice the size, you could set up an easel, like a real painter. There are two beds, we could divide the rent, which would be good for both of us since neither of us is exactly rolling in it."

His offer was so unexpected that I could hardly keep from laughing. Why would I want to share with someone who I had only just met?

It's out of the question, I said. I like my privacy. Besides which I have the whole roof, I pointed through the window.

"Roof?" He pushed past me to the window and looked upwards. He put one leg over the window sill, dragged the other leg behind him and with two more steps he was already on the roof. I wasn't at all pleased that he was acting as if my room was his; I decided to ignore him. But this wasn't easy, since he was walking up and down on the roof in his leather boots, looking around and saying admiringly: "If this isn't a room with a view, I'm the wart on my nose, not the greatest Russian writer of the 20th century. Willy Wow, do you know what you have here? I could write here, my writing would flow like wine. Shall we swap rooms?"

No, I said, I need that roof, I'd fall ill without it.

"Of course you need it," he continued, "you have a blanket laid out, you probably bring girls here, where you can make love naked in the centre of London in the middle of the day and no one can see you – it's crazy. I must put it in the novel I'm writing. Where are you hiding? Come on up."

I lost any hope of getting rid of him soon, so I crawled after him. He was sitting calmly on my blanket, rolling a cigarette.

"Sit down, Willy Wow, we'll smoke a pipe of peace, like brothers, and then we'll tell each other everything that's bothering us.

Something tells me that yours is an interesting story, that you're in a shitty situation, that you don't have many friends, that one might come in handy – and that's true for me, too. Sit down, you're blocking the sun."

Amazed at my own obedience, I sat beside him on the rooftop.

"Don't you want to sit with me on the blanket?" he asked, as if it was his. "Are you afraid of Solouhin? Dear Willy Wow, you've no idea who you have met. This blanket could become a magic carpet on which we fly towards the realisation of all our dreams. But first we shall loosen our imaginations and relax our brains. Here, have a drag," he offered me a joint.

I don't smoke, I said.

"The best hashish in the world," he said, his eyes drilling into me, "you're not going to reject something for which I gave half the money from my last story."

I don't smoke, I repeated.

"Right," he said, taking a deep drag, "I won't call you Willy Wow any more but Willy Potty. The whole world smokes. What century is it in Slovenia? Would you rather try LSD?"

I don't want you to call me Willy Wow or Willy Potty, I said, I want you to call me Vili.

"If you share this joint with me," he said. "Let it be the start of our friendship."

Who's talking about friendship, I wanted to say, we don't even know each other, but his self-confident forcefulness disarmed me, as if I had been hypnotised by the gleam in his eye. Of its own accord, my hand reached out and took the joint.

It's not the first time I've smoked, I said.

"I'm glad to hear that. It would be difficult to be friends with a weirdo."

32.

We stayed on the roof until the sun had passed its zenith and began to shine on us, when it became too hot. During this time we had smoked three joints and my head felt somehow full of air and light; I was afraid that the slightest breath of wind would blow me away. Meanwhile Solouhin talked without interruption, telling me so many details of his life that by the end I wasn't sure whether I was dreaming or listening to a summary of some barely credible adventure story.

He had been one of the best students at Moscow University and at twenty-three had published a novel that had sold a hundred million copies; he had become the most promising name in new Russian literature. Then a collection of his satirical poems about Khrushchev had appeared in *samizdat* and he had ended up in one of the notorious Siberian gulags, where he had to cut stone ten hours a day. His novel was removed from every library and bookshop, and placed on the list of banned books; anyone who kept a copy risked a year in jail. Thanks to riots and his rebellious behaviour in the gulag he was being transferred to a punishment camp in Novaja Zemlya, where he would have to work processing seal blubber in sub-zero temperatures. During the boat ride to the island he was just enjoying his ten minutes of "fresh air" on the deck when a Norwegian cruise boat went past – so close that he could wave to the officers on the bridge. With no thought of the possible consequences, he hurled himself over the side into the freezing sea; before the guard could trigger the alarm and the prison boat could stop, the Norwegians had already lowered a boat, pulled him from the water and taken him to the cruise ship.

From Norway he travelled to England, where he got temporary political asylum, without employment rights, but that didn't bother him since he had not the slightest intention of looking for work; he thought that he would soon become rich and famous as a writer. He began to learn English, attending a course, speaking from dawn till dusk with whoever he could find, preferably with strangers in Hyde Park and drunks in pubs; he read until four in the morning and learned to write in the new language as Conrad and Nabokov had done before him. He learned words from the dictionary by heart and began writing short stories, radio plays and dramas. He sent them around, but they all came back to him – some within a week, some two weeks, some in a month and some three months – but without exception they were either unread ("Thank you for thinking of us, but unfortunately this does not suit our requirements") or with comments that were polite, but for a writer who had sold a hundred million books in Russia immensely insulting ("The writing seems to be rather flabby, and the story line hardly credible; we do not publish beginners."). He had papered the walls and ceiling of his previous room with rejection letters. Welcome to the free world, here you can succeed like nowhere else.

References to his successful novel were no help, since he didn't have a single copy that he could show or translate; he tried to write it again from memory, but realised in time that what he was producing was merely a clumsy imitation, so he decided to write a new one. And that was what he was working on now. With it, he would conquer the world. In the meantime, things had shifted a little: he had sold a half-hour radio play to the BBC, although in order to accomplish that he had had to give the editor a blow job ("The BBC is a bastion of gays, Willy Wow, avoid those predators."), while an extremely stupid, amateurish story that he'd trotted out in two hours had appeared in an extremely stupid magazine for semi-literate women. That was the extent of his current literary success in London. But despondency was the last thing that Dostoyevsky had in mind: the greater the odds, the greater his determination to beat them. The novel he was writing now would trigger tectonic movements in the understanding of literature;

it would fly off the shelves and the critics would have to come up with new ways of expressing enthusiasm.

Of course, the English were not interested in anything that is not English or that does not have at least an English angle; publishers were petty traders who would not recognise a bestseller if it bit them on the nose; they didn't read anything themselves, but employed semi-literate readers, unpublished authors who were offered texts by other authors to give them at least some consolation for the fact that their own works would never get published.

That can't be true, I said.

"Listen, Willy Wow, do you know what they gave me at the BBC when they rejected my tenth play in a row? A stack of radio plays from all over the world to read and write a short review of. For each one they paid me two pounds. Can you imagine? Of course, I rejected every play as the utter delusion of a beginner."

That means that they see you as a semi-literate, unperformable author and are trying to console you, I said.

"Stop making fun of genius, Willy Potty," he tore the second joint from my hand, "and tell me something about yourself."

So I told him. Almost everything. About my plans, my arrival in England, Sandrina, what had happened to me, how I had lost all my pictures, about Jimmy and lastly about Cleo. He listened with great interest, even with strangely zealous attention.

When I had finished he sat up, took a deep breath and said: "My dear Willy, you have surprised me. While I'm writing my novel you have been living yours. Do I have your permission to include some of your experiences in my story? That's the same as you painting my portrait, which I hope you will do."

Be my guest, I said. It all seems pretty boring to me. I'm not exactly a classical hero.

"What are you talking about, what time are you living in – there are no classical heroes. But I'm also talking nonsense: you are interesting to me because of what you are, as if some centrifugal force had hurled you from the Zeitgeist and cast you many light years away into some world that is yours alone. In reality you are Willy Outsider, hero of our time, and you know why? Because you do not sense what is happening around you, what people are thinking, what interests them, what is in the air. Unusual, but beautiful, almost moving! I bet you don't go to rock concerts but alone, away from the noise of the world, listen to Mozart."

I nodded.

"But Willy," he said, "someone needs to look after you, the world is a wicked place, behind every corner lurks the Wolf waiting for Little Red Riding Hood. You must allow me to protect you. You are too precious as an artist to be left to the mercy of scavengers and to go forward as if your fate is of no consequence to me."

From his shirt pocket he pulled a notepad and pencil. "First we'll get your paintings back. Without them you are nothing, dear Willy. At every step you get asked *what are your references? No references? Sorry, but we don't deal with beginners*. Palisander, you said? Hotel *.o.el* near Victoria. Then the Lost Property Office at Paddington. Then Mrs. Henderson in Chiswick…"

No, I interrupted, not there. Those are not stolen, they were given.

"Okay," he said. "You know best. And the last theft of your paintings? Alan McClelland."

It's actually like this, I said, some were seized, some I forgot under my bed, some I left in Cornwall, some I left on the train, some I gave to Jimmy's mother, some stayed in the house that I fled from – none of them were actually stolen.

"Leave it to Dostoyevsky," he said, putting away the notepad. "The next thing. This Sandrina of yours would be an ideal model for a novel I'm writing about a clever woman in a world of stupid men. If she is really as you describe her, then she is very much like my heroine. Who currently has no name. So I see no reason why I shouldn't just call her Sandrina. At the beginning I thought of calling her just She, so that she remained archetypal. But Sandrina, that sounds very distinguished. And I'll change the beginning, so that She is travelling by ferry to Dover, She will meet a young painter from, I don't know, maybe Slovenia, why not, and that painter will fall in love with her at first sight as you did. She will become his muse, his ideal of pure femininity, while She is living a completely different life at the other end of London."

Will they ever meet? I asked.

"Perhaps. Or maybe not. Wait, the idea is still new, it came like a bolt out of the blue, give me a day or two before I tell you more. And while we wait for the development of imaginary events, we can devote ourselves to real women. And the most real is your Arab girl. My dear Willy, you made a big mistake. Why didn't you let her suck you off? Now she would be eating out of your hand, tidying up after you, cooking for you, you could send her for cigarettes, you could say jump and she would jump. You really don't understand women. But hardly any artist does, not to mention philosophers: since the days of Socrates, they have a tradition of marrying stupid women. You know, I'll act as a go-between. I'll go to her and ask discreetly what's bothering her, what she wants, what she expects from you."

No, I said, you're certainly not going to do that. She'd never forgive me if she found out that I had told you virtually everything.

"You really are Willy Potty, I won't tell her."

No, I said decisively. I'll write her a letter.

"And you know what she'll do?" he laughed. "She'll bring it back and stick it to your door unopened. I know her sort. Back home in Russia I brought together more than twenty couples, they called me a matchmaker, but if you don't trust me, okay."

It's not that, I said, I've decided to write her a letter to begin with, if I may.

"Go on then," he said, getting up. "I'm going to write my novel, I've already wasted half a day with you."

The exchange of letters with the Queen of Egypt was brief and to the point. In the first letter I wrote: "Cleo, stop sulking and give me at least five minutes, we're friends, we can't split up over something stupid." I stuck the letter between her door and the door frame; half an hour later I went to look and saw that it was no longer there. When two hours later I opened the door of my room and envelope fell to the floor; I thought it was her reply, but no, it was my letter, returned unopened, just as Dostoyevsky had predicted.

In the second letter I changed my tone: "My dear, unforgettable queen. Why are you being so cruel to your vassal who wants nothing more than to serve you faithfully to the end of his days? Allow me to become worthy of your love. Please, Cleo."

This letter, too, was returned in the same fashion; God knows when she brought it back and stuck it in the door. The same thing happened with the third letter in which I threatened to throw myself off the roof: did she really want the death of a friend on her conscience, someone who respected and might even love her?

It seemed to me strange that she had not opened a single envelope: how did she know they contained letters from me? After all, they could have been from anyone. I tried something else: on all three envelopes I wrote her full address and stuck stamps, then I put them with the letters on the shelf in the hall, where Mrs. O'Riley left the tenants' post. Cleo used to get a lot of post, every day at least five replies to her ads, it would be strange if she did not think that my envelopes contained something similar.

But the unbelievable happened: next morning I found all three letters in front of my door.

During this time I saw Dostoyevsky only once. We said hello on the stairs, he said he was in a mad rush and his interest in me seemed to have mysteriously diminished. But now I hammered on his door until he opened it, clearly angry, and rebuked me: "You know what, Willy Potty, if it was anyone else at my door now I would break their nose – you can't disturb a writer in the middle of his most fruitful work. What do you want?"

I can't tell you out here, I looked around, it's personal.

"Oh," he sighed. His great paw gripped my shoulder like a vice and dragged me inside. There were papers everywhere and I don't think I had ever seen greater disorder, but the room was spacious, almost three times as big as mine, and really was suitable for two.

"Sit somewhere," he said, "I won't apologise for the mess, you're an artist."

I told him about the letters, how Cleo had not even opened them, how she had returned them, how I couldn't understand why she wouldn't open them, since she couldn't know they were mine.

"Wow, Potty Willy," he gave an almost malicious laugh, "why didn't you listen to me? But now I'm too deep in work to act as a go-between for two lovers who do not want to admit that they're in love. Maybe next month."

I said I was asking for nothing more than that he take the letters to her and persuade her to open and read them and, if possible, to answer them. That was all.

He took a half-full sheet of paper from the typewriter on the desk and said: "listen to this. *I have always found the English a rather graceless people; the sort of people who would resent you for telling them they were graceless; and who would see no reason why they shouldn't resent you; and would fail to realise that by their reaction they were confirming the very charge for which they resented you.* Good, isn't it?"

Excellent, I said. Will you give her these letters? It won't take you more than five minutes.

"Oh, okay," he got up and took them from my hand. "Wait for me in your room."

He locked the door after him and started down the stairs. Then he suddenly turned and asked: "Which is her room?"

Number three, I said, just after the stairs.

I waited ten minutes, then half an hour, then an hour. When I finally heard his clumsy step I rushed into the corridor in the hope that he had an answer for me. But his hands were empty. What took you so long? I demanded.

"I tried to convince her to write back," he said, rolling his eyes. "A tough case. Otherwise, a woman who according to all the usual rules should be able to find the kind of husband she wants. And she asked you to teach her how to give blow jobs? Willy, you can be thoroughly disappointed in yourself. Anyway, she said that she may write tomorrow."

Without another word he went into his room, locking the door behind him.

The next morning around nine, I knocked on his door and asked him to go and check whether she had written anything yet.

"She has already brought a reply," he said, handing me a white envelope. "I had to swear not to open it."

259

Thanks, I snatched it from his hand and rushed back to my room. With trembling fingers I opened the envelope and pulled out the letter. It was short. "When you come for me in a Rolls Royce and invite me to a mansion in Primrose Hill or a nine-room flat in Mayfair, then you can knock on my door. Until then, I will see every attempt to reach me as harassment and I will report you to the police. The Queen of Egypt does not consort with beggars."

The words really did sound like hers, but the writing surprised me: letters clumsily leaning left and right as if drunk, each third letter bigger than the ones before – the writing of a child who does not have handwriting classes at school.

(So, "beggar", what will you do? asked Willy II.)

I climbed onto the roof, tore her letter into tiny pieces and threw them down onto Nevern Square at exactly the moment when Cleo came out of the house and headed along the street towards the Tube station. The scraps of paper were so small that they fluttered across the square, but some of them landed on the pavement where she was walking in one of her ten pairs of shoes; perhaps one of them caught in her hair, which was more luxuriant than ever before; she was wearing a tight dress that I did not even know she had, evidently on her way to meet some suitor that she was very keen to impress.

33.

I suddenly sensed a large shadow on my back. Fearful that someone was going to shove me off the roof, I turned and saw Dostoyevsky with a stupid grin on his face. "Willy, don't be Potty," he said, "lock your door, otherwise sooner or later you'll be left without money or documents in this house of thieves."

You frightened me, I managed to say, moving to the middle of the roof and sitting. Then I got up again to go and lock the door.

"I've already done it," he said, sitting beside me. "Isn't it normal for a neighbour to worry about your safety? What's happening with the Queen of Egypt?"

Nothing, I replied. End of comedy. I'll start painting again.

"Willy," his paw fell on my back with such force that I jumped, "that is music to my ears – if I wasn't tone deaf I would sing along. A wise decision. We can stage a joint parachute drop on the English cultural establishment."

I don't care about culture, I said, I'm a painter, I only portray my vision, which is often a thing of the moment.

"I agree with you, I too care nothing for culture, I too simply put my vision into words, but that, in contrast to you, is anything but a thing of the moment. For I don't write only for money, I write for eternity and that is what you should paint for. But let's leave that for now. The cultural establishment, my dear Willy, is something that stands in our way: it will be hard to go round it, we have to break through it, deceive it – I don't know how, but we'll find a way. Let's also leave that for now, because I came to see you as a writer in distress. I need your advice with regard to Sandrina."

Sandrina? I was startled.

"Yes. I advised you about the Arab girl, you advise me about the girl you sailed to England with."

Do you know her? I began to stammer. When did you last see her?

"Not long ago, in my room," he grinned inanely.

And what was she doing? I asked, although my voice was barely under control.

"Something she's used to. She was riding a fat American tourist, making noises to try and convince him that he was the best lover of all time, even though she was doing most of the work herself. But with each ah and oh she earned a few extra dollars."

That's not my Sandrina, I hurried to her defence, she'd never do anything like that.

"How do you know?" he asked with a smirk. "Anyway, I'm not talking about your goddess, but the heroine of my novel who has borrowed her name, have you forgotten?"

If you're writing a novel about a prostitute, I snapped, then you can't call her Sandrina, I won't allow it.

"Oh, you're such a child, Willy Potty. A bad-tempered, stubborn, refractory child. I really don't know what's going to become of you. First, I can call the heroine of my novel whatever I want, you don't own names. Second, Sandrina is not a prostitute."

What then, I snapped again, the patron saint of love?

"Why are you so peeved? She's not the patron saint of love, but a seductress who tries to show men that they are nothing, otherwise they would be able to resist her charms, and at the same time she wants to punish them by making them pay for the realisation that they are nothing. And when I say pay, I have figures in mind that would make you dizzy."

Not very suitable material for a novel, I replied, especially for an author who fled the gulag, but I suppose you know what you're doing. I don't know what kind of advice I could give you because I don't frequent prostitutes.

"Willy Potty, sometimes you say things that make it difficult to believe that you are an artist. Without breadth, without heart, without a wish to understand people, awkward for no reason, uptight and closed, as if someone has trimmed your feelings – or rather shaved them. Not to mention your sense of humour, which remains stubbornly out of sight. But never mind, I still like to think of this as a transitional phase, the consequence of Arab culture shock if I may joke a little, and that you will soon shake off your belated puberty."

What about my paintings, I asked, did you get them back?

He remained silent, he swallowed to control himself and then said: "Things are in hand. You can expect results soon. Well? Do you want to listen or not?"

Go on then, I said.

He began to roll a joint. "So, Sandrina came to England and is now working as an exclusive call girl in a luxury London hotel. She first started working there as a chamber maid, and when she saw what was going on in the rooms, she decided that life could be more interesting if others made the bed after her, rather than the other way round. This hotel is frequented only by the rich, directors, sports celebrities, singers, artists, even politicians. But Sandrina does not want to become a cheap tart, she wants to make an art of the world's oldest profession. When, still as a maid, she offered her sexual services for the first time, she asked the exorbitant price of three hundred pounds an hour, thinking that she would be shouted at and driven from the room. But no, the man calmly counted the money onto the bedside cabinet and said that there would be another hundred if he was satisfied. And thus the first time she earned four hundred pounds, three months' salary for a secondary school teacher. And right at the beginning she put in place the rule that the man must be satisfied; she had been raised as a Catholic and would otherwise feel guilty. Very soon, she trained herself to be an ideal lover for every man who had the money to pay for her services. She has strict rules for both them and herself: no one could stay in her room more than two hours; she limits herself to three clients a day and the rest of the time devotes herself to a correspondence course in psychology. When she stops doing this in four years, she will find employment as an adviser in a centre for battered women. Until then, her life runs smoothly: she has a notebook with a list of regular clients who come to her at a specified time and for each one she knows what pleases him, how she must dress, how she should greet him, what she should say, how she should lie on the bed, what she should cry out at the moment when she fakes orgasm; and from time to time, each of them introduces a new client. But her schedule is so full that she can afford to be choosy; her price is fixed and she cannot be tempted with higher offers, she is more interested in who the man is. Member of parliament is okay, state secretary better, a well-known rock artist or opera singer not bad, a newspaper magnate, why not, the ambassador of an important foreign country, let's be kind to foreigners. A high court judge who wants to be doused in ice cold water and whipped, okay, evidently he doesn't find what he is looking for at home. Thanks to all her professional care for their pleasure, not one of the men even imagines that Sandrina despises him the more he enjoys her company; her Catholic reflex does not allow her to respect someone who is normal enough to get for free what he is paying for. And here is the heart of my story, actually the bud from which the story will grow. I'll tell you some of the possible scenarios and you tell me, as a friend and a potential reader, which seems best. In the first version Sandrina is a KGB agent, who while making love to some of her clients is teasing out state secrets and passing them on to her contact, the writer Solouhin, who is supposedly an escapee from the gulag, but in reality is a KGB agent. In an extension of this version Solouhin is a double agent, who is also working for the CIA and, without Sandrina's knowledge, sending false information to Moscow. In the second version Sandrina, who may or may not be a KGB agent, is madly in love with a young painter whom she met by chance on a ferry from France to England, but now she cannot find him even though she does nothing but look for him. This painter, let's say he's called Willy, comes across KGB agent Solouhin, who is pretending to be a runaway Russian writer, and this Solouhin tells him that he knows where to find his Sandrina, but he cannot take him to her until he paints a convincing fake of some well-known painting, let's say Vermeer's *Christ with the Adultress*, that he can sell for two million pounds to an American institution, not only robbing them, but also humiliating them. For Solouhin is not only a double agent, but a triple agent who is pretending that he is not pretending. Which of these ideas seems the best?"

None of them, said Willy, who had decided to be cruel. Expensive prostitutes, spies, secret agents, war secrets, sexual perversion, deceit, cheating – there's nothing wrong with any of it, but to me these are only colours that I put on my palette in order to mix them more easily; none of them is yet a part of a picture and none of them can be part of a novel. And I won't allow you to make use of me as one of your characters; in that way you distort me, because you twist the little that is visible into a whole which is completely different – it is actually more complex, which your novel evidently isn't. So any advice I might give you would be superfluous. And I don't even like this kind of blending of reality and imagination…

"Which you have no doubt done many times as a painter," he cut in. "What is fiction other than a crocodile with feathers that has left the ground for the trees and learned to chirrup? Can't you see that the real story is somewhere else, not in the bare bones that I sketched? The decision of a woman that in the male world of deceit and lies she will play a role in order to punish men and open their eyes? Although I've already told you too much. The fact is, Willy Wow, that when I seek a story it's not the story itself, but its meaning and purpose. I'd hoped that I could talk to you as one artist to another."

Maybe some other time, I said, at the moment I'm in another world.

"I know," he said, "the Arab world, but if I were you, I would leave it."

I have, I said, but there's still a strange echo inside me.

"Paint it. Cover the old painting with another. You know how to do that, don't you? Now I'm off."

He threw aside the remains of the joint, got up, climbed onto the window sill and into the room.

"What's this?" I heard his voice.

I hurried after him and saw that the door to my room was wide open.

"I'm almost certain I locked it behind me," he said. "I keep telling you to do the same. Anything missing?"

What could be missing? I made a vague gesture. I don't have anything.

"You're not penniless, check anyway."

I lifted the mattress, pulled out the leather bag, opened it and – found it empty. Well, not completely empty, my passport was still in there but the money, the five hundred in five pound notes was gone!

It's not possible, I said.

"Under the mattress, dear Willy, you must be mad! That's the first place that anyone wanting to steal money would look."

But who would come into the room, look under the mattress and take the money? You said you locked the door, but you can't have done!

"You didn't lock it," he said heatedly, "otherwise I couldn't have got in. I said I was *almost* certain that I locked it, but perhaps I didn't, perhaps the key didn't turn, I don't know. So now it's *my* fault because you don't lock the door?"

No, I said quietly and lay on the floor, it's not your fault. But it must have been someone who lives here, the front door is locked.

"Not always," said Dostoyevsky. "I've often seen strangers on the stairs, although it's hard to say, as I don't know most of the tenants."

Oh God, I gasped. What will I do now?

"Don't you have any backup?"

No, I whimpered like a child whose toy has been stolen. I kept all my money in the same place. I should have opened a bank account, but I didn't.

"What's happened has happened," he said, patting my shoulder. "You can move in with me, one way or another I'm already paying rent, and you'll earn that money back, somehow. I'll help."

I raised my head and looked at him through my tears. Why?

"Because you ask stupid questions," he said with a friendly smile. "Because I'm strange. Because I help those in need."

34.

The following day we put up notices in five newsagents saying "writer and painter lead visitors hungry for culture through artistic London – cheap, intensive, witty, unforgettable". To our great surprise, on the first day at the recommended meeting point beneath Nelson's Column in Trafalgar Square there were twelve people waiting, half of them retired American couples, but also some young Japanese and a few hippies from different parts of Europe. They were so enthused by Solouhin's Rasputin-like appearance that they forgave him his impossible accent, especially when he explained that he was a Russian writer who had fled from the Siberian gulag and in the free world was enslaved by the stupid need to make a living – at least until the publication of his magnificent trilogy of novels, then his home would be one of the London sights.

"Just call me Dostoyevsky," he said in passing.

In a moment of inspiration he presented me as a painter that Tito had exiled from Yugoslavia because I had disobeyed an order to paint the president's wife as slimmer than she was; I had shown the sufficient level of patriotism by offering to reduce her by five kilos, but certainly not the twenty that had been demanded of me. And that was the reason why, in this fine country of absolute freedom where the authorities cared not a jot if we died of hunger, I was struggling for my five minutes of fame that would come when the gallery owners, all hostages to the latest fashions, recognised my genius and declared me to be a wonder of the modern world.

His anecdotes at my expense were very presumptuous but I couldn't find the strength to object, especially when I saw that the two of us exerted a magnetic pull that attracted an increasing number of people on our tours.

And so now each day, for three pounds a head, we led people round the parts of London that Dostoyevsky had arbitrarily labelled as "important milestones in the cultural history of one of the most interesting cities in Europe." Between the locations that were reasonably close to each other we walked along the crowded pavements. So that no member of one of the groups we were leading, which were every day larger, would lose sight of us, someone had to carry a placard bearing the words *London Literary and Cultural Tour.* That honour usually fell to me. The greater distances we tackled by Tube. The tour began at ten in the morning and lasted till three, with a stop at the Amalfi Italian restaurant in Soho, where Dostoyevsky had negotiated ten per cent commission on whatever our tourists spent. In addition, he usually managed to persuade the more generous members of the group to cover the cost of our lunch. In doing this, we remained tactically modest and always ate somewhat less than the greediest, except when some generous and benevolent American patronisingly encouraged us to build up our strength, then we went beyond all reasonable bounds and ordered three portions of cannelloni or spaghetti bolognese in a row, each one accompanied by a beer. Most of our clients thought that the chance to do something good for two rather comical refugees from behind the Iron Curtain was a real experience. Almost all of them wanted their photos taken with us: for friends and neighbours, relatives, grandchildren – just in case we ever did become famous.

However, Dostoyevsky somewhat exaggerated our role of "dissident artists", for sometimes sarcastic comments could be heard from among the group accompanying us. This did not bother him, but it did me; a number of times I warned him that we weren't clowns escaped from a Russian circus, but serious young men who were earning a crust in an imaginative fashion so that we could at least a few hours a day devote ourselves to art. The important thing was not to jeopardise our dignity.

Art is not framed, was his predictable reply; art is and should be everything that we do, every step we take, every gesture, every word, the whole life that we create as we go along, as if we were writing a novel – not by writing in advance schematic narratives, but in an open way, by exploring every possibility, by seeking the current of events that would carry us forward according to our own internal dynamics. And if that demanded that we should abandon writing and painting, then so be it. Dedicating art to life was our goal, not dedicating life to art, since we had outgrown primary school didactics; and particularly because the times were eminently favourable to improvisers.

Each day his words caused me more and more concern, even fear, for Solouhin was the most eloquent example of a man without a centre that I had ever met – a man who could improvise himself each day anew with the same ease that he brushed his teeth. In reality, I did not really know him; all that remains in memory is a sequence of improvisations that had in common only the fact that he was fond of me in his fashion and felt responsible for me, in the same way that an older brother would care for a younger one entering the wider world for the first time. The problem was that he took on this responsibility of his own accord, without my consent, not even implicit, simply because he wanted to play the role of someone generous who meant to initiate a less adroit acquaintance into the secrets of the wicked metropolis. My mistake was not to revolt against this as soon as it began to happen, when I could have done it without jeopardising our friendship, which was precious to me and which I had an increasing need for.

At the beginning, Solouhin did not reveal all his cards and we slipped into mutual dependency almost by the by, while looking for what we had in common – although almost from the start I had a feeling that he was taking over my life, that he saw in it replacement material for the novel that he could not get written, and that his daily attempts to shape my ideas and plans brought him pleasure and a sense of achievement primarily because I was (as he himself emphasised) fundamentally less stubborn than his heroes. With increasing frequency I felt that my life should not become merely another of his improvisations and that we must soon, perhaps the very next day, talk about this.

What is more, it was not at all clear to me why he insisted on dragging me on his tours, which he could easily have led himself: after all, he demanded of me nothing more exacting than collecting three pounds from each participant and making sure that, as far as possible, no one got lost in the crowds. Also, that I say a few enlightening words whenever Canaletto and Constable became relevant; and even then he often intervened with some spicy tidbit of information that he had dug up God-knows-where the day before without telling me – as if he felt the need to keep reminding me that he was unsurpassable and that I was in all respects only his assistant. It's true that he fairly divided the spoils with me and that every day in the Amalfi he strove to ensure that I ate as much as possible. Considering that the whole idea was his, I should have been grateful to him. At times, it seemed that he was doing it all out of a feeling of guilt because he was not sure whether or not he had locked the door when my money disappeared and that in this fashion he wanted to help me replace it.

In one way or another, something in addition to tourists walked the streets of London with us, something that was ours alone: something undefined, an embryo, a complication or perhaps the beginning of the end of something, accompanying us like a shadow that we were both afraid of; and often, when Solouhin looked at me in passing, I felt a reflection of it in his eyes.

The London that the self-declared escapee from the Siberian gulag presented to the largely misinformed foreign visitors was of course, or so it seemed to me, rather than the real London, an invention of a writer eager to seek revenge for the unenthusiastic way that the city had responded to his attempts to become part of its elite: a sought-after person, someone, Aleksej Ivanovič Solouhin, a successor to Conrad and Nabokov, a widely read and idolised novelist who was perhaps one of the reasons that people came to visit London. This was of course not obvious, but I could identify with his pain since it was a mirror image of my own; and often I thought that it was also felt by the more perceptive members of the tour groups.

In spite of this Dostoyevsky, as a natural performer, never slipped from irony into cynicism; his heightened sense told him that a negative tone as a London guide could lead to a loss of clients as fast as a writer loses readers, so he remained (regardless of the fact that from day to day he had to repeat himself like an actor who is somewhat tired of his role) entertaining and smoothly omniscient.

"Look," he would say, when we got to Ebury Street, "this friend of mine who likes to listen to Mozart – his wife says that he breathes it in from morning till night – was walking with his five-year-old daughter around the city and when they passed by here he pointed to that house and said: You see, in that house over there Mozart lived for some time and wrote his first symphony at the age of eight. His daughter was surprised and said: I didn't know that Mozart was a man, I thought it was just another name for music!"

Most of our clients liked this so much that they expected more anecdotes. And so gradually Dostoyevsky, without them being aware of it, steered them away from the desire to ask tricky questions about more specific matters that he would not have known how to answer. His skills as a raconteur never wavered; at times I got the feeling that he made things up as he went along and, if they met with a good response, incorporated them into his repertoire, like the story about Marx, who "lived for five years in poverty in Dean Street, where he stole from others for his most famous work *Das Kapital*. That was the conclusion reached by Mr. Leoni, the current owner of the house (and the Italian restaurant Quo Vadis on the ground floor), when he rummaged through Marx's former rooms and found a box of books in which many paragraphs were heavily underlined and the margins full of Marx's comments in German. Mr. Leoni was very disappointed when he realised that the great thinker had not written his best known works using only his own ideas and from that point on always voted for the Conservatives."

It happened sometimes that Solouhin's hypnotic voice captured me and I slipped into the role of one of the tourists who experienced London through the eyes of the sardonic Russian in a completely new way. Dostoyevsky had the rare gift of imbuing the words that he more or less repeated every day with a special, always genuine enthusiasm. I was not at all surprised that so few of our clients asked to be taken to Highgate Cemetery, where they could see the bust of Marx and the grave into which his bones had so long ago been interred: Solouhin knew how to confuse most of them so much that they forgot about Highgate or (and I can't get over this) they began to believe that they just returned from there to Soho, which was Solouhin's favourite area.

"Ladies and gentlemen, we are in the heart of the most scandalous square mile in London." The ladies blushed, the gentlemen would be happy to keep on walking along the narrow streets filled with flashing neon signs offering "porno film", "peep show", "topless bar", "Swedish massage". Of course Solouhin, to assuage any possible feelings of guilt, rapidly hurled at them data about the history of the area: how the avalanche of debauchery was triggered by the well-rounded Italian Teresa Cornelys (the lover, among others, of Casanova and the mother of one of his numerous daughters), who arrived in Soho in 1760 and, with her rich experience acquired in the beds of numerous European capitals, established a career in which she was celebrated in succession as Madame Pompeati, Madame Trenti and the Sultana of Soho. She moved into the luxurious Carlisle House and staged there notorious masked balls attended by, in addition to English aristocrats, foreign ambassadors and figures from the theatre such as Garrick, Sheridan and Goldsmith. At that time Soho was a mixture of palaces and sheds, the homes of the eminent rich and the ragged forebears of the lumpenproletariat, but also a refuge for the persecuted from every corner of the world. In the sixteenth century came French Huguenots, and later Greeks fleeing Turkish violence; one of the streets is still called Greek Street.

"And a year ago there arrived the gifted writer Aleksej Ivanovič Solouhin, known to his friends as Dostoyevsky, who did not remain in Soho, but moved thirty-two times in twelve months, as much as Dickens did in his whole life," he said every day in the same tone at the same spot, in front of 21 Doughty Street, which is now a museum where you can see the high desk at which Dickens always wrote standing up, often chatting with visitors at the same time. "Geniuses have at least one privilege: they do not have to act like normal people."

And onwards along literary paths: to Southwark, south of the Thames, that Dickens described in *David Copperfield*, and where his

272

father spent half his life in debtor's prison; and then to Kensington, to the house on Young Street, where Thackeray wrote *Vanity Fair*. On a later occasion, as he passed by with a friend he supposedly called out: "On your knees, man, don't you know that *Vanity Fair* was written in that house?" Then he added: "I'll kneel with you, because I too have a very high opinion of that book." And then to Chelsea, Tite Street, where Oscar Wilde lived, and round the corner to Tedworth Square, where Mark Twain once stayed. Legend has it that these literary giants, then in the greatest crisis of their careers and their lives, once met by chance and raised their hats to each other, "but this is not possible," announced Solouhin triumphantly, "for when Twain travelled to London, Wilde was already in Reading gaol." Twain came to Europe to escape the creditors that had bankrupted him; in the house on Tedworth Square he had tortured himself with the only bad book he wrote: *Following the Equator.* Word got out that he was ill and dying; the *New York Journal* sent a correspondent with the instruction to send five hundred words if the writer was ill and a thousand if he was dead. Twain received him with the words that have become immortal: "The news of my death has been somewhat exaggerated."

By this point the tourists – each day at least ten and at the most twenty – were already so tired that some of them at least did not care to go on. It seemed to me that more than the walking and the wealth of information, they were tired from Solouhin's manic verbosity; not for a moment was there a lull in the flow of words – he spoke, narrated, improvised, lied, entertained, made witty comments as if he was fighting for his life and I was surprised that he could not see how tiring it was to listen to him after the first hour, when he was saved by being new and amusing, especially when he took them somewhere by Tube, where the other passengers looked at us as if we were members of an alternative theatre group that London Underground had hired to entertain them.

All my attempts to restrain him fell on deaf ears and were completely misunderstood ("We can only lose through silence, my dear Willy; words are the rope with which we bind them to us"). In vain did I tell him that once they had paid their three pounds, there was no point in binding them to us any longer than they wanted. Although he agreed with me, while walking round the city he was always gripped by the same fever – as if a motor had started inside him that could not be stopped. I increasingly felt that Solouhin had no control over himself; or that there was someone else inside him, an intruder who borrowed his body and fed on his blood.

And at this point in the tour, in front of the house where Mark Twain stayed, it was not only our clients who were overcome by tiredness, but we ourselves, particularly Solouhin. The growing tension suddenly dissipated and in his eyes I sensed a mixture of despair and rage, which were so uncharacteristic that they could not belong to him, at least not to the Solouhin I knew. "Now I'd shoot every last one of them," he whispered to me once. Undoubtedly, there was not only Willy I and Willy II, but also two Solouhins. The only difference was that we two (the two Willys) were somehow connected and worked in harmony, although argumentatively; it never happened that one of us was completely unaware what the other was doing.

In the case of Solouhin, I did not have this feeling and I was increasingly afraid that Solouhin II, when his moment came, would manifest himself in a way that would stun even Solouhin I, and that it would be a dramatic, spectacular event.

35.

I don't know why from the very beginning I sensed that the setting for this event would be Tedworth Square; perhaps because at that point on the chart of invested effort, the psychological capacities of the participants were at their lowest ebb and some, if not all, replaced the lost enjoyment with a feeling of resentment – as if Solouhin had suddenly changed from a witty guide to a disagreeable interloper. Almost every time there was someone in the group who began to grumble or somehow to express the general dissatisfaction, and almost every time I felt that Solouhin could hardly restrain himself from striking back like a snake.

Well, yesterday it finally happened: some smoothy from Boston, who from the very start had received all of Solouhin's explanations with a superior smile and in between exchanged comments with his tiny, bespectacled female companion, when Solouhin quoted Twain's celebrated words added nonchalantly: "In your case it would sound a little different, wouldn't it? *The news of my gulag experience has been somewhat exaggerated.*"

For a moment, all eyes were Solouhin. Surprisingly, he did not even frown, he actually managed an accommodating smile, as if he wished to participate in this joke at his expense. This smile stayed in place even as he took a step towards the Bostonian and delivered two blows, one with his right hand, one with is left. At first the victim could not believe what had happened. The group, which this

275

time numbered twenty, was struck dumb. The first to react was the smoothy's companion, who leapt at Solouhin and jabbed the pointed end of her shoe into his shin. As if in passing Solouhin's paw, which always reminded me of the appendage of Frankenstein's monster, grabbed her glasses, crumpled them and threw them to the ground, where the remnants crunched under the heel of his enormous shoe.

Now the stunned Bostonian reacted, but no sooner had he reached out than Dostoyevsky, who had never mentioned that he was a master of kung fu, threw himself into the air and with both his feet smashed into the man's face with such force that he somersaulted over and then lay on the ground with bruised cheeks and a bloody nose.

"This is terrible," said someone in the group and a woman shrieked "We must call the police!" Another, a fat lady from New Zealand, began to rush around the square shouting "Help, help, help!"

At that moment Solouhin hurled himself at the tourist from Boston and began to jump on him as if he was trying to flatten an uneven paving stone. With his gorilla-like weight he must have broken three or four ribs at the first attempt; I was afraid that he would eventually smash his breastbone.

Then three male members of the group tried to restrain him. Solouhin shook them off with a wide sweep of his arms and continued with his rib-breaking; he obviously intended to kill the unfortunate wretch who had dared to insult him. The three men again threw themselves at him, joined by two others, and it seemed as if the wild Russian would finally be tamed. But no, Solouhin rushed over to me, as I stood there watching events unfold as if nailed to the ground, and snatched from my hands the placard saying *London Literary and Cultural Tour*; he brandished it and with one swing flattened all of his attackers. I had never before seen such controlled, cold-blooded rage accompanied by such a friendly, albeit icy smile.

Then we both noticed that the woman who had been screeching for help had managed to attract the attention of a plump bobby, who was rushing towards us, truncheon in hand. With long, kangaroo-like bounds Solouhin headed for the nearest corner and disappeared from sight. And although I had been as shocked at his outburst as anyone else, I had no choice but to follow him.

I barely managed to catch up with him; I don't know if either of us had ever run any faster. We galloped along the Thames towards Earls Court, only stopping when we heard a police siren above the noise of the traffic; at that, we ducked into the nearest pub and headed for a table in a dark corner. We immediately noticed that some guests were clearly wondering whether our gasping for breath might be connected with the sound of the police vehicle that had just whizzed past. To nip any kind of suspicion in the bud, Solouhin suddenly launched into a lecture on health.

"Jogging, dear Willy," he said in a loud voice, "jogging is the answer to the world's problems. Although we have, to put it mildly, seriously overdone it today. And we have inhaled too many exhaust fumes – next time we should find a park."

We drank our beers and then went on, to put as much distance as possible between ourselves and the location of the incident, and to become lost among the crowds. But outside, the sense of vulnerability only increased; we knew they were looking for us and at every corner I had the feeling that we would be apprehended. We went into a half-empty pub in a side street and sought out the darkest corner.

There, we finally dared to look each other in the eye.

We both knew that much of what we could read in our looks would have to remain unspoken. Words would not allow us to pretend that we had not reached a critical point in our relationship. And then each word would have to be justified with a new one, until we had built a wall over which only insults could be hurled. Of course, I could have asked: Why did you do that? And he would contritely reply: I don't know, something snapped inside me, I'm sorry, but it's too late now. We both knew that there was no rational explanation for his action, at which he himself was more and more surprised. At the same time, we both felt that the eruption of violence had its roots in the growing chasm between the dreams that had brought us to London and the cold reality, in which not only had we begun to run out of hope, but even air to breathe. At that moment, words would have brought us to the point where we would have to face up to the fundamental question: was there any sense in persisting? And since we felt that the response would not be a positive one, we wanted to avoid it at any

277

cost. Evidently we could summon up enough strength for illusion, but too little for the truth. And so we concluded a silent conspiracy to give each other our last hope.

When we finally spoke, we did so simply and practically, like cautious villains who wish to avoid the long arm of the law. We assessed whether there was any chance that the next day the police would knock on our door. In a city of eight million that would be a small miracle. Doubtlessly they could try to trace us through the newsagents where we had placed ads, but among the mass of people that they had to deal with every day the owners would probably not be able to describe us. They could get a description from the more observant members of the last group, especially of Solouhin, who was such a striking figure that he would be impossible to miss even in the middle of a crowd. But probably only an unlikely coincidence would bring the pursuers to us. Alongside all the violence that happened daily in London, our case would not be tackled by Scotland Yard's finest. An immediate relocation was not necessary; it was more important to avoid for some time the places where we had led our groups of tourists. That source of income was now closed to us, but we felt relief rather than regret; our days had started to become terribly repetitive and we were ready for something new. We had earned quite a bit of money: not as much as had been stolen, but enough to afford a break. And to do some creative work.

I in particular felt that I had to devote myself once more to painting; not only in order to protect my fragile reputation as an artist, but in the unshakable faith that art, at least in the long run, was the only thing that could bring in more money than I needed for mere survival.

Dostoyevsky could not find enough strength to carry on writing his novel or looking for an agent and sending his work to addresses where it had not yet been rejected. "I need to clear my head," he said. "I need to dig myself out of the hole in which I've fallen. Above all, I need enough money for at least six months: I'm not the kind of author who can write after work. When I write I need to live with my characters day and night. And this intrusion of the real world has confused me so much that my imagination is in ruins – first, I must heal it."

The next day he vanished and I could only surmise where he had gone and how he intended to carry out this healing. Like me, he was one of those who could deal with reality only in small doses: a drop too much and he found himself in a place where he could no longer maintain his balance. But while Dostoyevsky experienced the events of recent days as reality, to me they seemed illusory, like one of his narrative improvisations, the ending of which, as if he was writing a story with a twist, he had spiced up with a brutal physical showdown. Only in this way, by placing the events beneath an imaginative veil, was I able to keep them at a sufficient distance so that they did not completely throw me off course.

In spite of that, the painting that I slowly daubed in the days of Solouhin's absence, which contained ever more elements of Munch's grotesque, took on of its own accord the shape of a cry of protest intended to force the world to pay attention, to respect the rights and the dignity of the rejected, among whose ranks it was now more than obvious, after all our peaks of euphoria, Solouhin and I belonged.

The figures that were appearing on the canvas assumed their clearest expression around two in the afternoon when the sunlight fell on them through the window; at that point, the first impression was that they were not holding umbrellas but placards; they were rushing aggressively forward, somewhere to the left, towards an invisible fortress of resistance, with gaping mouths from which came orders and ultimatums, blind and deaf to their immediate surroundings, while beneath the feet of the humiliated and outraged, carelessly trampled on, were a small white dog and a pink baby that had fallen from its pushchair, its horrified mother standing alongside it, and finally, similarly trodden on, the reflection of the sun in a puddle. A sun that the figures rushing towards it had not even noticed.

36.

The next two days I devoted to shades of colour, finessed small details, varied the expressions on the faces of the protestors, sharpened
some, changed others into silhouettes, strove to ensure that each figure told its story of misunderstanding, dejection, thirst for revenge,
rage – and the painting so drew me in that I was unable to separate
myself from it even for the fifteen minutes I required to pop to the
nearest shop. So I ate slices of stale bread and waited impatiently for
Solouhin to return. I felt the urgent need to show the picture not just
to anyone, but precisely to him, since he was the creator of its content
as much as me, and more than anyone it was dedicated to him.

But the escapee from the Siberian gulag had mysteriously disappeared. When on the third day he was not there and had not even
called, which he always did whenever debauchery shackled him
somewhere for a few days, I anxiously began to consider the possibility that he had been recognised and arrested. That he would be
tried and sentenced.

And I with him, because I had been there, I had fled with him
instead of reporting him. But at that moment this worried me the
least, I was much more troubled (and astonished) by the thought that
without Solouhin London would become so grey and empty that I
would have nothing to do. In the course of our short acquaintance,
without trying to do so, Solouhin had become the central figure in
my life – not only an irreplaceable mentor in practical matters, but a

faithful comrade on the path to equally elevated goals that made sense (or so it seemed to me) only because we were both pursuing them. Without him alongside me I would have to rethink what I was doing from scratch, set other goals or, if I stuck with the old ones, lay them out on other terrain. Without wishing to (or had he?), he had become a kind of proprietor – and if not the proprietor, the administrator – of my attempts to achieve success, satisfaction and happiness; and I let him hold the reins, in spite of my serious doubts that perhaps his charisma was hollow in the middle.

Maybe the strength of his self-confidence was rooted only in my uncertainty, or perhaps it was great enough to overshadow my own sense of confidence and put me in a subordinate position. One way or another, at that moment it became clear that I must, even at the price of my own safety, find him as soon as possible, rescue him if he was in difficulties and hide him or in some way protect him from the worst. He too, I was convinced of this, would find it hard to survive without me, at least not in the context of the story that we had woven in London, since I was the only one who knew how to mitigate his excesses, to "hold him together" as he once put it himself.

But where should I look for him? He avoided the Russian community in the same way that, to use his words, the Catholic devil avoids the Orthodox cross, while he had never mentioned, let alone introduced, the friends he had before we met. Nor was there a woman in his life, at least no one specific, at least not since we had known each other. The only possibility was that he had gone to find solace, as he had done a number of times before, with Soho prostitutes and that they had recognised him and reported him to the police. Unless he wanted to lengthen his days of debauchery until he was penniless – then he would have no choice but to find another way of making a quick buck, and perhaps subconsciously he manipulated his fate in such a way that every so often he found himself on the edge, from where he could stare into the abyss. Perhaps this was the only way of staying alert and conserving his energy at its peak. And of avoiding, once more, a final showdown with his novel.

I thought that perhaps I would find a trail that led to him, or at least that showed where he might be, in his papers. I had never looked through them: I felt that, although we shared a room, or perhaps because of that, both of us were entitled to some privacy. I also expected him not to go through my things. Of course, I had no guarantee that he respected my privacy as much as I did his, but it seemed to me that between two people who sleep, cook, and work in the same space, there was a need for mutual trust. And so I hesitated for some time before I approached his desk, on which, beside the typewriter, lay a confusion of papers, newspaper cuttings, magazines, bills, letters and notebooks.

I knew that I would not find his address book, because he kept that in the large shoulder bag without which he never left the room, even if he was only going to the corner shop. The bag always looked so full that it no doubt also contained everything else of importance, so I had no particular hopes of finding anything useful on his desk. More than anything, it was full of fresh rejections from various magazines, publishers, newspapers, theatres, agents, radio and television stations, including the ones that he had used to cover the walls (or so he said) of his previous room – for they still had remnants of dried up Sellotape attached to them. "Dear Sir, Thank you for letting us read your story ... Unfortunately this isn't quite what we are looking for ..." and so on.

In my case rejections were always verbal and there were fewer of them, whereas Dostoyevsky could supplement on a daily basis the visible extent of his lack of success, leaving it on the desk where it would constantly be in sight – perhaps as a reminder that he must try harder, or a warning that his obstinacy was ruining his life. When I read these short, negative, falsely friendly and rather patronising letters, probably sent out by a poorly educated secretary, I was overcome by a crippling feeling, as if someone was pouring freshly mixed concrete down my throat.

I rummaged among the papers, choosing at random some pages torn from a notepad. They were covered with scribbled ideas, thoughts, drafts, plans, quotes. *"We must all be good men first and only then think about the other things we find important, said the missionary."* And some dialogues: *"How much longer?"* – *"You mean, how much longer is mine? Probably a good three inches."* – *"Are you kidding me? How much longer are we going to sit on our*

posteriors, that's what I want to know." – "Ask the boss. He's the
boss."- "You mean bums. How much longer are we going to sit on
our bums." – "Okay, you can sit on your bum, but I'll sit on my
posterior. Any objection?"

It struck me that while Solouhin was capable of writing witty and adept dialogue in English, it remained somehow empty, focused on word games, without the charge that would come from directly experienced reality. Real people, at least in my experience, not even the English, who were inclined that way, did not indulge in wittiness ad nauseam, but tried to communicate through conversation at least an opinion on something concrete. Upon reading Solouhin's texts, I could not shake off the feeling that his words were trapped in a kind of verbal cage and that, more than anything, were an attempt to prove, perhaps to himself as much as anyone else, that he mastered the language. This seemed narcissistic and insufficiently convincing for literature.

I thought what an advantage a painter has over a writer. A painter can move anywhere in the world and carry on painting in the same way. In a foreign language, a writer has to change completely: he has to move into a new culture, he has to reinvent himself, first as a person who is completely at ease in the new environment, and then as a writer who knows how to portray experience directly and not through the filter of his own language. Is that even possible? It's true that some have succeeded, and Solouhin never tired of mentioning Conrad and Nabokov, but a number of times I had already thought, and never more markedly than at that moment, that Solouhin would achieve more if he wrote in Russian and then had the texts translated into English. He had not given me the novel (which he seemed to speak about more than actually writing it) to read, so that I could not say with any certainty that he had made no progress, but I had never before felt so acutely how Quixotic were his goals and how obsessed he must be with his ambition of recreating himself as an English writer. Of course, I was most interested in the novel, which could not be found among the mountain of paper on his untidy desk. He probably carried it with him all the time in his shoulder bag.

I put the handful of papers back on the desk, my curiosity diminished. Then my eye was caught by the corner of a suitcase protruding from under the bed. After a moment's hesitation I suppressed any feeling of bad conscience, pulled it out and opened it. At first glance it contained nothing of interest: some Russian magazines, newspaper cuttings, old letters, keys, socks, handkerchiefs, developed films – disorder. But in the midst of all this I found a fat notebook containing dated entries, first in Russian, then in English. I had evidently found Solouhin's diary.

I opened it somewhere in the middle and read:

"Last night my rheumatism moved to the left side of my breast-bone; the pain is worse than if Nikita Khrushchev was sitting on top of me for five days after stuffing himself at a state banquet. I didn't sleep all night. In the morning I spoke with the decorator who is painting the hallway and stairs; he recommended a hot water bottle. And so I am now sitting at my desk, staring through the window at the damp grey English weather, while between the edge of the desk and my breastbone I am clutching a hot water bottle as if it was a newly found bastard child. Pondering. I feel like an invalid. I, Aleksej Ivanovič Solouhin, a tall (too tall), healthy young man, with enough energy for five people, feel as if a centuries-old oak tree had fallen on top of me and shattered not only my bones but my will. I cannot shake off the feeling that I have manoeuvred myself onto a totally irrelevant side-track. Maybe I should not have left Russia. Maybe I should think about my immediate return. No one responds to my letters. As if I had drowned. Soon I shall be completely alienated from the world that should be my arena. Do my friends, acquaintances, relatives feel some kind of resistance towards me, hate me because I have realised a dream that was also theirs? If only they could see the reality of this dream! I live in a vacuum, I have no one that I can call a friend, I have no contact of any kind with my relatives, I have no idea what English authors of my age write about and I have done absolutely nothing to change the world, to make my mark on history. Everything indicates that this is how it will remain. I could console myself with the thought that in Russia, the way it is, I would achieve even less and I would not see the world, thanks to which I am in a better position than my peers who remained faithful to the Party and their home town. But that would be only a transparent manoeuvre, not a comfort. Actually, the only real achievement is understanding people and the forces that create history. I have decided that I will be an artist and nothing else. Does that not mean that I have to resign myself to a lack of lustre in my life? Not only because I know that all lustre is false, but also because it is completely unnecessary for a happy existence. I will not pretend that at moments I do not wish that I was famous, successful, rich, the talk of the town – but how would I benefit from that? Would I then not spend most money trying to *buy* the solitude that I enjoy now? So what do I expect from life? Never what it brings me…"

I turned the pages and stopped again.

"For two days I have been suffering from serious depression. What am I doing in this city? Would it not be more interesting living somewhere in the East? On Bali, in Thailand, Lake Toba? Certainly a lot cheaper. And I would meet a lot of interesting people, a lot more than here, where everyone hurries past as if looking for someone who just hurried past them. Why can I not summon the courage to more aggressively include myself in the life here, find more friends, or at least one that I could be open with, be myself, without pretence? Why do I feel as if I would die of shame if someone saw me the way I think I am? Maybe I'm wrong about myself, maybe the aversion I feel towards Solouhin is completely unjustified or at least exaggerated; maybe a good, sincere friend would know how to help me conclude at least a temporary ceasefire with myself. The tarts drawn by my magnetism are no help; they are stupid, vacant, self-obsessed (except for one that I cannot mention because I am writing a novel about her). I need a friend with a soul that is at least as deep as mine; who suffers for the same or similar reasons; who has exceptional, elevated goals inappropriate to these insipid times. It seems to me that two who are equally talented and committed, a support and a consolation to each other, as well as a correction, could overcome the indifference and resistance of this town. But where to find such a person in this deaf, empty, satiated city? In this London fog that is something completely different from how I imagined it, except that no one within it sees more than two metres in front of themselves. Including me."

I stopped reading; I felt as if the wet cement in my veins was beginning to set. I peeped only at the end. The diary entries stopped the day after our chance meeting. The last entry was: "Today I met a young painter from Yugoslavia, his name is Vili. A rather unhappy lad who would like to vanquish London in a similar way to me. He hasn't actually said this to me, but I can see it in his eyes. His soul is not at all Slav, it seems narrow and restrained, somehow sketched in (maybe because he is a painter, just as mine is constructed). He speaks English almost without an accent, much better than me – quite ironic, considering our goals. I don't know what he thinks about me, but I get the impression that he is slightly afraid of me and does not completely trust me. He's right. After all, when have I ever been worthy of trust?"

I put the diary back in the suitcase and pushed it under the bed. I crouched down and thought it over. Why was it that I found the real Solouhin only in the hidden diary? Why did he not open up to me, why did he bluff, swagger and puff himself up, why did he invent a Solouhin that he thought would impress me?

Because in spite of everything, the "unhappy lad" was not "a friend with a soul that is at least as deep as his"? I was overcome by something that could (if I let it) turn into resentment, but the very next moment I thought: what about me? Was I also not acting out a role in front of him that was quite a long way from what it ought to be if I wanted him to trust me as he would trust a friend?

37.

The next day he had still not returned and my presentiment that I would never see him again slowly hardened into certainty. At the same time, the feeling grew within me that I could not simply abandon him to his fate, since among the millions in London I was certainly the only one who missed him. Even if he had been recognised and was in jail, I would find a way to help him – after all, he had helped me more than once.

I don't know why it took me so long to think of the Queen of Egypt. Many things had been left unresolved between us and the effort she put into ensuring that we never met by chance in the hall, where she sometimes collected her post, gave little hope that she would know where Solouhin might have gone, let alone that she would want to tell me if she knew. Since there was no other possibility, towards evening I knocked on her door.

I thought she would slam it in my face when she saw me, so I was surprised when she eagerly grabbed my hand and pulled me inside, as if she had something confidential to tell me.

"Oh, you Silly Boy," she said. "If you only knew what danger you're in."

Her room, with the small kitchen in the corner, still smelled of Arabic spices and had not really changed at all, except that Cleo had added two new pairs of shoes to the row of ten beside the bed, while two older pairs had probably been given to a charity shop ("Ten pairs of shoes is the most a non-wasteful woman can afford.").

She commanded me to sit on the bed and put the kettle on. "English tea or *Egyptian* coffee?" she asked. She emphasised the penultimate word as if to imply: I dare you to say "Turkish instead of Egyptian". When we were still friends, I had often teased her in this way. This time, it seemed safer to opt for English tea.

I waited for her to clarify the warning she had greeted me with, but she was so engrossed in her tea-making that she didn't say a word. Actually, more than tea-making, she was preoccupied with sudden dark thoughts – I could see that from the bitter set of her mouth. There was also no sign of any efforts to transform herself into an "article" (as Solouhin had put it) that might convince some mature wealthy gentleman ("if at all possible an aristocrat, but at least upper middle class") to propose to her. She had completely let herself go, her hair was sticking out in all directions, her thighs were lumpy and she was bent over as if carrying the burden of a hundred generations of her predecessors.

More than anything, she had aged: lines had appeared on her smooth olive skin that previously would have been hard to imagine. Her face was oddly creased, bitter, tearful, flattened – now, suddenly, a face that I would like to paint. Cleo, I asked (in order to say something), when can I paint your portrait?

For a while she said nothing while she poured boiling water onto the teabag. Then a strange smile appeared on her face.

"From memory, Willy," she almost shrieked in a hysterical voice. "Paint me from memory. Can you not see that I have stopped being me? I realised it's safer to be someone else. For now, I'm not sure who it is that is here instead of me, but I know it isn't me. Can't you see? Has your Russian friend blinded you so completely that you see nothing but him and his crazy ideas?"

She brought me a cup of tea on a saucer and as she handed it over I saw her hands were trembling and her scarlet nail varnish was flaking off.

Thanks, I said. Have you seen him recently?

She moved back, dropped onto her knees and nervously began to rearrange the row of shoes next to the bed. "I'll publish an ad that I'm looking for a fetishist," she said. "There would be a scrum of guys in

288

front of the door. There's not one normal Englishman, did you know that?"

She fell silent, picked up a black pair of high-heeled shoes and with the edge of her cardigan wiped some dust from the toes. Then she carefully put it back.

"No, I haven't seen him, but I have read about him. In the paper. I'm so glad that his wish has finally come true. After all that effort he deserves his moment of fame." When she saw the surprise on my face, she quietly added: "Willy, Willy, why are you pretending that you don't know what I'm talking about?"

She reached towards the pile of newspapers on the floor and picked up a copy of the *Daily Mail*; she turned a few pages, folded it and held it out towards me.

My eye was immediately caught by the headline: "The Latest Crime and Punishment of Dostoyevsky". I quickly read the article and saw that the American tourist from Boston, who had been brutally attacked a few days earlier in Tedworth Square by a self-declared tourist guide, had died in hospital from his injuries. The police were now conducting a murder investigation. Unfortunately, they had little to go on, except that the suspect was a Russian immigrant, supposedly a writer who had fled from the Siberian gulag, who went by the name of Dostoyevsky. He had advertised guided tours of the city on cards in newsagents' windows and had been accompanied by a bearded young Yugoslav, supposedly a painter, who had not taken part in the attack, but the police would very much like to talk to him, as well as with all those who had any information that might lead to the arrest of this undesirable alien.

My first thought was that Solouhin would be hurt by the words: *... that might lead to the arrest of this undesirable alien.* Solouhin wanted to belong, he wanted to make London his home, the base from which he would launch his campaign to conquer the world. As did I. *Undesirable alien* was the official term used to label those that the Home Office had a right to banish from the country and forbid them the right to return.

It was only then that I began to realise that Solouhin was not a candidate for expulsion, but rather for the gallows, for they still had the death penalty in Britain. And simply because for once in his life he'd had enough and had cracked. I don't know why I did not feel sorry for the supercilious tourist from Boston. I couldn't say that he deserved it, but if he had held his tongue he would still be alive. And our lives would not have been changed so irrevocably.

Cleo took the cup and saucer from my hand and put them on the floor. She probably feared that they would slip from my fingers and leave a tea stain on her carpet. Then she retrieved the newspaper, carefully folded it and put it back on the heap.

"Well?" she asked in a smug tone. "How do you feel now, when it is finally clear that you are hanging around with a murderer?"

You don't even know what happened, I sprang to Solouhin's defence. It was self-defence.

"Poor Willy," she said, briefly stroking my knee. In fact, her gesture was more as if she was trying to remove an invisible bit of fluff from my trouser leg; she wanted to have an alibi in case she was too obviously rejected.

"Will you now do what's expected of you and report him?"

I won't, what are you thinking of? Nor will you. In any case, he vanished a few days ago.

"Of course he did," she said with an unconvincing laugh. "And you helped him, I know you. Not just you, I know the both of you."

What do you mean? I asked. You've only seen him a couple of times.

"It doesn't matter," she said, strangely thoughtful. "Twice can be worse than a hundred times. Do you even realise that instead of an American tourist it could be you lying in the mortuary?"

I leapt up and headed for the door.

"Wait," she said, coming after me. "We were friends once. Are we still?"

At first I did not know how to respond to her question. I could say: Of course, Cleo, until death do us part, but now I must go, and I would go, but I felt things between us had not reached the point where I could simply push past her and leave. Although I was still full of Solouhin, somewhere inside me there still hovered the memory of those night hours that Cleo and I had spent on the roof together.

290

She took my hand; her fingers were still cold and damp, and that combination still smarted, as if her hand was burning hot.

"Do you know that I met someone who almost fits the profile of the man I could marry?"

No, I took the opportunity to retreat from the other risky topic. I'm very happy for you. Who is he and why almost?

"A very rich French man from Paris," she said, "who comes for me in a large black Mercedes and takes me to restaurants, where I feel very uncomfortable because I don't know how to eat snails and shellfish. You have to use strange pieces of cutlery and once a shell flew from my grasp and hit the man at the next table in the eye."

Oh, I said, I hope you didn't blind him. Congratulations, Cleo, when will the wedding be?

The corners of her mouth turned down, as if she was trying to stop herself from crying. "I hoped you'd be jealous, at least a little," she said accusingly.

Oh, Cleo, I sighed, how could I be? You know I only want what's best for you. The French man sounds just right: wealthy, cultivated, probably friendly – what does he look like?

"Toulouse-Lautrec," she said. "Do you remember the painter you told me about? You showed me his self-portrait. Like that." Impossible, I said, Toulouse-Lautrec in a Mercedes? That's too bizarre, even Dali would not paint anything like that. But the main thing is that he is kind-hearted.

"No," she exploded and began to pound my chest with her fists. "The main thing is that you don't like me and that's why I'm unhappy. And because you don't care about the Queen of Egypt, you will be punished: I shall betray your friend, I'll call the police today."

No you won't, Cleo, I said. I stroked her unwashed hair. She had probably made up the French suitor. No, you won't. The Queen of Egypt has high standards, she's not a malicious little weasel.

"But I am," she protested, with tears in her eyes. "That's exactly what I am and want to be. A malicious little weasel. So tell your friend when you find him that he has three days. If he has not turned himself in by Saturday, then I shall be forced to do my civic duty."

Oh, Cleo, I said, where did you get that expression from? Your only duty is to stay true to your nature. You're not a traitor or a weasel. You are a good fairy from the banks of the Nile who has found herself in the wrong place and in the wrong century.

"Fellatio," she said. "I know what it means."

I'd had a feeling that this would happen, but I'd hoped to get to the door before it did. It was too late: she was already on her knees, already eagerly unbuttoning me, already sucking and chewing on the head of my penis as if it was a tough chicken leg; and my reservations were disappearing as my delight increased. For a moment she removed her mouth and recalled Matthew Arnold: *I must not say that she was true, Yet let me say that she was fair; And they, that lovely face who view, They should not ask if truth be there.*

She bit me so hard it hurt and I thought that she could, if she wished, bite off at least half of what she was tackling with ever greater haste. Once more she removed her mouth and looked into my eyes. *Truh – what is truth? Two bleeding hearts, Wounded by men, by fortune tried, Outwearied with their lonely parts, Vow to beat henceforth side by side.*

I could not bear the look that she gave me; it was too bitter, too accusatory, too full of demands that were unclear even to her; I felt only that she wanted something, something more than my swollen penis between her teeth, my semen in her throat; not only more than the world could give her, but more than she was capable of receiving.

Oh, Cleo, I thought, God help you, God or Allah, because I can't, stop it, please. I closed my eyes and succumbed to the firm caresses of her mouth, waiting to explode, but of course, like one cursed I could not reach a climax – the more I pushed my feelings towards the point of eruption, the more it seemed to retreat from me. And so our grimacing and panting lasted a lot longer than we expected; she tried every trick she knew to make me come – soft, firm, slow, fast, gentle, violent; she used her hands and embraced me, stroked me, squeezed me from all sides, until eventually she gave up.

She simply withdrew, leaving me with a painfully erect penis, red and marked as if a pack of hungry dogs had attacked it; she wiped her mouth with a tissue and pushed me through the door.

"Go," she said, "go to your Russian, let him finish devouring you."

Wait! I said, trying to fasten my trousers, for someone could come past at any minute, but it was almost impossible, since my swollen member refused to subside. I waited in the corner for my blood to withdraw to other, less problematic parts of my anatomy. It was five minutes before I could make myself decent and go back to my room.

38.

The key would not turn and I thought that, confused and in a rush, I had left the door unlocked and in my room were the new picture and my new savings. Numb at the idea that I had lost everything again, I slowly pushed open the door. The shock was greater than I expected. On Solouhin's bed sat a strange man of frightening appearance: a long aggressive face, head almost shaven, with the beard covered in red blotches (as if he had shaved in a mad rush), piercing eyes that bored into me and a smile that was simultaneously challenging and mocking.

"Why are you gawping at me as if you'd never seen me before?" he asked. His voice and tone were oddly familiar and his clumsy posture also reminded me of someone; I thought we must have met before, but I could not for the life of me think where.

"I knew there would come a moment when you would deny me," he said. He got to his feet and his towering height, well over six feet, and his crooked legs put the idea in my head that I was looking at a shorn and shaven Dostoyevsky. His terrible stance, with his hands hanging by his side and his fingers loose, as if he wanted to strangle someone, strengthened the impression that my lost friend had returned. On the other hand, I could not shake off the conviction that a stranger had come to kill or rob me, and I stepped back into the corridor. But his paw reached out and dragged me into the room. And the other one reached past me, closed the door and locked it.

"This is too much," he said. "Maybe you thought that the beard covered more attractive features, but you're a painter, you can cope with ugliness."

I can't believe it's you, I eventually managed to say, evidently in such a scared voice that he burst out laughing.

"And you think I can?" he said. "But if we can't believe that I'm me, then it will be even more difficult for someone else. Which means that we are, at least for now, completely safe."

No, I said, automatically checking whether the door was locked, we're not at all safe, we have to leave this minute and erase any trace. I collapsed onto my bed, shaking and overcome with nausea. Solouhin went over to the window and stared for some time across the rooftops. Then in his usual abrupt fashion he turned back to face me.

"Dear Willy Wow," he said, "I can't allow your fate to be interwoven with mine into a rotten basket. In a rotten basket you cannot carry healthy fruit. And the fruit of your labours must remain pure, no worm must be allowed to enter it, no fly shit on it. On the one hand, I feel responsible for you because you are lost in this world, or you forbid yourself to manage because you're afraid of getting your hands dirty. And on the other hand, because you are the fortunate possessor of the kind of talent that I will never have. But my envy has never been malicious, quite the opposite, because of it I felt an even greater obligation to shield you from the evil that lies in wait on the streets of this city. And I really enjoyed the role of protector. But now I have squandered the right to play that role, don't you see? Now fate has handed me the role of a murderer who needs to evade the long arm of the law. How can I remain your guru when no word of mine has any credibility? We have to separate, otherwise part of my guilt will rub off on you. I see no reason why you should sacrifice yourself for me. You have no choice but to black out the memory of our friendship and report me."

Please, I replied, how could you even think that I would betray you – do you know me so little, do you hold me in such low regard?

"I hold you in too high regard, so I don't want to demolish the walls of your future because the ground is shaking beneath my feet.

If we part, you will find a more worthy friend. If not, then everything that befalls me will also befall you. Why would you stay stubbornly loyal to me?"

Because it's not in my nature to let a friend down, I said. After all, you didn't do what you did deliberately. Of course, it's bad that you can't control yourself, but that's the way you are, it's part of the story you once told me. Everyone at some point does something that they're ashamed of, we all have skeletons in our cupboard – even me, so don't think you're the only one.

"But you've never killed anyone, dear Willy," he said. "Whatever you've done was only the result of weakness: you don't have enough courage to show yourself and the world your true face. In that regard you're no different from millions of others. My flaw is more fatal – I'm violent. Not because I enjoy violence, but because I have a devil inside me who at times leaps out in order to run wild. And whenever it happens, I am pushed aside, I am not there. I return only when it is time to take responsibility for his rage."

He scowled at me for some moments. He seemed to be trying to connect my words with the Willy he knew. Then he said: "I know that now I will become very heavy and Russian, but your soul is also Slav and you won't be afraid of the profundities that you hear. But not in this room, there are too many ghosts here from our shared past. It's time for fresh new contexts, for sowing new ideas, for harvesting new crops. We need a space that is open, where words will not bounce off and return to us disfigured. Come."

I still don't know what awoke within me, but I suddenly felt the need to rebel against his leadership, the ease with which he almost always got me to follow him and to do what he pretended we had both agreed to do.

No, I said, let's stay here, it's too dangerous outside, someone may recognise you.

He laughed: "If you, who know me, did not recognise me, how would someone who does not know me at all?"

It doesn't matter, I said, I'm not leaving this room until we decide what to do.

"Okay," he said, barely concealing his reluctance, "but not without the usual encouragements." He reached into his pocket and pulled out some tobacco, hashish and cigarette papers, and then he began to roll a joint.

"Listen, Willy," he said. "Are you even aware that we live in an age when freedom is not only predicted, but even realised? *Tune in and drop out* are not only the empty words of hippy gurus, but a mantra that has changed freedom into an obligation and a burden. Holding on to freedom is almost as tiring as longing for it without the hope of achieving it. And what is freedom, anyway? That we can lay five girls a day, even though we don't feel like it, and because we don't feel like it, we don't do it? Basically, it is as if that possibility did not exist. That we can smoke a joint in peace without regarding it as a mortal sin or someone else regarding it as such? Give me a break. This hippyish concept of freedom is a great hoax against the mass of young people who know how to regard the world with curiosity, but lack the capacity to look inside themselves and see what drives them. You and I are artists – admittedly unrecognised except by our friends – but nevertheless artists, not only in spirit, but also by definition, who do not delude themselves that the meaning of life can be anything other than flight from the cog wheels of the machine which drives that which we call the self. *Tune in and drop out* has for some time already been part of this system of cogwheels and today if you want to be really free, you buy yourself a three-piece suit, put on a tie and get a job in a bank. And you know what? That's what most hippies do, sooner or later. They carry within themselves the seeds of everything that they most hate and when these seeds sprout they will hate most of all what they are now. That's not freedom. Real freedom lies in deciding something and carrying it through, regardless of the consequences. I, of course, who always thought that I was free, have indisputably shown that I am not. The attack on that arrogant bastard from Boston was not carried out deliberately, heedless of the consequences, it was an automatic reaction by the cog wheel that drives the automated me. And that is what is causing me the most torment. I don't care much about the death of a worthless tourist; the world won't miss him, the space created by his departure can be filled by a million others. No, my dear Willy, your friend Dostoyevsky is suffering because his life is unfolding of its own accord, instead of me deliberately living it. Here."

He offered me the first drag on the joint, but again an inner voice whispered that I should reject the offer and question it. But I didn't. I inhaled and passed the joint back to him.

"Dear Willy," he said, deeply inhaling with closed eyes the sweetness of the tobacco and grass, "your attempt to distance yourself from me is too feeble to succeed. You are stuck to me, which in one way I like, but in another not, because it makes us both less free."

I asked him why he became or wanted to be a writer because, as capable as he was, he would surely have been successful sooner in some other field.

"Successful?" he said, taking another deep drag. "Every day I am successful in a hundred different things. I successfully cross the road without being run over by a car; I successfully write two or three sentences that in the right context could become literature; I successfully evade arrest. You know what, my dear Willy, we've known each other long enough to dispense with this bullshit. Why did you become a painter? To be successful?"

That was one reason, I replied. But not the main one. And maybe not even a reason at all. Maybe there were other, deeper, inexpressible reasons.

"Rubbish," he said. "Everything can be expressed. I'll tell you why you became a painter and then you'll know why I became a writer. For the same reason that God created man. God created man because he loves stories. Maybe what I tell you now isn't my idea, maybe my father told it to me and maybe his friend told it to him and that friend his father. But it doesn't really matter who tells the story and to whom, what matters is that the story gets told, stays alive, stays with us. We are all pilgrims, even you and I. Metaphors and allegories are fine things, almost literature, but a pilgrim gets to the essence by telling his own story. On the one hand you and I are omnipotent – and that's good, because otherwise we'd never get out of bed in the morning. On the other hand, we are incredibly vulnerable, which is also good, because otherwise we'd encounter catastrophe around the first corner. And we need to find a balance between the two, to stop us from going mad, which would happen overnight, I guarantee it. When God was still alive and man belonged to him, there was only one story and that was the myth of salvation. At that time we didn't need psychologists, art was in praise of God and the story was the meaning of life. Now everyone who wants to know who he is must try to tell his own story. Or to revive, in his own way, that primal story lost in the mists of time. Once, it was possible to keep bad luck at bay by going into the woods, lighting a fire, saying a prayer beside it and God would hear you. Then the moment came when we no longer knew how to make fire, but we knew how to pray and that was enough. And then came the day when we no longer knew how to make fire or to say a prayer, but we did know where to go in the woods and that was enough. Finally, there came the moment when we no longer even knew where to go – all that remained was to tell a story about this. And to see how merciful God was, and that was also enough. From that day on, the story is all that saves us. But not everyone has the time or the ability to tell stories, and so the responsibility for maintaining the meaning of the world and of life itself has been taken over by artists. In other words, you and I. Through our work, we enable others to put their experiences on Earth into meaningful order and to free themselves from the past, which would be their prison. The meaning of life is not something supernatural – transcendence is the greatest fraud of all times – and don't say that you don't agree with me because I know you do. The meaning is nothing more than a spirit-friendly pattern that it is possible to conform to without any great effort. But that pattern has to be created, it has to be gleaned from the teeming life that surrounds us. And so someone must listen to your story and mine, bringing it to life not only for themselves, but for us. Do you know that old Jewish saying? Whenever two Jews meet and one has a problem, the other automatically becomes a rabbi. In other words, the essence of everything is empathy. Our stories are proof that we are not indifferent, that the world touches us, that we feel for others."

When I could finally get a word in edgeways, I said that that probably held true for a writer, but not for a painter, and even if it did for some of them, it did not for me. Brueghel tells stories, and perhaps Rembrandt, but my paintings – and I was not trying to compare myself with them – are more about bearing witness than storytelling, more statements, more a way of communicating to the world how I think and feel about this or that aspect of man's fate.

"Well," he cut in, "you've put it nicely: not your personal fate, but *man's* fate – although it's one and the same thing, you have to acknowledge that. What you call a statement is a concentrated story in images. Each painting of yours – in fact, every painting that attracts my attention – tells me something. It poses a question that disturbs me and then offers an answer. Maybe it isn't the painting itself that does that, maybe it is only my interpretation of what I see, but in any case the answer is the point of the story: what you have communicated to me. Both of us strive, regardless of the final result, to confront people with the basic colour of life, which is sadness, the eternal sadness of lost hope, the eternal sadness of the unattainable. It's not an easy colour, it's far from the false cheerfulness of our generation and perhaps even further from the pragmatic, self-centred generation that will no doubt follow ours, but people really do feel the need to face up to it, even if they are not aware of the fact, even if they deny it. We all want to know where we are and what lies in front of us. Regardless of what happened on Tedworth Square, regardless of the fact that the police are looking for me and I'll end up, sooner or later, on the gallows, regardless of the fact that I am possessed by a demon that challenges me to a duel because it wants to become my master, regardless of all that and much else, I can say, my dear Willy, that we belong among the thirty-six righteous ones, among the thirty-six hidden saints that hold the fate of the world in their hands. We belong among them even if we put forward a hundred rational arguments why it is not so. They are known as Lamed-Vav. When one dies, his place is immediately taken by another – always someone who is in the right place at the right time and in the right spiritual and blessed state."

Now he had so much hashish inside him that his eyes were glowing with a strange, obsessive brilliance, while his tone became ever more sermon-like, prophetic. I could feel the effects of the drug, but much less, since Dostoyevsky was handing me the joint ever less frequently and each time he soon snatched it back. In my case the effect was diametrically opposite: an increasing scepticism, against which his raptures beat like waves against impermeable rocks.

If at first I had trouble following his train of thought, I now clearly felt that it was carrying him into the realm of fairy tales – perhaps interesting ones, but with no connection to our role in the world, let alone the position we had found ourselves in, largely thanks to him. I suggested that he write a story about these righteous ones, but some other time, since our current hard reality demanded immediate and specific solutions.

"The only solution for me is to give myself up to the police," he said, staring at a point in front of him as if he had only now recognised the seriousness of his situation. He sighed and added, barely audibly: "Damn. Shit. Fuck, damn, shit." Then he sighed again and returned to the wave of energy vibrating inside him.

"But Willy, why not avoid the worst while there is still a sliver of hope that it is possible? Each man's first duty is to himself, otherwise how else can he care for others? And the legend of Lamed-Vav speaks precisely of that. On his death bed my granddad, one of the Lamed-Vav, named me as his successor. Can you imagine the horror of a seven-year-old boy when he is told that he must spend the rest of his life as one of the thirty-six righteous ones? Forget about your goals, your pleasures – care for others. But my granddad consoled me, saying that he did not expect anything like that, for the thirty-six righteous ones together cannot save anyone, cannot change anything. There was no need to scourge myself, no need to seek suffering, since life itself would bring it to me, as it did to all. My only duty, he said, was to feel empathy for the suffering of others, so that they did not suffer alone, but each particle of their suffering would be divided among the thirty-six righteous ones. Empathy is what God expects from these chosen ones, thanks to which the end of the world is occasionally delayed by two or three minutes. Of course, the lot of the one you feel empathy for is not greatly changed, but God is satisfied and while God is satisfied his grace helps us to keep on suffering. Is that not the only meaning of life? To keep on suffering? And for you and I, who are certainly among the chosen ones, to feel not only our own suffering but the suffering of others?"

His final words triggered within me a great desire to escape from his forced embrace; his emphasis on "you and I" was increasingly smothering me; he had taken so much sovereignty from me that I had to win it back.

You do that, I said, you be one of the thirty-six righteous ones, although I'd stake my life on the fact that you are quite the opposite. But let that remain a question for you to deal with yourself. I'm not on this Earth to suffer with others and make God happy, since I don't even know who God is or could be. I'm on this Earth for me. I've had enough of my own suffering, although it's not so great as to be unbearable. As for the suffering of others, I have neither the time nor the inclination to observe it, let alone incorporate it into my life. And I don't think that because of that I'm bad or worse than anyone else. Every hour that I devote to others – either you as a friend or a complete stranger – is still an hour of my life and I'm the one who is responsible for seeing that it is not wasted, and I've wasted countless hours already. You yourself said that we must each first look after ourselves and I do that too indecisively. Whenever I offer too large a part of myself, to establish and then maintain a relationship, I get the feeling that I am selling myself, while others see in my openness an attempt at manipulation or, even worse, an opportunity for their own bit of manipulation. So I am afraid to offer anything at all, or to be the first to be open, to take the first step – I'd rather not dance than have someone dance with me. And that's true for both of us, I said. I've never before had a friend who usurped so many of my thoughts and consequent decisions. It's still not clear to me – and is perhaps even less clear than it was – where our friendship begins and ends, at what point it transcends the desire for company, the fear of loneliness, the domain of selfishness and becomes what you call empathy. I wonder whether the story that we are telling each other is honest enough, developed enough, or whether it is a matter of coincidence and the need of the moment. I know that I would never betray you, but I'm not sure that you would not cheat me. Maybe I'm doing you an injustice, but I value you too highly to dissemble, and you are far too bright not to notice if I did.

He took a final drag from the joint and threw the end into the corner of the room, as if trying to hit an imaginary basket with an imaginary ball. Then his paw was on my shoulder, his fingers massaged me slightly and he gave me a gentle pat.

"Willy," he said, "being honest with someone is not the same as being honest with yourself. The first is easier than the second, but the second is higher on the scale of values, because it brings you closer to the truth. You have mastered the first, because it is one of your defence mechanisms and defence is a basic reflex. Since you were little, you have been convinced that the world is a vicious beast that wants to bite off your head. But if you knew how to be even a little honest with yourself, you would see that what I am telling you is true. It's no fairy tale, it's merely a matter of choosing words, just as in your case it's a matter of choosing and combining paints. If you knew how to be a little bit less literal, if you saw metaphors for what they are – in other words, signposts – you would realise that you and I *are* two of the thirty-six righteous ones who feel the torments of others. You express it through your paintings, I through my stories. A suffering person sees your painting and realises he is not alone – someone has been there before him, someone has expressed his pain. A suffering person reads my story and realises that he is the author of a literary work – it seems to him that the story is his personal confession, something that he would entrust only to his diary and even then only when he knew it was safe from prying eyes. What's important is that the suffering person, on encountering our work, knows that he is not alone. That someone is depicting stories that he would otherwise have to live and bear completely alone."

And how does that help? I asked argumentatively. How does it help us? Does anyone care about your stories, does anyone publish them, read them? Does anyone care about my paintings, does anyone want to buy them, to hang them on the wall at home? No. A hundred thousand books are published in Britain every year – is yours one of them? The museums and galleries have at least that many paintings – are mine among them? No. When will we drop this pretence that we are artists? How long will it take before we're capable of acknowledging that we are nothing more than dreamers?

"And what then?" he asked abruptly.

He suddenly got up and his face glowed above me, red with anger. "Are we going to cut off our ears, like Van Gogh? Commit suicide? None of his works was sold during his lifetime. He had plenty of reasons to doubt whether he was an artist. Now everyone knows the story in his paintings. Great and small. The stories of your dear ones, your predecessors, friends, mankind. What is it with you, Willy? Are you really so small, so impatient that everything must be now, now, now? What if it's fated that our *now* is tomorrow? Or the day after? Look at this painting of yours. You painted it, but do you even know why? Do you even know what story you are telling with it? How do you feel our suffering through this painting?"

He went over to the painting, which was not only unfinished, but I had no idea what I wanted to say with it. "Three things being trampled on by the hurrying crowd. A small white dog, a pink baby, a reflection of the sun. An anthological story, my dear Willy! A personal confession *par excellence*. In our haste to achieve the goal that hovers on the horizon like a fata morgana, we trample on precisely those things that we are rushing towards: the inner child, which represents the innocence that we are constantly longing for, as well as the hope that we shall grow up innocent. The small white dog represents the purity of the playful, uncorrupt soul, which we hope will never be bitten by adulthood. And the reflection of the sun, which is a reflection of the never achieved future in the always achieved present – in short, the moment in which we are. And you're trying to tell me that your paintings do not tell stories that are proof of empathy for the suffering of all those who live on this Earth?"

Now I scrambled to my feet. Evening was falling and my painting was glowing in its own strange, veiled light, as if radiating precisely what Solouhin had ascribed to it. But what it seemed to be radiating was precisely what I wanted to deny.

No, I said, no, no, no. The story you are forcing into my images is your own projection, what you see, elevated into understanding of art. This painting tells thousands of stories, a different story to each of us, but never the one I wanted to tell. Between me and what you refer to as my empathy lies an endless ocean of misunderstanding, speculation, wilful interpretation. And for many there is no feeling here, no content. Ascribing meaning to a random arrangement of colours, lines and shapes is a simple, innocent, non-binding game: I like to play it myself, when I look at clouds and see the shapes of animals, birds, people. That has no connection with art and art has no connection with empathy.

"Oh Willy," he said, "it is so disappointing to listen to you. What about Munch's *The Scream,* Picasso's *Guernica*, Van Gogh's self-portrait? Compassion is not pity, it does not relate only to suffering, you can identify with thousands of shades of feeling – including pleasure, rapture, ecstasy, fear. And what does it matter if each person sees a different story in your painting? Be glad: we writers are more restricted, words are always more specific than images, it's harder for us to be ambiguous, let alone achieve multiple meanings, which even the most average painter can achieve. You also misunderstood the metaphor of the righteous ones. It's not a matter of an actual number and actual things – obviously leaning towards the actual is an occupational hazard of all visual artists. It's about general categories, and perhaps it would become clearer if we connected it with the number of possible stories, narrative developments, dramatic situations described by the Italian Gozzi, which is also thirty-six. And don't think that it's a matter of coincidence: God does not reveal himself through coincidence, but through meaningful correlation. The kind of empathy that pleases God can only be expressed in thirty-six ways and it doesn't matter whether it is expressed through narrative or dramatic twists, through a painting, a sculpture, a piece of music, a way of living, which can also show empathy, or through sin, which can be an exemplar and a spur to compassion. In every case the point is the same: that we do not suffer alone, that there is a bond of understanding between us, that the worst has not yet happened to us only because our fellow sufferers have attracted parts of the lightning bolt to themselves."

More than ever before, it seemed to me that Dostoyevsky could not be pinned down, that he was chronically slippery, different every moment, at every moment a different one of the thirty-six. I felt the need and just enough courage to tell him.

You know what, I said. I've realised that you make things up as you go along, you create yourself as if you were improvising a story, or like I do my paintings, one stroke at a time, one idea at a time. You are constantly evaluating what you could be, which story you could be the hero of, and then you become that, at least for a moment, perhaps for a few days, until a new opportunity arises. There is nothing constant about you, you are in a constant state of flux, and your internal conflict is not like mine, where Willy I and Willy II are fighting to see whether morality or effectiveness prevail. Your conflict is more brutal: whether illusion, which nurtures hope, will prevail, or the truth, which could destroy you.

"You blame me for changing?" he said haughtily. "You want me to be frozen, like a statue that always reflects changes in the same way? You expect too much of me. You accuse me of precisely that which you see as good in yourself. We all keep changing, because we all keep growing, thank God. Or do I not have the right to reveal my consciousness and act accordingly? My dear Willy, you completely fail to understand me: if I want to live without a mask, I have to face up to my entire self, all the oppositions and contradictions, all that is ugly and evil and that shames me. How can I be honest with myself if I dare not be honest to you? And vice versa. If you see nothing constant in me, but just a sequence of faces, that means I am constantly searching for and testing the characteristics of the hero who enters my life story as me. And therein lies the only true freedom, since the awareness of what is being born and growing within me enables me to choose how and with what feeling I shall react to external challenges. If you cannot accept me as I am and at the same time allow me to be different the next moment, then you'll never feel comfortable in my company, you'll always feel threatened. So I repeat the advice that triggered this whole conversation: staying with me would be too difficult for you. Let's embrace and say our goodbyes."

It was then that I realised for the first time that he was rejecting me because he was afraid that I would reject him: he wanted to maintain his primacy, his role of teacher to the less experienced pupil, but at the same time to leave himself an honourable way out. This gave me the chance to win some advantages.

So I said: I don't need advice on how to behave. I decide myself what is a sacrifice and what isn't; I decide when I go out, when I come back. I'm not saying I feel responsible for you and we maybe would achieve more if we went our separate ways and saw each other once a week on neutral territory, but this does not seem the right moment for that: before, I needed protecting, now you do. And one other thing: I wasn't condemning your metamorphoses, I was merely mentioning them. I, too, want to be frank. The thing is this: you are not a single person, but a sequence of test sketches that fade before they have the chance to be reinforced by paint. And because I don't know who I'll be dealing with tomorrow, I'm slightly confused. That's all. The fact is, we can't stay in this room – every trail leads here. I recommend that we relocate.

He came over to me, put his arm around me and squeezed so tightly that my bones almost creaked. "Willy," he said, "you are a friend like no other. A friend with a soul at least as deep as mine. Perhaps fate, which is wilful but more generous than either of us, will reward you with what you most desire. Perhaps soon in this labyrinth of streets you will by coincidence and God's mercy meet your muse, Sandrina. Then it will be the end of our friendship, that much is clear to me. But because that won't happen tomorrow or the day after, for each thing comes to us in life when we are ready for it, we have before us at least one more episode together as misunderstood artists. I've already found a flat, we can move in today under cover of darkness, as befits criminals, and my new name, which you need to remember, is Aleksander Sergejevič Stavrogin. And not only that, dear Willy: as well as a flat I've also found work. Not just for me, but for both of us. And this time, believe it or not, you're going to be employed as a painter!"

39.

The flat was in an abandoned house on a neglected street in Kilburn, where Dostoyevsky (now Stavrogin) and I got a room on the first floor. The other rooms of this large house, which the unknown owner had abandoned to its fate, although the doors and windows had thick boards nailed across, were occupied by at least a dozen strange and somewhat suspicious-looking individuals. The facade, including the front door, was completely covered by rampant vegetation and so we crept in and out via the back door and the narrow path through the impenetrably overgrown garden.

There were hundreds of abandoned houses in London and squatting was one of the ways of solving your housing problem if you were without money, or preferred to spend it on other things. Every few months the squatters, who were organised and who even had their own publication offering information on new opportunities, took over some building in which they were not welcome. If after three official requests they did not withdraw, the police came and forcibly evicted them, almost always accompanied by a large media presence. Our house was too insignificant to be threatened by such a fate, but in spite of that every evening, before turning on the lights, we drew the curtains at the front of the house or, where there were no curtains, covered the windows with pieces of cardboard.

This was one of the house rules. In fact, there were no others and they would not have been respected if there were. Dostoyevsky had arrived there thanks to "connections" and had taken over the largest room where, in addition to two dusty mattresses on the floor, there was a table with a wobbly chair.

"Camden Market is close by," he said. "A few days ago I saw a cheap easel. I'll go and get it for you tomorrow, I don't like that sour expression on your face."

You surely don't think that I'm going to paint here? I responded. I'm not staying in this house a minute longer than necessary.

"Oh, Mr. Artist with your bourgeois pretensions, I'm sorry that I could not find you a palace with a view of the park," he replied sarcastically, even aggressively. "It was you who insisted that we move as soon as possible."

But not into such a house and among such people!

"What's wrong with them?" he wanted to know.

I actually did not know them well enough to condemn them like that, but it was true that I did not feel safe among them. They lived in some kind of hippy commune where everything belonged to everyone and where each one belonged to everyone else; the only personal belongings were clothes and shoes. Eight guys shared four girls and vice versa. The company was richly international, including a Japanese girl, an Indian guy and a black guy from the Caribbean, while there were two more girls from Australia and one from the States.

I never managed to work out what they lived on, since they rarely left the house, and when they did so it was usually in the evening or at night. Alcohol, drugs, sex, lying around, music, the smell of incense, long-winded discussions, occasionally an Indian mantra and strange ceremonies; jointly prepared vegetarian meals; that part of their life was visible. About all the rest I could only surmise. At night the girls might have hung around street corners in Soho or danced in night clubs, while the guys maybe dealt drugs or worked as waiters or even night watchmen – but I never found any evidence for my suppositions. Perhaps it was as Dostoyevsky said: that they were merely travellers who had got stuck for some time in London, since I often heard them say: "I like it here, but I think it's time to be moving on."

Dostoyevsky and I were a kind of addition, almost a disturbance. He did actually visit them on the ground floor, smoked and sometimes ate with them, perhaps even slept with one of the four girls, but in general they left us in peace, especially me, whom they often regarded warily, even with suspicion, as if they sensed that I did not approve of their way of life. Just once it happened that one of them, the American Danny, came to me in the room and said: "Hey, man, my girlfriend would like you to come to our room tonight. She likes you because you're different. I can go out or I can join you, it's up to you."

I have a better idea, I replied. You two go out and I stay in my room.

After that they left me in peace, even though their mistrust deepened and more than once I got the feeling that I'd be doing them a favour if I left.

I would have done that with the greatest pleasure, if it wasn't for Dostoyevsky. Without him I didn't want to go anywhere, since it would mean I was leaving him to his fate and I had no wish to do that, especially when I saw how doggedly he defended me against the members of the commune. "Where did you find that weirdo?" I overheard one day. Dostoyevsky responded vigorously. "Willy Wow Potty is no weirdo and I'd like you all to remember that. Willy is a talented painter who has got into difficulties. He's also my best friend, so any negative comment about him is a personal attack on me. And that, I don't recommend." This was followed by conciliatory murmurs and one of the guys, judging by his accent Australian, muttered: "Stop threatening us, you crazy Russian, no one's going to do you any harm."

Fortunately, we were out most of the time during the day. Every day at nine we walked to the famous zoo in Regent's Park, where Dostoyevsky, through connections that he refused to talk about, had arranged us the kind of work that comes along once in a lifetime. My job was to paint pictures of the animals for the London Zoo's gallery and for sale to the public – realistically, with no artistic pretensions or additions, standard format. Dostoyevsky had a less gratifying but more intriguing task: he joined the team of keepers charged with counting all the zoo's residents and bringing the list up-to-date. This stocktaking had to be done every three years because the number was constantly changing: animals died, fled or produced offspring and new ones were acquired; some multiplied too vigorously and the management had to work out how many it could afford to keep.

At that time London Zoo contained more than six hundred animal species, more than a hundred of these threatened in the wild – altogether, more than ten thousand creatures. And all of them had to be categorised, counted and recorded – every turtle, every lizard, every bird, every snake, every insect, every fish. In doing so, you had to take care not to be bitten, stung, scratched, kicked or trodden on. You also had to ensure that your trousers were not invaded and that you did not leave work with some hairy creature hiding in your pocket. The hardest was counting insects, lizards, frogs, birds and fish; some of them never stayed still, others were so alike that it was hard to say whether the specimen you were looking at was not the same one that had a moment before disappeared from view.

In spite of this, Dostoyevsky enjoyed the work and every evening he told me how animals were helping him to understand the nature of people. I was finding something similar myself. Dostoyevsky was not earning much, while for each painting I finished, alongside material costs, I was paid three pounds. Since the average monthly wage at that time was less than a hundred pounds, I thought they were being quite generous. I calculated that if I painted at least one animal from each species, I would earn sufficient money for at least two years of relatively worry-free life; above all, I would soon have enough to leave the squat and move into somewhere more comfortable. But it quickly became apparent that this was not to be, because the whole thing was a kind of experiment; they already had in their archive paintings of most of the animals and all the rest was dependent on how much interest the public showed. If apes proved most popular, I would have to paint mostly apes; if giraffes were a hit, I would be painting giraffes; I was told that sooner or later I would be working solely on the basis of supply and demand.

Among the apes it was easiest to paint gorillas and orang-utans, who did not move around too much and stared at me in fascination,

311

while the chimpanzees and baboons jumped around their enclosures like mad creatures; some of them reached through the bars and tried to grab their portraits in order to rip them to shreds. One of the baboons was quite malicious: he would hold onto the bars with all fours and wait for a passing visitor, often a child, to offer him a banana, nut or other snack; he always took the food gratefully and extremely cautiously, then he would wildly bite his benefactor's fingers. Even though there was a large sign on the cage saying "This animal is dangerous", visitors either did not see it or did not take it seriously, since the baboon had a very friendly, almost human face.

Whenever I was painting outside, I soon attracted a small crowd of curious onlookers, especially children, whose mothers could never persuade them to leave me alone; they wanted to see whether my final product really resembled the model in the cage or enclosure, while I constantly had to listen to comments – from encouraging to critical to destructive – that made it impossible for me to concentrate on my work. Eventually, I'd had enough and I hung a sign on my back saying "Do not disturb the painter at work". This led to no great improvement, I still had to listen to a range of comments, often stupid ones, and the questions of pesky children, such as: Daddy, what's that boy painting? Mummy, why does it say don't disturb the painter at work? It was true, however, that they no longer came too close, looking over my shoulder and breathing down my neck.

My most successful animal portraits in the first two weeks were those of the lions and tigers, the giraffes and zebras, the rhinos and hippos, whereas the crocodiles and snakes were somewhat less satisfactory, and some residents were never available for their portraits. Others were too quick to be captured when they displayed their most interesting behaviour, such as the chameleon, who flicked out his tongue at a cockroach with such rapidity that the hapless victim both was and was not almost in the same moment. The exotic mice and rats were almost never to be seen, similarly the crickets and frogs, while the fish in the aquarium were simply too numerous to be able to follow only one of them with your eyes.

Whenever Dostoyevsky and I talked in the evening about our work, he almost always ended with a statement that one way or another was connected with his current predicament. Once he said: "If I had at least a tenth of the capabilities that animals have I would never be caught. Have you ever thought that man is actually the least qualified to survive in the world, where he is most endangered by his imaginings?" And another time: "If there is reincarnation, I'd like to come back as an animal with the defence mechanisms of all animals, from claws to horns to poisonous fangs, and with gills and feathers, with the capacity to take on the colour of my environment and a tongue I could swish round the corner and finish off my enemy before he even knew I was there."

I wouldn't, I said. Animals don't form friendships. That is what saves us. I'd rather come back as a person.

40.

Two days later, along the corridor of the Reptile House, where I had just finished painting a python, came two men with close cropped hair accompanied by a bobby in uniform with a truncheon in his hand. They were accompanied by the director's assistant, who was just explaining something as they walked past me and when I caught his words my stomach lurched.

"We took him on to help us inventory the animals. He was recommended by an acquaintance of the director's, we never imagined there could be anything wrong…"

I knew that Dostoyevsky was somewhere in the Aquarium and my first impulse was to run and warn him. But then I thought that this might only attract attention. They were heading in his direction and I would have to run past them, which would have aroused suspicion – they would want to know who I was and it would emerge that they were looking for me, too, primarily as a witness to the incident and a possible source of information. In spite of my concern for Dostoyevsky, my own life suddenly seemed more important: I had earned quite a tidy sum at the zoo, I could look for somewhere more comfortable to live, start to pursue my artistic goals once more…

And so, although with a heavy heart, I left Dostoyevsky to his fate. Although I hoped he would manage to get away, I was convinced that he could not be helped, as the director's assistant knew where to lead the officers, whereas I would have to search the whole Aquarium before I found him. Poor Solouhin, I thought, while counting fish he would also be netted. I quietly tidied away my palette, paints and brushes, and put them in a plastic bag. I left the unfinished painting and the easel, which belonged to the zoo, in the corridor. I calmly walked towards the exit and told the guard that I was going for lunch. After turning the first corner, I took to my heels and headed for Kilburn.

In front of the house I was met by one of the squatters, the guy from the Caribbean, who seemed the friendliest. "Don't go in," he said. "They're looking for you and the Russian. They're interrogating everyone. The Russian got away in time, he asked me to give you this."

He handed me a sheet of paper that had been folded five times. I opened it and read: "The hounds are on our trail. Flee, I have already. Rendezvous: below Nelson among the pigeons."

What about my things? I asked the guy.

"If I were you, I wouldn't waste any time," he said. "I'll keep my fingers crossed."

I hurried down the street. Thankfully, because of the drugged-up hippies in the squat I had my savings and my documents with me, otherwise I would have been once more without money and perhaps even without a passport. But everything else stayed in the house: all my modest possessions, especially my paintings, including the last one, which I had done after Dostoyevsky disappeared and which, I don't know why, I had entitled *Tea With the Queen.* I knew that I couldn't go back to the house, it was too risky, so my only hope was my friend, who a little earlier I had abandoned to his fate; he knew the squatters much better than I and might be able to get my things back.

I took the Underground to Trafalgar Square and looked for Solouhin's horsey face among the crowds feeding the pigeons. I was sure that he, too, would have gone straight there. But he was nowhere to be seen. I waited an hour, two, three, but in vain. Had they caught him and I would never see him again? I refused to believe it. Was he perhaps afraid that I was being followed by one of the detectives and dared not come near me for fear that he would be pounced upon?

I had not imagined that without him I would feel so lost, that London would seem once more so indifferently empty, noisy and too full of everything that did not interest me, that did not touch me. I watched the visitors from every corner of the world going up and down the steps of the National Gallery, and for the first time I thought that I would never cross the threshold of this austere institution, that I would never summon up the courage – that I would never have anything worthy of being hung on the wall of a toilet, let alone a painting that would one day hang in the National Gallery. Although when I first came to Britain I knew that everything would not go according to plan, it never occurred to me that several months later, in the middle of September, on the cusp of autumn, which I could already feel in the cool gusts of wind, I would be sitting beneath the statue of the famous victor as one defeated, without friends, or paintings, or a future, and even without a roof over my head. I felt like bursting into tears, but there were too many people around me, so I kept my emotions to myself.

This effort left me feeling strangely agitated and nervous. I went round the square four times, I climbed the steps of the National Gallery, determined to go in and look at some paintings, but just before I got to the front of the queue I changed my mind and went back out. I went towards Piccadilly Circus and noticed a bank; I went in and said that I wanted to open an account to put my savings in. The short-haired young man in jacket and tie asked me for proof of my address and a recommendation from an existing customer, otherwise he would not be able to help me. Okay, I thought, if you don't want my money, I'll have to carry it with me.

I walked on, ending up in China Town, where I went into a restaurant and ordered duck with rice, but I found I couldn't eat it. I then went into a pub, ordered a beer, sat in the corner, hung my head and tried to make sure that no one could see the tears falling into my beer. But one of the bar staff realised that all was not well. She kept looking in my direction and eventually she took a minute's break and sat down beside me.

"What's wrong?" she asked. "Can I help?"

I shrugged. I noticed that she had a kind, concerned face, covered with freckles, tousled red hair and large, dangly earrings. It's nothing important, I said. "Okay," she replied and went back behind the bar.

But she soon came back and asked whether I wanted another beer, even though customers were supposed to get their own drinks at the bar. Please, I said, and when she brought me a pint she sat down beside me once more. Whichever way I looked at it, the only possible explanation was that she liked me. I liked her too, but just as my thoughts were elsewhere, so was my heart.

"It's ages since I saw such an unhappy looking lad," she said. "Did someone die?"

As a matter of fact yes, I replied. Quite a number of people who I thought would be my friends have died. Leaving without saying goodbye is also a kind of death, isn't it?

"You sound a like a poet," she said. "Are you?"

I'm a painter, I admitted modestly. A painter without paintings, without anything, especially a roof over my head. I've no idea where I'll sleep tonight.

"I thought it would be something like that," she sighed and returned to the bar, from where her colleague was giving us black looks.

She wasn't absent for long: as soon as she got an opportunity, she was back. "Where are you from?" she wanted to know.

Russia, I said. I didn't want to waste energy giving a lesson on the lesser known countries of Europe.

"Really?" she responded with enthusiasm. "I've never met a real Russian before! But you look quite human, considering all I've heard about Russians. I'm from New Zealand, from a small place near Wellington, which even the inhabitants of Wellington have never heard of, let alone someone from Russia. My name's Sandy."

Nice to meet you, Sandy, I said. I'm Vaclav Kandinsky.

"Oh," she said, "what an interesting name. I'll ask my colleague behind the bar if he knows of a room, people often put up notices."

She returned to work, pouring beer, mixing cocktails, opening bottles of juice and Coca Cola. I noticed that she had freckles even on her legs, she was probably freckled from head to toe, Speckled Sandy, my new friend. When she once more headed towards me I

317

noticed that she had shapely legs, a nice walk, a nice figure, a nice smile, friendly but melancholic eyes (as if they reflected an inner sadness) and guessed that she felt lonely in this soulless city, although she tried hard not to show it.

"No room," she said. "The only thing available is a studio, not far from here, on Greek Street, but you probably already have a studio, if you're a painter."

After a moment's silence, I took a breath and almost shouted: You're pulling my leg, someone's renting out a studio in Soho? Can I see it now?

"I'm afraid not, because my colleague has the key and we only finish just before midnight. Can you wait?"

Absolutely, I said, for a studio in Soho I'll wait all night if necessary... to the end of the month, the end of the year! A studio in Soho is something I barely dared to dream of. And probably the rent is so high that it would have been better for my peace of mind that you hadn't even mentioned it.

"I'll ask," she said and went back behind the bar.

When at around midnight we turned into Greek Street, Jeremy, her colleague, explained that the studio had become available because the previous tenant, also a painter, had been murdered. The owner didn't want this mentioning, but he wanted to be open with me – in any case, sooner or later Sandy would have told me.

That's not such a big deal, I responded, there must be at least five murders a day in London. But I'd like to know who murdered him and why, so that I don't end up as the next victim.

"As far as I know, it was something to do with borrowed money and extortion," said Jeremy. "Not the kind of thing likely to be repeated."

I hope not, I said.

We went down some narrow steps to the entrance and when Jeremy unlocked the door and turned on the light, at first I could not believe that what I saw was real: a basement about thirty feet by fifteen, with reflectors in the ceiling that gently illuminated the whole space, particularly certain points where there stood three easels holding unfinished canvases – evidently the murdered man had been working

318

on three paintings at once. Sketches, engravings, drafts, finished and unfinished paintings lay all around.

It isn't empty, I said, someone's living here.

"No," said Jeremy, "the dead one's brother looked through everything and took a few paintings away, but he wasn't interested in the rest. The owner said the new tenant should decide what to do with what was left."

But there are paints, brushes, canvases, all sorts, I said. It's strange to leave these to a stranger. And the pictures are not at all bad – in fact, I'd say that they are good, very good.

"I don't think him and his brother got on too well," said Jeremy. He showed me a small side-room with a toilet and shower; next to it was a kitchen area with a tiny fridge and a double hot plate.

One could even live here, I said.

"The previous tenant did. His brother took away the bed yesterday."

I can't believe it, I said, he took the bed and left the paintings?

"He can use the bed because he rents rooms out to students. Evidently, he didn't like the pictures."

He opened a door at the other end of the studio. I squinted into the dark and saw a disorderly, heavily overgrown garden, at least fifty yards long and six wide.

I'd like to take it, I said. Immediately. Can you find out what the rent is?

"I daren't call the owner now," said Jeremy, looking at his watch.

"Oh, go on," said Sandy, "call him, he'll be glad – didn't he say he's been trying to rent it out for six months?"

"Okay," agreed Jeremy and reached for the phone.

Impossible, I said, a phone as well – what luxury.

While Jeremy was on the phone, I discovered other things: an ancient, but comfortable armchair, a heap of art books with full page reproductions, more than twenty tins of beans, four bottles of wine, a stained t-shirt, a pile of worn shoes, a heap of newspapers and magazines – as if the person who lived here had been forced to leave in a hurry.

"He's not answering," said Jeremy, putting down the phone. "Tomorrow."

319

I could sleep here, I've nowhere to go, I got evicted today. Jeremy began to fidget as if he was being bothered by a particularly troublesome flea. "I don't know," he said. "Without the owner's permission, I daren't. I only have the key for viewings – that was the agreement."

Okay, I said, I'll sleep on the street. Jeremy turned off the light and locked the door. One by one, we went up the steps to the pavement.

"You can come home with me," said Sandy, after Jeremy had said goodbye.

She lived in an attic room above the pub where she worked; her room was even smaller than mine at Mrs. O'Riley's on Nevern Square. When we had finished making love, which started off polite, friendly and considerate, but ended in a violent climax, driven by her passion (mine did not completely come alive, although I dutifully went through the necessary motions), Speckled Sandy burst into tears in my arms.

What's wrong? I asked, removing the tears from her cheeks with my lips.

"Oh nothing," she lamented, "I had pictured this damned London so differently. I think I'll just go home."

Maybe not a bad idea, I said.

"What about you?" she sobbed.

I can't, I said. The fight is still on. London has given me a few kicks, but I'm not yet on my knees, I still hope I might win.

"Can I visit you in your studio?" she said, snuggling up to me. "It's the first time in ages that I'm with someone who can give me a bit of warmth. I need that, otherwise I'll die."

My warmth is actually sadness, I said. My sad life is hugging and stroking you. I'm a peddler of desolation.

"Don't say that," she said, "I have enough sadness of my own. I want joy, I want hope, I'm sick of emptiness."

But there are many kinds of sadness, I said. Some are quite pleasant. You're welcome at the studio any time, day or night, although it's probably only a dream, since I doubt I have enough money for the rent.

And the next morning it seemed as if I really couldn't afford the studio. The owner was asking fifteen pounds a week and a year's rent in advance. My savings amounted to four hundred (mainly what I had earned at the zoo) – that was enough for six months, with ten pounds left over for food (for the first week or so, and then what?).

"It's too much," said Sandy, "the guy's taking advantage, tell him to lower it a bit."

He refused to lower the rent, but he did give some ground regarding the deposit, accepting only six months' rent.

And so by midday I was the proud owner of a studio in the heart of Soho (and a large jungle-like garden). I had already started tidying up and thinking where I could get a cheap mattress, so that I wouldn't have to sleep on the floor. I had begun to realise that I had as much good luck as bad: I had Sandy (who found great pleasure in helping me); I had the canvas, paints, brushes left by my predecessor, and could start work immediately; but I didn't have anything else, apart from the trousers, shirt and shoes I had fled in (and no money to buy new ones).

And I still didn't know what had happened to Dostoyevsky. That was the greatest loss. But at least during the first few days, the studio outweighed everything else: I sent my parents my first and only postcard of London.

"I have rented a large studio in the middle of London, where I am living. I'm painting every day and my paintings are selling. I'm doing well."

At the beginning, the telephone was a toy that I could not resist. I called Mrs. Hudson and hung up when she answered. I called Stella Henderson to hear her voice, but Conchita answered the phone. I called Alan's and for some time listened to Marisa's voice ("Hello, who's there? Who is it? Mr. McClelland is not at home, please call later."). I called Cornwall and put down the phone when Mr. Denton-Barker answered. Only Cleo remained unreachable: although there was a phone at Mrs. O'Riley's on Never Square, I didn't know whose name was listed under in the directory.

The possibility that I might get in touch with people from the past, if only to hear their voices, made me feel somehow grounded: the past, which at times seemed so remote, was not a hallucination, it was real and very close. The phone was also useful because Sandy could call me several times a day. In the pub she learned many useful things from the customers and with her friendly manner she managed to scrounge for me quite a good mattress, which someone brought to my door two hours later. She "borrowed" four sheets and two pillows from the pub, she told me where there was sale of pots and pans, and then every day she cooked a little something for me. She also brought me food from the pub: a sandwich, some salad, chips – whatever was left at the end of the day and would end up in the bin.

Precious Sandy, how hard she tried to look after me and create a normal life for us! Even though I knew it was only temporary, since Dostoyevsky could turn up at any moment and I've have to take him in, her presence had a beneficial effect and our nights became ever more pleasant.

I'm sorry, Sandy, I whispered into her ear at an appropriate moment, my name isn't Kandinsky, but Vaupotič, and I'm not Russian but a Slovene from Yugoslavia, if you want, you can call me Willy Wow Potty.

"It doesn't matter where you're from" she said, "even if you're from Mars. In any case, I prefer the name Willy, it's easier to pronounce. There's one other thing, my dear: you're penniless, you'll have to start earning some money, they've started giving me strange looks in the pub, the landlord asked me what I was doing with the leftovers."

I know, my little Freckles, I replied, I know you're supporting me and taking risks for me, though I've no right to expect you to do that. Tomorrow, I'll start painting, to justify having this studio. Maybe this wasn't the most sensible move, but what's done is done.

"Start painting," she said, "but it may be months before you sell anything. Look what the last guy left behind."

That's nothing, I said. It's not bad, but it's derivative. His figures are reminiscent of Dante Gabriel Rosetti and his dreamy women among kitschy natural details. Faithfulness to nature is unfaithfulness to art. My paintings are much more original.

"How come you have none to show?" she wanted to know.

322

Let's keep that a secret, I said. Whenever I've told anyone the details about my past, everything has gone wrong. I don't want that to be repeated, I'd like us to stay together at least some time.

"Then you need to do something," she said, trying hard to maintain a patient tone. "I can't support both of us. The cleaner at the pub handed in her notice, you could apply for that, you'd get ten shillings an hour."

Ten shillings an hour, I tried to stop myself from laughing (and crying at the same time). Four pounds a day, twenty per week, not bad, we could eat spaghetti every other day and I could buy some shirts, jeans, shoes.

"And sometimes we could go to the cinema," she said. "You'll have to say that you're an experienced cleaner, otherwise they won't take you on."

Of course I'm an experienced cleaner, I said, who has cleaned more paint from the floor or from clothes, who has washed more brushes, who has scraped off more badly applied layers of paint?

"You know I'm not saying you have to do this," she said, "but you could start tomorrow and get paid in cash each day."

I'd be honoured to be employed as a cleaner in a pub, I said. But I'll keep painting, especially when you're not around – I prefer painting when I'm on my own.

"What will you paint?" she asked.

I'll start with the story of my recent past, I said. I must transform it into an image, I must condense it in order to see it – to be able to look at it at all. I have a feeling that I am constantly falling into the arms of people who take advantage of me to some extent, even those who have the best intentions. As if I'm incapable of standing up for my rights. As if I don't know what I want. I hope a painting will reveal all that."

"And how am I taking advantage of you?" she asked.

Not you, Freckles, I said, giving her a hug. You're the first one that is asking nothing worse of me than that I become a cleaner.

41.

In the pub at seven the next morning, armed with brushes, cloths, sponges and cleaning fluids, I attacked the dirt from the previous evening: full ashtrays, beer-stained tables, messy floor, toilets covered in vomit and shit, the filthy kitchen and bar; I washed the windows, took out the rubbish, dusted, trying so hard that everything shone and when the landlord came to assess the results of my work he laughed, took a fiver from his wallet and said: "Carry on like this, lad, and the two of us will remain good friends." When Freckles came to work a little before eleven, he asked her: "Where did you find him? Make sure he doesn't escape. Give him a beer if he wants one."

I didn't want to drink before midday and was in a hurry to get to the studio, where I first showered thoroughly, to turn myself back into an artist and then, feverish with enthusiasm, started painting. In the middle of September it was quite cold in the basement, but I was burning with energy: on the unfinished canvas on one of the easels I began to sketch the outline of the story of my time since my arrival in London. I envisaged the painting as a kind of mass picnic in front of the statue of Peter Pan in Hyde Park, with all the people that I had met, from the important to the less important, and I would give each of them a representative characteristic.

In the midst of the crowd, just beneath the statue, I intended to paint Cleo as the last Queen of Egypt; I don't know why it seemed to me that she must be the central figure. I didn't know where to put

Sandrina; I thought that perhaps she did not belong among the others, but rather above them, like a kind of permanent presence, as a face that benignly observed the goings on below through a gap in the clouds, the sunny face of a goddess. I didn't want to rush, I wanted to ponder each small detail before I started the composition. And where should I put myself?

An unusual vision offered itself: all those in front of the statue would have a fishing rod and I would be a fish in the pond, with one eye on the heavenly face among the clouds and the other staring in horror at the hook dangling before my mouth. Had not everyone I'd met tried to hook me in some way, to pull me from the water, to cook me? The idea was over the top and I pushed it to one side, but it stayed there like a stubborn beggar who is unwilling to leave.

And where could I put little Freckles, the simple girl from New Zealand, who had never completed her course at the college of design and who had come to "Swinging London" to study fashion, but ended up behind a pub bar in Soho? And who had now, or so she said, reduced her goals to only one: saving enough money to buy a plane ticket home. Should she also be holding a fishing rod? Without her, I may well be on the street; without her, I would certainly not have found the studio, nor the cleaning job, although it was true that I needed the work because I'd used my savings to pay for the studio. From the very beginning she had only wanted to help me. Wasn't it now my duty to help her? Had I not, with all the people I had met, too often seen only what they expected or demanded of me, and rarely what they had given me, which I had accepted as my right, because I was Vili Vaupotič, artist?

I felt the need to redeem myself, to still my conscience, so I decided to use the money I saved from the cleaning work and any pictures I might sell to buy a plane ticket for Freckles, so that she could return home. I didn't tell her this because I wanted to surprise her. Of course, I had to take care that she did not notice how part of my earnings was disappearing, for we used the five pounds per day for food and cinema tickets and for gas, electricity and phone bills, while at the start quite a bit of it went for a modest renewal of my wardrobe.

But as if sensing that I was saving for her, she soon found me additional work and at a better rate: for an agency that cleaned offices in the centre of London. If I had not already decided to surprise her as soon as possible with an airline ticket, I would have gladly rejected the opportunity, but as it was I expressed my delight and that very evening joined the team of six working for Cleaners Limited. I thought that I would still be able to paint in the hours between the end of my shift in the pub and the start of cleaning the offices, at 6 p.m.

The team was led by the domineering and tetchy Mrs. Penhaligon, who was never quiet for more than half a second: "Empty that basket under the desk... don't lean out the window, we're on the tenth floor... don't jumble up the papers on the desk... polish that lino again... Mary, I don't care what ideas of cleanliness you have in Ireland, but that's not good enough... push the vacuum cleaner under the desk – God, why do they send me only incompetents... what have they had here, a party with red wine, the pigs, look at that upholstery... Willy, dust the *frames*, not the actual pictures, for God's sake, have you never seen a painting before, don't you realise how valuable they are... empty that vase, Helen, the flowers are completely rotten... let's get on..."

And thus one evening, in the offices of an American bank, on the third floor of a building in the financial centre, I found myself dragging a feather duster across the expensive frame of a painting, which seemed strangely familiar. I thought that it must be a copy, since the original of an old master would not be hanging in the office of a bank, where it might easily be stolen

I took a step back for a better look and froze. On the wall in front of me hung an image of three dancing virgins in veils that were swirling around them, like the misty edge of a galaxy that is densest at the centre, in front of an orangey red cloud that could be a fire or a stellar explosion.

What a coincidence, I thought, I painted something like that when I was at the academy. The simultaneity of ideas, the simultaneity of styles – the words of Alan MacClelland echoed in my memory. I remembered that I had named my picture *Bad Luck Comes in Threes*, and it was one of those that were seized in Dover.

I went close to the painting again to see what it was called, since it was so similar to mine. But there was no title anywhere: all that could be seen was the artist's signature in the bottom right corner: Vili Vau – the rest of the surname was covered by the frame. I felt as if struck by a bolt of lightning.

"What are you staring at, Willy, we're going to the fourth floor," I heard Mrs. Penhaligon say. Her voice sounded as if it was coming from a great distance. So Mr. Palisander does exist, I thought (as if I didn't know that before), my paintings really were collected from Dover (as if I had not already received an official notification about this from the customs office), Mr. Palisander had sold my paintings (and how much had he got for the one that hung in front of me?).

I'm sorry, Mrs. Penhaligon, I said, I suddenly feel sick. I'd better go home, I'll see you tomorrow. And I wandered towards the lift.

In the studio, I stared at the draft sketch of the painting that I was going to title *My Life So Far* and wondered how many of my paintings were hanging on the walls of London offices and homes, and who was making money from this and how much. It was highly unlikely that only one had been sold, there must be quite a few in circulation – maybe all of them! But alongside anger and disappointment, I discerned another feeling inside me, a completely different one, and the more it came to the forefront, the more it came to resemble delight, even ecstasy. Vili Vaupotič is being bought, Vili Vaupotič hangs on the wall of an American bank, Vili Vaupotič is a commodity! Vili Vaupotič can live from his paintings!

When, just before midnight, Freckles returned from the pub with a bag of cold chips, she was almost scared by my manic mood.

"What is it?" she said, taking a step back.

I took the chips from her and threw them in the rubbish bin. We don't need leftovers any more, I said, from now on we're going to live in style. I grabbed her hand and fell with her onto the mattress.

"Wait, let me have a shower first," she said, trying to extricate herself, but I said: No, listen.

And I told her the story about my confiscated, forgotten, locked away and stolen paintings, from beginning to end. And how two hours earlier I had been dusting one of them.

"Bastards," she said, immediately on my side, as always. "Actually, I'm not all that surprised, but you must get the pictures back, you must show that they're yours –after all, they have your signature on them."

It won't be easy, I said. For now, I've found only one of them and why should the bank care if I painted it, they'll say they paid for it, they're sure to have a receipt, and if I say the picture was stolen, they'll say: prove it, take us to court. I don't have the money for that, nor the time, nor the energy – and I doubt whether I'd succeed.

"Then you'll have to steal it," she said, "and sell it to someone else."

I thought of that, I said, but now I'm thinking differently. The picture is where it belongs: it has found a home, it hangs on a wall, where someone put it who likes it – perhaps one of the directors of the bank, who knows? The best thing that can happen to a painting is that it comes into the hands of someone who is proud of it. Now the picture has found its place, I couldn't take it away.

"You're right," she said, "I hadn't thought of that."

But Sandy, I said, I would like to steal the painting – for you.

"For me?" she asked in surprise.

For your plane ticket, I said. And if there was anything left over, I could stop cleaning for some time, I could just paint. I miss a normal life.

She turned away from me, with a strange look on her face. The next moment, she burst into tears.

What is it, Freckles? I tried to stroke her, but she pushed my hand away as if I was a leper.

"You'd steal the painting for that reason? To get rid of me as soon as possible?"

Hang on a second, I said, I'd like to help you, as you helped me – a favour for a favour. Didn't you say you'd had enough of this city and that you'd like to return home as soon as possible?

"But not now," she blubbered like a child. "Now I have you, now I want to stay."

Oh my God, I thought. Why had it not occurred to me that something like that might happen?

That will be difficult, I said, because I … I didn't know how to continue.

"Don't you like being with me?" she said through her tears.

I do, very much, I said, but … and again I stopped.

"But what? Don't you care for me?"

I do care for you, Freckles, I said, but from the beginning we knew that this was temporary. Coincidence brought us together when we both needed support, but in the long term, as well as the short term, the situation is that … And again I had no idea how to go on. I knew that whatever I said would hurt and I didn't want to hurt her, she didn't deserve it.

(Go on, tell her, said Willy II, suddenly coming awake. Tell her that she's not cultured enough; that you can't have a long-term relationship with a barmaid who hasn't even finished college; that you haven't got anything to talk to her about, that she doesn't understand art; that she has dragged you – albeit for noble motives – into the underworld, among the uneducated, the humiliated and indigent; that if she is in love with you she needs to fall out of love as soon as possible, because you have other, higher plans that she cannot even begin to comprehend… Oh, shut up, responded Willy I, I refuse to listen to such nonsense. Shut your arrogant mouth, it's because of you that we're in the mess we're in.)

I hugged her close. I didn't know you were happier with an office cleaner than being back in New Zealand.

"Idiot," she said, with great relief, pressing her tear-stained face to mine. But I'd still like to steal the painting, I said. And sell it. To buy myself time for painting. I wasn't sent to this Earth to work for Cleaners Limited. It's also true that I could paint a new one and try to sell that, instead of masturbating over the stupid story of my life so far.

"You keep on painting," she said. "I won't force you to go cleaning any more. And I'll find someone to steal the painting for you from the bank. Every evening I serve about five guys who would do it just for a nice smile."

Don't sacrifice yourself even more, I said. You've already done too much.

"A nice smile doesn't cost anything," she said. "All the rest is reserved for you."

329

42.

The next morning I didn't go cleaning. Sandy telephoned to say I was ill and we stayed in bed until it was time for her to go to work.

"Maybe I'll stop soon and do something else." Before she said goodbye she gave me a long look.

Intoxicated with the intensity of her love and wounded by the realisation that I could not respond with the same degree of feeling, I sat for some time, staring at my draft sketch for *My Life So Far.* The idea of the fish hooks suddenly seemed misplaced. I knew that I needed to rethink the whole thing and in the meantime tackle something else. Or finally pluck up the courage to go to the National Gallery for inspiration. And straight away, in case I had second thoughts after less than five minutes.

I was already at the door when the doorbell rang. I remembered that after Sandy left I had forgotten to lock it, but it was too late – the door opened and in stepped a young man with a red beard and hair, in an elegant white suit.

"I hope I'm not disturbing you," he said in a slightly foreign accent. "Allow me to present myself: Aleksej Ivanovič Solouhin."

He grinned and offered me his enormous paw, which I gripped as if I never intended to let it go. "Hey," he laughed, "give me back my hand."

He walked around the studio, examining everything with great interest and nodding with approval. "Finally, a studio worthy of your talents," he said. "How did you manage it?"

By leaving myself penniless, I replied.

"Penniless" he said with a laugh. "Here I see a bra and over there women's panties, here a t-shirt that is too small for you, so you cannot be without feminine company. Is she worth the sinning?"

And you? I asked, ignoring his question. Why the red hair and beard all of a sudden?

"Disguise," he said. "I have to stay one step ahead of them."

Why didn't you come to Trafalgar Square? I asked. I waited for you. And where have you been all this time, why didn't you get in touch? I was afraid I'd never see you again.

"And what if you hadn't? There's no indication that you would have suffered because of that."

You've no idea, I said, you've no idea what happened.

"My dear Willy Wow Potty," he said with one of his usual broad gestures, "do *you* know what has happened this year?"

The Americans landed on the moon, I said.

"Forget the Americans," he said. "At the same time, the Russians sent an unmanned probe to the moon, which landed not far away – they might even have collided. But that's not important, only idiots look beyond – we who know where the real secrets are hidden, search the depths of the soul. Many other things unimportant happened even before your arrival here. At the end of January, the Beatles made their last public appearance. In February, George Harrison had his tonsils out and the first jumbo jet flew in the United States. But in March, the supersonic Concorde made its maiden flight in France. Up, up and away! People would like to be elsewhere, as far away as possible, as quickly as possible – why? John Lennon married Yoko Ono, and a week earlier Paul McCartney married Linda Eastman, the heir to the Kodak empire. How lucky some people are! Anyway, in May the Russian space ship Venera 5 crashed into the surface of Venus. At the beginning of August, Charles Manson murdered Sharon Tate, and a week later Woodstock took place, man, Woodstock, man, you know. Half a million people at a rock concert! Compare that to the fact that at Mozart's funeral his coffin was accompanied only by the gravedigger and a stray dog. But all that is nothing in comparison to two events. The first was that Solzhenytsin was expelled from the

331

Association of Russian Writers and will soon be following in my footsteps. But how will that help him, because I was here first – before he gets here, I'll publish my novel and there'll be nothing left for him."

Come off it, I said, how many joints have you smoked? Have you forgotten that the police are looking for you? Who will publish your novel?

"Dear Willy Wow," he said, hugging me so tightly that for a moment I could not breathe.

His violent proximity was beginning to put me off a little. Not so close, I said. I'm in a fragile state and need a little distance.

"Sorry," he said, stepping back. "There are some Russian habits I can't shed. But allow me to mention one other event that is more important than everything else that has happened this year. I heard that in two months at the latest, Parliament will vote for the current trial prohibition of the death penalty to become permanent. I'll stay alive, Willy! Whatever happens, I'll stay alive! Maybe in jail, but Wormwood Scrubs will be a fairy tale in comparison with the gulag. They cannot take this away from me. In jail I will write ten timeless novels. And you will be my agent. In fact, you could be my agent now, while I'm still free. Willy," he adopted a serious look, "in the name of our friendship, I ask you to become my literary agent."

Don't be ridiculous, I said, I don't know the literary scene, I've no idea who I could offer your novel to. Which in any case, you'll never finish.

"I'll tell you who to offer it to," he said. "It's true I haven't finished it, but only because I'm reworking it. Sandrina will no longer be an exclusive call girl, she'll no longer be a secret agent, she won't arrive at Dover by ferry, she'll no longer meet a painter called Willy, nor will I appear in the book as a double or triple agent. You were right, that was insufficiently thought through, unselective, somewhat popularised, rather cheap, inappropriate for Solouhin who, by the way, is now called Ivan Aleksandrovič Tatarski, which will be my *nom de plume*. No, not long ago I picked up a book with an unusual title: *Twiggy: How I Probably Just Came Along on a White Rabbit at the Right Time and Met the Smile on the Face of the Tiger*. Of course, you've heard of Twiggy, that skinny girl who is now the most famous model of all times and who is referred to as the Face of the Sixties. Do you know what she said about herself? "It would be hard to call this a figure." A modest girl. She's been referred to in all sorts of ways – the frail torso of a teen-age choirboy, four straight limbs in search of a body – but the fact is, Willy, that she did nothing to achieve what she has. She simply appeared with the right body at the right place and the right time, and the market turned her into an icon. This is where my novel begins. Imagine that into this environment, where all the models are like skeletons, there comes, let's say, Cleo, the Arab girl that I carried your letters to. Extremely beautiful, there's no doubt, but a completely unsuitable figure for modelling clothes for today's girls. Too large, too shapely, too heavy, almost clumsy, although with the right grooming she could be elegant. And this young Arab woman, let's call her Cleo, gets it into her head that she wants to become London's most famous and best paid model, a supermodel. The question, Willy Wow, is simple: how to succeed when all the odds are stacked against you. Is it possible to achieve your goal and remain pure and innocent, or is it necessary to be at least a little corrupt along the way, to sell yourself at least a little, to lie at least a little, to forget your principles at least a little? And above all: how to get the world to value something new and different from what it values now? A different female figure, a different way of writing, a different way of painting. Do you see what I'm trying to say?"

How far are you with this novel? I asked.

"Further than you think," he said. "A lot further. Recently I've been circulating in the world of high fashion, collecting material, getting to know interesting people, interesting women. You've got to understand: when they catch me – and some time they will – I won't see any twenty year-old women, let alone touch one. In the world of fashion there's no shortage of them and there are even more waiting in line outside the door. And they are prepared to do anything. I set up an agency, Willy. From each one I take fifty pounds for a professional portfolio of photographs and an introduction to three agencies who employ models. Fifty pounds is quite a lot, some of them have to borrow the money, but I have to give the photographer half of that. And about a third of them, in their impatience to become the new Twiggy, give me a night or two of love. Do you want me to send you one?"

No, thanks, I snapped. What's happened to you? You're embroiled in lies and exploiting young girls – that's not like you! Or is it? Maybe you were always like that.

"You're too much of a moralist. That's a great flaw if you want to become an artist. Do you not see that I'm acting like one of the characters in the novel I'm writing? How can I understand the way he thinks if I don't live according to his principles, at least for a while?"

Wonderful, I said, a great philosophy: the artist is permitted any-thing.

"That's it, Willy Potty, everything. If you don't understand that, you're pursuing some other goals, not artistic ones."

Well, I said, you follow yours and I'll follow mine. It doesn't re-ally matter because in the end, the result will be the same – a big, fat nothing.

"A big fat nothing? Look what I brought you," he said, going to the door. He opened it, reached out, picked up a large tube-like package and returned to the room. Then on the floor in front of me he unrolled my painting *Tea With the Queen*.

Oh, I couldn't conceal my delight, did you manage to bring any-thing else from the squat?

"Sadly, that's the lot," he replied, kneeling over the painting. "By the way, I stopped at a small gallery and asked how much they'd offer for it. Guess how much they said."

Two pounds, I said.

"Five hundred, my dear Willy," he said. "Five hundred pounds."

Why didn't you sell it? I wondered out loud.

"Because it's not mine," he said. "It's yours and I don't cheat my friends. You sell it if you want, it's sufficient reward to me that I brought it back to you. Definitely your best picture. Am I your friend or am I not?"

He rolled up the painting and put it on the work table. "Okay, I'm going now. If you don't want to be an intermediary between me and the publishers, I'll stop bothering you."

It's not that I won't, I said, but first bring me something to read, stop talking all the time about what you're writing. Where are you living?

"Here and there," he replied. "You know, a man on the run. *Au revoir, mon ami*, I'll be back soon." And he went.

Wait! I called after him. He immediately came back.

How did you find me? I asked

"How did I find you?" he responded, surprised. "Do you mean to say that I wasn't supposed to? Were you hiding from me?"

Okay, I said, let's drop the subject. You're very difficult at times and this is one of them. I wanted to ask you if you knew that my pictures were in circulation.

"Of course they are, Willy Wow, people are not so stupid to have them locked away in a cellar for longer than necessary. And now you can put into circulation the one I've just brought back. Recently, my hearing hasn't been so good and so perhaps I didn't hear you say thanks."

You know that I'm grateful, I said, raising my voice slightly. I wanted to tell you that one of the paintings confiscated in Dover is hanging on the wall of an American bank in the City.

"Good for you," he said, as if the news did not surprise him. "Evidently that Alexander or Palisander or whoever he is, has pulled his finger out and is starting to make your name."

Okay, I said, my pictures obviously don't interest you much, you're living in another world, one that I don't know – you've changed, but so have I. In spite of that, I'd like to ask you a small favour. Can you help my flatmate? She really wants to break into the world of fashion. And since you said that you're moving in that world, that you know people, you might be able to give her an idea who to turn to.

"And what is she doing now, your flatmate, who has, judging by that bra provocatively staring me in the eyes, just the right tits for a model?"

She's working as a barmaid; she has to do something to survive. I'm cleaning offices – all my money went for the rent of the studio.

"Poor Willy," he said. "How unwise. You could go to Leicester Square and do portraits, it's much easier work."

335

He reached into the inside pocket of his jacket and pulled out a brown leather wallet. He took out thirty pounds and put them on the table. Next to it, he put his business card. "Have her call that number. Aren't you worried that I'll take advantage of her?"

Not at all, I said. I know her, she wouldn't let herself be taken advantage of. Don't leave the money, you might need it.

"A small advance, for your flatmate," he said. "What's her name?"

Sandy, I said. And I'm serious: take the money, it's enough that you brought the painting.

"I'll leave the money, because I don't like being told what I may or may not do with what I have earned. Allow me at least that luxury – there are precious few in my life. You can throw it in the rubbish bin, if you like. And because I know you, that wouldn't surprise me. Just as I wasn't surprised that you didn't ask which gallery had offered five hundred pounds for your *Tea With the Queen*."

He turned and made for the door.

Which? I asked.

"Do you really intend to sell it?" he asked, turning. "Your best painting? I wouldn't. Certainly not for five hundred. Maybe for five thousand. Learn to value yourself, for once." With these words, he left and through the window I saw him going up the steps to the street.

I reached for his business card. "Tatarski Modelling Agency" it said. It was the address that surprised me most: Grosvenor House Hotel, Park Lane, one of the best in London. I couldn't help myself: I picked up the phone and dialled the number on the card to see who answered. But just then, I noticed through the window that Solouhin was coming back. He opened the door and marched in.

"I forgot something," he said and pulled from his pocket a worn paperback book. "As well as the painting, I managed to retrieve from the squat your favourite poet. Have I ever told you what I think of Arnold? The most clumsy, naively pathetic and verbose English poet of all times. Listen to this."

He opened the book and read: *"And women – things that live and move / Mined by the fever of the soul - / They seek to find in those they love / Stern strength, and promise of control. / They ask not kindness, gentle ways - / These they themselves have tried and known; / They ask a soul which never sways / With the blind gusts that shake their own."*

He closed the book and put it on the table next to the money. Willy, Willy," he shook his head. "I, who know nothing about painting, know more about it than you know about poetry."

When he had gone, I dialled the number on the card. It rang for a long time and I was about to put it down when someone answered. A warm, friendly female voice said: "Yes?"

A moment of silence, I could hear her breathing. Then I put the phone down.

43.

Sandy was not very enthusiastic when I told her my lost friend had reappeared – perhaps she feared that he would come between us and that she would no longer have exclusive rights to my time and company. Nor was she very keen on the painting ("Terrible! Trampling on a baby – why can't you paint lighter things?") She was even less pleased when I told her that Dostoyevsky was ready to help her to achieve what she had always wanted to.

"Once," she said. "Not any more. There's no place for me in that world and now that I've come to terms with that I don't want to start again, there have been too many defeats. And now everything is okay, I'm kind of satisfied."

Listen, Sandy, I said, I can't be a replacement for all that you haven't achieved – that is a recipe for disaster and I won't take on that burden. If someone is prepared to help you, you must at least try. If it doesn't work out, then things can always be as they are now. And if it does, the world will be a very different place. You can't give up this opportunity, it's your duty to take care of your future, just as I must take care of mine.

"You mean we don't have a future together?" she asked, again on the verge of tears.

Sandy, I raised my voice, our future together is dependent on how much desire you show to get out from behind that bar and go elsewhere! I don't want you to be stuck and I don't want to be stuck with you. If you really care for me, then you'll call this number first thing in the morning.

"I found someone who is prepared to steal the picture from the bank," she said. "If we sell it, we can live on the money for quite some time."

No, I said, no one will steal my painting and we won't be selling stolen goods. If needs be, I can sell *Tea With the Queen,* but for now there is no need. Please let *me* decide what to do with my pictures.

"I'm glad," she said, "because until now others have decided for you."

And that was the end of the evening. In bed, she turned her back to me and I to her.

Next morning she was very quiet, but she still prepared breakfast as usual. Then she spent some time shifting Solouhin's business card from one hand to the other. Eventually, she grabbed the phone and dialled the number. She spoke to someone who obviously wasn't my Russian friend – perhaps the same woman from the day before, his secretary (or lover, or both?) – who said that Mr. Tatarski was not there, but to come to Grosvenor House Hotel at one and ask at the reception for Selena. She would arrange everything.

"How can I go at one," said Sandy when she put the phone down, "if I start work at eleven?" I'll say you're ill, I said. You've got to go and when you do, you must insist on seeing my friend, say it's all arranged.

"Why don't you call him if you're such good friends?"

I'll call him when it's necessary, I said. He doesn't make empty promises, he's a man of his word.

In spite of her reservations, a little after twelve she made her way to Oxford Street, to catch the bus for Park Lane, while I walked to Leicester Square to see the portraitists. There were five of them, sitting on small stools on the busiest part of the square, with mini-easels in front of them holding drawing pads on which, with crayons or felt pens, they quickly and skilfully sketched the portrait of the tourist perched on the plastic chair in front of them. I saw them sketching a large American woman, a slender Japanese girl with her boyfriend at her side and a red-faced man with a Bavarian hat, while two chairs remained empty.

"Your portrait in 10 minutes – only 80 pence," it said on the pieces of cardboard leaning against the easels. A standard price, probably by agreement. Two of the artists were very good and the portrait captured the model, although with a hint of caricature.

How many customers do you have a day? I asked the closest, a long-haired lad with glasses.

"Depends on the weather," he replied, without removing his eyes from the man in the Bavarian hat.

I wasn't convinced that this would bring me more money than cleaning offices with Mrs. Penhaligon, but I decided to give it a try – with one small difference. I returned to Leicester Square with ten small canvases, a palette, bottles of oil paint, brushes, rags and white spirit, and against my easel I leaned a piece of card saying "Your portrait in the style of Hans Holbein – only five pounds."

I joined the line and waited for customers.

"Hey, you," said the nearest portraitist, "have you got a permit?"

I have, I said, what about you? He fell silent and carried on drawing.

In reality, none of them saw me as a serious competitor. They looked at each other and sniggered and kept on drawing, while for the first two hours people queued for them and basically ignored me. I was all ready to pack up and accept the fact that some ideas are better in theory than in practice, when I was approached by an imposing middle-aged woman, accompanied by a slightly bent older gentleman, who was probably her husband.

"Who's Hans Holbein?" she asked in an American accent and in a voice used to giving orders, although still polite and friendly.

Hans Holbein was the most famous portraitist of his time, named as court painter during the reign of Henry the Eighth. His portraits of Henry and his wives are thought to be the best portraits of all times.

"Five pounds is quite a lot," said the man, although I saw that the woman was already half-decided.

It is, I said, but instead of a sketch on thin paper that will get creased in your luggage on the way home, you will have an oil painting that you can frame nicely and hang over the fireplace in the living room, where it will delight visitors forever.

"Right," said the lady and sat down on the rickety chair that I had bought two hours earlier in a second-hand furniture shop. The portrait took quite some time and after forty minutes the woman started to shift restlessly, but when I eventually handed it to her, she was at first lost for words.

"Much better than I expected," said the man, reaching for his wallet. "Here," he offered me a five pound note.

"Give him six," said the lady. "The boy is a genius. I never would have thought…"

Her husband decided to give me seven!

Now please be very careful, I said, the oil paints need to dry and that can take a few days. You must hold the painting away from you and make sure you don't knock it against anything. I recommend a taxi and straight back to your hotel.

"John," she said to her husband, "will you?"

I'll never forget how they made their way towards Piccadilly Circus: the man holding the painting in front of him, with the painted side towards him so that nobody would bump into it, and the woman trotting beside him, giving instructions.

Before evening, I got one more customer: a ten year-old girl who I had problems with because she could not sit still. Her proud parents were very satisfied with the results, but she showed no interest ("Is that me? That's not me, I'm not like that. Shall we go, mummy?") And so in one afternoon I earned twelve pounds, half an average weekly wage – why hadn't I thought of this before?

Sandy returned shortly before midnight and described to me the events of the day: She had felt completely out of place in the luxury hotel and could not shake off the feeling that people were looking at her as if she did not belong there. A young woman by the name of Selena came for her and took her to an apartment on the sixth floor. There she was offered tea, her details and measurements were taken and she was told that the chances were slight, it all depended on the good will of Mr. Tatarski, who arrived a little later. He was the ugliest man she had ever seen, so ugly that he was quite interesting and in a strange way attractive, whereas Selena was definitely one of the

341

most beautiful girls in the world, and if she really was just a secretary what chances did she have, who was only average? Whatever, my friend had been very friendly, he had told her that she needed a professional portfolio, he gave her the name of a photographer who would cost thirty pounds and as my friend he would not charge the agency's usual fifty pound fee – that was his present. He would do his best, but he could not promise anything. She should come back when she had the photographs.

You see, I said. Satisfied?

"It won't come to anything," she said, "I'll just waste thirty pounds."

Here, I offered her the money that Dostoyevsky had left on the table the previous day.

"Where did you get it?" she wanted to know.

I told her I had earned it doing portraits in Leicester Square.

The next day, she went to the photographer's and I back to Leicester Square. I had to wait for my first customer until eleven and then there was nothing until two. While waiting, I watched the bustling crowd, the jugglers, clowns and buskers who performed close by, the waves of people surging from left and right, passing each other, coming together and struggling to get past. At times (usually around lunch) the crowd thinned out and there was a lull for the row of portraitists; some of them nodded off, some of them ate the stale sandwich they produced from a bag or pocket, while others counted their meagre earnings. I sat at a slight distance from the others, since I felt that they did not want me among them; I was different, I was better, I was *far out, man* – the wonder of Leicester Square.

A little before two o'clock, as I was looking to my right, towards Charing Cross Road, Solouhin went past in his white suit. Beside him was a slender young woman, swaying on very high heels; her black hair was in a pony tail that bounced up and down as she walked. Bastard, I thought first, how does he manage to find them, although I didn't really envy him, but then the young woman looked to her right, towards the square and it struck me like a knife, that she was like Sandrina – not only like Sandrina, it couldn't be anyone but her!

Although it was months since I saw her for the first and last time, her striking face was engraved on my memory with such precision that I would recognise her even in poor light, even in thick fog, even among a crowd of thousands. Her most distinctive feature was a pucker on the left side of her face, the lower part of which did not turn towards her mouth, as it did on the right, but slightly away and outwards; for this reason, she always attracted a second look and a third, because it gave her a slightly cynical, but at the same time childishly trustful appearance – a striking combination that was impossible to resist. It's true that the young woman and Solouhin were quite some distance away and I couldn't see any such details clearly, but the face as a whole could only be hers; together with her characteristic swaying walk and rolling hips, there could be no doubt.

As soon as they disappeared round the corner (they were going along Charing Cross Road towards the National Gallery), I leapt up and rushed after them. In so doing, I almost knocked over some careless children, earning a rebuke from their parents, I bumped into a traffic warden who got in my way and a number of people I simply elbowed aside, because I had no choice. When I got to the corner, there was no sign of my friend and his companion. This was no great mystery; they had doubtless entered one of the many available doors – perhaps into a shop or restaurant – or simply turned into a side street. I hurried across the road and looked around near the Wyndham and Garrick theatres; I turned into two side streets hoping to find them in one of the many antique shops; then I ran to the corner of the National Gallery, where I could see the whole of Trafalgar Square and its hordes of people.

Nothing, I'd lost them. But I was so agitated that I could no longer sit waiting for customers. I put my things away and went back to the studio. I immediately called the number on the business card that Solouhin had left. Although I let the phone ring for about ten minutes, there was no answer. I tried again half an hour later, with the same result. And again two hours later.

The twelfth time I called, just before eight in the evening, I heard a warm female voice that I recognised.

Selena? I asked.

"It depends who's asking," she said.

Just someone, I said. A painter, no one special, but he is the best friend of your well-known Russian writer in exile.

There was a silence, she covered the mouthpiece with her hand and spoke to someone; I heard muffled voices.

Then Solouhin came onto the phone. "What can I do for you, Willy Wow?" he asked. "It's odd that we are talking on the phone after all that we've been through, it should hardly be part of our fate, should it?"

I saw you, I said. I'm painting portraits on Leicester Square and this afternoon I saw you going past along Charing Cross Road with a young lady.

"Really?" he said, without the slightest hint of discomfort or of concealment. "If I'd known you were there, I'd have come and said hello. Why didn't you shout?"

That young lady, I said, was Sandrina, the girl from the ferry I told you about.

"Sandrina?" he exclaimed. "The heroine of my novel? My dear Potty Willy, you are obviously bowing beneath the pressure of this ungenerous city. For the time being, I am not walking around with imaginary people – I think you need professional help."

You know very well what I mean, I shouted down the phone. Sandrina is the girl I met on the ferry and I never gave you permission to use her name for the heroine of your novel, which you will never finish, if you're writing it at all, if you're not just talking about it.

"Calm down," he said, "otherwise you'll destroy the membrane in the phone. If I'm not writing the novel, then the non-existent heroine cannot be called Sandrina, nor can the girl from the ferry, since didn't you tell me that it was you who gave her that name? The whole thing is fiction from start to finish – is that what's tormenting you?"

The girl is real, I said more quietly, regardless of what she's actually called, and today she was with you. Why are you denying it, are we no longer friends?

"No, my dear Willy, I am your friend and I always will be. You should ask whether you are still mine. The young woman who was with me today is called Selena and is sitting here beside me. Your

Sandy spoke to her today. You should come and see her, too, so that you are not living under some bizarre delusion – I wouldn't like you to lose your mind because of some strange fixed idea. Has it occurred to you that your obsession with a non-existent woman could be an early sign of schizophrenia? And you have Sandy, for God's sake – a lovely girl, hold on to her."

We were both silent for some time. Sorry, I said quietly and put down the phone.

When Sandy got home around midnight I asked what kind of hair Solouhin's secretary had. "Why do you want to know? she asked in surprise. Just because, I said, I'd like to know.

"Long, wheat-coloured," she said. "And a small plait."

Are you sure she doesn't have black hair and a pony tail?

"Are you okay?" she asked, giving me a concerned look.

No, I wanted to say, I'm not okay. I wanted to tell her about Sandrina, about how I saw her everywhere, how I also saw Sandrina's features on her face, but at the last moment I realised that this would cause her pain she did not deserve. She was good and caring and in love with me, and I was fond of her. I said nothing and thought: if Selena has wheat-coloured hair and a plait, how at two this afternoon could she have had a black pony tail?

Something was not right, but Sandy looked so concerned that I didn't want to upset her any more.

Come on, I held out my hand, let's go to bed.

44.

The next morning she went to the photographer's and I went early to Leicester Square, so that no one would take over my space, since almost every day some new portraitist appeared, although it was true that some had already left and that the number remained relatively constant, fluctuating between five and ten. There was nothing for some time, then at around eleven an odd looking little man appeared in front of me: protruding ears, a round hairless head, with no eyebrows, but with a moustache beneath his turned-up, almost childish nose, of indeterminate age, but probably over forty, with hunched shoulders and wearing a sailor's t-shirt, from which emerged a narrow, tortoise-like neck on which his head nodded the whole time, this way and that.

"Einmal, bitte," he said. "Ein Portret für mich." I got to work and made rapid progress. I had always liked faces that themselves bordered on caricature, which could be reproduced much more accurately than those with regular features. The nodding of his head bothered me a bit, but not so much as to interfere with my portrait. I was more bothered by the exceptional garrulousness of the little man, who was no bigger than a twelve-year-old. Obviously in puberty some illness or genetic fault had restricted his growth. "Ich kom' aus Deutschland," he said, "aus Bingen, weisst du wo das ist? Nein, du weisst nicht, das ist ja ganz normal. Ich spreche kein English, das ist eine schreckliche Sprache, aber die Leute sind ganz normal, denkst du nicht?"And so on, with barely a pause. And every third phrase was "ganz normal". I remained stubbornly quiet and pretended to understand nothing.

He only became a little less talkative when he saw that a group of curious onlookers had gathered, drawn by his unusual appearance. Some of them came round to see if the emerging portrait resembled him or not. This eventually inspired him to get up and come closer. "Ja, gut, sehr gut," he said, standing behind me, "ausgezeichnet, weiter, bitte." He returned to his seat, looked at the gathered crowd of onlookers and pulled his head in like a tortoise that does not like attention; his head stopped nodding and he became almost motionless. The onlookers slowly drifted away, but new ones appeared, although in smaller numbers. Eventually, there was just one eminent-looking man standing there: late middle age, corpulent but not fat, slightly bent shoulders, as if frozen in an attacking posture, in check trousers and jacket, indicating that he was "an English country gentleman", although not the kind that loved pheasant shooting, but with a sharp eye that spoke of sophistication, independence, self-confidence.

He also came over and looked over my shoulder at what was developing. "Well well," I heard him say. Then he took a step or two away, took out some tobacco and started to fill his pipe. When he had lit it for the third time without moving on I thought that he was probably queueing – he wanted his portrait painting.

I was not wrong. When the German from Bingen had left, satisfied, the man with the pipe authoritatively (but not arrogantly) pushed aside an American woman who wanted to install herself on the chair in front of me, saying "Madam, I'm terribly sorry, but this is England – here we form a queue." He sat on the rickety chair and crossed his legs, not the slightest concerned that the woman had puffed in an offended manner and stalked off. That was her problem, not his. He looked at me expectantly, as if to say where shall we begin?

I don't know why, but with his self-confident look he made me feel uncertain, almost afraid; he was no tourist, he was on home ground, where he felt completely at home; he gave the impression that he was in control and that he never needed to negotiate. He spoke in a clear, comfortably restrained voice of medium depth and with one of those plummy English accents characteristic of aristocrats.

"How long will it take? I can't sit more than half an hour, I have back problems." He said this without embarrassment in front of the crowd of onlookers that had gathered again.

I'll try and finish in half an hour, I said.

"If you can," he said, "but don't rush, if I'm not satisfied you will pay me for the loss of my time." When he saw my face, he gave a friendly smile and said: "No sense of humour? We can't have that."

Then he relaxed and smoked, the whole time looking me straight in the eye, as if trying to discern what was going on in my head. I'd never been stared at so relentlessly before. I felt an extreme discomfort; if he had watched my hands closely, or my brush, it would have disturbed me less. The whole time I had the feeling that he was monitoring me, that I was taking an examination and that I would be happy at the end if I got a pass grade, let alone a grade A.

"Half an hour has just passed," he observed. "How far are we?

Just a little, I said; I'm having problems with the eyes and the end of the nose.

Some of the onlookers laughed and the sitter indicated with a glance that he was aware of the public. "You're not having problems with the eyes, but with the lines on my face," he said, "there are too many of them, but there's no need to paint them all." He acknowledged the laughter that his comment provoked with a slight incline of the head.

What would need to happen in my life for me to mature into someone so relaxed, so self-assured that I felt no need to defend myself against anyone or anything? I wondered if it was already too late for me, such qualities should be inculcated in childhood. I would never so comfortably and unquestioningly occupy space like this gentleman. The only reason that I might be of interest to him was my original offer of portraits in the style of Hans Holbein and that only in passing, to kill the time between two meetings.

But I was wrong. He was not only satisfied with the portrait, he was not only over-generous (to the envious looks of my fellow portraitists and the general approval of the gathered crowd, he gave me no less than ten pounds!), but he wanted to know what else I did, whether I painted anything else, whether my pictures were for sale, where he could see them. When I told him that I had a studio close by, on Greek Street, he did not even ask whether he could invite himself round and thus interrupt my working day. He beckoned to a young man standing among the onlookers as if he just happened to be passing by and handed him the painting, saying: "Be careful, Jonesy, it's still wet." He told him to lay it carefully in the car and then to drive to Greek Street.

"What number?" he asked, turning to me. Twelve A, I said. And he added: "Twelve A, Jonesey, don't forget. And don't hurry. We shall walk back through Soho, shall we?" He gave me a look.

I had no choice but to put away all my things, stuff them in my travel bag, pick up the wobbly chair and easel, and follow him. Actually, I did have a choice, but what he said seemed so self-evident that my reaction couldn't be any different. I was neither angry nor happy, but acted as if I was following orders, like Jonesey, who was evidently his chauffeur.

"I'll carry the bag," he said, taking it from my hand, "you can't manage everything. By the way, I'm Lord William Hattersley. Who are you?"

William Vaupotič, I said. But my friends call me Willy Wow Potty.

He laughed so loud that people on the pavement turned their heads. "Two Willys in the heart of Soho," he said, "what a coincidence, or perhaps not, eh?"

When we got to the studio, Jonesy was already there. In front of the entrance stood a large white limousine, not a Rolls Royce, but a Bentley – an even more renowned vehicle for people with no shortage of money.

"Wait, Jonesey," said the gentleman, "and make sure you don't get a parking ticket."

"Right, Sir William," said Jonesey through the open window, "I'll do my very best to avoid it."

When we got to the studio Sir William looked around and the first thing he saw were the paintings left by my predecessor; I could feel his face contort with unpleasant surprise.

Those are not mine, I said quickly, those are canvases left by the previous tenant. There are very few of mine – in fact, only two and one of those is only a draft of a draft.

"What about the others?" he asked, putting my travel bag on the table. "All sold?"

I'm afraid not, I said, but it's a long story, maybe too long. "Hm," he turned his sharp gaze to the canvas on the easel, the draft for *My Life So Far*. "The style seems strangely familiar, but it's not Holbein, that's not an exercise in imitation, that's for real, and that's you, if I'm not mistaken."

Yes, I said, that's me. *Trying* to be me. And that, too, I directed his attention to the painting that Dostoyevsky had brought and that I had already fastened to a frame. Sir William looked where I was pointing and flinched – I'd almost swear that he flinched.

"It's hard to see a painting if it's on the floor, leaning against the wall," he said. "Let's put it on the easel, help me, we'll move this one elsewhere for a moment."

We put *My Life So Far* on the floor and lifted *Tea With the Queen* onto the easel. Sir William took two steps back, supported his chin with his right hand, which leant on his left arm, folded across his stomach, and stared at the painting. "Well," he said and then, after a long pause, another "Well." I didn't get the impression that he particularly liked the painting, I thought he was merely evaluating the style, the details, identifying inadequacies, but not mentioning them out of politeness.

"Interesting," he said finally. "Have you promised this picture to anyone else?"

No, I said, I wasn't planning on selling it for now.

"Shame," he said. "A real shame, because to me it seems, not to waste words, excellent. Although I don't know what or who your style reminds me of. And if you decided to sell, what price would seem to you reasonable?"

I'm not sure, I said with a shrug and remembered Solouhin's claim that he could have got five hundred for it. Probably, he had been greatly exaggerating: he saw that I was having a crisis and he wanted to encourage me, so I didn't want to quote that price out loud, in case Sir William burst out laughing.

I really don't know, I said with another shrug.

"I know that you artists are very sensitive," he said, "and I don't want to offend you, but I'll take a risk and offer you one thousand five hundred."

The silence that followed his words evidently seemed too long to him and he sighed deeply. Just a moment, I said and rushed to the toilet. I felt dizzy, there was a strange pressure in my head and I was overcome with nausea; I fell to my knees and began to throw up into the toilet. I coughed and spat and hawked for several minutes before I summoned enough strength to wipe my mouth and return to the studio.

"What's wrong? You look green around the gills," said Sir William.

I had a ham sandwich earlier, there must have been something wrong with it, I improvised.

"You know what: I'll give you two thousand pounds and write the cheque now." He reached into his inside pocket and pulled out a leather wallet.

A cheque's no use to me, I said, because I don't have a bank account.

"Why not?" he frowned.

When I had the chance to open one, I didn't want to. Now, I don't know anyone who could recommend me.

"We'll soon sort that out," he said, returning the wallet to his pocket. "We'll go to the nearest branch of the National Westminster. Where do you keep your money, in a safe place I hope?"

Most of my money has been stolen, I said. Most of my paintings, too. Or I lost them, forgot them on a train, all sorts of things. Nothing stays with me very long. That's my fate.

"Nonsense," he said. "Too romantic, even for a painter. I don't believe in the kind of fate that can't be improved with a little goodwill. For quite some time, I've been looking for a painter to employ as a family portraitist. I'm thinking of my aunts, uncles, cousins, their children – there's more than enough work. In addition, he would paint

351

the gardens at my country house. And of course, he would still have enough time for his own work. If there's nothing important holding you here, than perhaps we can come to an agreement. At least for a trial period, you can always say 'this is not for me' and leave."

My eyes strayed to the bed near the door, where Sandy had left a messy heap of clothes that I had not had time to tidy away, which I was doing ever more often recently.

No, I said. There's nothing important holding me here.

45.

The rest of the day passed as if in a dream: I placed a cheque for two thousand pounds in my first English bank account, signalling the end of living from hand to mouth (in the worst case scenario, I could live on that money for three years!). The sudden absence of worry freed within me unimagined reserves of empathy, understanding and generosity; and my gratitude did not stop at Sandy, Solouhin and all the others who had helped me in any way – it was directed at the wider world, the universe, God, fate! But above all at Lord Hattersley who, in spite of his corpulent presence, did not seem entirely real: he had appeared too unexpectedly, he had offered me too much money, my life had changed too quickly and I wasn't at all clear what I was getting myself into.

When I told him briefly about Sandy, he said that I should say goodbye to her in person, Jonesey would drive me to the pub where she worked; he would wait for me, since what was five minutes in the context of eternity, especially when love was involved?

No, I said (fearing the scene that I knew Sandy would cause), I'll leave her a letter. ("Dear Sandy, I have got an offer I cannot refuse and am moving to the country for an indefinite period of time. The rent on the studio is paid, stay here, make use of it, I'll call you. I'll also call Solouhin about helping you – you can't stay behind that bar. I'm sorry to leave so suddenly, that's how things turned out and I have no choice. I won't forget you. Take care of yourself.") I put the letter on the kitchen counter.

"How much does the girl earn?" aksed Sir William. When I said five shillings an hour, he shook his head and once again pulled out his leather wallet. "Gestures, Willy boy," he said, "gestures are very important when it comes to women." And he put beside the letter five ten pound banknotes.

No, I picked up the money and gave it back to him. She would think that I was trying to buy her off or to redeem myself – she's not like that and neither am I.

He looked at me for some time and his sharply inquisitive eyes suddenly softened, even moistened. "Willy boy," he said, "I think today is a fine one for both of us. I'm as proud of you as if you were my own son. Which I don't have, because God saw fit to bless me with five daughters. And two of those are extremely disagreeable. Shall we go?"

His country house, Lockwood Manor, was an eighteenth century palace, in Palladian style, with classical Greco-Roman elements, twenty-five acres of parkland and gardens extending right up to the back door, endless, spacious, richly decorated reception rooms on the ground floor, bedrooms and other private rooms on the first floor, and a kitchen and servants' rooms in the basement. Wherever I turned, I saw paintings in elaborate frames, from portraits of his ancestors all the way back to the fifteenth century, to what were no doubt originals by Constable, Turner and other British artists. In the corridors (where the parquet creaked beneath my feet as it had in Hampton Court Palace), I had the feeling that I was walking round a gallery, the walls were literally covered in valuable paintings.

Suddenly, the two thousand pounds I had got for *Tea With the Queen* did not seem so much; Lord Hattersley's wealth, most of which he had no doubt inherited, far exceeded the capacity of my imagination.

"I need a massage," said Sir William, whose face showed that he was in extreme pain, although he was trying hard to conceal it, "I've been on my feet for too long. Spikey will show you your room. I'll see you at dinner. The green room, Spikey. Please check that every-thing is okay."

354

"I will, Sir William," said Spikey, with a slight bow, obligingly but without servility; he was a slightly clumsy, elderly man, evidently a butler, a gentleman's gentleman. He took me to a spacious room on the first floor, pulled back the curtains on an enormous window so that the soft early autumn light of the sun just about to set flooded in, then he turned to me, scanned me with a slightly critical eye from head to toe and asked: "Will that be all, sir?"

Since I didn't know what to say, I merely nodded. He gave a barely discernible bow and said: "Thank you, sir. Dinner is at seven." And he went.

The room was no different from the other parts of the palace that I had seen on the way; the wallpaper and other decorative elements exhaled a sedate combination of good taste and the desire to exhibit wealth, the antique furniture seemed cumbersome, uncomfortable, non-functional. I couldn't shake off the feeling that I had wandered at least a hundred years into the past; even the bathroom fittings looked as if they belonged to times long gone – nice to look at, but impractical. Although there was no reason for me to think so, I had the feeling that I had been kidnapped, torn forcefully from the world that, in spite of everything, I somehow coped with or at least knew how to cope with, and brought into an environment that I knew only from films and books. It seemed impossible that such a world could even exist.

I stared through the window, my eye following the gravel driveway lined with poplars that climbed a slight rise and then disappeared into the distance. The September sun was setting exactly at the point where the avenue of trees met the horizon. On the right, behind the poplars, on the freshly mown grass, I saw two female figures on horses, probably the Lord's daughters; bouncing in the saddle, they receded into the distance and disappeared behind the tall trees. I felt unbearably lonely, perhaps because of the unfamiliar dimensions and vistas.

Or perhaps they had only deepened the feeling that was perhaps always inside me, the colour of my soul. I always saw the world most clearly through myself and through myself back into the world, which was no longer what it would have been if I knew how to perceive it directly – it was painted over with me, with the colours of my feelings. Whenever I painted, I was almost always depicting externalised elements of myself: almost every one of my paintings was a kind of self-portrait.

I felt tears running down my face. I should be feeling happy, but I did not know how to feel happiness and that was perhaps why I was crying. Lord Hattersley had offered me board and lodging plus fifty pounds per week to paint what he requested, but only five hours per day, the rest was mine to do with as I saw fit – for my own work, for sleep or for walking. I told him that my residence permit was about to expire and he immediately asked me to give him my passport – he was a member of the House of Lords and he knew the Home Secretary.

"There's a solution to every problem," he said, "remember that." Perhaps there is, I thought, if you have sufficient money. But now I was going to be in a position, although on a lesser scale, where money would not be a problem, so why couldn't I relax, stop worrying, enjoy myself?

Before dinner, I took a bath in the old-fashioned bathtub (there was no shower) and dressed the best that I could, in a check shirt and grey linen trousers. In spite of this, when I entered the dining room I was greeted by eight pairs of amazed and sharply critical eyes, which immediately became mercifully forebearing.

"Willy boy," said Lord Hattersley, who sat at the head of the endlessly long table, "sit there next to my wife and try to entertain her – you might succeed, I haven't been able to for years, so I stopped trying."

"Don't take that feeble-minded old man seriously," said Lady Hattersley, when I cautiously sat next to her on the heavy upholstered chair at the corner of the table. She was much younger than her husband, with short hair and warm, friendly eyes.

"We're quite informal here," she said, "so please call me Mary. On your right are our three youngest daughters, Phoebe, Jenny and Diana; the oldest two are married and live elsewhere. On the other side of the table are my older sister, Elisabeth, who lives with us and who you can call Elisabeth, then my cousin Lord Macauly, who you will call Sir Andrew, and lastly, on my right, his younger brother, who you can call Michael, while the head of the household insists on being called Sir William."

"Pay no attention, Willy boy, if you make a mistake, I won't have your head cut off. Two Willys will be tolerant of each other, considering that they share a love of art, which to everyone else around this table is unknown territory."

"Sir William likes to exaggerate," said Lady Hattersley. "He learned that in the House of Lords, where they compete in exaggeration. And you? What do your parents do?"

I noticed that they had all raised their heads from the soup and were looking towards me; there was a tense silence; even Spikey stopped pouring the wine and was looking at me, while two maids who had brought the food were standing in the doorway.

Then Sir William said: "Don't embarrass the boy, Mary, you can see that he's a bit lost, wait a few days before you bombard him with questions. You can do it when he's painting your portrait. You're first in the queue."

"Sorry, Willy," said Lady Hattersley, "very tactless of me."

No, no, I said quickly, I'm not embarrassed, it's just the soup is hot. My father is a general in the Yugoslav army, a member of the general staff. During the war he was a close collaborator of Tito's, they planned Neretva and some other battles together, and he was there when Tito met Churchill on Corfu.

"Oh," replied Lady Hattersley tersely, "Churchill was a fool." Sir William laughed. "I like this lad, he's very sharp and, I suspect, not without a sense of humour. I'm not embarrassed, it's just the soup is hot! Bravo, Willy, keep it up!"

Then we sipped our soup; Spikey finished serving and went for more wine. On the table were three large legs of lamb, potatoes, cauliflower, broccoli, carrots, kale, three different sauces, five different salads, and the food kept coming. While eating, my eyes wandered around the room: the three crystal chandeliers above us were so heavy that they would have smashed the table and us with it if they had all fallen at once; on the wall hung an enormous painting, at least ten feet by seven, in a gilt frame, a dark oil painting depicting lords and ladies fox hunting on horseback – an English classic, nothing special.

"Willy, do you have a suit for more formal occasions, we have quite a few of them here?" Lady Hattersley suddenly asked. "At least once a week we have distinguished guests."

"Don't ask stupid questions," said Sir William from the opposite end of the table, "of course he doesn't, what would he do with one? I'm going to London again in a few days, I've got business at the Lords. Jonesey can take him to my tailor and he can get kitted out for any occasion."

"Well, you know what you're doing, I suppose," responded Lady Hattersley drily, as if she was not too pleased with her husband's generosity.

"Almost always," said Sir William, "you, rarely."

In spite of this goading, which at times became quite sharp, they were clearly fond of each other and probably staged these verbal skirmishes out of habit or to keep boredom at bay, since none of the others was exactly talkative – not the three young ladies, aged from twenty-five to thirty-five who, although not unattractive, were not the type to set male hearts beating more rapidly, nor Sir Andrew and Michael, who were keeping up a murmured conversation between themselves, nor Elisabeth, who kept her eye on me the whole time.

"Actually, our young guest is very good looking," she said when dessert arrived on the table, don't you think, Phoebe?" she said across the table to the youngest daughter.

"Nothing will come of that," Sir William intervened quickly before Phoebe could respond. "He has a girlfriend in London, and in any case Phoebe and Jenny are off to America in two weeks, while Diana... well, let's leave that..." he concluded, reaching for his wine glass.

The oldest daughter suddenly gave a loud sob, pushed back her chair and dashed towards the door.

"Congratulations," said Lady Hattersley, "I'm amazed that none of your daughters have killed themselves yet."

"No," replied Sir William, "but they're slowly killing me, which is worse."

Then his wife turned to me: "Probably you're taken aback by our discord, I'm sure that in Macedonia family relations are much warmer."

"What do you mean, Macedonia," roared Sir William, "the lad's from Bosnia, from the Dinaric Alps, where did you get the idea he was from Macedonia?"

Actually, I'm from Slovenia, I was bold enough to correct him, far from Macedonia and in the real Alps, not the Dinaric.

"Well, as I said," Sir William continued to rebuke his wife, "far from Macedonia, don't talk such nonsense."

"We've often been to the Alps skiing," said the lady, "although only the French Alps."

"This pudding is awful." Sir William pushed the silver dish away from him and got up. "Have you finished, Willy? I'd like to show you something."

"There's no need to leap to your feet," Lady Hattersley chided me, "finish eating. And you stop dealing with him as if he was your dog," she told her husband.

No, no, I said, quickly getting up (the pudding really was awful), I've had too much, I'll burst, thank you, my apologies. I followed Sir William down the long corridor into a wing of the palace. Just before the end, we turned to the left into a shorter corridor and went through an arched entrance way into a gigantic conservatory. It contained not a single plant: everywhere there were stacks of pictures, framed, un-framed, empty frames, brushes, bottles of oil paint, palettes and other materials, and a large easel, on which stood an unfinished painting of a sunflower.

"The family studio," said Sir William. "We all do a bit of daubing here, particularly my talkative wife, myself less frequently recently and even, believe it or not, Spikey, who has the most talent among us. But from now on, this is your space, here you will paint, and all the others will have to fit in with your schedule. If you need anything, make a list and Jonesy will go to a supplier's and bring it within an hour. Come, there's something I want to show you."

He led me back along the corridor and through a spacious reception room with bookshelves to the ceiling, except on the wall opposite the entrance, which was reserved for paintings. And there, hanging in a place of honour in the centre, I saw a painting that pinned me to the floor.

"That's the painting that your style reminds me of," said Sir William. "A work of genius. I jumped on it as soon as I saw it, although the painter is unknown."

On the wall hung my *Venus with Dog and Lambs*, for which Julia's mother had posed in Cornwall. I held my breath.

"I knew you'd be stunned," said Sir William. "The artist took the image of Velazquez's *Rokeby Venus* and created a painting which, in this age of psychoanalysis that we all grumble about, can say a thousand things, be interpreted in a hundred different ways, all equally valid, all equally likely. It's a painting that tells a more complex story than any novel could. Unbelievable. I'm really pleased with myself that I managed to acquire it."

It is unbelievable, I said, although I was saying something completely different. How much did you pay for it, I asked, if it's not a secret.

"One doesn't normally talk about such things," he said a little coolly, "but since it's you – five thousand pounds. A lot, I admit, but if I organise a sale at Sotheby's I'll get at least three times as much, I promise you, in spite of it being an anonymous work."

No painter would paint something like that without signing it, I said. Did you buy it already framed?

"Yes," said Sir William, "but there's no signature, have a look," and he went closer, "usually the signature's in the bottom right-hand corner, but there's nothing."

Whoever framed it wrapped too much of the canvas on the stretching frame, I said. If you take it out of the frame, you'll find the signature.

"Is that so?" said Sir William. "I hadn't thought of that. I'm extremely interested." He went to the door and called: "Spikey!"

"Immediately, milord," came Spikey's voice and rapid footsteps. He almost ran, trying hard not to show how heavily he was breathing.

"Spikey, you're a handy type, would you know how to take this painting out of its frame without damaging it?"

Spikey shrugged uncertainly and said: "I think Jones would be more suitable for something like that, if you don't mind my saying."

I'll do it, I said. I need pliers and a screwdriver, but first we need to take the painting down. We did that together while Spikey went for the tools. "I hope you're right," said Sir William. "I don't want anything to happen to the painting, but I'm sure you know what you are doing."

Don't worry, I said, I know very well what I'm doing. It took me ten minutes to remove the stretching frame from the decorative one. And there, on the wide, too-wide fold of canvas that the framer had stapled to the back of the frame, was the painter's signature, clearly visible.

"Wait, let me see." Sir William put his glasses on. "Vi … what's that … li or ti … Vili Vau … go or po … Vaugotic … Vaupotic. Vili Vaupotic!" He straightened up and stared at me through his glasses. "What's going on?"

Just that my paintings are living a more interesting life in England than I am, I said. This is one of those I left on the train. I'm glad it ended up in good hands. If I can say the same for the others, then I'll be satisfied.

"You painted this?" asked Sir William, looking once more at the signature. "Of course, it's your style, I recognise it immediately. Now I'm ashamed that I employed you as a portraitist. But that's only temporary. You must move forward and I shall help you, Willy boy, really – I'll do everything for you and more."

PART FOUR

46.

Sir William was not one of those people who make empty promises – if he said he would do a thing, he would do everything, including the impossible, to make good on his rash promise, whatever the consequences. This is what happened with regard to the extension of my residence permit. When a Home Office lawyer told him that he could not employ me as a family portraitist, but he could employ me, for instance, as a restorer of the frescoes in his house, which was a protected building under the provisions of the National Heritage Trust, he decided to ignore the fact there were no frescoes and, through a legal contract witnessed by a notary, employed me as a restorer for a period of five years.

"After that, you can ask for citizenship," he said. "I probably won't go to hell because of these lies, I'll go there for other reasons, although I'll have to live with the bad conscience. But for you, Willy boy, I would do worse things."

He called at the art dealer's where he bought *Venus with Dog and Lambs* and tried to find out where the picture had come from, but the dealer was not willing to divulge this information, since in this business, it was "completely normal not to tell who you bought something from, unless compelled to do so by the police, which we don't want – after all, Sir William himself had said that the paintings were forgotten, rather than stolen." He checked whether the man had received any other paintings from my Cornwall period (I made a list), but he insisted that he had not, "or that he had already sold them on," commented Sir William, "in which case, there's nothing we can do."

And then he did something else: he hired a private detective, a Mr. Gray, to whom I had to describe all my misadventures with paintings down to the last detail; he carefully noted everything down and said that he would get straight onto it. "First we need to establish what the current state of affairs is," said Sir William, "only then can we decide what action to take."

At this point I was painting a portrait of Lady Hattersley, who was reading Henry James's *Portrait of a Lady* while posing, putting it down every so often to talk about her husband and the hard times that had befallen the British aristocracy. These hard times were not at all evident in the palace or its immediate environs and Sir William did not give the impression that he was facing bankruptcy – quite the opposite – but Mary (as she kept insisting I call her, although I don't know why) saw them in the wider, historical context, as the unstoppable decline of the great families of a great nation that was now ruled by a "half-educated lower class" lacking in taste and any sense of aesthetics or "real values". And then there were the hippies, who were a living reproach to everything that the best sons of England have fought for!

"And how many foreigners," she said, "how many foreigners had moved here? You cannot go anywhere, Willy, without seeing a black face."

Perhaps that's not all that bad, I dared to comment. Black faces are interesting and often beautiful.

"You speak as a painter," she said, "and that's as it should be, but imagine what it will be like in twenty years – suddenly all the foreigners will come together and demand their rights and what then? Where can we go, those of us who created this kingdom? To Australia, where we once sent only convicts?"

I don't know, I really don't know, was all that I dared say.

"Of course, there are no longer any real aristocrats left," she said, "with a few exceptions, the most notable being the Hattersleys. Some say that there is only an upper middle class. The Queen, of whom I think only the best, keeps producing lords as if there's no tomorrow, she keeps on naming them, picking them up on the streets, trade union leaders, socialist politicians, traders who got rich dealing in plastic dishes or condoms – what have we come to? The essence of a true aristocrat is that money means nothing to him. I don't mean that he does not want any, that he does not know how to spend it, but that a real aristocrat feels no obligation to work for money. He does many things, but not for payment. And my husband is one of those who adhere most closely to this principle. His greatest talent lies in spending what he has inherited from his predecessors. It's true that English aristocrats were always patrons of the arts and collected the works of the best painters in their luxurious homes, but Sir William has elevated this natural tendency into a way of life. He'd rather be a painter, but because he lacks the talent, he admires that of others and praises them to the sky. And because he doesn't know what is good or what he wants, he goes round exhibitions and galleries and auctions buying everything on offer, including the unknown work of completely unknown young painters. I admit that he often sells these on for twice the price and thus at least partly finances his hobby, but the money melts away – last year we were forced to sell five of our best horses. What shall become of our daughters if we don't find them suitable husbands? Today, there are not so many dukes and counts and barons around as there used to be and the sons of artificially created lords are quite willing to marry a girl without blue blood in her veins, as long as she is good looking. Some of them marry models, who are little more than walking clothes hangers – can you imagine what is happening in this once great country? How can Phoebe, Jenny and Diana compete with girls who show themselves off shamelessly in women's magazines? The oldest two, thank God, are by some miracle provided for, while Phoebe and Jenny are going off to study in America. There they'll have to get to know some short-sighted stockbroker who wants to marry into an aristocratic family – Americans love that kind of thing – and then our blood will be even more diluted. It's no surprise that my migraine is constantly getting worse."

In the end, it'll all turn out how it should, I tried to comfort her with a bit of stupid philosophy; nothing else came to mind.

"My husband is very fond of you," she said. "He is thinking of adopting you. He always wanted a son and I think he is so brusque with me because I failed to give him one. Henry VIII had his wife beheaded for the same failing. Of course, Sir William isn't Henry VIII, although he is one of his distant forebears and often acts like him. Above all, the times are somewhat more just than they were then, so he has to make do with beheading me verbally. I am against the idea of adoption, although I have nothing against you personally. I'm against it, because it seems unnecessary and because Sir William has completely incomprehensibly fallen in love with your talent, which I acknowledge is exceptional, but to him – and please remember this – you are nothing more than a toy, while my husband is and will always remain a child. Whatever, we shall all resist his idea, but please don't take it personally. We are happy that you are here, we like you, but I must think about my five daughters – I hope you understand."

Absolutely, I said, I'm not an orphan who needs adopting, I'm actually a stubborn young man who decides his own fate. For now, I like it here, but tomorrow something may get into my head and I may take off for Greenland to paint walruses. I would be a very unreliable adopted son and so that is one of Lord Hattersley's less happy schemes, although his ideas are usually good, even exceptional.

"Oh, I'm so relieved by your words, Willy boy, and so happy that you understand the interests of the women in this family."

Maybe it isn't that, I said, maybe it's that I understand where *my* interests lie.

(No, Willy II once more broke into my thoughts, you don't, that's the problem. You'd like to be noble, but unlike Sir William you can't afford to be. He can support his nobility with actions, you can only blabber about it. Think about it: from a basement in Soho you have made an amazing leap to the trough – will you now act like a good little piggy or will you once again convince yourself that you're an angel and flutter back among the clouds? Do you realise what adoption would mean, however unlikely it is? Inheritance rights – all this could one day be yours. Don't make your greatest mistake at the age of twenty-three, you'll have to live with it for too long. Let it be Sir William who makes his greatest mistake, he's near to seventy, he'll have much less time to grieve. What are you on about? replied Willy I. In return for everything he has done for me, I should lumber him with you as a replacement son, officially and for all time? Shut up and let me do the work for which I'm paid in peace. Isn't that more than we dared expect even a week ago? Why do you always want more, more, more? You fool, said Willy II. You'll be sorry, and when you are don't come to me looking for consolation.)

"And one more thing, Willy," said Lady Hattersley. "If one of my daughters should want to use you to get rid of her frustration – most likely it would be Jenny – you must resist at all costs. It's true that in that regard they are all three of them extremely deprived – poor Diana has never even touched a man yet – but you are here for other reasons. Sir William would be, to put it mildly, disappointed if something like that took place. He might even terminate your work permit and then you'd have to go back to Macedonia, which you probably don't dream about every often."

That's true, I said, nor about returning to Slovenia, for I've never actually been to Macedonia.

"Anyway," she said, "to wherever it is you are from – there are too many unimportant places in the world for one to remember all of them."

As far as your three daughters are concerned, you don't need to worry, I said. I don't think they even like me, they give me only black looks.

"What do you expect?" she said. "If Sir William were to adopt you they would be disinherited – not completely, but to a great extent. I shouldn't actually be telling you this, but the girls are cunning and will try to prevent your adoption in any way they can, even by accusing you of something, such as harassment, or they will try to seduce you and then accuse you of rape. I know them and what they are capable of when they feel threatened."

I didn't understand why Lady Hattersley was telling me all this. If she wanted to prevent the adoption, it would make a lot more sense for her to support her daughters' conspiracy, instead of warning me about it.

As if she read my thoughts, she added: "The only luxury I shall never deprive myself of is the right to always speak frankly. For many that is embarrassing, including me very often, and perhaps not always in the family's interests, but I made this resolution when I was very young. I know all too well that nothing would sway my husband if he had definitely decided to adopt you. Not even if you really did rape one of his daughters – he'd merely say she should be happy. You are the only one who can drive the idea from his head. That's why I'm being open with you. I want you to resist my husband in gratitude for my openness. And above all, I don't want any dirty business going on in the house, can you imagine how difficult that would make our lives?"

I was grateful to her anyway, since I could have been drawn into all sorts of things if she hadn't warned me; I now watched my every step. When I finished Lady Hattersley's portrait and it was the turn of Jenny, the middle daughter, I requested that someone be present in the studio throughout – either Spikey or one of the maids. Spikey said that as the head of the staff he could not play such a role and in any case it seemed totally unnecessary ("Miss Jenny is a grown-up person and does not need protection"), while the maids didn't have the time to sit for hours in the studio – whatever next?

Lady Hattersley had to intervene and recruit her sister to play the role of chaperone. This was an even better solution, since Jenny and Elisabeth spoke almost exclusively to each other and I could work uninterruptedly. Their questions, when they were directed at me, were strictly neutral and without pitfalls.

When Sir William found out what was happening he laughed and winked at me. "Far from being naïve, our Willy," I heard him say later to his wife in the library. "He knows how to look after himself, I'll give him that. It's a good job we didn't have a son, he'd have been completely different from him. *You*'d have made him different, completely unworthy of the family name."

"If the family name is still worth anything," she responded, "you'll make sure that it soon won't be and the main reason will be your blind worship of this boy. Sooner or later, he will disappoint you. How will you bear it?"

"Willy boy won't disappoint me," he said with confidence. "A hundred others he might, and why shouldn't he if they are not as important to him, but he'll never disappoint me."

"I'm afraid that you are digging a large hole for us to fall into," she said.

I insisted on the same arrangement when it was the turn of Phoebe and Diana; and although some thought the whole thing absurd and often teased me about it, especially at dinner, saying that I was afraid of girls, I was not to be swayed. The girls tried to get their revenge by relentlessly criticising their portraits, saying that I had deliberately distorted their faces; that I was depicting them as horrors and how lucky they were that mirrors don't lie. And then Jenny came and offered to teach me to ride, saying it was a basic skill if you ever wanted to be worth anything. I don't, I said, and I don't like horses, I prefer to walk.

This was not strictly true, for when Jonesey offered to teach me to drive the Bentley, I grabbed the opportunity with both hands. Jonesey (Trevor Jones) was only a few years older than me and had no company in the house, and in my approachability he saw an opportunity for friendship, which I was not against, since in my luxurious surroundings, almost cut off from the world, where nobody did anything worthwhile, except for his lordship, who was often absent, I felt increasingly lonely. And so, whenever we had the time, we would drive around the local roads, through villages and market towns, stopping now and then for a beer and a chat, and generally enjoying ourselves, although I could not convince him to stop calling me sir.

"I can't do that," he said, "Sir William would be very angry if he found out."

Jonesey, I said, I'm younger than you. My father is a builder by trade and my mother a seamstress.

I let him have his way and always acted towards him as if we were complete equals, with the difference that he knew how to drive (and repair) the Bentley a hundred times better than me and I was a hundred times better at painting. When I made this comparison we had a good laugh together.

47.

And then, after it had been put off four times, the moment finally arrived for me to go to London with Lord Hattersley, so that Jonesey could take me to the tailor's. And of course, the tailor was located on the famous Saville Row. We arrived more than an hour late. He measured me for a dinner jacket, tails, five shirts, four pairs of trousers, four jackets and some sports clothes. This all seemed far too much to me, but the tailor had received written instructions from Sir William and was reluctant to deviate from his intention of dressing me for the next thirty years.

To take a break from this effort, Jonesy and I had a beer in a nearby pub, and then London was ours until five o'clock, when we were due to pick up Sir William from in front of Parliament.

Jonesey, I asked, would you do me a favour? Of course, there was no likelihood that he would refuse, but he was happy to oblige me and also take part in a small conspiracy. First I asked him to drive me to the studio in Greek Street, which I was still officially renting. So as not by chance to bump into Sandy, I asked him to go first, to ring the bell and, if anyone came to the door, to ask for me. Since no one did answer the door, I was able to go down the steps myself, unlock the door and enter.

I could not understand how it could once have seemed luxurious – it was a dark, damp smelling hole. Almost nothing had changed: everything lay about willy nilly and in the kitchen there were rotting leftovers, which at one time had not bothered me, but now evoked in me a mixture of despair and anger; the creased clothes of my Kiwi friend were still scattered around, particularly on the unmade bed on the floor near the door. But (oh ho!) there was something new: beside her bra there now lay a pair of man's underpants, plus a man's shirt and jeans. I opened the wardrobe and found further evidence that freckly Sandy was not pining for Willy: two jackets, a coat and a tracksuit.

Do you believe women who say that you are the only one and that they would die without you? I asked Jonesey.

"It depends, sir," he said, "but generally not."

Has one of his lordship's daughters ever invited you to bed? I asked.

He went bright red. "I don't know if I can talk about such things, sir," he said.

Oh come on, I said, you know that I'd never tell anyone.

"There were some attempts," he said, trying not to seem too pleased with himself. "Especially by Miss Diana."

I can't believe it, I said. Diana, the oldest and least attractive? How did you react?

He shrugged: "As Sir William ordered me to – I went to him straight away for advice. He asked me to do my duty and keep quiet about it."

Poor Jonesey! I said. But do you have a girlfriend, I mean one you chose yourself?

"I go to this widow in the next village," he admitted. "Otherwise there's no one less than ten miles away."

Some paintings by the previous, murdered tenant were still leaning against the wall. But against one of them rested some new A4 size black and white photographs, evidently those that Solouhin had instructed Sandy to have made to aid her assault on the world of fashion. The most visible thing on the photos was her freckles, sown so thickly that it looked as if someone had scattered barley across her face. Come on, Jonesey, I said. Let's continue our nostalgic journey around London.

The next stop was Paddington, the Great Western pub, St. Michael's Street. We parked the Bentley right in front of the door, so Jonesey could keep an eye on it ("Unsavoury neighbourhood", he said). I was ready to flee through the side door at any moment should Alan decide to come into the pub. But the house looked deserted and even more neglected than before: the windows were covered by torn curtains, faded by the sun, some of them hanging from the curtain rail by only a few hooks, the remnants dangling down in ugly folds like tattered rags. In that house, I said to Jonesey, something happened to me that I would rather forget about forever.

"There are things like that, sir," he agreed. "There are things we would rather forget, but we can't."

I felt I had no choice but to go up to the bar and ask the barman, who I remembered from before, whether Alan still came in.

"Alan?" he said in amazement. "Alan is in hospital. He was attacked by thieves, who broke his bones and almost cut his throat. They emptied the house. Luckily, Marisa was at her mother's, where she then stayed. Terrible thing."

When I went back to our table by the window I emptied my glass and said: two lots of bad news so far, Jonesey, the second considerably worse than the first, I hope that there will be no escalation. Shall we go?

We drove to Chiswick and sat for some time at the roadside close to Marie Hudson's house, not far from the Rover in front of the door, which meant that she was at home. But she obviously had no intention of coming out; Ana and Harry were at work, Gerry and Christopher at school, there was no point in waiting; if she had a new lodger in my former room I wouldn't even know him. We moved on.

Oh, Jonesey, I said, do you know the pain of nostalgia? As if honey mixed with iron filings was flowing through your veins? I don't know why I can't get rid of the feeling, it keeps pulling me back to where I experienced something, to the people I experienced it with, almost as if it wanted everything to be repeated, but with a different outcome. Do you ever wish there were different versions of your life story?

"I can't say that I do, sir."

Then you don't even know what you're missing, I said. Of all the attractive things in this world, nostalgia is the most beautiful. It is also the most comforting, for once you have satisfied it, the way forward is once more clear, open.

"And is yours satisfied, sir?" he asked, consulting his watch.

No, Jonesey, I said, there are still some places to visit.

We had no luck in front of Jimmy's house in Ravenscourt Park. There was no sign of Stella, she was probably at the school for those with speech difficulties; but at the cemetery, Jimmy was still where they had buried him, the grave freshly planted with flowers and greenery, and the inscription was still the same (I don't know why I thought it would be any different). Do you like Matthew Arnold? I asked Jonesey.

"Can't say I've ever heard of him, sir," he said. "Painter, is he?"

No, a poet, I said, perhaps rather old-fashioned, pathetic and verbose, but he wrote some really good poems and even more very good lines – he is problematic only when taken as a whole.

"That's true of many things." Jonesy offered a pinch of wisdom, which was closer to true wisdom than he perhaps realised.

I knelt at the grave, head bowed, hands together and in my mind said an Our Father and a Hail Mary, both of which I remembered from religious instruction as a child. Then we drove to Earls Court, to Nevern Square, and parked in front of Mrs. O'Riley's boarding house, so that I could establish whether the Queen of Egypt was still in residence (or had she found her prince on a white horse and moved out?). It seemed almost unfair that I was now living in the kind of house where, according to all the rules (if wishes were rules), she should be; for the first time in a while, fate once again seemed to me capricious and even wicked. And more than ever before, her longing seemed ridiculous in its absurdity, primarily because she was unwilling even for a moment to consider the possibility that it *may* be unrealisable.

Oh, Jonesey, I sighed, if you only knew how many nice things happened to me in this house.

And then I noticed Cleo walking along the street. She was coming from the direction of the Underground station, probably from lunch with one of her always unsuitable suitors, her head down, as if tired from whatever she had been doing, worn out from relentless incursions of reality, but stubbornly determined not to give in.

She mustn't see me, I said, turning and leaning over the seat as if I was looking for something in the back, but you take a good luck at her. I heard her heels click past and from the corner of my eye I saw her go up the steps, looking over her shoulder at the luxurious limousine, rather unusual for Nevern Square. When I finally dared to look round, she had already unlocked the door and gone inside.

What do you think? I asked Jonesey.

"More beautiful than most of the women I've seen," he said.

Oh come on, I chided him, there's no need to lie. She's too fat, too tall, too clumsy and other things as well.

"She seems pretty slim to me, sir," he said, sounding almost guilty for being unable to agree with me. "Maybe she has lost weight. She is tall, but I've always liked tall women with black hair, who do not walk, but who roll along like ships in a storm. But above all, I like her face! Those large, dark, sad eyes. And how she looked at me! Not as if I was a chauffeur, but as if I might be the owner of this car."

Would you let her suck you off? I asked.

He blushed so extremely that I feared the blood would seep through his skin. "I wouldn't think twice," he said. "Even if I had to die immediately afterwards."

Oh, Jonesey, I said, you've become slightly poetic, which shows that the young lady made quite an impression on you, but now let's go somewhere else, where we shall possibly meet the woman for whom I would be prepared to die *before* she sucked me off.

"You seem to know quite a few women, sir," he commented.

A handful, I said, but what does it matter when the only one that means anything to me is the one that I met only fleetingly? Grosvenor House Hotel, Jonesey, I said, Park Lane.

"What would we young men do without women, eh sir?" he asked as we drove. "The world would be very empty."

Undoubtedly, I said, but it's terrible when it seems empty in spite of being full of beautiful women.

"But that only comes later, doesn't it, sir? When we reach Sir William's age, around seventy, don't you think?"

I don't know if it's a matter of age, I said. Maybe it depends on what kind of soul the Creator gave you. If he painted it with melancholy, you'll always want what you don't have. And as soon as your wish is fulfilled, you'll want something else.

"That's difficult," he said, as we drove past Hyde Park. "Then I should be grateful that my soul is relatively simple."

No soul is simple, Jonesey, I said. Not one.

When the Bentley stopped outside the entrance to the Grosvenor House Hotel, a uniformed doorman immediately opened the door on my side and said: "Good afternoon, sir, welcome. Sir, what can I do for you, sir?"

Before I had the chance to reply that he had probably confused me with someone else, Jonesey said: "Nothing special, Mikey. Keep an eye on the car, the gentleman wants to ask something in the reception."

"Of course," the doorman obligingly straightened up, "no problem. And how is Sir William?"

"So-so, Mikey, so-so," said Jonesey, as we went towards the entrance, where Mikey returned to his usual place.

I didn't know that Sir William also came here, I said, as we entered the sumptuous lobby. He must be a regular guest, if the doorman recognises his car.

"Not a regular," said Jonesey, "but they do have business meetings and conferences here. The hotel has twenty-two conference rooms and the largest banquet hall in Europe, which holds two thousand guests. It has a ballroom for more than five hundred and a twenty-yard swimming pool. It has seventy-two suites and almost four hundred luxurious rooms. Rich people from all over the world come here."

Then we're probably in the wrong place, I said. And he: "You probably not, but me certainly, since chauffeurs are not allowed past the entrance. I know Mikey because we usually have a chat while I'm waiting for Sir William, who always presses a fiver into his hand when he leaves."

In the middle of the spacious foyer, amidst the intrusive and almost aggressive luxury, I felt very alien, so out of place that I would have happily fled; and that was in spite of the luxury I had become accustomed to at Lockwood Manor; that seemed harmonious, calm

377

and natural, perhaps because the house was somewhat neglected, but here newly earned money screamed at you from every side, money that wanted to show off and, in doing so, went too far. We hardly dared to approach the long reception desk, behind which were three black-suited male receptionists and a grey-haired lady, also in black, as if they were all employed at an undertaker's.

"We can't linger too long," said Jonesey, "sooner or later someone's going to come over and ask us what we want." We went over to the desk and spoke to the youngest of the three men.

Tatarski Modelling Agency, I said.

"Yes, and how can I help you?" asked the receptionist with a slightly superior air (he obviously did not realise that we had driven up in a Bentley).

Could you call Mr. Tatarski and tell him a friend is waiting for him in reception? I squeezed a hint of impatience into my voice.

"Room number?" he demanded.

I've no idea, I said, you probably have a guest register.

"We probably do," he said, "but even more probably we don't have the time to look at it for just anyone."

Oh, this is unbearable, I said more to myself than to him. And then Jonesey spoke up: "We shall have to inform Lord Hattersley about this rudeness. I doubt he will come here again." He turned as if to move away from the desk, as did I.

"Just a moment," we heard behind us. "What do the young gentlemen want?"

These words came from one of the other receptionists, who had evidently caught Jonesey's words. "My young colleague has been here only a few days and is still finding his feet. I apologise."

The insolent receptionist sank into the background, while the older, more friendly one gave such a wide smile that he was in danger of beheading himself.

Tatarski, I repeated, Ivan Aleksandrovič Tatarski.

The receptionist's smile narrowed somewhat, he bent over, threw onto the desk an enormous guest register and ran his finger down the list of names.

"No," he said, "that name is not on the list."

What about Solouhin? I asked. What about Dostoyevsky?

Once more he ran his finger down the list and once more he shook his head. "I'm sorry," he said, pushing the register back beneath the desk.

What about Selena. I decided to be direct. Could they call Selena?

The receptionist barely discernibly flinched, took a breath and said: "I'll try." He picked up the phone and dialled. I thought: Dostoyevsky is staying here under God knows what name – he has to keep erasing his traces, so as not to get caught. When I thought of my fortunate retreat to the country I felt almost guilty, although it was more than clear that I could not help him.

"Sir," the receptionist leaned across the counter towards me, "I need the password."

Password, I looked at him in surprise, what password?

"You don't know the password?" He seemed slightly shocked.

I shook my head and he said into the phone: "The gentleman does not know the password. What shall I do? Yes, yes… I understand."

Once again he leaned towards me and in a slightly lower voice, as if he wished to keep this between ourselves, he said: "The young lady is asking who recommended you."

Oh, I felt suddenly lost. I looked at Jonesey, who shrugged help-lessly. And then I grabbed at my only chance. I was recommended by three gentlemen, I said, Aleksej Ivanovič Solouhin, Fjodor Miha-jlovič Dostoyevsky and Ivan Aleksejevič Tatarski. The receptionist repeated only the surnames into the phone. He listened for a moment, then put the receiver down and once more leaned across the counter towards me. "She'll come down," he said, "please wait over there." And he pointed towards four armchairs near one of the pillars that supported the arched ceiling of the foyer. They were so comfortable and soft that Jonesey and I were almost swallowed up.

Jonesey, I asked, how do you like all this luxury, doesn't it seem a bit over the top?

He shrugged: "I'm used to all sorts of things, sir. I prefer sitting on a wooden chair. I like it when I smell of oil, when I'm repairing engines and cars. The rest of the world I see as a place where I must try not to die of hunger. I think with that my duty to society is done and the rest of the time I can devote to my hobbies, or stare into space, which I also like doing."

There's a lot of wisdom in your words, I said.

"Oh", he shrugged, "the wisdom of chauffeurs is not very highly rated."

Jonesey, I leaned towards him, for me this is the most important moment since I arrived in England. In a minute or two the woman of my dreams, my muse, will appear, the woman who I have in a deep sense dedicated my life to and all my goals, although I barely know her.

"Congratulations, sir," he said, "I'm honoured to be present at such an important moment."

A young woman emerged from the lift and walked towards the reception desk. She was tall and slim, with wheat-coloured hair and a small plait. She stopped at the desk and spoke to the receptionist, who indicated us with a slight jerk of his head. Jonesey remained seated, but I got up and went towards her.

I immediately saw that it wasn't Sandrina. She was not ugly, quite the opposite, she was exceptionally beautiful, but in an intrusive and at the same time somehow jadedly erotic way, so that she was light years apart from my Sandrina.

"Are you looking for me?" she asked, barely audibly.

I'm looking for Selena, I said.

"I am Selena," she said slightly impatiently.

Actually, I'm looking for my friend, I said, the friend who owes me his life and I perhaps, him. I know that he's in big trouble and is constantly on the move, but I have to find him on behalf of a friend who is looking for work as a model.

"The friend you're looking for is no longer here," she said, glancing left and right. "For reasons you are familiar with he had to move out. He hasn't yet passed on his new address. Get in touch in a week, there might be some news then."

And you, I asked, what's your connection with him?

"For some time I did secretarial work for him," she said. "And we were lovers, I won't deceive you. Otherwise, I am employed here as a masseuse. I wanted to help him. As you did. That is a connection between us, so please believe me when I say I'm not hiding anything from you. As soon as he gets in touch, I'll let him know you're looking for him. Can you give me your address or phone number?"

It's difficult, I said. I'm the guest of a prominent public person. I'd rather come back in a week's time. "Okay," she said, turned and went back towards the lift.

Jonesey, I said, as we drove back to the country, I am a fool. I see things that aren't there. I imagine conspiracies all around me and believe that my best friends are getting ready to stab me in the back. I must put an end to that, I must calm down, look to the future. That ought to be the simplest thing in the world.

"I agree," said Jonesey, "no woman is worth behaving like an idiot for. That's what I think, but I'm just an ordinary chauffeur, maybe I'm wrong."

No, Jonesey, I said. You're not just an ordinary chauffeur. You are a fount of wisdom.

48.

October brought autumn rain, real downpours, with wind whistling round the corners and shaking the tops of the trees like an irate teacher trying to punish a disobedient pupil; in between there was heavy drizzle, which mingled with the dampness of even the wallpaper in my room and narrowed the misty horizon to a few hundred yards. The atmosphere in the house changed in harmony with this: because it was not possible to ride or go on walks, the three daughters became restless, touchy and slightly malicious; Jenny suddenly got it into her head that her portrait was bad, much worse than those of her sisters, and gave as the reason the disturbing presence of her Aunt Elisabeth, who had constantly broken her concentration. She demanded that I paint her afresh, but without her "governess", in the complete spiritual fusion of artist and model, since posing was also an art and required optimal conditions.

"What do you say, Willy boy," asked Sir William, "is it doable?"

I'm afraid not, I said, I paint more easily if the model is not at peace, but absorbed in something or someone else – direct confrontation often confuses me and I lose control over the brush.

"Right," said Jenny, "then I'm not going to America."

"Then don't go to America," said Lady Hattersley, "who will get worked up apart from you, when you find that Phoebe has had a serious offer of marriage?"

Jenny laughed out loud and her laughter sounded like a scary mixture of despair and evil: "By the time one of my sisters receives a serious offer of marriage, I shall be a grandmother with at least nine grandchildren."

"Thanks, little sister," snapped Phoebe, while once again Diana sobbed and fled from the table.

"Oh, God," sighed the bland Michael, Sir William's younger brother, himself also unmarried, "when will all this stop?"

"Excuse me, Sir William," said Spikey decisively; he had evidently learned when to intervene in family discord. "This wine seems a little suspicious, rather bitter and perhaps a little fusty, will you permit me to go to the cellar for another one?"

"Thank you, Spikey," said Sir William, "we shall drink what you have poured for us. If there is anything wrong with it, then one of us – or perhaps all of us – will fall ill and one of us might even kick the bucket, which would certainly spice up the traditional autumn party that is only five days away. Have the invitations been sent out?"

Spikey gave a concerned look at Lady Hattersley, who said: "This year, I took over the invitations. The list is ten years old, some names needed to be crossed off and new ones added."

"I hope you haven't crossed off my colleagues from the Lords and gallery directors and all my foreign contacts," bristled Sir William. You can't deny me all pleasure in life."

"I wouldn't even dare think of such a thing, my dear." Lady Hattersley emphasised the word dear. "I crossed off only those who are dead, or have moved away, or who said something horrible in the newspapers about you or your political speeches. And I added the sons of some eminent aristocratic families. As well as the sons of some people who got rich selling Persian rugs or marijuana, since the time for compromise seems finally to have arrived, wouldn't you agree?"

"I have been making compromises all my life," said Sir William, "and you are all the result of such compromises, except of course Willy. Now pudding, and then all to your rooms."

Half an hour after dinner, Sir William knocked on my door. Together with him, the room took in the pleasant aroma of the pipe he was puffing on rather nervously and so enthusiastically that it was whistling.

"Willy boy," he said, "a small consultation. I'm not disturbing you?"
Not at all, Sir William, I said.

He sank into the only armchair in the room, while I perched on the edge of the bed. "Jonesey says that you were looking for some Selena in London," he said. "You mustn't hold it against him, the boy is as fond of you as if you grew up together, but he is contractually obliged to inform me about anything that might concern me one way or another."

Actually, I said, we were not looking for Selena, but another girl who I met briefly on the ferry when I was coming to England almost six months ago. Due to some strange coincidences, I thought it might be Selena. Now I know it wasn't. And my obsession is over, as well. Now I know that the person who for some reason I named Sandrina has disappeared into her own life and I will never see her again, which is as it should be. Until recently, I thought there was something wrong with fate; now I know there's something wrong with me. I stubbornly and persistently fled from what is towards what might be. Delayed puberty. It won't happen again.

"There's no need to abandon your dreams just because they seem childish," he said. "What do you think keeps me going at my age? But I'm known at that hotel, I take part in international conferences there, meetings with eminent foreign representatives, sometimes I treat myself to a sauna and a massage – I wouldn't want my name to be connected with anything questionable, unpleasant."

That won't happen, I assured him. I'll avoid the hotel in future. And I would have avoided it in the first place if I knew you were connected with it in any way.

"Willy boy," he said, "forget we ever had this conversation. The matter is of such marginal importance that it's really not worth mentioning. I came to see you for a much more important reason. I've noticed that since you came to Lockwood Manor, you haven't painted anything of your own. You haven't even touched the painting you had started in London – what was it, *My Life So Far*?"

I looked down, searching for the right words. I realised that I could not find them, since I had not succeeded in thinking about the problem, which had begun to trouble even me. It's true, I said. Since I met you, *my life so far* has been literally turned on its head, it has taken on dimensions of experience, values and feelings which have half erased, overshadowed and perhaps even re-valued all that happened before. Certainly, it has reduced it to something transitional, to initial steps, to draft figures whose real form are still unclear to me. The reason that I have not started anything new is the same. The pace of events has blurred my vision. Before, I noticed details: in the small room where I could barely turn round, I thought for hours about the edge of the hot plate that was being attacked by rust, about how I could use the rust-brown patches on the black background to make a general statement about my experience of the world, but now I had lost that capacity. I had a blind spot that prevented me from seeing more than what was right in front of me.

"Willy boy," he said. "I wanted to help you, I hope I haven't made a mistake that you'll never forgive me for."

No, I said, it's not that. It's like a centrifugal force has flung me into a distant orbit, far from the world that I know and that I had somehow domesticated. Now I have to get used to this new world, to adapt to it. The same would happen if I was in prison. That doesn't mean I'm comparing life in this house with prison, it's just that I've been carried into depths where my feet no longer touch the bottom. But I think it will all sort itself out.

He got up and went towards the door. He opened it, turned, took his pipe out of his mouth and said: "Willy boy, do you know how much of value you have taught me in the short time you've been here? I admire your ability to speak openly, to reveal your deepest feelings without effort, without wishing to achieve anything or to make a good impression. That is a rare quality, I don't know if I've seen it in anyone to the degree I have in you. Is that your usual nature or is it reserved for me?"

No, I said, not just for you, although I must admit that others experience it infrequently, while with you it's all the time. Don't ask me why that is. Perhaps you're the first person in my life who deserves complete honesty.

He came towards me and, judging by the expression on his face, he intended to embrace me, but at the last moment he thought better of it and merely patted me on the shoulder.

"How would you feel," he asked, his voice becoming very soft, but at the same time fragile, breakable, "if I said I would like to adopt you?"

Bad, Sir William, I said, I'd feel bad. Not because of you, but because of your family.

"Do you know," he said with a hint of bitterness, "that I knew exactly what your answer was going to be? Your problem is that you're too honest, mine is that I long too much for a real son. Just as you cannot shake off the dream about the girl on the ferry."

He went through the door and closed it behind him.

49.

In the following days, the weather improved and Spikey was asked to move the planned party from inside to the large lawn in front of the house. Since the preparations were almost made, he was not too happy about this, but not a glimmer of dissatisfaction appeared on his face. "Very good, milady, we'll do as you ask."

Of course, this meant a great deal of effort and rushing around: new serving staff had to be taken on, tables and chairs ordered, marquees and awnings erected; Jonesey had no time even for a brief chat, let alone a joint excursion. I spent most of my time in my room or the studio, where I worked on a portrait of Lord Macauly, who stubbornly read the paper the whole time and did not say a word.

My clothes came from London (the bill paid by Sir William), but I refused the request from Lady Hattersley and the girls to try them on and show them; I said that appropriate clothes were worn only on the appropriate occasion. The day before the party, it started to drizzle again and it seemed unlikely that the weather would quickly improve again, so Spikey was instructed to forget the outdoor arrangements and move the whole thing back inside.

"Very good, milady," said Spikey, this time, too, without the slightest hint of reluctance, "we'll do as you ask."

Plans regarding what to offer the guests also changed; at one point, cucumber sandwiches were enough, but the next day there was talk of roast beef, and then of twelve different kinds of salad; the first idea was that they would drink only champagne, then red and white wine as well as champagne; at first, Spikey was supposed to order bottled orange juice, but then the gardener was supposed to bring five sacks of oranges in his van and they would be squeezed freshly in the kitchen.

In the end, or at least that was my impression, there was more than enough of everything, especially guests, more than were invited (Lady Hattersley rebuked Spikey in the corridor). The men were in a range of outfits, some very buttoned up, others in hunting gear, some in V-neck sweaters and others in riding boots and jodhpurs; the women were in suits, flowered dresses, some younger ones in mini-skirts, although none in trousers, but almost all in hats that would require at least two days' attention if I wanted to portray them; I had never imagined that there was such a range of millinery available. Jonesey became a traffic policeman and had to see to the parking of cars and directing latecomers, of which there were quite a few; and Spikey discreetly commanded the team of hired waiters and tried to keep a cool head, in spite of the fact that nothing was going as he had planned.

The hubbub kept getting louder and soon became noise, increased by the string quartet, which stubbornly stuck to Baroque pieces – that seemed quite rebellious to me, at a time when almost everyone had succumbed to the Beatles and the Rolling Stones. Across the waves of noise there were sudden loud exclamations in shrill female voices: "Oh my God, haven't seen you for ages!", "I heard you were splitting up!" "Just back from Bermuda, it was glorious.", "Damn this socialist government!", "Where are you hiding your new husband?"

Suddenly, the afternoon sun broke through the clouds and larger groups of guests began to move outside, the crowd thinned out, Spikey had to see to it that some tables were carried out, too, to hold the rich array of food, from legs of lamb to smoked salmon and lobster, from unusual salads to tasty desserts and fifteen kinds of cheese, from apples and pears and grapes to exotic fruit I had never seen before.

Dressed (on Sir William's advice) in grey linen trousers, light blue shirt and a brown jacket with white stripes, all of which fitted me very well (the tailor had evidently tried hard), I was sufficiently unremarkable to be able to walk through the crowd, pausing now and then to watch people, who increasingly began to form in my eyes a barely real, exaggerated, almost Bosch-like grotesque picture, a dance of trivial stupidity, since among the social chatter I heard nothing that you might call significant, serious or profound – only business, gossip, backbiting and politics.

No one made any effort to introduce me to anyone, it was expected that I would manage on my own, going up to different people, engaging them in conversation, and that was fine by me, since I did not need to talk to anyone who did not address me, which in the first hour happened only once: I was followed by two young girls from among the handful who were weaving among the older guests, looking for someone they might be able to talk to differently from the majority of the guests.

"You look good," said one of them, and the other: "Do you want to go with us to a disco, it's boring here."

When I shook my head, the first one asked: "Do you like this music?" and when I nodded, they looked at each other and moved on.

Soon after, Sir William came up behind me. He put his hand on my shoulder and said: "Willy boy, I'd like to introduce you to Lord Fontleroy, an old acquaintance and political opponent with whom I have been friends for many years, perhaps because we agree about nothing except one thing, which has just emerged. Come with me."

I followed him to the library, where there stood a tall, thin man with a glass of champagne in his hand, staring raptly at my painting on the wall; not at *Venus with Dog and Lambs*, but at *Tea With the Queen,* which Sir William had had richly framed and hung near the door. The grey-haired gentleman, who looked every inch the classic English aristocrat, was so absorbed in the detail of the painting that he almost failed to hear when Sir William said: "Here is my consolation for my old age, my Willy boy. And this is Sir James Fontleroy."

The man, the only guest who had come in a smoking jacket and white bow tie, turned and examined me with a sharp, but friendly and then soft look.

"Willy," he said, but he did not offer me his hand, which was holding the glass of champagne, "Did you explain to him what it was about?"

389

"Not yet," replied Sir William, turning to me.

"Willy boy, the thing is, and please hear me out, so that you don't misunderstand me. Sir James is one of the richest and best known, I could say infamous collectors in the kingdom. If he wants something, there's almost no way to stop him. We have unsettled accounts going back twenty years – the details are not important."

"Except one," added Sir James, "that I owe you nothing, but you owe me a favour of my choosing, that was the agreement."

"Okay," admitted Sir William, "let's resolve the misunderstandings in the Upper House, to the entertainment of our colleagues, but let's stick with the facts. And the fact, Willy, is that Sir James has fallen in love with your *Tea With the Queen* and wants to have it at any price. I told him that it was probably the only one you wouldn't want to part with, but he wants to negotiate." And he gave me a barely discernible wink, as if to say: strike a hard bargain.

But the painting is yours, Sir William, I said, you're the only one who can –

"Willy boy," he interrupted me in a tone intended to make it clear that I had made a mistake, "are you artists all so forgetful? I returned the picture to you, don't you remember? I returned it to you because you are so attached to it and in return you promised to paint me twenty family portraits. We agreed that ten days ago, surely you can't have forgotten?"

He emphasised the last words to leave me in no doubt that he would be *very* disappointed, perhaps even angry, if I didn't suddenly *remember* that he was speaking the truth. Since I couldn't imagine putting my benefactor in an awkward position, I slapped my forehead and said: Yes, of course, I don't know what's wrong with me recently, I'm sorry.

"The boy's in love," Sir William explained to Lord Fontleroy, "he's dreaming about some young lady in London. What can you do, life is on the side of the young, we can console ourselves only with art."

"Whatever," said Lord Fontleroy, "love of art is perhaps less orgasmic, but is therefore more elevated." He turned to me: I'll give you three thousand pounds, which seems very generous to me, but I'm keen to have it for my collection of recent art, so I'm prepared to pay over the odds."

I was all ready to say that it was a very generous offer, when Sir William once again intervened, this time almost violently. "Don't insult the boy, whom I look upon like a son," he said, "and don't think that you can acquire almost anything in the world for some trifling sum. The sum that I paid and that Willy will pay off in portraits was ten thousand and I know of no reason why he should sell it to you for less – if anything, it should be for more, if of course he wants to sell it, which I doubt."

"Why are you interfering?" responded Sir James, showing signs of annoyance. "You're not his agent."

"In a sense I am," said Sir William, "I am his employer. And your offer, my dear, sly old James, is anything but an honour to you. But what can we do, that's the way you are. Actually," he suddenly remembered, "we did consider selling the painting at public auction, at Sotheby's."

These were the words that broke Lord Fontleroy's resistance. "I could not come up with so much cash at the moment, my investments are too dispersed. But I do have a flat in Mayfair with twenty years rent paid, which I no longer use and which I actually no longer need. It is fully furnished and twenty years is not such a short period, I could sign it over tomorrow at my solicitor's. You know what flats in Mayfair are worth and you must admit my offer is a sure sign of suddenly clouded judgement. As a friend, you should find me a good psychiatrist, rather than standing there grinning in satisfaction."

"Oh," said Sir William, "I'm grinning because you have once more demonstrated how shrewd you are and how cheaply you would like to acquire a unique work of art..."

"Sorry, old chap, a four-bedroom flat in the most select part of London with a view of Grosvenor Square and furnished in true style – Bidermayer throughout – is *not* cheap, as you well know. And so I have an additional condition: right of first refusal to the next twenty paintings produced by your boy. I insist upon that as part of the contract for transfer of property."

Sir William looked at me with an unusual, hard to judge expression and said: "A flat in Mayfair is certainly not something that every young man can afford. Although Willy does not need it, since he lives here comfortably enough, at least he'd have somewhere to sleep when he was in London. As for first refusal, let Sir James have it, what do you say, Willy boy?"

I was completely confused, everything was happening too quickly and I still thought that they might be joking, that it might be some kind of game. I don't know, I shrugged. If anyone is entitled to first right of refusal on my next twenty paintings, it's you.

"I'll wait for the twenty-first," said Sir William, winking at me on the sly. "It won't be long, you'll now start painting like one possessed, I know, I can feel it in my bones, as is always the case when better weather is on the cards. In short," he turned to Lord Fontleroy, "tomorrow at ten at my solicitor's on Curzon Street."

"Certainly not," replied Sir James, "at my solicitor's on Brook Street, and not at ten but at twelve."

"Have it your way," said Sir William. "And with that the favour is returned, is that right?

Sir James turned and looked at the painting on the wall. He sighed and I suddenly no longer recognised him: from an excellent negotiator, he had become a child who has received a toy from his older brother that he has longed for all his life.

"Completely," came the barely audible reply. He remained in front of the painting, while Sir William took my elbow and steered me to the door.

"An interesting day," he whispered. "Let this remain our little secret."

50.

In spite of the late hour (it was seven in the evening, just before sunset), the day was far from over, for twenty minutes later Spikey knocked on the door of my room, to where I had retreated to recover from the latest developments, and said: "Sir, two gentlemen from London are looking for you, they say it's urgent."

Close to my heart I felt the stab of the cold blade of reality. What are their names? I asked.

"They didn't say," said Spikey.

Have them come up, I said.

But his slightly horrified response was: "Guests are not allowed to come to rooms, sir, that's not the custom in this house, I'm very sorry. I'll put them in the library."

I heard his footsteps retreat along the corridor. I took a deep breath and followed him.

In the library I found Dostoyevsky and an unknown young man with slick black hair, considerably smaller than the Russian and darker skinned, like some Sancho Panza to the Russian Don Quixote, whom my strange friend increasingly reminded me of.

"Willy Wow," said Dostoyevsky, jumping to his feet and giving me the usual, bone-breaking hug. He was not exactly dressed for a garden party, his previously elegant white suit looked creased and worn, as if he had been sleeping in it; his beard was no longer red, but black with grey streaks, which made him look older; but above all, he had aged because he looked tired and this, together with his weak, slightly hoarse voice, gave the impression that his life had taken a turn for the worse.

But he still was not short of his usual imperiousness, for when Spikey looked in and asked "whether the gentlemen would like anything to drink," Dostoyevsky straightened up like an officer at a military parade and said: "Butler, what is your name?"

"Spikey, Sir," replied Spikey without any particular emotion, used to all sorts.

"Spikey," said Dostoyevsky, taking a step towards him, "bring two bottles of champagne, three glasses and some snacks on a tray. Thank you, that will be all."

Spikey withdrew as if this behaviour was completely normal, but I did not like Solouhin's arrogance. You can't carry on as if you were at home here, I said. But first of all, tell me how you found me.

"Aren't I at home wherever you are at home?" he asked with the same self-evident tone as before. "Wasn't that our agreement? Or do you no longer recognise your friend now that you've landed in clover?"

Tell me how you found me.

"First I'll introduce my friend and colleague," he nudged the leg of the slick, dark-haired young man. "Bruno Marchisetti."

The young man offered me his clammy hand, withdrawing it immediately after a light squeeze and sat down again. "As to the other question," said Dostoyevsky, "it's not difficult to find someone who turns up at the Grosvenor House Hotel in a Bentley and questions my former secretary."

I was looking for you, I said, and she was the only possible contact. What about the world of fashion and my friend Sandy? And what about your novel?

"Your Sandy is fine, great figure, great legs, very cooperative, but those freckles, Willy Wow, freckles are not currently in fashion and I doubt they soon will be, at least not in such numbers. In any case, I have abandoned that world of false appearances, because the tracker dogs were hot on my trail and forced me to look for a new hideout. The noose is tightening and the day will come soon when my head is in it. That's why I came, Willy Wow. You must help me."

At that moment, Spikey appeared at the door with a large tray.

"Thank you, Spikey." Dostoyevsky took it from him. "We'll serve ourselves. That will be all. Lock the door when you leave."

This was the first time that Spikey barely visibly blushed. "We don't lock doors in this house, sir, except when ordered by Sir William, who would do so only in exceptional circumstances. You will not be disturbed." He raised his head, went out the door and almost slammed it behind him.

"Conceited creatures, these English butlers," said Dostoyevsky with a frown, as he poured three glasses of champagne. "And what are you doing here, Willy Wow, are you going to marry one of the lord's not-so-beautiful daughters?"

No, I also made my voice a little sharper. He hired me as a family portraitist. Do you have anything against that?

"Me?" he said in surprise, passing me a glass. "Look, I've only just got here and I'm already serving you, I've always done everything for you, protected you, can't you show even a glimmer of gratitude? Has this over-inflated world corrupted you so quickly? Cheers, friend Willy."

He and his smooth friend drank; I gripped the glass and remained silent. Dostoyevsky took a cheese sandwich from the tray, threw it into his mouth and gulped it down like a wolf, without once chewing it.

"Willy," he said, "I see that you've done alright for yourself. Congratulations, I hope that on the way you haven't sold your soul, although if you have that's your affair. I'll be brief, because I can see that my presence is an embarrassment to you. I must get out, away from this country, I don't want to spend twenty years behind bars, I don't deserve that. And I hate the English, I can't stand that false friendliness, which is in reality arrogance, I want different people around me. Brazil is the only country where they won't be able to get to me. But all that costs, Willy – from a passport to a new identity, to safe passage without the risk of being captured at the last moment. I've got to bribe at least a hundred people. And I don't want to arrive in Brazil penniless. I want enough money to last me at least a few years, I don't want to go there to starve."

I don't have that much money, I said. I can give you a little.

"Who's talking about money, Willy?" he said in surprise, devouring yet another sandwich. "I'm just saying I need help and you start talking about money. Is that all that's left between us?"

Listen, Dostoyevsky, I said, don't try and make me feel guilty. The fact is, I'm a lot less naïve than I was and I can no longer stand such games. Tell me as briefly as possible what you want, otherwise I'll call Spikey and have him escort you out.

"Uuuuuh," he emitted a strange noise and leaned back in the armchair. He pulled his head in like a tortoise under attack and exchanged a quick look with his accomplice. "The sandwiches are good, Bruno, help yourself, I doubt we'll get any dinner today."

The smoothie nodded and pulled from his pocket a folded newspaper cutting. "May I?" he looked at Dostoyevsky, who waved his hand in approval.

Bruno unfolded the cutting and held it out towards me. I saw the headline in Italian and some columns of text with sub-headings. All I could read in the headline was the name Caravaggio. I don't know Italian, I said.

"Tell him, Bruno," ordered Dostoyevsky.

Bruno folded the cutting and put it back in his jacket pocket. "Two days ago Caravaggio's *Birth of Christ* was stolen in Palermo," he said in a heavy Italian accent. "The picture has disappeared."

And what's that to me, I asked Dostoyevsky in surprise, surely you don't think that I took it?

"I wouldn't dream of such a thing, Willy Wow," he replied, recovering from his embarrassment as soon as it appeared, "although I can see that there are quite a few valuable paintings in this house. No, what it means, my friend, is that the stolen painting is now on the market. Someone will try and sell it, and the art collectors know that. Each one silently hopes that the thief will contact him. At this moment, if we had another Caravaggio's *Birth of Christ* we could sell it immediately and the price would be more than the value of this house."

Possibly, I said, but unfortunately we haven't, because there is only one.

"*For the moment* we haven't," said Dostoyevsky with emphasis. "The situation can change. Some painters make such good copies. Often there are a dozen originals in circulation."

Only then did I realise why they had come and what they wanted from me. That's impossible, I said, no expert would believe that a copy in acrylic paints on a modern canvas was a seventeenth century original.

"Bruno," Dostoyevsky turned to his colleague, "explain the technique to him."

Bruno obliged without hesitation. He leaned towards me and lowered his voice almost to a whisper. "You need to use fast-drying paints. You need to mix synthetic phenol formaldehyde dissolved in alcohol with lavender oil and then with hand-ground pigments. That produces a kind of pitch. When it is heated, its chemical composition changes so that it will no longer dissolve in alcohol or other solvents. Then you need to paint the copy of the picture on a canvas from the seventeenth century. The original painting needs to be rubbed off with pumice, but in such a way that you don't damage the small cracks that show its age. Then it has to be painted over before you start the copy. And when the painting is finished, it needs to be heated for an hour in a special stove. Then it needs another topcoat, but dispersed so that the old cracks show through. And no one will guess that the painting is not an original."

"Bruno is a goldmine of information about forging paintings," added Dostoyevsky. "But unfortunately, he can't paint."

Nor can I, I said. I have done some copies and sold them as such, but I certainly don't have the skill, let alone the desire, to paint a forgery. You've come to the wrong person.

"Oh come on, Willy," said Dostoyevsky, getting up to pour him and his friend some more champagne – I hadn't touched mine. "I know what you are capable of, what you have painted. I'd prefer it if you said honestly that you don't care if I rot in an English prison. Besides which, you have enough money now, you no longer need Sandy to bring you leftovers from the pub – you don't need anyone. But if someone needs you, that's his problem, when was friendship anything to do with mutual help? You're not even tempted by the third share of the million that the Caravaggio would bring…"

Stop, I interrupted him, stop, because you don't understand. I'd do anything to help you, but you can't ask me to break my most solemn pledge: that I will never devalue the work of other painters by stealing their genius. I simply can't do it, because something inside me would die, wither away. I'd rather rob a bank for you than forge a Caravaggio.

"Bullshit, my dear Willy," he said. "High grade bullshit. A third of the paintings hanging in the homes of the rich are forgeries. The same is true of museums. But they will never acknowledge this, because then the value of their paintings would plummet. A Matisse, as long as it is an original, is worth a million dollars, but as soon as it becomes clear that someone else painted it, it becomes worthless. Even though it's still the same painting! People don't buy art, they buy the prestige that comes with a name. Some will happily pay millions for a painting that they find so ugly they have no desire to look at it. The main thing is that they can boast about owning it. Do you want to support such nonsense with your moral stance?"

That may all be true, I said, but the immorality of others is no excuse for my own…

"Fuck morality," he interrupted. "Who is moral? Are you? Don't make me laugh. I could enumerate at least a hundred slips in the time since I've known you. It's simply that you don't want to help me."

I could no longer hold back the tears. They poured from me into the glass of champagne that I was still turning in my hand. Dostoyevsky was suddenly on his knees in front of me, his face close to mine, his paws on my shoulders.

"Willy," he looked into my eyes and I could suddenly feel all the fear and all the pain that had brought him to this. "The Lamed-Vav, the thirty-six righteous ones, empathy, have you forgotten? Do you want me to end my days like a caged rat?"

You know I don't want that, I sobbed, hugging him.

"Willy," he whispered in my ear, "you are my only hope."

I need to think, I said and slowly pushed him away. That's all I can promise.

He got to his feet and said: "Bruno, show him."

His sidekick put his glass down and opened the green folder that sat on his knees; from it, he took a sheet of drawing paper and handed it to me with a strange gleam in his eye.

At first, I thought there had been a mistake, a time shift. In my hands I held the drawing of Sandrina that I had done with a marker pen at Dover harbour when I arrived in England. In the bottom right-hand corner was written *Piccadilly Circus, tomorrow at 11.00 a.m.*

I looked at Dostoyevsky. Where did you get this?

"He who seeks shall find," he said. "I made a promise that I would bring you close to realising your dream; the last step you must make yourself. You can keep the drawing. The person on it is prepared to meet with you. Perhaps for dinner in London. Maybe she can be persuaded to pose for you. Perhaps, even in the nude, you never know. Now that she has changed from dream to flesh, anything is possible."

Where does she live, I jumped up, what is she doing, can I see her? You owe me that.

"I owe you?" he said with a smile. "I'll certainly think about what I owe you. Now we have to go, don't we Bruno? We've lingered too long in a place where we don't belong." They moved towards the door.

Where can I find you? I almost yelled after him.

"I'll call you," he said. And they left.

51.

The days that followed were full of intense feelings of at least twenty different shades: from the anxiety triggered by the avalanche of events, to the fear that I would suddenly wake up in the studio in Soho, with Freckles beside me, and everything that had taken place after my meeting Lord Hattersley would turn out to be a dream, a recognition of how unripe and unprepared I was for a life with my wishes granted.

Suddenly I was sought after, suddenly I owned things, suddenly I had the chance of meeting the girl that I had been dreaming about ever since I came to London. Longing, which I remembered as a pleasant and lively experience, abruptly became fear of loss; if the first feeling stung but at the same time invigorated, the other crippled me, bearing down on me with its crushing weight. I kept having to convince myself that it was all true: that I had a passport with a five-year residence permit, that I had an employment contract with Lord Hattersley, that in return for one painting Lord Fontleroy had handed over a flat in Mayfair.

The transfer of ownership had gone without a hitch; the solicitor had promised to deal with all the formalities. Then I had spent three hours wandering around the large rooms on the fourth floor of an excellently maintained town house on Grosvenor Square, on carpets into which I sank almost to my ankles, among pieces of furniture which I didn't particularly like, but which were authentic, in perfect condition and infinitely expensive (and many would like them, I thought – particularly Cleo, perhaps even Sandrina). I explored the kitchen, which had all the latest gadgets and was so well equipped that there were even silver spoons for ice cream; the dining room, with its oak table and eight chairs; the bedroom, with its comfortable, luxurious bed opposite an enormous mirror; the living room, where the various sofas and arm chairs would seat at least twenty people; the shining bathroom, full of Italian marble, where on the shelf beneath the mirror I found two toothbrushes and some bottles of perfume; and the library, floored with parquet rather than carpeted, which would be my studio, since I intended to spend at least half my time in London.

The flat gave the impression it had a history – not distant, but recent; perhaps it had served as Lord Fontleroy's love nest, although not just for secret brief encounters, since there were hundreds of books on the shelves and quite a few tasteful paintings on the walls, although none of great value; in the linen cupboard there were mountains of unused bedding; in the main wardrobe, three Japanese robes, two of them women's; in the kitchen there were at least a dozen bottles of excellent wine and exotic liqueurs. There was almost no doubt that a woman had been living here who Lord Fontleroy visited at his convenience. That it was not his aunt, cousin or niece, I discerned from the words he had used when handing over the flat, in response to my discreet question about the things that were not part of the fixtures and fittings.

"I've nowhere to take them," he said, with a shrug of both impatience and melancholy. "Let them stay here. We'll sort it out with the next painting, if I decide to buy it. Don't forget that for the next twenty projects you are *my* painter."

Although it was one of the main clauses of the agreement we had signed, I intended to keep quiet about the first of these projects, since it was not intended to promote Vili Vaupotič the artist, but to save the life of his friend. Dostoyevsky had once more disappeared from sight and my assistant in painting the forgery had become his 'Mafia' acquaintance Bruno Marchisetti. He supplied me with an appropriately sized canvas from the seventeenth century, an easel, brushes, palette, cleaning fluid and everything else I needed (I said that I would prefer not to move things from Lockwood Manor to London, since this would trigger unnecessary questions and, above all, the suspicion that, now that I had a flat and money, I wanted to wriggle out of my agreement with Lord Hattersley, which was far from my intention); he also brought his mysterious paints, and then we got to work.

We covered the parquet in the library, which became my London studio, with old newspapers; Bruno brought from the kitchen silver dishes and bowls in which he mixed the ground pigments with synthetic phenol formaldehyde, while I studied closely the details of the reproduction of the *Birth of Christ* in a book on Caravaggio that I had found in the library at Lockwood Manor (and which, besides my clothes, was the only thing that I dared to bring to London). It soon became clear that without the original, on which I could see the actual shades of colour, it would be extremely difficult to produce a convincing fake and that the whole project was a great waste of time. Bruno, I said, why are we doing this? People who buy old masters are not fools – the prices are too high for them to afford naivety.

But Bruno vehemently protested, with eloquent Italian gestures. The first time we had met, when he came with Dostoyevsky to Lockwood Manor, I had though him very taciturn, but in London it was almost impossible to shut him up. At least part of the reason might have been the wine that he soon discovered in the kitchen and which he then proceeded to open, bottle after bottle, without asking for permission (since the wine had been given to me, it didn't seem right to draw attention to this). Almost every other word he spoke was 'fuck' (fuck this, fuck that, fuck everything) and every third word one of the innumerable Sicilian blasphemies that I didn't understand, but which sounded as rich and melodic as the most noble opera aria.

"No, no, no," he yelled, waving the hand holding his wine glass so violently that some drops fell into the carefully mixed red-brown pigment. "Fuck them all, they're all idiots. You are an artist, bravo, but you don't know what happens in the world of art. Swindles, I tell you: one before breakfast, three after lunch, five after dinner. Collectors and museums hire experts to confirm the authenticity of the paintings they intend to buy, but the experts are few and often the expert is a cousin or nephew of some dealer. Fuck the art scene, I know it and I'm telling you that dealing in drugs is a hundred times more honest. There simply isn't time for someone to check whether the stolen Caravaggio is genuine: they all know it was stolen, they all want to get their hands on it so that no one else does. The contacts are already made: the painting will be bought by someone who will sell it on to a third person, who'll sell it on to a fourth. No one will be able to say that I am the first in the chain or that you painted it, so fuck it all, relax, and work."

Painting a Caravaggio is, of course, not a simple matter, especially with the paint mixtures that Bruno prepared more by feeling than from the extensive experience that he boasted of. The first three attempts I had to remove from the increasingly unconvincing canvas and only at the fourth attempt did I find the right balance of dark and light; then things went more smoothly and quicker than I had expected – although I still did not believe that anyone could confuse my daubs with a genuine Caravaggio.

While I was painting I couldn't help reflecting on the deeper meaning of the coincidence that I was forging the *Birth of Christ* to save a friend, who in terms of character and fate was very similar to Caravaggio: both were dreamers, both explosive, both accidental killers, both fugitives from justice, both enemies of bourgeois norms (although they perhaps longed for them). I told myself that by saving one I was saving both and at the same time my own soul, which had perhaps not been sold (as Dostoyevsky had said in passing), but it had certainly (of this I had no doubt) taken a great step towards that point where creative fever is replaced by a desire for safety and comfort.

"Fuck all that," said Bruno, as if reading my thoughts, "we'll sell the painting, buy ourselves expensive cars, go to the seaside, hire *bambine bionde* and have a good time."

My *bambina* is not *bionda*, I said, my *bambina* is *negra*. You know her, you've seen her, have you ever seen a more beautiful creature?

He said that he had never seen her in the flesh, only my drawing, by which he could judge my talent, but not her beauty, and that was a matter for his Russian friend, who was a juggler with the lives of others as well as his own. He would sort everything, he never broke a promise.

And he really did not, for when the Caravaggio achieved the maximum level of similarity and Bruno had loaded it into a van saying "Window Repairs" on the side and driven it off to be "heated" in a special stove, Dostoyevsky rang me and offered two options: that Sandrina meet me in the restaurant at the Ritz (which would have cost me about a half of my share when the painting was sold), or at my flat where, in addition to sandwiches, I could offer her "other services". Or she could offer me – you never knew, life is unpredictable, women especially.

I chose the second option, not because of the "other services", but in order to make on her the biggest impression, since she remembered me (if at all) as the clumsy lad who had vomited on her on the ferry. I wanted to show her what she had missed out on. And discreetly hint that it was not too late, that the future was still open.

52.

I was just thinking about what I would cook for my guest when the phone rang and a woman's voice asked: "William Woopitic?" Probably, I said. In the vicinity I see only one person who at least approximately answers to that name. "Lord Fontleroy wanted to let you know that on the inside of the fridge door there is a list of people who may be of use to you. Please check." Click and silence.

I opened the fridge and on the inside of the door there really was an unusual list: John the plumber (and phone number), Mac the electrician (and phone number), Simon the barber (and phone number), Sharon the cleaning lady (and phone number), Wang Choo Chinese takeaway (and phone number), Sunandan Shetty Indian takeaway (and phone number), Nigel the courier (and phone number), Mario Vedutti complete Italian catering (and phone number), Pavel Suhanek boiler repairs (and phone number), Kari Kekonnen Finnish sauna (and phone number).

I called Mario Vedutti. "Sir James," he said, "welcome. The usual dinner?" I put on my most upper class accent and said that I was certainly not Sir James, who had gone bankrupt and left me his flat in part payment for a loan; I was Sir William Wowpotty and I needed a delicious Italian dinner for two, with ice cream, a top class red wine and an exceptional aperitif. "No problem, Sir William," said Mario, "just say when."

When the doorman called on the intercom and announced "a very beautiful young lady", everything was already on the table: salmon for the starter, saltimbocca alla romana as the main course, mixed salad, tiramisu, five bottles of the best Italian wine, ice cream, which I had put in the fridge, and a flickering candle on an elegantly set table. Three of Mario Vedutti's employees withdrew a moment before Sandrina stepped from the lift.

"Oh," she said, "it smells good, and what a flat!"

Her tanned legs emerged from a short light skirt, even though it was already cold outside, and she took off her leather jacket and handed it to me, revealing a half-open yellowish blouse that showed off her well-rounded (though not too much so) breasts; two strands of her stylishly tousled black hair fell across her left eye, so that she could push them aside and not get bored; she had a crocodile skin handbag over her shoulder that she wanted to hold onto, three rings on her left hand and three on her right; and her perfume was redolent of youth, sex and forbidden fruit – all exactly as I had remembered her from the ferry, but less reserved.

She wandered around the rooms and said: "How the other half lives! And what a bed, God knows how many women have memories of it!"

Then she sat at the table and said: "Surely you don't think we're going to eat all this!" First she tackled the salad, as did I. "What did you do to make God smile on you like this?" she asked. "When you drew me in Dover harbour he still wasn't, am I wrong?"

I'm honoured that you kept my drawing for so long, I said.

"I waited for you. The next day, at eleven, as it said on the drawing. Beneath Eros."

That's not possible, I said, I was there, I waited, you didn't show.

"I came at exactly eleven o'clock, I sat on the steps for twenty minutes and I'd still be there if I hadn't begun to think that you were only toying with me."

But that's not possible, I repeated; even if we were each sitting on different sides of the steps, we wouldn't have missed each other because I walked around the monument every five minutes, just in case.

"Me, too," she said, "at least three times."

How did you know that it was eleven? I asked. She looked at me strangely, the pucker on the left side of her face trembled a couple of times. "I looked at my watch, silly," she said with an impatient smile.

Did you put your watch back an hour when we landed in Dover?

"No, I did it three days later, when someone reminded me. But that…" Her words sank in a confused look.

If you were there at eleven on your watch, I said, that was ten English time. That means I came a moment after you left.

"But I was sure that at eleven meant at eleven on our watches," she said, "after all, we came with the same ferry, I never imagined that you would put your watch back an hour."

I didn't, I said. A taxi driver told me about the time difference. I was actually a bit late.

She started on the salmon, eating it with her fingers. I felt so disturbed that I had to get up from the table. That's not possible, I said; my life changed because of the damn clock? I went over to the window and looked at the square, so that she wouldn't see my tears.

Damn clock, I repeated.

I suddenly felt her standing beside me. From behind, she laid her left hand on my left shoulder, her right hand on my right shoulder and pulled me towards her. She did not remove her hands, she stood right beside me, her left hip against my right, her face so close to mine that I could feel her breath.

"Don't talk nonsense," she said. "Your life is what has happened to you."

If we hadn't missed each other then, it would have been different, I said. And yours, too.

"Maybe. We might have fallen in love, grown tired of each other and split up. All that has happened to you would not have happened, nor to me either. Look what you've achieved during this time. You're rich, successful, important people value your paintings. In any case, we haven't missed each other – if we met today beneath Eros we could say that we have come six months late, but we have come and that is the main thing – that we are together."

She lowered her eyes to my mouth, opened hers slightly and approached mine. We sucked softly on each other's lips, our tongues cautiously exploring, caressing each other; I could feel her with my whole body, but then without warning she withdrew her mouth and gently pushed me away.

407

"Enough of that for now," she said. "Just so you don't think that what has been missed cannot be compensated for. Men are not supposed to cry."

She went back to the table and threw me a linen napkin; if I hadn't caught it at the last moment, it would have flown through the window. I wiped my eyes and sat back down at the table. I downed my glass of wine in one; she smiled and did the same. I poured her another, and then myself one.

"I think you're trying to get me drunk," she joked.

At least tell me your real name, I asked.

"I quite like Sandrina. Maybe I'll keep it, because of us."

Is there an 'us'?

"Maybe not before," she said, "but now there definitely is."

I told her I'd had that feeling since I first met her on the ferry, in spite of the fact that our encounter had not been a very romantic one, and then my tongue loosened like never before. I invited her to bring her glass to one of the comfortable couches in the living room and there the speech poured from me, words overtaking each other, getting stuck, overtaking their meaning and intention, tying themselves in knots that I had to unravel and explain. I offered her selected details of almost everything that had befallen me between our first and second meetings, not even omitting the sexual encounters, although with regard to them all I emphasised was that they revealed to me my vivid memory of her face, which stubbornly attached itself to every woman, even the ones I merely portrayed. I was a bit less generous with details when I spoke of Cleo and Dostoyevsky. I felt that by describing Cleo's hunt for a husband I might ridicule her, which I did not want to do. In the case of Dostoyevsky, it was clear to me how close he and Sandrina were, and what had happened between them: if she did not know the "criminal" side of his London story, I didn't want her to hear it from me.

As I talked, I couldn't help feeling that she was bored, since her eyes kept wandering over the walls, the furniture and other items, as if evaluating them, but at the end she exclaimed: "What a story! Enough there for two novels!"

And you? I looked at her expectantly.

"Me?" she twisted her wine glass between her fingers and then put it on the coffee table.

I had hoped that she would respond with an equal degree of openness, but it soon became evident that she did not like talking about herself, that certain things – perhaps crucial ones – she dressed up and blurred, that she wanted to keep something important, perhaps central to her story, to herself, as if fearing that the truth would hurt me too much or cool my ardour for her.

You can be honest, I said. Whatever happened is in the past now and cannot influence what I feel about you.

"My story is a pathetic one, really pathetic," she said, reaching for her glass. "Could you pour me a bit more wine? I think I'll get drunk, partly from sadness, partly from joy."

Cheers, I said as we clinked glasses, and be brave – I'll understand everything, forgive anything.

"That's the trouble," she said, "nothing dramatic has happened to me. I've been surrounded by boredom since I was born. I come from Bucharest, my mother's Russian, my father Romanian, although not a real Romanian, he's the son of a Hungarian and a Transylvanian gypsy, while my mum is a quarter Tartar and a quarter Finnish. There's not a drop of pure blood in my veins, God knows what genes I carry, but I'm sure there are some robbers and murderers among my ancestors. Shall I stop there or carry on?"

Go on, I said, go on. I imagined something like that, perhaps even wanted it. I knew that you weren't from an ordinary family, the first time I met you I saw something wild in your eyes, something that men either flee from or fall on their knees before.

"You're too romantic," she said. "You probably know what things are like in Romania and that I'd never have got out of the country if a high ranking politician hadn't fallen in love with me and taken me on a trip to Paris, where I ran away from him. Since he intended to go from France to Belgium and then back, I had a French visa in my passport permitting two entries and so I was able to persuade that woman in Dover that I was only going to have a look at London and then return. Which of course I didn't. And now I'm an illegal immigrant. You can report me if you want. Do you mind if I smoke?"

She rummaged in her handbag and pulled out a packet of Benson & Hedges. She looked again and produced a lighter and with it, unintentionally, a pack of condoms. She quickly pushed it back and threw me a glance to see if I had noticed. I pretended to be brushing some crumbs from my shirt, although we hadn't eaten anything that was likely to leave crumbs.

"Anyway," she said, blowing smoke towards the centre of the room, "can you imagine how hard it is to be cheerful when you might be arrested at any moment?"

And then? I wanted to hear the rest of the story.

"You've probably heard how pleasant life is in Romania. You can imagine that I didn't want to go back, even though the three years of law I studied there are no use to me in London. But I managed. It's easier for girls than boys: bosses are almost always men and they almost always hope that they might get something. I learned that it was best to keep them hoping right up until the moment that I fled, which I usually did at night. Once I jumped out of a car as it was driving down Regent Street. Look."

She transferred her cigarette from one hand to the other and with her right hand pulled up the hem of her skirt above her thigh, almost half-way up her hip. In so doing she revealed not only the scar on her tanned skin, but also a substantial part of her black underpants, although only at the side, because she had her legs crossed, but enough to make me feel dizzy and to fill me with the wild hope (and fear) that she was trying to seduce me with discreet movements, gestures and words.

"Of course, I didn't do anything special. I cleaned houses and offices, worked in bars, sold toys – I even danced for a couple of weeks in one of those booths in Soho, you know, peep shows where men go to see naked women and to masturbate. I still regret it, but I had no money even for food. Throw me out if you want, probably you will, but you yourself told me to be honest, and I am being."

I wasn't completely sure, but I though her eyes glistened, as if she wanted at all costs to hold back her tears. Sandrina, I said, taking her hand. I know how hard it was for me and I did have some money. I don't blame you for anything.

410

"I don't know," she sighed. "You seem so clean and innocent. Life hasn't knocked you down."

I'm not clean and innocent, I said. Like you, I carry a heavy load of regrets – I'm a sinner, not a saint.

"If you're a sinner, then what am I? Do you have any gum? Whenever I'm nervous, I like to smoke and chew gum at the same time."

Sorry, I said, just about everything apart from that.

"Maybe I have," she rummaged through her bag again. This time, too, in addition to the gum, she managed to pull out the pack of condoms, and once more she shoved it back with an apparently careless movement and a quick look in my direction. But this time I thought that she was doing it deliberately, sending me a signal, offering herself.

And Dostoyevsky? I asked.

"Oh, Dostoyevsky," she blew a bubble with her gum until it burst, "he's a bastard, as you well know. I liked him because he is so terribly ugly, almost a monster. Until then I'd only had smooth types drooling over me, who thought that as soon as I saw a handsome face I would throw myself on my back. They were all like decorative containers that someone had forgotten to fill. Dostoyevsky, as you know, has a big personality. You can defend yourself in a hundred different ways, but he breaks you with one look, one word. Besides which, he's Russian and, perhaps because of my mum, I've always had a strange attitude to Russians – half fear, half respect, half longing. I know that's one-and-a-half, but Dostoyevsky always affects me as if there was one-and-a-half of him."

Once more she blew a bubble and popped it, then she emptied her glass and held it out: "A little more, please. Whenever I talk a lot, I get thirsty. If I lose control, just throw me out."

I filled her glass to the brim, my own a little less. Of course I won't, I said. You can stay as long as you want.

"Nice to know." She took a sip of wine, put her glass down, leaned back, blew smoke at the ceiling and said: "You're right, if we hadn't missed each other that day because of the stupid clock, my life would also have been different. Never mind life, *I* would be different. Your Sandrina could have been someone else, someone you could have loved."

411

I do love you, I said. I've never loved another woman as I love you.

"Don't be in too much of a hurry," she said. "I've heard similar words too many times and perhaps they bother me a little, even coming from you. We can agree to sex whenever, in five minutes if you want, but let's leave love for a more appropriate time. I want to give you the opportunity, when you find out what I'm really like, to reconsider and say: Sorry, Sandrina, you're an interesting girl, but I'd rather marry a lady."

How wrong you are, I said, intoxicated (from the wine, her bare legs, the apparently casual words about sex, even the word marry). You can become a lady any time, I am attracted to you as you really are.

"Do you know who you really are?" She turned her slightly troubled eyes towards me. "Dostoyevsky doesn't. He says he is trying out different roles to see which suits him best and when he finds it he'll know who he is. Me, too. Have you ever seen those metal pastry cutters for cutting out different shapes? I'm something like that. I have met a lot of people who thought I was something special and with each of them I *was* something special. But the whole time I was just a different shape, cut from the same pastry. Which of those figures is me?"

In other words, I said, Dostoyevsky has completely taken you over.

"Dostoyevsky takes over people who *want* to be taken over. It's a good job he is choosy or he would take over the whole world. But be careful, he did it through his goodness. I've never felt such a strong urge in anyone before to help people, to rescue them from distress. When I was in a complete fix he brought me money. He didn't have any himself, but he found some somewhere – maybe he borrowed it, maybe he stole it – and he gave it to me so that I could buy bread and milk. And cigarettes, which I can't do without. And he expected nothing in return. When I first offered to have sex with him, he turned me down. I was offended. I was furious. But he said, you know what he's like: I decide about such things, not you. Okay, I said, then decide. But do it before I'm a hundred and fifty years old."

And did he? I asked.

412

"Of course," she stared with troubled eyes at the ceiling. "But I wanted to tell you something else. Without Dostoyevsky, I would have stayed an ordinary illegal immigrant. He organised my life for me. He filled me with hope. He took me in hand and made a saleable article out of me, as he likes to say."

And what does that mean, exactly? I asked.

"Oh, silly Willy," she said, "that means that Dostoyevsky knows not only a lot of people, but also their weak points. Dostoyevsky is a gifted chess player, like all Russians. He knocked on a door here, a door there, whispered in this ear, in that ear, and Sandrina not only had the door opened for her, but an incredible opportunity."

For example, I said.

"Oh, for example," she blew smoke straight at me, "you really are funny – for example, that I am now head chamber maid at the Grosvenor House Hotel. Do you know what that means? Board and lodging and a regular wage. Why are you suddenly so downcast? Disappointed because your Sandrina is not a princess?"

Did Dostoyevsky ever speak to you about me?

"He mentioned you for the first time ten days ago. Why?"

When did you show him the drawing I did in Dover?

"Wait, let me try to remember," she tried to think back (or gave the impression that was what she was doing). "It was the only thing I had that I could boast of. I showed it to quite a few people, so I can't remember exactly when I showed it to anyone in particular, Look, I said, I was sketched by a well-known artist. I was a model. And would like to be again. Your model. Not for a drawing, but for a big canvas, six feet by nine."

That's the size for a gallery, I said.

"My flesh it beautiful, look" – and suddenly she raised her t-shirt and showed off her tanned bosom – "and this", she raised her skirt above her hips to blind me with the beauty of her thighs. "But all this will decay, become wrinkled and old. Only if you paint me as Venus will my beauty be eternal. Maybe it will hang in the National Gallery or in some museum in the United States and people will stand in front of me in two or three thousand years and admire me. Mainly men, of course, but that's the way the world is. Maybe women as well, with

413

bitterness in their hearts at the thought of how unjust God is when he dispenses beauty."

One other thing, I said.

"What, my dear," she leaned towards me and kissed me on the mouth, tasting of cigarettes and wine.

Do you know Selena? I asked.

"Selena is a little tart," she said with a frown, "Dostoyevsky came up with the idea of an agency for fashion models and she helps him because she knows how to lie and has a pleasant, English accent. I've said a hundred times that I will scratch her eyes out, but he says there is nothing between them. Anyway, it doesn't matter, I've had enough of all that, I want out, I want to live a normal life, I want to be the model to a painter who I'm married to, his only model."

She sighed. "Those, in brief, are the dreams of your Sandrina."

She was still chewing gum, smoking and flicking the ash straight onto the carpet; her blue-grey eyes darkened and she turned to me as if expecting an immediate answer.

Are you in love with Dostoyevsky? I asked.

"No," she said, reaching for her glass to finish her wine. I noticed that her movements were becoming rather uncertain. "I'm in love with you, with the idea of a shared future in this flat, with the possibility of pure existence, which Dostoyevsky is always singing the praises of, but which he does not know how to achieve. If you say to me: throw Dostoyevsky away like a dirty tissue, kick him into the gutter like a lump of mud that has got stuck to your shoe, I'll do it. Be my master. London has revealed many things to me, it has taught me that I have to look after myself, because others will only take advantage of me, and so, dear Willy, be my saviour. It's your fault that my life is like it is, because you arrived too early or too late for our rendezvous at Eros and left too early. Men should know what time it is, from a woman you can't expect anything more than love, but you have to earn it. My dear Willy, you must paint me as Venus, Odalisque, Leda, Naked Maja, Mona Lisa, as all the beauties from the history of art that Dostoyevsky spoke about … sorry, I think I'm going to be sick."

She rushed to the bathroom and slammed the door behind her. I went into the kitchen, so as not to hear her vomiting. Somewhere

414

above my stomach, perhaps in my heart, I felt an unbearable weight. It hurt as if someone had driven a sharpened stake through my entrails. Between one vomiting and the next – mine on the ferry and hers in the bathroom – my dreams had drifted up to the sky, so high that they had been struck by lightning and were now charred like wood in a fire. It was her, but it was not her; she had come (or was she sent?) to play a role, to involve me in some new plans (whose?), but the role was not convincing, as she had finally realised herself.

At that moment the door phone rang.

"Sir," said the doorman when I answered, "Lord Hattersley and Mr. Gray are here. They wonder if you can receive them."

Of course, I said.

At that moment Sandrina came out of the bathroom, deadly pale, blotchy, wiping her mouth with a tissue.

I have visitors, I said. Lord Hattersley and Mr. Gray.

"No!" she cried and grabbed her handbag. "Lord Hattersley is a regular guest at our hotel, he mustn't see me here. How are they coming up, in the lift?" She rushed to the door, grabbed the handle, turned the key, dashed into the hallway and hurried down the stairs. For some time I could hear two sounds: the clacking of her heels, fading down the stairs, and the hum of the lift coming to my floor, until it stopped with a slight squeak.

"Willy," said Sir William, "Mr. Gray has some very interesting information."

53.

I kept them in the living room, so that they would not see the remains of dinner on the dining table; I offered them wine, but they both declined; Mr. Gray pulled a small bottle of whisky from the inside pocket of his leather jacket and took a gulp. Lord Hattersley and I looked at each other.

"I always carry it with me," explained the bald Mr. Gray, whose large stomach hung aggressively over the waistband of his trousers. He had terribly scruffy shoes and a round, red face, from which his slightly squinting eyes kept exploring the space around him; he looked as if he was afraid of being followed, although it was him who was supposed to follow others.

"Willy boy," said Sir William, "sit down, please, for the news is rather shocking."

Mr. Gray pulled two folded sheets of paper from his right-hand pocket, placed them on the table, smoothed them and from his other pocket took out his glasses, which he put on and adjusted twice; his nervousness was making me anxious.

"Let's begin at the beginning," he said. "The customs office in Dover confirmed that they confiscated the paintings on this list…" He pulled from his pocket yet another sheet of paper and held it out towards me. "Is that your signature, sir?"

I nodded and he placed the list on the table beside the other papers. He straightened them as if to ensure that the distance between them was the same; to achieve this, he had to move the glass that Sandrina had been drinking wine from.

"Mr. Gray," Sir William cleared his throat "could you stick to the point? Time – if you permit me a small cliché, which no doubt you've heard before – is gold and we may suddenly run out of it, especially a man of my age."

"Sorry, Sir William, but I have my system and if I don't proceed in order, things soon get confused and I can't find anything. The young gentleman has not heard what you have heard, perhaps he may be interested."

"No doubt," replied Sir William, standing up, "I apologise, but this couch is torture for my back, so I shall walk around the flat and you two carry on."

It's not very tidy, I said quickly, but he gave a dismissive wave: "Tidy at a painter's? A contradiction in terms, Willy boy."

He opened the door to the library, where after painting the Caravaggio there remained a total mess. "Oh, the artist is working again, well done!" he exclaimed and closed the door behind him.

"To start again," said Mr. Gray, who seemed relieved that Sir William had withdrawn, "the paintings on this list, with your authorisation – I have a photocopy," he reached into his pocket and produced yet another sheet of paper, which he held out towards me: "is this your signature, sir?"

When I nodded, he placed the paper on the table beside the other three. "With this authorisation, the pictures on the list were collected from Dover by a Mr. Richard Whitehouse. He is actually a Pole by the name of Palisander, who has a small hotel in Pimlico, not far from the Thames."

That's not possible, I said, I searched the whole area around Victoria Station and didn't find it.

"It is quite a distance from Victoria. Above the door there is a neon sign with two letters not working, so that it reads like *.o.el*. Mr. Palisander is a friendly gentleman, he tried to convince me that he was looking after the paintings, together with those that you left under the bed, but unfortunately you never returned. Two months ago, two

417

men finally appeared with your authorisation. Mr. Palisander handed over every single one of your paintings."

He pulled yet another sheet of paper from his pocket and held it out towards me. It said: "Due to restricted mobility, I authorise the bearer of this letter to collect in my name the paintings that Mr. Palisander collected in Dover, together with those that I forgot beneath the bed in his hotel." And my signature, forged, but only a graphologist would be able to prove that it was not mine.

What were these two gentlemen like, I asked.

"I was unable to find out," said Mr. Gray. "Mr. Palisander claimed that he had been involved in a traffic accident, since which he re-members almost nothing – he showed me the scars and the bumps. But between the two of us, sir, I would say that there was no accident and that they had come for the paintings, beat him up badly, and threatened him to keep his mouth shut. That is confirmed by my later findings."

Sir William emerged from the library and asked: "Are you near the end yet?"

"No, Sir William, things don't proceed that fast," said the detec-tive, a little ruffled, so that Sir William gave a sigh and returned to the library. This time, he left the door open.

"The lost property office at Paddington Station," Mr. Gray contin-ued. "You said you'd called there and they claimed that they hadn't found any paintings."

Actually no, I admitted. I thought about going a number of times, but each time I decided not to because it didn't seem likely that someone would take a painting they'd found to the lost property, they would rather keep it, I know I would.

"A pity," said Mr. Gray. "Obviously they were found by someone honest, or someone who knows nothing about art. Less honest and clearly knowing more were the two young men who came for the paintings with your authorisation. I have a photocopy of it."

He produced yet another sheet of paper from his pocket and showed it to me. It said: "Due to my limited mobility I authorise the bearer of this letter to collect in my name the paintings that I left on the train from Penzance to London at the end of May. The paintings are signed with my name, Vili Vaupotič. Thank you." And a signature, again forged, as successful as the other one.

Was it the same men? I asked.

Mr. Gray shrugged: "No one was able to describe them, a hundred people go to the office every day, but enquiries elsewhere lead me to believe that they were. I first called to see Mrs. Stella Henderson, to check whether Alan McClelland really had returned the paintings from the *Simultaneity* series. She confirmed what I had suspected all along: that he had not. She added that she had been asked the same thing before by two young men, one tall, one short. I visited Mr. Mc-Clelland to confront him with the facts, but I came too late: he had been viciously attacked and even his daughter had been threatened. I traced him to the hospital. He confirmed that a few days earlier two young men had come to his house with an authorisation supposedly written by you to hand over your pictures to them. Because he suspected that fraud was involved, he refused to do so. Three days later, in the middle of the night, his house was broken into and he was attacked trying to defend the paintings, which were then stolen. Mr. McClelland described the young men who spoke to him in some detail. One was big, well over six feet tall, with massive hands. The other was smaller and swarthy, and spoke with an Italian accent. He could not confirm whether they were the same two who attacked him."

And where are the paintings now? I asked.

"I visited almost every gallery in London, from the biggest to those that aren't even in the phone directory. I omitted only the major ones such as the National, the Tate and the Hayward. I'm sorry to say that I didn't find a single one of your paintings. I assume they are looking for buyers via the usual secret channels. If we knew who the thieves were, I'm sure we would soon find where they were hiding them, because they knew exactly where to go. It's clear that the information could only have come from you. You probably remember to whom you mentioned the details of your lost paintings."

Oh, I said vaguely, quite a number of people and no one in particular. You know how it is: you drink a bit too much in the pub and it loosens your tongue, you want to boast a little and the damage is already done – someone overhears, recognises an opportunity and makes a plan.

"Well, that's true," said Mr. Gray and then he took another gulp from the whisky bottle that he produced from his inside pocket. "But it's more likely that you entrusted someone specific, perhaps a friend, perhaps a girl, with the details and they passed them on."

At that moment Sir William returned to the living room: "Have you finished?"

"You could say that," replied the detective.

Sir William sank back down onto the uncomfortable couch and said: "By the by, Willy boy, who were those two young men who were looking for you at Lockwood Manor during the party? They were rather an unusual pair."

I don't really know, I said. Someone had sent them to the wrong address, I think there was a misunderstanding… excuse me, I drank too much, I feel a little sick.

I rushed to the bathroom and locked the door behind me. I thought I was going to throw up, but once I had splashed some cold water onto my face, the urge faded. I squatted and rested my chin on the edge of the washbasin; I stayed like that for some time, thinking about my next step. When I returned to the living room, only Sir William was there, his face slightly distorted in an expression of pain, which I could not say for certain was coming only from his back.

"Willy boy," he said, sitting up. "I sent Gray home. He's done his bit, he can't help you any more, now it's up to you."

I sat on the edge of the armchair and stared dully at the coffee table in front of me.

"I'd like to say a few things before I leave," he said.

Judging from the tone of his voice, I expected that he was going to announce the end of our friendship, cancel my employment contract, sever all contact. He got up with difficulty and went over to the window. For a while, he stared at the Roosevelt Monument on the square, sighing deeply a couple of times. My heart had never felt so heavy.

"We all have a past," he said. "That's inevitable. We may dream of sainthood, but we live what we call life. To the pasts of others we

420

must be at least as understanding as the extent to which we would prefer to forget our own. Listen, forgive, move on – that should be the rule. When I in a sense took possession of your life and talent, I thought I was doing something good for you. I forgot that you had a life before we met. Evidently, some things from the past have now caught up with you and you need to deal with them. That you can only do yourself. I won't push you, I won't ask for details. I am always available should you need advice, money or protection. I've got to stay in London for some time: if I'm not at the Lords or in business meetings, I shall be contactable at Grosvenor House Hotel. Which of course you know. Jonesey and the car are at your disposal whenever I don't need them, which is most of the time. Do what you think you need to, then return to Lockwood Manor, at least three days a week, we all miss you. At the same time, we know that you must live your own, parallel life, appropriate to someone your age. London is more than suitable for that. The only thing I fear is this: that at the moment when you are in a situation of extreme risk, you would not want to call. I ask you not to be so proud."

He went towards the door. I stood up and took a step towards him. He turned and looked at me. For a moment, our eyes met: mine full of gratitude and repentance, his full of love and forgiveness. I realised that never in my life had anyone loved me so unconditionally. Awkwardly, we both took a step forward and embraced.

Sir William, I whispered, I'm so small in comparison with you.

"Nonsense," he said, pressing me to him once more, "quite the opposite. I am just an aristocrat, a rather strange beast in this moment of the kingdom's history. You are an artist. You understand the nature of the game in which we are engaged. Learn to play it a little more skilfully than I have been able to. And don't forget: if things go awry, call me. I am proud of your pride, but don't overdo it."

With these words, he gently pushed me away from him, gave a fleeting smile and left. But within a moment, the door opened again and he came back. "I'm glad that you are painting again," he said, "I see you are mixing some special pigments, I hope you will tell me what you are planning."

I will, Sir William, I said quietly, but not right now.

421

"And I don't see any painting anywhere," he said. "Have you not even started, or has Lord Fontleroy already taken some away?"

He hasn't, I haven't even started.

"I won't be intrusive," he said and closed the door behind him. But after less than ten seconds, he opened it again. "By the way, did you know that Caravaggio's *Birth of Christ* was stolen in Palermo? It's in all the papers."

No, I said, I don't read newspapers. But I like Caravaggio, he is one of those that I could still learn from.

"Undoubtedly," said Sir William. "But learn from the original – now the market will be flooded with forgeries."

He looked down, closed the door and this time really did leave; I heard the sound of the lift descending to the ground floor.

54.

After his departure, I immediately opened another bottle of wine: I felt an urgent need to become even more inebriated, to sink into forgetfulness, lack of feeling, absence. I had been in situations before where too much seemed to be happening and too quickly, like hailstones gathering in heaps in the garden, but this time it felt as if the hail had broken through the roof and was falling on my head and piling up around me as if it would never stop. Retreat, although temporary, felt like the only option. I sank into a twitchy state between sleep and wakefulness; in the meantime, I dreamed that I was trying to finish a painting for an impatient commissioner, but the paints would not hold, the more I put on the brush, the less stayed on the canvas. Castrated! I yelled in my dreams, Castrated! Why can I no longer leave any traces behind me? So many schemes and plans, so many wishes and so much striving – and in the end nothing? It's not fair!

I heard shouting, ringing, banging and then nothing for a while, and then once more shouting, ringing, banging, and a distinct female voice: "It's not fair! It's not fair!" I started awake and staggered to the door. I opened it and Sandrina almost fell onto me: "It's not fair!" she repeated. "Why won't you open the door to me?"

It's open, I managed to say and made to return to the couch, from which I had risen with such effort, but Sandrina grabbed my hand and dragged me to the bedroom, pushed me onto the bed and started to unbutton her blouse.

"You must make love to me now!" she cried. "It's your fault that we missed each other at Eros. It's your fault that my life strayed so far from what I deserved because of the innocence of my dreams. It's your fault that I'm no longer me. Love me, rescue me from my sins, bolt the door to hell, show me the doorway to heaven!"

Sobbing and naked, she threw herself on me and began to smother me with wet, slobbering kisses, but all I felt was the desire to flee, to avoid a confrontation, to avoid promises, to withdraw into a world where the memory of what I had got myself into was just a temporary delusion.

"Don't you want me?" I heard next to my ear and at the same time distantly, as if her voice was coming through a stone wall. "Don't you want for free what everyone else pays for?"

She grabbed my right hand and pushed it between her legs; I felt the soft hair, the slightly uneven labia, the bulge of her mons veneris, the silky, muscular smoothness of the inside of her thighs. "Take hold of me," she demanded. "Take hold of me and never let me go. From now on you are the master of my body, don't reject me because you will regret it – you will regret it so much!"

I waited for her fingers to relax and then I withdrew my hand. I had often dreamed about this, but it had come at the wrong time and not in the way I imagined – roughly, almost violently, without any attempt to find out whether I wanted to cooperate. It was like a final warning that my web had been spun by the wrong spiders.

"So," she said, after a long silence, "all those dreams about the goddess Sandrina were simply hot air, male exaggeration – how could I expect anyone to see me as anything special? No, my fate is to be a body, but only as long as that body is beautiful. I have no right to be a person. Oh God!"

She turned, slid off the bed, crouched on the floor and sobbed loudly.

You're drunk, I said. Me, too. When we're drunk there are many sins we can commit, but there are none we can atone for.

"No, no, no," she kept repeating and wiping away her tears with the bed cover, "we can't, but I would like to atone for all my mistakes, but I can't do it alone, someone has to help me. Where is that prince that my stars foretold? Who will watch over me, who will lead me?"

She was still talking to herself, leaning against the bed, but ever quieter and less understandably, while I, from extreme tiredness, was sucked into a drunken sleep that lasted all night and part of the next day, for when I opened my eyes, the sun was shining through the window at quite an acute angle. At first, I didn't understand why I was lying on the bed in my clothes; it was only when I moved my head and realised that it was full of gravel that I recalled the volume of wine that I had poured down my throat the previous evening. And then I recalled what else had happened.

Sandrina was no longer beside the bed: she had probably gone in the middle of the night.

But when I was on my way to the kitchen to get some coffee and went into the living room, I saw her on the couch. She was sitting bolt upright, her legs slightly apart and her hands on her knees, motionless, staring into space as if turned to stone. My first impression was that she was dressed extremely gaudily, but then I realised that she was still naked and coloured from head to toe with green and brown lines, yellow and red circles, black crosses, and blue and violet triangles; her nipples, her navel and her pubic region were coloured bright red. She reminded me of the living statues that I had seen a number of times in the centre of London, but also of a warrior of a primitive tribe, ready for a clash in which she might die.

I immediately guessed that she had smeared herself with the remnants of the paints and pigments that I had left in the library when I had finished the Caravaggio. Her eyes, outlined with orange marks, damp from tears and darkly melancholy, slowly turned and fixed on me. Then she asked: "Am I dirty enough?"

For heaven's sake, I said, do you have any idea how difficult it will be to wash that off?

"I don't want to," she said. "Dostoyevsky once said that a painter displays his soul through his paintings. So I decided to show people mine like this. Do you like it? You didn't like my body, what about my soul?"

I don't know what you're talking about, I said. My head is killing me, I desperately need coffee. I'll make you some as well if you cover yourself. Cleaning you up will take ages and will sting like hell.

"Will you clean me?" she asked. "I'll be eternally grateful. A girl who would rather be elsewhere. A girl who would rather be different. Are you kind enough to clean me even though I was dirtied by others?"

When I returned to the living room with coffee, she was nervously smoking, wrapped in a bathrobe she had found, holding the edges together, as if she wished to conceal the worst consequences of her painterly zeal. Actually, I should take your photo, I said with a laugh. The whole thing reminds me of a scene from our friend's novel. He thinks in this dramatic way.

"He was writing a novel about me," she said, taking a sip of coffee. "Didn't he tell you?"

He mentioned something, I said, but there were quite a few different versions. I couldn't decide which was most believable.

"Neither could he. In fact, he wasn't writing a novel but recording real events. He didn't change his story, but me: I had to be one thing this moment, something else the next – the clay from which he moulded now this, now another character. He acted like a god who is dissatisfied with what he has created and must put it right."

Why did you allow it? I asked, not entirely without reproach.

"Because I'm weak," she said. "Because I had nothing inside me to hold onto. Since I've been studying psychology, I understand a lot more. When I was three, I lost my father. I've always been looking for someone who could hold my hand, tell me what was wrong and right, and bring me presents. Once, for a few fleeting moments, I hoped that someone was you. Although you were terribly clumsy, I felt in you a strength, a persistence, a stubbornness. Then it all went wrong because of the stupid clock. And the stupid English, who refuse to use European time."

Did he force you to become what you have become? I asked.

"You mean a whore," she said so self-evidently that I was startled. "I wanted to become a singer. I had a nice voice, maybe some time I'll sing you a Transylvanian folk song. But there was no opportunity. And he thought that there's no point taking the footpath when you can turn onto the motorway. For him, the motorway meant quick money, with perhaps a bit of blackmail to increase earnings, and then at the right moment, withdrawal from the scene to a decent life. Into some old, distinguished house in the country. And then I would be a lady of leisure, he said, while he would start writing seriously. He said he couldn't write when he didn't know if he would have enough money for his next meal."

Did he arrange for you to live at the Grosvenor House Hotel? I asked.

"No, I was already a chambermaid there when he found me. But he did organise my employment as a masseuse. I received clients in my room."

Is Lord Hattersley among your clients?

"Oh," she gave a brief laugh, "once he came for a massage, because he has back problems. He immediately guessed that in this case massage meant something more. He was angry at first and then he said that he had nothing against sex with young women, but that he didn't want to be a member of a club where he did not know who the other members were and for the same price he would rather send me his chauffeur, who had no such reservations."

And did he? I asked. Jonesey?

"Twice a month," she said. "Always on a Tuesday. Never misses. Why are you so shocked?"

Actually, I'm not, I said. Jonesey and I were looking for you once. We found Selena instead.

"I'm Selena," she said. "Selena Marinescu. The other girl is Susan Jackson, an American. She was my cover, I hid behind her. Dostoyevsky was very cautious."

Yesterday, when you arrived, you were different, I said.

"Very," she said. "I was told to convince you that with me as your model you should paint some of famous nudes, which in the end would turn out like forgeries. You've no idea just how cunning your best friend is."

I've known that for some time, I said. But I didn't realise the scope of his depravity.

"Don't judge him too hastily," she said. "He always speaks about you in a special tone. He makes fun of your honesty, which he sees as naivety, but at the same time he respects you for it, envies you.

He was grateful that you did not abandon him after that unfortunate incident. He keeps saying that he should repay you for everything you've done for him. He has a special plan."

Really, I said. What kind of plan?

"It would work like this: we would meet by chance and I would invite you for two weeks of love in a seaside hotel and then I would mysteriously disappear."

And you agreed to that? I asked.

"With him it's not a matter of agreeing or not – he is the writer and we are all just characters in his story. Although I did want that to happen. And for the two weeks to be extended forever and I would mysteriously escape from him."

And now, I asked, why are you here? Have you got some new plan?

"No," she said, busying herself with lighting a new cigarette. "Yesterday Sir William was here, didn't you agree anything?"

With regard to what, Sandrina? I asked (and then suddenly remembered that her name was Selena, although it seemed impossible that I would ever be able to call her anything other than Sandrina).

"About getting Dostoyevsky out of the way. He's been saying for some time that he has the feeling that someone is making enquiries about him, but not the police looking for him because of the murder. Didn't you and Lord Hattersley agree yesterday to get rid of the crazy Russian?"

How could you think something like that? I retorted. How can you accuse people of something they're not even capable of? But our friend is capable of many shady things: he has stolen or extorted from people a whole load of my paintings, to profit at my expense.

"He did that for you," she almost shouted. "You gave him the list. All the paintings are waiting for you in a garage in Hammersmith that he rented for the purpose. He wanted to get just one more, the one that some Palisander sold to an American bank, and then he was going to hand them over with a celebratory bottle of champagne as a present to his friend."

But that can't be true, I said, with the sudden hope that I was wrong about Solouhin. What about *Venus with Dog and Lambs* that

428

Sir William bought in a gallery? How did it end up there if it was part of the collection that I left on the train?

"I've no idea," she replied quickly in a dejected, weary tone, "I'm just telling you what he said. And he seemed so eager to surprise you. But Sir William wants to have those pictures to himself and that's why he reported Dostoyevsky to the police. They came for him yesterday evening to the hotel. It's all over for him. And I'm alone. And you don't care for me."

She threw her cigarette end in her cup of coffee, which she hadn't touched, and once more burst into tears.

He's been arrested? I asked very quietly. Where have they taken him?

"I've no idea," she howled through her tears. "Ask your Lord, he'll know."

Sir William is innocent, I raised my voice. He wouldn't benefit in any way and even if he did, something like that is quite out of character. You know that yourself. The police have been looking for Dostoyevsky for months. Why didn't he escape to Brazil when he had the chance, did he say anything about that?

She bowed her head. "We meant to go together and write to you from there and apologise for everything."

I must go to him, I said. I must find out where he's been taken.

"What about me?" She turned to me like an abandoned child. "Can I stay here?"

I'll give you some cleaning fluid to get that off you, I said. I'll be back by then.

55.

Grosvenor House Hotel was close enough for me to walk there briskly in ten minutes. But it was almost 11 a.m. and I thought Sir William would already have gone out. However, as soon as I turned the corner I saw the Bentley parked outside, with Jonesey and Mikey standing beside it.

"Sir William," I said, when I ran up to them, out of breath.

Mikey turned towards the hotel entrance; Sir William was just coming out. He did not seem surprised to see me, I even got the feeling that he had expected me. "Willy boy," he said somewhat coldly, haughtily, as if he wanted to remind me of the gap between us.

I rushed up to him and grabbed hold of his jacket sleeve; although he started slightly, he did not remove his arm. Sir William, I said, lowering my voice, I must see him.

He hesitated slightly. I could see that he faced a dilemma: at one moment he had almost decided to pretend that he did not know what I was talking about, but the next moment he succumbed and squeezed my elbow just as I stopped squeezing his.

"Of course, my boy," he said and indicated that I should follow him back inside. "Telephone," he said to one of the receptionists when we got to the desk. The man responded immediately. "Anything else, Sir William?" he asked obligingly.

"I'd like to make a call!" For the first time since I'd known him Sir William raised his voice beyond the level of politeness; the receptionist fell back in fright, at any other time the expression on his face would have seemed extremely funny. Sir William dialled the number, waited and spoke into the phone. I was standing close enough to hear what he said.

"Gray, where is he being held?" He waited for the reply and then asked: "What is the head of the station called? Okay. I might need you again."

He said he had to make some other calls, but from his room; he took the lift to God knows which floor. He soon returned and handed me a note in a handsome envelope on which was engraved *Lord William Hattersley, OBE, MBE, Lockwood Manor, Berkshire*.

"Jonesey will drive you to the police station in Kensington," he said. "I'll go to parliament by taxi. Give this letter to Inspector Robins."

Half an hour later I was sitting in a small room with bare walls, behind a wooden table with two chairs; the window looked out on an untidy yard full of old car tyres; the bars were the only sign that I was in a police station and not a hospital waiting room, although the sharp smell of disinfectant reminded me of one. When they brought him in he was at first startled to see me, but then in a resigned way, almost shamefully, he smiled and hung his head. He was thin, pale and unkempt; he had bruises on his face, probably from resisting arrest – I couldn't imagine that he had been beaten later, in the cell.

The police officer who brought him removed his handcuffs and said: "You've got ten minutes!"

That's not enough, I replied. At least half an hour, please!

"Impossible," the man straightened up stiffly, "it's an unusual concession that you can talk without an official person being present. One of you must have friends in high places! Ten minutes," he emphasised before leaving.

"We're not alone," said Dostoyevsky, without looking up. "They're listening in. Be careful what you say."

I won't, I said, it's time to speak the truth. Why won't you look at me?

He slowly raised his head and directed his deep dark eyes straight at me. They were terribly empty and hollow: there was no trace of

431

the fire that once burned in them. No trace of the former superior, at times arrogant self-confidence. I was shaken by the thought that such a man could be broken.

"You look at me as if you don't recognise me anymore," he said. "Give me a minute to collect myself – I didn't expect you to come and visit me. Do you want to prove to me that it wasn't you who betrayed me?"

No, I said, I don't have to prove anything. I came because there are things we need to talk about. We were friends, have you forgotten?

"Then it was her, the bitch," he said, as if he had not heard my words. "Your Sandrina, who you dreamed about like some goddess, when she's not even worth your dirty socks. Well, now you have her, you can dream on together. I've long had the suspicion that she was planning to get rid of me. I made a mistake, I trusted her too much. That is always men's downfall. Never make the same mistake, Willy Wow."

I don't know what went on between you two, I said, but I'm sure you didn't trust her as I trusted you.

"Everyone trusts at their own risk," he said, the old fire slowly returning to his eyes. "Friendship is more risky than an international agreement with a gold seal. But there's really no such thing as love, do you realise that now?"

No, and I'll persist in the naïve belief that one day I'll find it. I simply don't belong in this time, I'm yesterday's or perhaps tomorrow's man. I'll keep on believing that one day I'll find what I naively thought had developed between us – true friendship.

"Oh, Willy Wow," he sighed, "how childish you are. Right, wrong, true, untrue – if you painted like that, with no feeling for the thousands, billions of shades, you would be an amateur. Which you are not, we both know that, as does your benefactor Lord Hattersley, who you trust as blindly as you once trusted me, although you should have realised by now that you are of interest to him only because he can exploit you. But don't think that I condemn him for that – we find a way of doing well for ourselves, isn't that our duty, to make the best of this world? I blame you for letting yourself be exploited in the naïve belief that someone loves you because, in your mind,

432

you have a pure soul. People don't care two figs about your soul. Do you know what is the most important event of this year? Apart from the Americans landing on the moon? That the singer Lulu – which mean two toilets, loo loo – won the Eurovision Song contest with the song Boom Bang-A-Bang. It's true that she had to share the prize with someone else, but the main thing is she got to the top and Boom Bang-A-Bang expresses all the incredible profundity of the time into which fate has placed us. If it is so shallow that even a frog jumping in would crack its head open, then that is something else. The fact is, Willy Wow, that in this world, this society, at this historical moment, you can only achieve anything if you are boom bang-a-bang. And only if that is the only sound you hear – each improvement to your hearing or ear for music brings with it a dangerous reduction of your capacity to survive. Boom bang-a-bang," he began to sing and bang his fists on the table, "boom bang-a-bang."

The door opened and two suspicious policeman's eyes peeped in.

Everything's alright, I said. The surprised face withdrew and the door closed.

You wanted to be a writer, I said. You spoke about a great novel, about how you would use storytelling to improve a world that seems to you too boom bang-a-bang –

"I am a writer," he interrupted decisively, his eyes glowing. "But, my dear Willy Wow, I'm not writing a novel, I'm writing life. My characters are real people."

I know that, I said.

"You don't know anything," he rebuked me. "Life retains some of the authenticity that language has completely lost. The writer no longer has at his disposal uncontaminated language: all the words, all the phrases have been taken from him, simplified and devalued by politicians, journalists, academics, advertisers. Boom bang-a-bang. There seems to be little sense in writing a novel that would just become my personal myth. And if I turned against that, the result will be anti-literature that will scorn itself as punishment for its independence from exhausted modes of expression. What do you do as a painter, my friend? Have you ever thought about the *real* background to your paintings? I'll use words that you understand, right – wrong,

433

true – untrue, sincere – false. What is your *Simultaneity* if not an expression of scorn for the inability of art to express anything new? Don't imagine that you are some kind of genius who will open the door to the next generation of artists. Not a chance, my friend. You have surrendered to the spirit of the times, your paintings are also boom bang-a-bang. But you are in a worse position than me, because you don't want to admit it. Just as you don't want to admit that your goddess is a whore who, now that she's swept me aside, is looking for a new pimp. Of course, you are more suited to the role: you have a flat in Mayfair, you have money, you know some influential people – even if she doesn't touch another man, she will retain at least one client. Friendly, naïve, obliging, undemanding – what could be nicer? For that kind of relationship they will sooner or later have to invent a new name – such as love. Don't imagine that next year the Eurovision Song Contest will be won by a different kind of song. It will still be Boom Bang-A-Bang, although under a different name. Time, dear Willy, has thrown back in our faces all that we have been serving it for too long as top class cuisine because it is simply dog food. Enjoy."

He stopped talking and hung his head. I looked at my watch and saw that our time was running out. Perhaps it already had and the police were giving us a little longer.

I can't believe that you think like that, I said. Bad things have happened to us, things that I didn't want to happen, either, but they have happened and there's no way back. All this is a reaction to something that seems unjust to you now, but you want to blame everyone other than yourself. After some time you will accept it as part of your life, as a stopping off point on your way to realising that everything we experience in life we take on board ourselves and that everything brings some benefit.

"Oh my God," he interrupted me, "they have sent me a priest – have I already been sentenced to death? Officer!"

The door opened and the police officer poked his head in. It's nothing, I said, how much longer do we have?

"Actually," he looked at his watch, but at that moment a man in civilian clothes came past and said: "Five more minutes." The police officer nodded and closed the door. Evidently, whoever was in charge had decided to give us an extension.

"What if I don't want five minutes?" shouted Dostoyevsky.

Then he calmed down and gave me a meek look: "Sorry. What can I still do for you, when I have already done everything that was in my power? You don't even know that I was collecting your paintings for you as a Christmas present…"

I know, I said, she told me. I believe you and I'm grateful. Who has the key to the garage?

"Your Sandrina," he said. "My Selena. Have you slept together?"

No, I said. And we never shall. Why are you interested, when she's been sleeping with five a day?

"It's different with friends. It's like a transfer of ownership. Was it her who betrayed me?

No one betrayed you, I said. And Sandrina is not your property – of all the illusions that you so stubbornly cling to, that is the greatest. Of course, mine were even worse. There are a hundred questions that I'd like to ask you, but our time is running out, so just tell me one thing. Seeing that there is so much good inside you, seeing that you know what good is, seeing that you had high, noble goals – where did it go wrong, what was the moment when the scales tipped the other way?

"Oh, Willy Wow. I'm very tired and your question is the kind of stupidity that I'm accustomed to from you, but let's leave that for now – after all, we're still friends, in spite of everything. There are no scales to tip one way or the other – you're using empty words that don't fit the reality. Boom bang-a-bang. The other side *is* this side, don't kid yourself that good and evil are two different things that can be clearly separated. Have you read Conrad's *Heart of Darkness*? You haven't, you read too little, like most artists. The story is about a naïve young optimist called Marlow, who goes to the heart of the Congo on the trail of a civilised European called Kurtz, an ivory trader who, faithful to his business interests, becomes uncivilised, he watches the dances of the African savages and feels within himself the same primitivism, the same savagery, but camouflaged in nice words and civilised gestures. Ask Sir William how many people he murdered on his way to the Lords. I don't mean literally – murder can

435

also be found in a black look, harsh words, a small act of unkindness, or false friendliness. Have you ever read Pliny, the Roman naturalist? You haven't, I don't really know why I'm asking. He describes the unicorn, a wild animal faster than any that would lie in wait for it, hoping to make use of the miraculous properties of its horn. But this perfect creature had a fatal flaw. It had stubbornly convinced itself that it loved nothing in this world more than purity and innocence. And so some cunning hunters used a young virgin as bait. The unicorn came, lay down, gratefully laid its head in her lap and fell asleep. At that moment the treacherous virgin signalled to the hunters, who threw themselves on the naïve creature and captured it. Don't be like the unicorn, Willy Wow. Don't try to be good at any price. Goodness has caused a lot of harm in the world. Be cautious, learn to recognise a lie before you respond to it. That is all you need to do to get to where you want to be: to trample on others more often than they trample on you. That's my only advice, if you want to listen to a friend. And what is your advice for me?"

For a moment our eyes were glued together as if we were in an embrace. He persisted and I was the first to withdraw. This time it was my turn to hang my head.

You don't need any advice, I said. For the next twenty years you will be completely taken care of, you won't need to decide about anything important. Although it sounds hard to believe, you'll be in a better situation than me. I will be faced with important decisions every day. You won't be able to make any more mistakes, but I can make three serious ones every day.

"You're wrong," he said. "The only important thing is being in the right place at the right time. That's real simultaneity, Willy Wow. That's what history is based on, that's what our personal stories are based on. Let's say that you had not missed Sandrina at Eros. Would she now be the most sought after prostitute in London? No. And us: if we had never met on Nevern Square? Would you then have tried to earn money by guiding tourists round London, which led to me being here now? Never. We would both have led different lives. And Sir William? If he had not by chance wandered across Leicester Square when you were painting portraits there in the style of Hans Holbein, would an eminent English aristocrat, who even preferred to give Sandrina to his chauffeur rather than get down from his moral high horse, be thinking of adopting you?"

How do you know all that? I asked him.

"Dostoyevsky knows everything," he said.

He stood up and looked at me. "Will you testify against me in court?"

I also got up. No, I said, I'll say that you were provoked, that I would have done the same in your shoes.

"And if I ever get fed up of prison and ask you to help me escape?"

Again I was silent for a moment and then I asked: Are you sure you will want to escape?

His eyes moistened. He took a step towards me and I towards him, and we embraced. "Hey, Potty Willy," he said and his voice softened so much that it was no longer his. "You might hate me, you might despise me, but I love you more than anyone. Promise me something. Take care of that part of my life that remains at liberty."

I promise, I said.

He pushed me away, went over to the door and knocked. "The extra five minutes is up," he said to the astonished police officer.

Before the door closed behind him he turned to me and winked. "By the way, have you visited the National Gallery yet?"

I shook my head. "That's wise," he said. "There lurks the greatest danger to your art."

Then the door finally closed.

56.

Jonesey drove me back to the Grosvenor House Hotel. On the way, he fidgeted and twitched as if he was trying to tell me something. There's no need, Jonesey, I said, your loyalty belongs to Sir William – who you go to bed with and who pays for it is your business and I'm not even interested.

"I just can't believe it," he said, "that in the middle of all this is the woman that you have long been looking for. My heart ached when I heard about it, especially because she is not what you imagined."

Maybe she is deep inside, at the core that life has buried under so much rubbish, and she can still be saved.

"A nice thought, sir, but if a chauffer's words are worth anything at all, I would say that when too much rubbish is gathered in one heap, then whatever is underneath it rots away."

I can't accept that, Jonesey, I said. Inside every one of us there is something that never rots, that can always be salvaged. But of course, it requires a lot of willpower, particularly from the one who bears it.

"That's what I'm talking about, sir. It seems to me that the will-power is simply not there. Maybe it was once, but now it would need a miracle to awaken it."

Miracles can't be excluded, I said.

"That's true, but Sir William has high expectations of you. You don't have time for rescuing prostitutes who would like to return to the path that, with a little good will, they could have stayed on – instead of leaving it after sober reflection."

438

After sober reflection, Jonesey?

"Those who have grown up in poverty value comfort more than anything else and often don't realise that they are selling themselves."

I'll think about that, I promised, shocked at the sudden question as to how much his statement could apply to me. But I was more interested in something else. Was it Sir William who had betrayed my friend to the police?

"Of course not. It was Gray the detective. Sir William objected, he even yelled at him, but it was too late. Between the two of us, Gray was doing what he had to do and Sir William wanted to protect you and Selena. That's how it was. I didn't have any say in what happened. I only watch, listen and do as I'm told."

I'm glad that you told me, I said. Can you take me to my flat and wait for Selena, or Sandrina, to drive her back to the hotel?

He nodded.

I found Sandrina in the bathroom, still trying to scrub off the oil paint she had smeared herself with in the wave of repentance in the middle of the night. "This is awful," she said, "what have I done? Help me."

I told you not to use water, I said slightly impatiently, weren't you listening to me? Here, I threw her a towel, wipe yourself.

I collected all the cleaning fluid I could find and brought from the kitchen a rough cloth; I covered the bed with a clean sheet and asked her to lie on it, then I scrubbed off the paint and the smears, stubbornly focusing on the surface of the skin I was cleaning; I did not want my eyes to take in her whole body since it was tantalisingly beautiful, aggressively erotic, as she carelessly offered it up to my hands.

I knew that I had to take care of that part of Solouhin's life that remained at liberty – I intended to keep that promise. But not by taking on something that belonged to him more than it had ever belonged to me in my dreams. As a fixed idea, Sandrina had fulfilled her role: she had given me the will to carry on that would otherwise often have been fatally lacking. As a living person she had sobered me and opened a door into a new, less juvenile perception of the world. I should be doubly grateful to her.

But as a woman who had found herself without support and had frantically grasped at things around her, grabbing at the first straw, she was already a third person, someone who was both too familiar and not familiar enough for me to want to bother with her any more than necessary.

"You're hurting me," she said, "can't you be gentler?"

Sadly, no, I said. The only way to scrape a badly composed painting off a canvas is roughly.

"Is that how you see me? As a badly composed painting?"

I don't know, Sandrina, I said. I don't know, Selena. Maybe. But you do have, according to our mutual friend, the key to the garage where there is a collection of my paintings that are not badly composed. I give them to you. All except the cycle of twenty called *Simultaneity.* Those belong to the mother of my only real friend in London. All the rest are yours. I'll give you the address of Lord Fontleroy, who will pay you more for them than you can possibly imagine. If you want, I can be there when you negotiate with him.

"You'll give me the paintings?" She sat upright. "But I've done nothing for you. We haven't even slept together – do you want to now?"

You've done a lot more for me than you think, I said.

"What about me? Don't you want me?"

At the moment there is no one inside me who *could* want you, I said. I have been temporarily erased, cancelled, withdrawn. I've got to find myself once more. That won't be a quick matter. In the meantime, you can sort out your life.

"Not even once?" she leaned on her elbow, her hip turned towards me. "A souvenir of our meeting?"

Our encounter was beautiful enough not to spoil it, I said. And in any case, my libido does not function as directly as with most other men – it takes some strange detours. And the most important thing, to repeat the words of Sir William: I don't want to be a member of a club where I don't know who the other members are. It seems that we are both a bit strange.

She got up and started to dress. Her face darkened. "I know I made a lot of mistakes," she said, "but I don't deserve this."

When she was ready she walked to the door. She opened it and then turned.

"You won't have second thoughts about the paintings?"

I'm not the sort of person who has second thoughts, I said. Jonesey is waiting for you downstairs: he'll take you to the hotel.

"You despise me, don't you?"

Far from it, I said. If I had the strength I would feel sorry for you. But at the moment I feel more sorry for myself.

She looked at me once more, sensing that it was the last time we would ever see each other.

Then she went down the stairs, the sound of her heels slowly receded.

And who remained in the flat?

I decided to think about that some other time. First I wanted to tidy up and clean: I opened the fridge and got the phone number of Sharon the cleaning lady. I said I needed some cleaning done immediately; she said it would be double the usual rate. I agreed, I had enough money. I left her the key and went to Hyde Park; I wanted to be alone, without anyone around me. After a short walk, it struck me that I *was* alone and without anyone around me: alone and lonely as never before – employed, materially secure, with buyers for everything I intended to paint, but alone like the young tree by the path, trembling in the October wind.

In the air I felt not only autumn, but also a hint of winter.

I had two possibilities: to return to Lockwood Manor and continue painting the portraits that I had not completed, or to return to the flat and start thinking about some new paintings for Lord Fontleroy. I was not particularly attracted by either option – wherever I looked I saw only a frightening emptiness. With a hollow feeling inside me I longed for those that were a link to my past, which now seemed so remote as to be almost a myth, but the only one that I could turn to in order to prove I was not totally rootless was Cleo on Nevern Square: the only one I had not fled from, the only one I had done nothing bad to, the only one that I could ask for company, perhaps friendship.

I have already decided to drive to Earls Court and knock on her door when a less mundane thought occurred. I returned to the flat, which had already been cleaned, tidied and aired, leaving not a trace of the recent past. I already felt easier and my idea of preparing a surprise for Cleo began to fill me with real enthusiasm. I looked through the phone directory and called the telegram office. I dictated the address and then the content.

"I saw your ad. I'm interested. I'm educated, young, pleasant to look at, from a respectable family. I have a four-bedroom flat in May-fair, servants, a Bentley, a chauffeur. My favourite poet is Matthew Arnold. I recommend dinner at the Ritz tomorrow at eight. Reserva-tion in the name of Sir William Butterfly. I expect you. *Au revoir*."

Be careful how you spell *au revoir*, I said to the woman who had answered my call.

"Don't worry, Sir William," she said. "By the way, I'm not mar-ried."

But you're not the Queen of Egypt, I said and put down the phone.

Then I asked Jonesey, who had no other work, to drive me to Harrods. In the shoe department I bought ten different pairs of shoes, size 6; in the food department I bought five packets of fresh imported dates; in the flower shop, advised by the manageress, I ordered a large bouquet of roses, asters and orchids; in the book department I bought the latest, leather-bound edition of the poems of Matthew Arnold. I had everything gift wrapped and was promised that it would be delivered to Cleopatra El-Kaffash within the hour.

Thanks, I said. Thank you, Sir William, said the elegant shop assistant who supervised the transaction, with a bow. Ah, I thought, the comfort of money. Let it last as long as I have it – in the long run we are all dead anyway.

Then I called the restaurant at the Ritz and booked a table for two, somewhere in a corner, discreet, I emphasised, with dark red candles on the table. Finally, I asked Jonesey to drive to Lockwood Manor and to bring back to London the full set of clothes that Lord Hatters-ley's tailor had made for me. He was somewhat surprised, but made no objection and set off straight away.

57.

When, at eight the following evening, I was sitting at the table in an intimate corner of the Ritz with an aperitif in front of me, what had begun as a mischievous whim had already taken on the dimensions of a more serious plan, although still not clear enough for me to know exactly what I intended to do. After all, it was possible that she had not received the telegram or the presents, or that the offer seemed sufficiently absurd that, if I gave it some sober thought, she had thrown it in the bin. And who would blame her? If she had any self-respect that's what she would do – altogether it was foolhardy, childish, risky. On the other hand, the elegant surroundings of the best restaurant in London was a safe enough place to meet with an odd stranger – especially since she had quite a few such (and more risky) meetings behind her.

Suddenly, accompanied by a waiter, she appeared from behind the pillar that sheltered the table. At the sight of me she started slightly, but gave no other sign of recognition. She seemed incredibly tall: evidently she had selected her highest heels (she wanted to be high in high society). She was slightly pale and strained, her hair in a tidy ponytail, fastened with a gold bow, in an elegant grey suit, which in spite of its excellent cut could not entirely conceal that she had put some more weight on, particularly around her waist, but I was the only one to notice, the other guests were staring at her as if she was Ava Gardner. Even to me her beauty, that I had somehow forgotten, was so stunning that at first I was lost for words.

I got up and offered her my hand; she sat on the chair that the waiter pulled out for her and placed her small handbag on the plate in front of her.

"Aperitif, Madam?" asked the waiter. And she replied: "A glass of water. I'm a Muslim, I don't drink."

"Sir William," the waiter turned to me, "another?"

Not for the moment, I said.

"Sir William," she said. "They are ten-a-penny in England, aristocrats have no imagination when it comes to names. And they get smaller every year," she measured me with her eyes, "evidently a sign of degeneration."

Not necessarily, I said, William the Conqueror was even smaller than me, haven't you seen him in the wax museum?

"Who needs to go to a museum," she said, "I meet enough wax dummies through my ads. Which one did you reply to? I haven't published one for ages."

Oh, I said with a wave, I was looking at some old magazine in the dentist's waiting room. Where are you from, while we're at it, Amazonia?

"We'll talk about that after dinner," she said. "What shall we eat?"

I motioned to one of the waiters standing nearby. He came closer, pencil and notepad in hand, inclined his head and said: "Sir?"

I looked at Cleo, who was observing me the whole time in amazement.

"I eat everything apart from pork," she shrugged, "I'll let you choose."

I was pleased: it gave me the opportunity to show off my gastronomical knowledge and that I was a regular guest of this elite establishment: "The usual," I said to the waiter.

He immediately recognised that we two strangers, an aristocrat and a waiter, could come together in a small conspiracy and both derive some pleasure from it, so with a meaningful twinkle in his eye he said: "I'm new, sir, my apologies."

Then please make a note: Ritz crab cakes, medallion of saute foie gras Strasbourgeois, sea bass flambe au fenoil, boulangere potatoes, fillet of lamb Nicoise, tian of provencal vegetables, Ritz raspberry souffle, chocolate feuillatine with lavender honey ice cream and caramelised pears.

"Very good, Sir. And the wine?"

Whatever you recommend, I said. I've never failed to be surprised.

"We're always pleased to see you, sir," he said with a bow and then withdrew.

"Who is going to eat all that?" asked Cleo. "It sounds as if you've ordered an aid package for Africa."

I really like your sense of humour, I said.

"Actually, there's something you should know," she replied. "I've been here five times before, so there's no need to try so hard to make an impression. And something is bothering me terribly. What you're wearing, is it called a tailcoat or a dinner jacket?"

A tailcoat has tails, I said. This is a dinner jacket.

"Very nice. In fact, you are an extremely handsome, well-mannered and elegantly dressed man. But young. I don't want to be personal, but I would say there is no need for you to look for a wife through advertisements. You will find one just like that," and she banged her hand down so hard that people at other tables looked around. "Is this some kind of hobby, leading on young girls who dream about marrying?"

Oh, I assure you it's nothing like that –

"Besides which," she interrupted me, "you remind me of an acquaintance of mine from the recent past. An incredible similarity. The only difference is that he is a pauper who does not know how to behave and you have manners that go back to William the Conqueror. And a chauffeur waiting outside in a white Rolls Royce."

Bentley, I corrected her gently.

Two waiters approached and began to serve the starter; a third poured some wine into my glass. This gave me a chance to think. Was it possible that she had not recognised me? If she had – although how could she not? – then she had obviously decided to play a game, which I was prepared to go along with. If she had not, then the game would be even more interesting; in that case, the advantage would be mine. I felt good in her company; she was sharp, self-confident and evidently weary of the endless encounters with flippant or inappro-

445

priate suitors, so that she was not prepared to be lenient. Let the lad take care of himself, I could read in her eyes; let him make an effort, if he feels like it, I am a queen, I don't need him.

We began eating. "One more thing that seems strange to me," she said. "How did you know where to send the telegram?"

I faked the most genuine surprise that I could. I don't understand, I said. I sent you dates, my favourite fruit; and Arnold, my favourite poet; and flowers, because I love flowers; the shoes were a shot in the dark, but women, as far as I know, are always complaining that they don't have enough of them.

"And why ten pairs?" she asked.

Oh, I said, in the hope that you will like at least one pair. A bit over the top, I admit. I apologise.

"Apology accepted," she said. Then she started to recite with her mouth full: *"Come to me in my dreams, and then / By day I shall be well again!"*

To give her time to swallow what she had in her mouth, I continued: *"For then the night will more than pay / The hopeless longing of the day."*

She closed her eyes and continued with a smile that expressed pure, almost childlike joy: *"Come, as thou cam'st a thousand times, / A messenger from radiant climes, / And smile on thy new world, and be / As kind to others as to me!"*

Longing, I said. The title of the poem is *Longing*.

"But when will it be fulfilled, that's the question," she sank back into a mysterious mixture of melancholy and uncertain satisfaction; as if something beautiful was happening, but at the same time she was afraid that it would all evaporate.

"Tell me something," she said. "How quickly are you prepared to marry?"

The question startled me. It depends, I said. Why do you ask?

"Because I urgently need a husband. I was selected in a lottery to attend the ceremony at Buckingham Palace when the Queen bestows honours. As an aristocrat you must be familiar with these events. Each time, in addition to those receiving awards and their immediate families, some ordinary people are invited, who are drawn from those who apply. I was stupid enough to do so and look at this."

She put down her knife and fork, opened her handbag, pulled out a folded sheet of paper and passed it across the table.

"*Dear Madam,*" I read, "*you have been chosen by ballot to attend in the company of your husband the investiture ceremony which will take place ...*" I stopped reading since my eyes had started to cloud over.

I handed back the letter and asked: You have been invited to tea with the Queen?

"Together with my husband," she said, replacing the invitation in her handbag. "So for me a wedding is a question of days. An awkward matter for you, who had probably counted on a more leisurely pace, a longer courtship, on visits to your family – that kind of thing."

I'm not committed to conventionalism, I said, I have a bit of a rebel inside me.

"You've probably already met the Queen."

No, I said. There was a time when I wanted just that, but now it seems like an inflated thing that has nothing to do with most people's lives.

"So you don't want to come with me?"

I will come with you, I said.

"When we come back from the Palace we can get divorced. That's not a problem here. We could also stay married, see how things develop."

There's just one problem, I said. I don't know if you'll like my flat. If we marry, we'll have to live there. And if you don't like it there, our union is bound to fail.

"Then let's go and see this flat as soon as possible," she said, "there's no point making plans in the dark."

Jonesey drove us to Grosvenor Square. "Will you need me any more today, sir?" he asked, his tone of voice indicating that the answer should be no.

I looked at Cleo, who quickly responded: "Oh, I can walk home or take the Tube, there's no need to worry about me."

Thanks, Jonesey, I said, the rest of the evening is yours. "Have a pleasant evening sir," he said and drove off.

"I think that my heels are too high," said Cleo in the lift, where the difference in our heights was very noticeable, particularly in the mirror. "I'll take them off." This she did immediately and then we were the same height.

You're still pretty big for a woman, I said, but that doesn't bother me. If we are ever attacked by thieves, two heavies like us would deter them more than one.

"Hey," she said, "if you hadn't just bought me an expensive meal I'd slap you for constantly insulting me."

Perhaps because you are constantly provoking me, I said.

"And is this the flat?" she asked, her shoes in one hand and her handbag in the other as we entered the hall. "Can I have a look around? That's why we've come, isn't it?"

I followed her from room to room, trying to guess what was going through her head. But her face was an immobile mask. "Oh," she said in slight surprise when we entered the library, "a painter's easel, are you an artist?"

I dabble a little, I replied. Amateur stuff. I've not enough talent for more.

"I like that," she said, "because that friend you look like was a painter, a real painter, and I'm glad you are alike not only in appearance."

We stopped in the dining room, where she put her shoes and bag on the table.

Then she said: "I'll be straight with you, but don't take offence. The flat is nothing special – a number of my suitors have shown me something better. I like the furniture most of all. Old-fashioned, elegant, dignified, but in spite of that full of life. You need a wife who is roughly like that, although such women are rare these days and even rarer are the men who know how to value them. But considering that this will be an emergency wedding, because without a husband I can't have tea with the Queen, I have no right to complain. Where are the servants you mentioned?"

I took her into the kitchen, opened the fridge and showed her the list inside the door.

"How ingenious," she said, "but impractical. I would have the list by the phone. What are you going to offer me?"

I don't know, I said, looking round the kitchen. Which would you prefer, English tea or Egyptian coffee?

"Really," she said in surprise, "you have Egyptian coffee?"

Of course, I said, my favourite, I couldn't survive without it. Although it reminds me of Nescafe, it's quick and practical – maybe the only practical thing in this flat.

"Actually," she said, "I'd prefer English tea. It's time I practised for my visit to the Queen. I wouldn't want to make any mistakes. You will have to teach me the etiquette, which I'm sure you're familiar with."

So tea, I said and began to make it.

She sat at the table watching me. "It's nice to see an aristocrat in the kitchen. I hope it's neither the first time nor the last, I'm not very good at such things, I prefer opening tins."

There are some things we have to learn, I said with emphasis. In fact all, not just some.

"So you expect me to learn to cook," she said. "And that I'll be cooking while you're doing your amateur painting."

We all have to make a contribution to the common good, I said.

"But we need to define what the common good is," she replied.

Not always, I said. Sometimes it is so self-evident that it's not worth talking about.

"It constantly surprises me how clever and proficient you are. For instance, how you managed to find the right address for the telegram and presents. I never include my address in my ads and all the replies go first to the post box given by the magazine, which then sends them on. You must have connections everywhere."

I do have some, I said with a shrug. Milk, sugar, without?

"Without," she said, "I already have the feeling that you think I'm too fat."

Not at all, pleasantly rounded, I would say, with a slight bulge around the waist.

"Oh," she said in surprise, "you've noticed?"

A painter – even an amateur one – notices such things, I said.

"And it doesn't bother you?" she asked.

In itself, no, I replied, it depends what lies behind it.

I poured her tea, pushed the cup towards her and poured my own. And then I sat down. Now there was only the corner of the table between us.

"Did you know that my painter friend who is so like you has a friend who claims to be a writer and insists that we call him Dostoyevsky?"

I think I've heard of him. It said in the papers that he killed someone.

"That's the one," she said. "There were times when I wanted to report him to the police to protect the painter friend that you look like and who, amazingly, is also called Willy. There seem to be too many coincidences in this story, wouldn't you agree?"

Who knows, I said. The main thing is being in the right place at the right time.

"This Willy was something special in my life. You won't be angry, will you, if I tell you I was in love with him?"

Why would I be angry, I said, we all have a past.

"But then something went wrong. Maybe it was all my fault. His friend Dostoyevsky came to act as an intermediary between us. But then, regrettably, things became even more complicated."

I can imagine, I said, the details don't matter.

"This Dostoyevsky taught me many useful things, as well as many that I would rather not know. Once he said to me: don't try to be good at any price, goodness has caused a lot of harm in the world. And he told me a story of a unicorn."

I know that story, I said. But Dostoyevsky told it incorrectly. Let's be honest: he also gets things wrong sometimes. And that's why I have given myself the opposite, perhaps absurd goal of being good at any price.

"But is that possible?" she asked, sipping her tea.

We won't know until we try, I said.

"For our friends?"

For our friends, hoping for love, I said.

"But what if these friends go and leave traces behind them?"

We shall take care of those parts of their life that remain at liberty, I said.

450

"Because of a sense of duty?"

Not at all, I said. Out of love for friends. Duty and friendship don't belong together.

"How nice," she sighed, laying her hand on her stomach. "Is it wise for us to get married, considering that we have nothing in common apart from unreliable friends?"

Why not? I asked. We're both equally naïve, we both believe that people are basically good. It would be hard to find someone who would help us maintain that belief as convincingly as we can ourselves.

"How unusual," she said, "that two Willys have combined into one."

Yes they have, I said, thinking of Willy I in Willy II. And now they are speaking with one voice.

"But this tea party at Buckingham Palace," she said, "I don't really know why we should go. In fact, I feel less and less inclined to."

I don't really care, I said.

"Do you think it's clear outside? If we opened the window would we see the stars?"

There's no need, I said. We can paint them in our thoughts and that's enough.

"An unusual day," she said.

An unusual life, I added.

"Unusually good tea," she said and reached her hand across the table.

With the Queen of Egypt, I said and took the offered hand.

www.ingramcontent.com/pod-product-compliance
Lightning Source LLC
Chambersburg PA
CBHW021841010726
47493CB00005B/1499